Praise for Tiffany L. Warren

"Filled with love, betrayal, heartbreak, and forgiveness."
—**Kimberla Lawson Roby** on *The Favorite Son*

"Highly entertaining. Captivating and compelling. Great book club option."
—**USAToday.com** on *The Replacement Wife*

"Warren explores the inner workings of a marriage between two talented and ambitious people thrust into a series of difficult situations. The twists and turns will keep readers engaged . . . Fans of ReShonda Tate Billingsley and Victoria Christopher Murray will find familiar characters and themes, but Warren's novel will appeal to any reader who enjoys stories about couples in crisis."
—*Booklist* on *The Outside Child*

"In a fine blend of suspense and inspirational fiction, Warren spins an entertaining tale about folks misbehaving behind the pulpit in a modern African American church."
—*Library Journal* on *The Pastor's Husband*

"I just love her work."
—**Victoria Christopher Murray**

"When I read a Tiffany L. Warren novel I know I'm going to get two things—a riveting story and a faith boost!"
—**ReShonda Tate Billingsley**

"It was refreshing to read about women of the same age and category as myself. The author did an amazing job with the characters in this story. I saw myself in all three of the main characters at one point in my life . . . This book is emotional and will have you in your feelings, depending on where you are at in life."
—**Black Bloggers Chicago** on *All the Things I Should Have Known*

Also by Tiffany L. Warren

TIFFANY L. WARREN

All the Things I Meant to Tell You

www.kensingtonbooks.com

DAFINA BOOKS are published by

Kensington Publishing Corp.
119 West 40th Street
New York, NY 10018

All Kensington titles, imprints, and distributed lines are available at special quantity discounts for bulk purchases for sales promotion, premiums, fund-raising, and educational or institutional use.

Special book excerpts or customized printings can also be created to fit specific needs. For details, write or phone the office of the Kensington Sales Manager: Kensington Publishing Corp., 119 West 40th Street, New York, NY 10018. Attn. Sales Department. Phone: 1-800-221-2647.

The Dafina logo is a trademark of Kensington Publishing Corp.

ISBN-13: 978-1-4967-2371-0
ISBN-10: 1-4967-2371-6
First Trade Paperback Printing: May 2021

ISBN-13: 978-1-4967-2372-7 (e-book)
ISBN-10: 1-4967-2372-4 (e-book)
First Electronic Edition: May 2021

10 9 8 7 6 5 4 3 2 1

Printed in the United States of America

Acknowledgments

Another book done. Whew! A little trivia: this is the longest book I've ever written. I could've gone another thirty thousand words too. These characters are so fun and familiar to me. I feel like Hahna, Twila, and Kimberly are in my bestie circle.

I'm so blessed to have a myriad of girlfriends that I can laugh, cry, drink, and travel with. Friends that I can vent to, and who can share their frustrations with me. This year, 2020, has been a lot. A whole lot. If it wasn't for my friends, I don't know what I would do. So here I want to say thank you to my girls (lord Jesus, don't let me forget anybody): Shawana, Tiffany (Tip), Afrika, The Bride Tribe (Brandi/bride, Tiffany/TLee, Jameeka, Kamilah), Da Baddest Authoresses (Victoria, ReShonda, Renee), Lucy, Nicole, Daveda, Leslie, Cybil, Staci, Karla, and Tonya.

As always, I thank my husband, Brent, who is Sam, Big Ron, and DeAndre combined, for tolerating all of my late writing nights (where I sit in bed dropping snacks on his side). I also thank my fabulous five chickadees for being the best kids ever.

Much thanks to the editorial crew at Kensington—Wendy, Elizabeth, and Rebecca, and to Sara Camilli for believing in my talent and pushing me to do more.

Finally, thank you to Lorisa, Courtney (RIP), John, Perri', Patricia, and the team at Swirl Films for bringing The Favorite Son to BET as a film. I can't wait for you all to get reacquainted with Camden and Blaine and their gospel singing group So G.I.F.T.E.D.

As I write this, I am so full and while dealing with the loss and anxieties of 2020, there was also much joy to be had. Also . . . Madame Vice President is a black woman. I just . . . whew! I keep saying that :)

Enjoy this journey of love and sisterhood.

Chapter 1

TWILA

Coffee, then meditation, and next my morning run. This was the ritual.

I stretched outside my brownstone, basking in the sunlight, and not giving a damn who admired my behind in these leggings. I inhaled moist air and exhaled. Mid-September, and summer's humidity hadn't gone anywhere. It was going to be hot as hell by ten, but at seven there was only the promise of the excessive heat.

I inhaled and exhaled again. Gave myself my morning pep talk, because there was a moment, right before every run, where I almost changed my mind and went back in the house. A little voice from somewhere deep down inside whispered, *You don't have to do this today. You ran yesterday. You're good.*

But I knew if I listened to that voice, even once, it would be easier the next time. And the next. And then I'd look down and see cellulite in place of my lean muscles. I'd end up looking like my mother and brothers—short and round. Shoot. I was fighting against generational curses and genetics. Principalities and freaking powers.

So, I quieted the tiny voice. Shushed her lazy ass. That shushing was a ritual too.

I took off, slowly at first, building momentum and dropping

into my cadence. I didn't listen to music while I ran. I counted in my head. Eight footfalls to cover three blocks of pavement.

As I hit the first hill, I picked up the pace. Still counting. A little faster. Two hundred and forty footfalls to the top of this one. Passed Karen (her real name) and her shiatzu, so I shifted right, but kept going.

Down the hill was my first resting period. On autopilot, I eased up on the speed to control my forward trajectory. My body knew this path. I'd run it every day for the last five years.

I rounded the corner, taking me to the front of my subdivision. The big Crystal Acres sign was the midpoint of my run. There was a car on the corner that I didn't recognize. Probably someone's Uber or Lyft to drive them to work before the Atlanta traffic got too thick.

At the corner, I prepared to cross. But a door opened across the street. A man laughed. The laugh made me stop in my tracks. Paused the count at three and dropped my foot to the ground in a thud.

I recognized that laugh.

My legs froze, then trembled with my entire body. A scream struggled to escape, but in my ears it sounded like a tiny whimper. I touched my waistband. The taser was there, but gave me no solace—not when my hands were shaking too badly to unholster the weapon.

Without warning, I was thrust back to the night at Phenom. The night that had changed me. The one I'd tried to forget.

I stood in front of the red door and grinned. Assured myself again that I was ready for this. The Halloween masquerade party had given me the perfect cover. No one would recognize me in my black, jewel-encrusted mask and long, blonde wig. As I glanced at the mirrored wall outside the door, I hardly recognized my damn self. Those were my beautiful and perky breasts sitting pretty in the black leather, barely-there bra. Those were absolutely my honey bronze thighs peeking above the knee-high leather boots. And yes, that was my round, bubble ass in all her glory encased in black leather.

I touched the door handle and felt a shock. No doubt from the static kicked up by my boots on the carpet. But, for a second it made me think of my best friends and sorority sisters, Hahna and Kimberly. I wondered what they would think of this leather-clad version of me. Then, I decided I didn't care what they or anybody thought. Well, I almost didn't care. I still cared enough to put on a costume and disguise myself. I hadn't even told my soror, Traci, the owner of the club, that I was venturing into the room behind the red door.

It would be my little secret.

I reached back down to the door handle. No shock this time, so I pushed it open and ventured into the darkness.

It wasn't completely dark in the large room. There was lighting along the baseboards that cast a glow all around. Along the perimeter of the room there were glass encased sections that almost looked like cubicles, although everything happening inside the glass was not-safe-for-work.

My planned role for the night was the voyeur. I'd gathered enough bravery to watch and consume the debauchery, but I hadn't committed to participating. I still had to work up enough nerve for that.

So, I watched the singles, couples, triples, and even more numerous groupings engage in every sexual act known to woman and man. More than once I had to block out my grandmother's voice in my head saying, Sodom and Gomorrah. *I discarded my upbringing. Dismissed sermons and my sporadic dealings with the women's ministry at my church.*

This had nothing to do with any of that.

Or maybe it did. Maybe I was tired of waiting on God to send me a Boaz. I didn't need the whole man anyway. Too much trouble. Just wanted to feel that part that made my body tremble.

I swallowed hard as I watched one couple who were into each other like there was no one else in the room. The heat surging in my lady parts wasn't caused by the leather.

I kept walking along the wall, vaguely aware of the people around me. Other voyeurs enjoying the exhibitionists. Maybe thinking of participating, or content to be outside of the action.

I stopped again, in front of a woman who was alone. She plea-sured herself and stared straight ahead, as if she was on a Broad-way stage. I tilted my head to one side and wondered if she was performing or if her face contortions were authentic.

I started to walk again, but I felt someone walk up closely be-hind me. Before I could turn and demand my personal space, I felt a burn through my spinal column. And I lost control of my body and consciousness.

I woke up behind glass, and to quiet laughter.

He laughed again as he walked toward the car. His red hair was the same and so were the freckles. He looked somehow smaller than he had on that night, but I was sure it was him.

The man who'd raped me at Club Phenom waved to a woman and little girl as he got in the car with his briefcase, probably on his way to work.

I couldn't move until the car pulled off, but when it did, I broke into a full sprint. No quiet voice now, no counting, no footfalls. Just pure adrenaline and terror as I raced back to my brownstone.

Getting behind my locked door did nothing to relax me. I couldn't stay here. Not today, maybe never again.

I grabbed a bag and shoved random clothing inside. Not even sure what came next.

But I had to leave. My sanctuary had been invaded.

Chapter 2

HAHNA

My office sanctuary had been overtaken. By Corden. And by Corden's reports.

I tried centering myself by looking out my bay window at the magnolia trees and the lake. It didn't work. Corden was still there, and so were his reports.

"Are you even listening to me?" Corden asked.

"I think it's obvious that I am not."

Corden leaned back in his chair and sighed. "You been like this ever since you and Sam got back from the motherland."

"Like what? Peaceful? Not worried?"

"Unbothered is the word I'm thinking about."

Corden was right. I was unbothered. I was trying to stay exactly where I was for two months in West Africa. I had explored all the places that contributed to my genetic blueprint. I'd gone to market with women who could've been my cousins and aunties. I'd tried foods that were seasoned in a way that was familiar, confirming that the Black women in my family had these cooking skills passed down through generations.

And the entire time I didn't think about saving my company. I didn't think about data breaches or The Data Whisperers at all. There were no strategy sessions or murder boards or plots or plans. There was rejuvenation, restoration, and relaxation, not to mention mind-bending, soul-rending, spirit-molding sex.

I needed someone to take me back to that oceanside rental and away from Corden.

"You preferred the frantic version of me?" I asked. "The one who was breaking down every five minutes?"

"No, but I need a version of you that wants to save this company. Me and Sylvia don't have millions in the bank, you know."

Corden was right. I was being selfish. Corden and Sylvia were my only two employees. Aliya, the one who'd caused the data breach, was long gone, and we were the ones left to pick up the pieces. Except I could go on trips for two months, while Corden and Sylvia had to make do with a combination of reduced pay checks and unemployment benefits.

"Okay, you're right. Tell me again about the government contracting."

"Well, we'd have to go through the process to get our certification, but there is a lot of money there for the taking."

"We haven't done anything in that space, though."

"But we have," Corden explained. "We've done financial analytics, human resources, customer relationship management and more. They need all of those things under the federal umbrella."

I started the pitch in my head. Big government, big data, and how we could help their efficiency and effectiveness—especially since the government was always trying to save money.

"And they're willing to pay our rates?" I asked.

Corden nodded. "From what I've researched, the federal offices are paying more for quality analytics than big corporations. And you know we're magicians with our stuff."

I laughed. "We are indeed magical."

"Just let me start the work on it, and if we decide it isn't for us, then we won't do it."

I smiled at Corden. He was a genius, and a godsend to me. He and Sylvia were the only ones I completely trusted with my life's work. If I had listened to him about Aliya and fired her when she first started slipping, we wouldn't be worried about generating revenue. Corden was the real deal, and I was grateful for him.

"Well, that's settled," Corden said. "Now what about my other idea?"

"To rent out our downstairs offices? To strangers? I don't know, Corden. That is . . . I'm not ready to go there yet."

"It's premium office space, in Buckhead. Centrally located and full of high-end décor."

"How much could we charge someone?"

"I've done the math. At fifty dollars a square foot for the two office spaces and conference room downstairs, we could charge over eight thousand dollars a month."

My eyes widened. "That's the mortgage and Sylvia's salary."

"Exactly."

"I hate that you're right about this, but we really could use that money just to float us between these low revenue engagements."

Corden looked pleased, probably more about me saying he was right than his actually being right. He loved when he could bring me around to one of his ideas, especially when I had opposed it at first.

"How does the rest of your afternoon look?" Corden asked. "I want to give you a break and then go over some more reports and projections."

"Ooh, let's do it tomorrow. I'm taking the afternoon off, because we're having a bridesmaid's meeting at my house this evening."

"Oh, for Ms. Kimberly's wedding?"

I nodded. "It's our line sisters mostly."

"This is gonna be a Gamma Phi Gamma affair, huh?"

"It is. Pink dresses, pale blue flowers in the bouquets. All of that."

"I know Kimberly is gonna go all out. All those new millions she's working with."

If anyone other than Corden had said that, I would've thought there was shade attached to the statement. But Corden was just being honest. Kimberly wasn't poverty-stricken before, but the money she'd earned with her distribution deal for her hair care products, CurlPop, had certainly come in handy for her wedding planning.

"Not just Gamma Phi Gamma. It's Omega Phi Gamma too. Big Ron is our frat."

"Y'all gonna be stepping and hooting and hollering. I can hear it now."

My cell phone buzzed on the table. Twila's name showed on the caller ID.

"Hey girl."

"Hey. I'm at your house. Where's your spare key?"

Twila's voice sounded wrong. Panicked, worried, or frightened. Or maybe all three. Twila was the warrior of our group. She was the kick ass and ask questions later friend. I had never heard her sound afraid.

I looked at Corden. "Can you give me the room for a second?"

"Everything okay?" he asked.

I shrugged but verbalized nothing. If there was something wrong, I didn't want to spook Twila into not sharing.

"Hahna? You there?" Twila's voice shook even more.

"I'm here. What's wrong?"

I could hear Twila's ragged breathing, but she said nothing. Whatever Twila wasn't sharing had her speechless.

"I'm not ready to talk about it," Twila finally said, "but I need to stay with you for a while. Is that okay? Will Sam mind?"

"Sam doesn't live with me, so I'm sure he doesn't have a say as to whether my friend can stay."

"You're a damn boss," Twila said, almost sounding normal, but not quite.

"The key is in the lockbox on the side of the house."

"What's the code?"

"Four, two, three."

"April twenty-third. The day we crossed."

We'd been so happy that day. Our sisterhood in Gamma Phi Gamma had been solidified. There were seven of us who'd pledged and seven of us had crossed. The numbers in our crossing date added up to seven—the biblical number of completion.

"I'll never forget that day," I said.

"Me neither."

"You might want to change the sheets in the guest room. I may have spent the night in there with Sam."

Twila chuckled. "Y'all just had to be freaks all over the damn house."

"I am unashamed."

"Well, then you've learned something from all our years of friendship. I'm proud of you."

"My housekeeper, Lauren, is on her way over. She's going to tidy up before the bridesmaid's meeting."

"Oh shoot," Twila said. "I forgot that was tonight. I'm totally not in the mood for those heffas."

"We can just drink and eat."

"Okay, girl."

"Twila, are you all right?"

"No. I'm not. Hurry home, okay?"

Twila disconnected the call, and I shuddered. This couldn't wait until after Kimberly's bridesmaid's meeting. It sounded like a sister emergency.

Chapter 3

KIMBERLY

Kimberly loved watching Big Ron eat. She'd been cooking for him at least four times a week since he'd proposed, and in those two months her man, who was usually thin, had put on weight. Kimberly had also, but she didn't want to think about that, or the inevitable diet she'd go on after the holidays. For the wedding.

The wedding where all her thin friends would be bridesmaids. Especially her two besties, Hahna and Twila. She wanted to lose fifty pounds by June, and she wouldn't officially start until after Thanksgiving in a few weeks. But she didn't want to tell anyone about her goal, not even Big Ron. Kimberly didn't want workout partners, diet tips, positive affirmations, or bootcamp style kicks-in-the-pants.

"You like the waffles?" Kimberly asked Ron as he happily chewed a mouthful. "I used a vanilla waffle mix from my friend Chef Tam's collection."

"Do I know Chef Tam? It's really good."

Kimberly shook her head. "No. She has a restaurant in Memphis called Chef Tam's Underground Café."

"We'll have to visit then."

"That's one of the things I'm looking forward to when we get married. Taking random road trips, just to find something yummy to eat."

Ron smiled. "I can't wait to spend the rest of my life with you Kimmie Kim, and yes to yummy food."

"Speaking of, I have been looking into caterers for the wedding. I think I want to bring someone to Jamaica with us."

Ron nodded, but gave no opinion like he did every time Kimberly tried to talk about the wedding plans. He loved talking about their plans for life after the wedding, but he never had an opinion about anything about that day.

"Ron, why do you never weigh in about the wedding plans?"

Ron placed his fork on the table and took a deep breath. Kimberly felt her stomach drop wishing that she hadn't posed the question.

"Do we really need to have a wedding?" Ron asked.

Kimberly glared at her fiancé. She picked up her bourbon punch and took a long swig, all while maintaining her glare.

"I guess that means yes?" Ron asked.

"Unless you don't think it's important for all of our friends and family to see us declare our vows, before God."

Ron sighed. "I'm just thinking about the cost of it all," he said. "We spend a hundred dollars a person feeding folks . . ."

"A hundred? Does that include alcohol and the cake?"

"Okay, one hundred fifty dollars a person feeding folks, for them to give us a tacky little gift. We have some great photos and end up with a bill. Make it make sense."

Kimberly balled her fists under the table so Ron couldn't see how furious she was. She bet he'd given his ex-wife—that white woman—a wedding. So why would he even think to steal this moment from her?

"First of all, there won't be a bill. We're paying for this out of pocket."

"I can think of a lot of good uses for forty grand that don't include doing the Cupid Shuffle."

Kimberly put her fork down. "Ron, have you had a wedding before?"

"I have had two weddings, babe."

"And do you remember how happy the bride was on that day? Do you remember her family and bridesmaids cheering for her joy?"

"I remember."

"Well, don't you understand that I want that too? I want to feel that joy and experience it in front of everyone I love."

Ron reached across the table and took Kimberly's shaking hands in his. He gave her a sad smile.

"I want you to have that, Kim. It's just that this will be the third time I stand in front of my family and friends and say, 'til death do us part.' I'm ashamed, I guess, about my divorces."

Kimberly blinked back tears. She heard the sadness and shame in Ron's voice, and wished he didn't have those feelings. She didn't want anything to detract from their joy at finding one another again.

"If you had done what you were supposed to do in college, I would've been your first and last wife."

Ron chuckled and kissed Kimberly's hands. "You're right babe, but you could've let a brotha know something."

"Did you have your frat brothers as groomsmen in your other weddings?"

Ron shook his head. "I didn't. With the first, well, that's kind of obvious. No one knew about the baby and her mom that I'd left behind while I was in college. And, the second one . . . well, I thought someone would object to her being white. I didn't want to hear that."

"So, then this is perfect," Kimberly said.

Ron sat back in his seat and seemed to mull over the idea.

"It would be kinda fun. Your sorors. My frats. Maybe the twins can be little flower girls or something."

Kimberly plastered a smile on her face. She'd have to consider having the twins in the ceremony, but she wasn't going to say anything to steal Ron's excitement—not when she'd just convinced him of the idea.

"Yes! It's going to be fun. And I think your family who saw you get married the other times just want you to be happy."

"They do. My mama is so excited about you. She hates Sabrina. I mean everything about her. Especially her cooking."

Kimberly laughed. "She puts raisins in potato salad?"

"Worse. She's a vegetarian. She asked my mama about meat-free options at a barbeque."

"Was that when you knew?"

"Knew what? That I needed to come on home to my sistas?"

Kimberly nodded. Ron was still laughing, but Kimberly's laughter had subsided.

"No, it wasn't her cooking, even though it was bad. It wasn't anything about her whiteness. We just weren't good for one another. I definitely don't think she cheated on me with her ex because I'm black."

Kimberly took another sip of her bourbon punch. It was difficult hearing about Ron having had other loves before her. Not that she hadn't had romances, but it was never anything that had felt like love. Ron had loved and lost.

"We can have a wedding, Kimmie Kim. I want you happy. And I'm not going to take this away from you because I made mistakes."

Kimberly smiled at his words, but mostly the love and kindness in his eyes.

"Don't worry. It will be your last time walking down the aisle."

She believed every word.

Chapter 4

HAHNA

When I got home from work, Twila had already started with the wine. She sat on the leather sectional in my family room, guzzling red wine out of a huge goblet (not one of mine, so she must've brought that from home), and watching a movie. I sat next to her. Didn't say anything, because I wanted to see if she would share first.

"That Lauren is a beast. She cleaned the hell out of your house in less than two hours," Twila said.

"She's in and out. That's what I like about her."

"I hope you don't mind, but I asked her to take a little extra time in the guest room."

I thought back to the fun night where Sam and I had anointed the guest bedroom and grinned.

"That was probably for the best."

Twila sighed and drank some more. "When is everyone supposed to be getting here?"

"Six, but you know Kim is the only one who'll be here on time. Everyone else will show up between seven and seven thirty."

"I don't really feel like doing this tonight, but for Kim I will."

My phone buzzed, and I read the text.

"It's Kim. She's here already."

"It's not even five thirty."

"She probably wants to help me set up. You wanna help too?"

Twila rolled her eyes. "Of course, I want to help."

I knew she didn't. When Twila was going through something, she liked to stew on it alone until she came up with a solution. We usually didn't even find out something was bothering her until after things were solved and her life back intact.

Twila went straight to the kitchen, but I stopped at the front door to let Kimberly in. We embraced, and I got a nice whiff of Kimberly's natural hair care products. Whatever she was using this week smelled like lemon meringue pie.

"Twila's already here?" Kimberly asked. "Is Jesus coming back?"

"She got here hours ago. With a suitcase."

Kim stopped and grimaced. "A suitcase?"

"She's going through something. Don't know what yet."

"Oh, okay."

Kimberly marched into the kitchen, arms swinging, head high, and on a mission. I should've let Twila tell her she was staying with me, because unlike me, Kimberly didn't play coy. Direct was the only way she knew how to be.

"Hey girl," Kimberly said to Twila while hugging her. "Hahna said you're staying over here. What's going on?"

Twila glared at me. "Big mouth."

"Sorry."

Kimberly tossed her purse on a barstool and washed her hands in the sink. She opened the refrigerator and started pulling out food.

"What all are we having Hahna?"

"All those trays. I got a sandwich tray, pasta salad, a fruit tray and a sushi tray."

Twila's eyes lit up. "You sprang for that fancy sushi tray? These girls don't deserve that."

"Yes, they do. This is the first bridesmaid's meeting," I said. "We'll make them bring potluck for the rest of the meetings."

"Twila, I'm not going to drop this," Kimberly said. "You can't just say you're staying over here when you own a whole ass brownstone."

Twila took her glass of wine and plopped down in a barstool. "I saw someone today, from my past, in my housing development. It spooked me."

"Spooked you? Not, I-know-a-dozen-ways-to-kill-a-man Twila," Kimberly said. "What gives?"

"I don't think I'm ready to share the rest of the story," Twila said. "Why can't you just let me do this in bits and pieces?"

"You can take your time, but we just want to help," I said.

"I know you do, and I love you both, but I'm going to see my therapist on Monday."

I locked eyes with Kimberly. Twila hadn't brought up her therapist in years. I thought she'd stopped going. And if she had stopped, who from her past could make her go back again?

Twila climbed down from the barstool and refreshed her wine. "It looks like y'all got this kitchen thing. I'm going back into the TV room so I can get my mind right for the rest of y'all line sisters."

"Our line sisters," Kimberly said.

Twila took her wine and a piece of cheese from one of the trays and sashayed out of the kitchen. I was just about to say something when we heard Twila's voice from the other side of the wall.

"Y'all heffas better not be talking about me."

"We'll talk about you later," Kimberly said.

I nodded in agreement as I covered up my mouth to stifle my laugh. We'd have an extensive conversation about this later, whether I wanted to or not. Kim wasn't going to let this go.

"In other news," Kimberly said, "can you believe that Big Ron thought he was going to talk me out of having a wedding?"

"He doesn't want one?"

"He didn't, but I helped readjust his thinking on that."

I pressed my lips together and let the air slowly out of my nose.

"What?" Kimberly asked.

"What if he didn't want his thinking readjusted? Did he tell you the reason why he didn't want a wedding?"

"He did, and the reason was invalid. Just because he'd already exchanged vows twice in front of his family. He'd said 'til death do us part with two other women, and was feeling some kinda way about it."

I didn't think his reason was invalid at all. I understood what he meant. Big Ron had a southern church family like mine. They didn't take too kindly to divorcing and remarrying. Even to the point of inviting all the ex-wives to all of the family functions. It was weird at Christmas when Bobby had two of his babies' mamas, his ex-wife, and his current boo all vying to make him a plate.

"You know Big Ron's family in North Carolina all go to the same church. They probably all have the same pastor."

Kim shrugged. "He gave that white woman a wedding, so he's giving my ass one."

Oh. That was what this was about. Poor Ron was going to spend the rest of his life apologizing to Kim about marrying a white woman. It wasn't enough that they'd gotten divorced and that Ron had clearly not sworn off black woman because of his choice. It also wasn't enough that Ron had chosen Kim. He had a lifetime of penance ahead of him.

"Well, if he's okay with it, good," I said, not wanting any friction with Kimberly ahead of this bridesmaid's meeting.

I needed Kimberly to know that I was clearly the choice for Maid of Honor. It was always going to come down to me or Twila, but our soror Samantha Pike seemed to be making a play for the coveted spot. I wasn't at liberty to trash Samantha, because she'd written the article in the Atlanta Star that cleared my name and The Data Whisperers' reputation of any impropriety. So, Kimberly was going to have to see, on her own, that I was the best woman for the job.

"We decided on a destination wedding in Jamaica," Kimberly said.

"Oh, I thought y'all wanted to do Atlanta."

I certainly wanted Kim to get married in Atlanta. Her status would bring out the black elite, and I could've used some referrals or some business.

"I want a beach, and he wants a small crowd."

"I know the perfect venue. It's a castle in Negril."

Kimberly stopped unwrapping the sandwich tray and laughed. "How do you do that? You're like google. My own personal search engine."

I laughed with her. "I was looking for my own venue when I was dating Torian, but you know how that went. I was thinking of marriage and he wasn't."

"He might've been, before he got cancer," Kimberly said.

I had no clue what Torian had wanted out of our relationship, but his ghosting me was the best thing that ever could've happened to me. Because he disappeared when he got his cancer diagnosis, I was free to find the real love of my life—Sam.

"Well he's in the past along with those wedding plans, so I'll send you the link to the castle."

"You sure? You might want to use it with Sam."

"Sam wouldn't want that kind of wedding," I said. "He'd want something minimal. Probably just the two of us and a minister."

"That wouldn't bother you?" Kimberly asked. "You love a party."

"Well yes, I do, but I love him more."

"Loving him doesn't mean you have to give everything up, though. That's not fair."

She was right, but there were some things that I didn't mind giving up. Sam had given up a lot for me too. He had to go on expensive trips, hobnob with rich people, and pass the time in my renovated mansion.

Wait. What was he giving up again?

"Enough about me and Sam," I said, not wanting to pull that thought thread any more than I already had. "Tonight is about you and my frat, Big Ron, and announcing the Maid of Honor in your wedding."

Kimberly laughed. Why was there laughter?

"I said something funny?" I asked.

Kimberly gathered the remaining plastic from the food trays and placed it in the trashcan. "I think I want two Maids of Honor. You and Twila. Why would I choose differently? You're my best friends."

"Oh, 'cause I heard Samantha called you with plans for a bachelorette party and a garden bridal shower."

Kimberly tossed her head back and hollered. I folded my arms and waited for her stop being so amused.

"Yes, she did, and I humored her. That's all."

"Mmm-hmm."

"Come on girl, and let's put this food out for everybody."

We carried the trays out to my entertaining space and placed them on tables all around the room. There were food stations set up with small plates, napkins, and bottles of wine. Kimberly wasn't lying about me loving a party. Even if it was just our line sisters, I wanted everything perfect.

"What do you think?" I asked. "Just like if I'd hired a party planner, huh?"

"Yep. You should probably be one," Kimberly said.

"I don't need another job."

Well, maybe I did. If I couldn't get The Data Whisperers back on track, maybe there was a career for me in party planning. Ugh.

The doorbell rang, and I could hear the cackling before I even got to the door.

"Wait," Kimberly said. "Let me have a second before I have to do this."

"You need wine?"

"I need something stronger. Bourbon."

We rarely brought all our line sisters together, and with good reason. But we'd made a pact in college to stand up at each other's weddings. We'd done the bridesmaid thing only once with Abena when she married Kyle. And that was a shenanigan from start to finish.

Twila emerged from the bedroom, still holding her glass of wine in her hand. "The doorbell rang. Might as well let them in."

Kimberly took a deep breath and exhaled. "My wedding, so I guess it's on me."

It *was* on Kimberly, but Twila and I had her back. No matter what drama was going to ensue. And the drama was inevitable.

Chapter 5

KIMBERLY

Kimberly opened Hahna's front door, but it wasn't all of the bridesmaids, only Traci and Abena, the sisters-in-law. Kimberly relaxed a little because they were not the ones who caused anxiety. There was only one.

They both hugged Kimberly, and she hugged them back. Even though they all lived in Atlanta, it was usually only on special occasions that she got to see Traci and Abena. They weren't as active in their Gamma Phi Gamma alumni chapter, except in their giving. They co-owned an exclusive nightclub, Club Phenom, where Abena's husband was the deejay.

"Is everyone here?" Traci asked as she walked into Hahna's house. "And why didn't we do this at your place?"

"Samantha and Debbie aren't here yet, but they're always late, right?" Kimberly said. "My house has boxes of CurlPop products all over. I need to get organized."

Traci and Abena took turns hugging Hahna and Twila. Kimberly's heart warmed to see Twila's ice melt a bit. She even gave everyone warm smiles.

But, unfortunately, this was the pregame.

If the bridesmaids number was going to stop at four and the final two weren't on the way, this whole thing would be peaceful and harmonious. Kimberly damned that stupid pact. Not all sorority line sisters ended up being best friends.

"Kim finally bagged Big Ron," Traci said as she sat. "I could've sworn y'all was hooking up when we were in college."

"What? I was the epitome of chastity, elegance, and grace," Kimberly said.

The other ladies chanted in unison, "Gamma Phi Gamma ladies run this place."

They erupted into laughter at the chant they said as they walked onto the yard. Samantha always led the line—her great grandmother was a founder of their campus chapter. She was Gamma Phi Gamma legacy and royalty. Hahna always brought up the rear, because she was the youngest of the line, by a couple months.

The doorbell rang again, and Abena hopped up to answer it. "Sit down, Kim," she said. "This get together is all about you. You don't have to play hostess."

Hahna gave Kimberly a sidelong glance, and Kimberly bit her lower lip to keep from chuckling. Abena's sweet admonition was a dig at Hahna *not* playing hostess. She didn't need to, though. It was a gathering of sisters.

As soon as Debbie walked through the door, hauling a car seat in one arm and dragging a toddler behind her in the other, Kimberly felt her headache start. Why would she bring her damn kids to a bridesmaids meeting?

"Hey y'all. My mama couldn't watch the kids. She going on a gambling trip to Mississippi. I hope it's okay."

Twila guzzled her wine to mask her smile, while Hahna's nostrils flared nervously as the little girl toddled towards her white couch while holding a red lollipop. Kimberly scooped her up before she made contact with the couch, and she expertly removed the candy from the child's sticky hand.

She started to scream. Debbie plopped down in a decorative chair and the baby boy in the car seat added his yells to his sister's.

"She gone keep hollerin' until she get another piece of candy," Debbie said.

"Can she have fruit?" Hahna said. "There's plenty. Does she have a playpen or somewhere we can sit her down?"

Debbie burst into laughter. "You can tell you ain't got no kids. She is way too big for a play pen."

"Oh, I didn't know. My white couch isn't kid friendly, though."

Debbie rolled her eyes. "I'll make sure she don't touch nothing. Come here Artalaysha."

"Named after her daddy, huh?" Twila asked.

"Yeah, girl. Art's ass got on my nerves the whole time I was pregnant with her, then she came out with his damn head. I was just gonna name her Laysha, but I had to put Art on the front of it."

Twila guzzled more wine, but Kimberly could see the way her body shivered, that she was holding in a monster laugh.

The toddler waddled over to her mother, and Hahna hopped up to give her grapes in a cup.

"Her hands are sticky," Hahna said. "Can I get you a paper towel?"

"There's a wet wipe in the bag."

The door rang again, and this time Kimberly hopped up to answer. She was happy to flee the uncomfortable scene with Hahna and Debbie. The scenes between them had always been uncomfortable, even when they were in college.

"Samantha, girl I'm so glad you're here."

Kimberly felt herself relax with Samantha's presence. While she was closer to Hahna and Twila, Kimberly and Samantha shared a special bond outside of the line sister circle. While she wasn't as social with Hahna or Twila, no one could say that Samantha wasn't always there when someone needed her. She was.

Samantha's life was just so different from everyone else's. She was a journalist and evangelist at her church. She never judged anyone on purpose but Twila, in particular, always *felt* like Samantha was judging her life. It was just best if they spent little time together. Small doses.

"I'm sorry I'm late y'all. I had a deadline at five and I had to get it done this evening."

Samantha made the rounds and hugged everyone, and it was evident that the only warm hug she was getting was from Kimberly.

Before she sat, she walked to the beverage table. "Is there anything non-alcoholic?" she asked.

Hahna finished with Artalaysha and stood. "I have lemonade in the kitchen. I'm sorry. I forgot you didn't drink."

"No big deal."

Abena shook her head as Hahna left the room. "How did she forget Evangelist Samantha was gonna be here?"

Traci jabbed her in the ribs, and Abena hushed. Kimberly wondered if she was going to be able to survive the catfighting up until the time of her wedding.

Hahna came back with the lemonade in a pretty glass and handed it to Samantha. Then she sat, but she didn't relax. She kept looking at little Artalaysha's little hands.

Kimberly just decided to get started. The energy in the room wasn't going to get any better, and there was a good chance if she didn't do something to focus everyone's attention that things had the potential of getting worse.

"I'm so glad y'all are all here with me," Kimberly said. "I couldn't imagine having a wedding without y'all being there."

"What's the date?" Debbie asked. "I need to get off work."

Kimberly swallowed her irritation. It was a valid question, but could she give her a second to do her introduction?

"The wedding is the third weekend in May, and it's going to be in Negril, Jamaica."

Abena did a little shoulder dance. "I love Jamaica! Can't wait. Are we doing an all-inclusive?"

"No, I mean you can if you want to, but I plan on booking a villa with enough space for all of us."

"For just us? Or for our men too?" Traci asked.

"Men too," Kimberly said. "It's not like you'd go out of the country for a wedding without your significant other."

"May as in this coming May?" Debbie asked. "Eight months from now?"

Kimberly knew that Debbie would have an issue with the wedding date and venue. She always had an issue with anything that cost money. Even if it had been a year out or two years out, she would've had a problem with it.

"Yes, but since I'm paying for the lodging for you, this shouldn't be a problem," Kimberly said, refusing to let Debbie's situation dictate the logistics of her wedding.

"Hmm," Debbie said as she shifted in her chair with the tod-dler thrashing about.

"Jamaica sounds wonderful," Samantha said. "And that's generous of you to pay for our lodging."

"I'm still looking for venues, but I think Hahna and I have got that covered," Kimberly said, to Hahna's apparent delight.

"So, is she the Maid of Honor?" Traci asked. "We're wearing pink and blue, right?"

"Yes, to the colors, although I haven't decided the configura-tion. We'll have silver accents for the frats."

"Y'all need to be getting married right here in Atlanta," Deb-bie said. "This is where it all began."

"We thought about that, but we'd end up having to invite too many people."

"Right," Twila said, "we know half of Atlanta."

Abena raised her hand, although no one was raising hands to speak. "You didn't answer about the Maid of Honor."

"Oh, right. It's Maids of Honor for my wedding," Kimberly said. "Hahna and Twila."

Samantha pressed her lips into a tight line, but she said nothing. Kimberly valued Samantha's friendship as a confi-dante, and a prayer partner. It was just that she was such a good prayer partner that half the time she wasn't any fun. Kimberly wanted her wedding celebration to be fun and a little wild. She wanted a bachelorette party that was full of debauchery and shenanigans. Samantha shunned debauchery and frowned upon shenanigans. Samantha was the friend that made every-one feel immature.

"I'm planning the bachelorette," Twila said. "You can do everything else, Hahna."

Traci and Abena high-fived Twila. That was the trio of terror during college. They were the ones who went to the frat parties and drank more than the guys. And even after graduation, they were the ones Kimberly lived vicariously through.

"Since you're not getting married in Atlanta, I do think you should, at least, have an engagement party," Hahna said. "It doesn't have to be big, but you should have some of your key business contacts in Atlanta to come and give you and Ron a toast."

Hahna was right, but Kimberly had zero bandwidth to plan another party. The party that she'd had for her product launch a few months ago had been too much work.

"I don't know if I can swing that. I've got so much going on with work," Kimberly said.

"We can host it at the club," Traci said.

The look that Hahna and Kimberly exchanged needed no explanation. There was no way Kimberly would have her engagement party at that freak nasty club of theirs. Twila may have been a frequent visitor, but Kimberly never planned to set foot inside of that place.

"That would be a no."

"Why?" Traci said. "It's really upscale. You guys should come out and see it. We all support everyone's business, but only Twila has been to the club. I mean, we know Samantha can't come . . ."

"You got that right," Samantha said. "It would be just my luck Jesus would come back right when I set foot in there."

Twila closed her eyes and shook her head. It was coming. The battle between the sinners and the saint. It happened every time the line sisters got together, so Kimberly didn't expect this time to be any different.

"Maybe if you came to the club, you'd meet a man there, or are you still saving it for Jesus?" Abena asked.

"I'm not responding to that," Samantha said to Kimberly.

"Let's talk about where we're actually going to have your engagement party."

The engagement party that Kimberly didn't want to throw in the first place.

"You never respond when I'm telling the truth," Abena said. "Truth hurts."

"No, that's not it at all. You're low, so I'm going high."

Abena rose from her seat and both Traci and Twila pulled her back down. Traci was always the first to pop off, and . . .

"Call me with the details," Samantha said.

. . . Samantha was always the first to leave.

Samantha stood and gathered her purse. Before Kimberly could talk her out of it, she was headed for the door.

"Let me walk you out," Kimberly said. "I'll be right back y'all. Can we come up with some alternate venues for the engagement party. Club Phenom isn't everyone's cup of tea."

Kimberly followed Samantha although she'd already gained a head start. Kimberly easily caught up, though, because out of all the line sisters, Samantha was the only one more plus-sized that she was. In the heat, Samantha slowed down whether she wanted to or not, and they both stopped at her car.

"I'm sorry about that, Samantha. You know how Traci and Abena are about that club."

"Club Sodom and Gomorrah, you mean?"

"That's not nice."

"You know I don't care about being nice when it comes to Jesus."

Kimberly sighed. "I know."

"Is that why you didn't ask me to be a Maid of Honor? Because you want to have strippers and carrying on and you think I wouldn't deliver any of that?"

"Would you have delivered that?"

"No. But I didn't think that's something you'd want. We prayed for you to find a husband and now he's here. This wedding celebration should give honor and glory to God."

"And it will. It's just that everyone isn't an evangelist, okay? You can't judge everyone and expect them not to be mad."

"Well somebody ought to say something. Debbie sitting up there on her third child and third baby's father."

"Her children are beautiful."

"I'm not judging them, Kimberly. It's just that you're my friend . . . they are my line sisters. They are my past and not my present."

"Not even Hahna?"

Hahna and Samantha attended the same church, which was why Samantha came through with that article in the Atlanta Star for Hahna's business.

"Sometimes Hahna."

"I love all of y'all," Kimberly said. "You, Hahna, and Twila are my best friends. You all serve a different purpose in my life, and I love you all separately and equally for those reasons."

"And I love you too. I wouldn't miss your special day for anything. But don't expect me to enjoy hanging with these girls."

"I am my sister . . . my sister and I are one."

Samantha rolled her eyes. "I put God first. Not Gamma Phi Gamma."

Samantha opened her car door and got inside. Kimberly waved as she drove off. It always happened this way, and Samantha's tolerance for everyone else was getting shorter and shorter.

Kimberly thought about how to create harmony with all her sorority sisters as she walked back to the house, but as she approached the door, she could hear Debbie's children wailing. Even closer and she heard Debbie's voice and Hahna's, and neither of them sounded friendly.

"I'm sorry, Kim, I've got to go," Debbie hollered as Kimberly walked into the room. "Hahna ain't gonna keep dogging out my baby over these damn material possessions."

"I just asked you to take that red juice away from her, because she was spilling it. I think you wanted her to spill it with your hating ass." Hahna was furious.

"Oh, so I'm a hater? Really, *soror*?"

"I said what I said," Hahna declared. She picked up the diaper bag and handed it to Debbie. "Next time get a babysitter."

Debbie's eyes watered as she grabbed her children and snatched the bag from Hahna. When no one moved to help her, Kimberly stepped up and took Artalaysha's little sticky hand.

"I hope you have the rest of the meetings at your house, Kim," Debbie said as she trudged to the door.

Kimberly glanced over her shoulder and gave Hahna a mean glare. Hahna's face softened a little, but only a little.

"Debbie, I'm sorry. Come on and stay. I'll put some plastic down for the baby," Hahna said.

Debbie, who clearly didn't want to leave, spun on one heel and rushed back to her chair. She plopped the car seat down on the floor and left Kimberly with the sticky-handed toddler.

Kimberly took a moist wipe from the diaper bag and wiped Artalaysha's hands. Then, she followed Hahna to the kitchen with the child in tow. When they were out of earshot of the other girls, Kimberly opened her mouth to speak.

"Don't even say anything," Hahna said to Kimberly. "I know. It's not her fault that the daddies aren't helping. She needs us. That's what you were gonna say, right?"

"I was gonna say that we've got a long road ahead of us until the wedding, so maybe we want to hold off on the high drama."

"High drama? Girl, you would've seen high drama if she had spilled that damn Hawaiian Punch on my seven thousand-dollar Horchow sofa."

"Do you know how much you paid for everything in your house?"

"What? No."

"Oh, 'cause for a second I thought that couch meant more to you than your line sister."

"You sound like Sam."

"Well . . . it can't be both of us. Maybe it's you, sis."

Kimberly lifted her eyebrow and waited for Hahna's retort. She couldn't have a valid one, because it *was* her. Kimberly understood why Hahna revered her things so much, but it just didn't always come across well to the people she loved.

"Wow. I didn't know you felt like that. You having second thoughts about choosing me as one of your Maids of Honor?"

Kimberly chuckled. "No ma'am. I accept you in all your flaws and brokenness, although Samantha sure would be ready to step up and take your spot."

"She's bothered, huh? That's the real reason she left, isn't it? She doesn't care about Traci, Abena and that club."

"She does care about that too, but yeah she just felt she should've been before y'all. Probably more Twila than you."

"But it's always been the three of us. Even in college. We were friends before we pledged. And when she got all the way evangelist saved, she ghosted all of us."

"Not all. She and I never fell off."

"Well, she fell off with me and we go to the same church and serve on the same ministries. It's pretty awkward. Especially when the other Gammas at our church find out we're line sisters."

Hahna took out a sandwich bag and filled it halfway with Cheerios. Artalaysha giggled as she put the unoffensive snack in her hand.

"I wish I had something for her to play with," Hahna said. "Or at least something for her to put her hands on other than my couch."

Kimberly spied some colorful plastic measuring cups on the counter. "What about those?"

Hahna shrugged. "Maybe."

She picked up the measuring cups and held them out to the little girl. She reached for them and handed back the cereal.

"Look at who's gonna be a good mom," Hahna said. "I would've never thought of that."

"I don't know about that good mom part. Ron mentioned having his daughters in the wedding, and I'm still trying to wrap my brain around what that even looks like."

"Will their mother have to be there?" Hahna asked.

"I'm sure she's not going to let him take them to Jamaica without her going along."

"Well, maybe y'all will have one of those Will and Jada type things. They're all one big family with his ex-wife. I bet if Tupac was still alive, he'd be in the mix too."

"Nah, Will wasn't feeling Pac all like that. But he wanted Jada to accept his ex-wife all up in her space, though."

Hahna laughed out loud. "Girl, we act like we know them."

"Shoot, you don't? I done watched every Red Table Talk. I know them."

Twila poked her head into the kitchen. "What's taking y'all so long? They in here drinking all the wine. We're gonna need replenishments in a minute."

"Debbie too?" Hahna asked.

"Especially her ass, but you know she don't get out much. Somebody gonna have to drive her home."

Hahna and Twila both looked at Kimberly.

"Y'all get on my nerves," Kimberly said.

"She's your bridesmaid," Twila said.

"Both of you need therapy and life coaches to fix y'all messy ass selves," Kimberly said.

Hahna laughed, but Twila did not.

"I start therapy tomorrow," Twila said. "Dr. Mays."

"Does this have something to do with the reason you're staying here," Hahna asked. "You know you can tell us, right?"

Twila took the last swallow of wine in her glass and shook her head. "I can't. I've tried to start the conversation so many times, and I know y'all are a safe place. I just . . . this requires a professional."

Twila's hands started trembling so hard that Hahna took the glass from her hand and set it on the table. Hahna smoothed Twila's hair out of her face and hugged her.

"It's fine. Whenever you're ready to share, you will."

Kimberly touched the middle of Twila's back and rubbed. She wondered if they could ever all be joyful at the same time. It seemed she and her two best friends always had to juggle sadness and joy at the same time—only allowing the appropriate amount of either emotion to come out in their conversations so as not to disturb the other's happiness or block their healing process.

Kimberly wasn't, however, surprised that Twila was on her way back to therapy. The multiple self-defense classes, the weapons, the twice-weekly gun range visits. All the signs were there of someone who had experienced trauma. Kimberly had been talking to God about her sister for years.

She was never surprised about an answered prayer.

Chapter 6

TWILA

I thought I'd never come back to this place. The office of LaTonya Mays, licensed therapist. She was the one who'd helped me put the pieces of my life back together when my mother died, and I couldn't get past the grief. I didn't see her after what happened to me at Club Phenom. Probably should've, but I didn't want to cross-pollinate pain. She had witnessed one tragic event in my life, and didn't need to witness another.

Plus, over the years, I'd built a friendship with Dr. Mays. Just like I didn't want my best friends to know that I'd visited the land of the free and the home of the nasty, I didn't want Dr. Mays to know. Everyone always said that they wouldn't look differently at you, but they always did. Unconditional love had conditions and they were usually tied to sex, crimes, and religion. My shit had all three.

But I wasn't going to get through this without someone who could reach down to my core, find all the sludge, and drag it to the surface. That was Dr. Mays. She was my own personal Iyanla. She didn't call me beloved, but she sure as hell made me own my shit.

Dr. Mays's receptionist showed me to her office, and I sat reminiscing. The décor was different, upgraded, but it felt the same. It still smelled like lavender and sandalwood, and there were still African masks on the wall. You couldn't come in Dr. Mays's presence as a person of color and not feel like you mattered. She dripped blackness and greatness and wrapped herself in the motherland. She was a masterpiece.

Dr. Mays walked into the office and parted her lovely strong African mouth into a smile. Her teeth were perfect. Of course, they were. I fixed them. I was the only orthodontist in Atlanta who cared enough about culture to fix her slight overbite while maintaining her small gap—a thing of beauty to her Nigerian family.

Dr. Mays extended her arms, and I jumped up to hug her. Her locs smelled like essential oils and heaven. This was a nontraditional practice. There was no distance between Dr. Mays and her patients. She didn't just help them heal with her education and degrees. She helped them . . . us . . . heal with love.

"I have missed you, Ms. Twila. How have you been?" Dr. Mays asked as she sat on the couch across from the one I'd chosen. I sat as well.

"I've missed you too. I've mostly been well."

"Is it right for me to assume that the little bit left behind after *mostly* is what you are here to talk about?"

"That would be an accurate assumption."

"Where would you like to begin?"

I took a deep breath and exhaled. I didn't know where to start. I'd been plugging my emotions up like the little Dutch boy who'd saved his town by sticking his finger in the dam. Except that story was a fraud just like my false cover. I was falling apart one leak at a time, and now the people closest to me knew because I couldn't hold it together anymore.

"I'm staying at one of my best friend's houses. I can't stay at home."

"Cannot or will not?"

"I would if I could. I don't feel safe there right now."

Dr. Mays nodded slowly. "Not right now, but you would like to feel safe again. That is the end state you would like to see?"

"Yes. I'd like to feel safe. Empowered."

"And did someone or something take your power away?"

I scoffed. "I am a black woman in the American South. My power is microaggressed against every day."

"Right. Agree. But be more specific. You have stayed in your own home until now even with the microaggressions of racism stealing a portion of your power. Who specifically made you feel unsafe and powerless?"

"The man who raped me."

The words shocked my ears as if someone else's voice had said them. It was the first time I'd said that out loud. I'd never even thought the word rape with reference to my being assaulted at Club Phenom.

"Did this rape happen at your home? Is he someone you know?"

I swallowed, suddenly not feeling as forthcoming about the rest of the story. "No, I don't know him. And it didn't happen at my home."

"And does he now know where you live?"

"No. I saw him in my housing development, but he didn't see me. I don't even know if he would recognize me."

Dr. Mays pursed her lips and moved them from side to side. I wondered if she was calculating what she should say next. She took long pauses all the time. She considered things and then considered them some more. There were no written notes taken, although she recorded every session. This was analysis in real-time.

"The reason he wouldn't recognize you?"

"When he raped me, I was wearing a mask."

"Tell me what you felt when you saw him. I know that you moved to your friend's house. But in that moment, what did you feel?"

I thought back to that moment. Standing on the pavement, at the intersection, unable to move. The terror.

"I was having my morning run, so my heart was already racing. But I felt the air leave my lungs, and I felt like I couldn't draw another breath. I couldn't move. My feet were stuck in place."

"What emotions did you feel?"

"Fear. Mostly fear. But some shame with remembering him . . . hurting me. The memory of it had started to fade, and when I saw him again it all rushed back."

There was another long pause, and more lip pursing.

"I'd like to try a technique with you, over the next few sessions. I think it will get you to the end state you desire. Empowerment and feeling safe again."

I was willing to give anything for that. I didn't know how long I'd survive living with Hahna and her bubbly goodness. I needed my own space back again.

"What is the technique?"

"It is called Cognitive Behavior Therapy. CBT. Basically, you recount the assault over and over until it no longer causes the fear and shame. You desensitize your emotions and your body's natural response to the stress of remembering."

"And it loses its power?"

"Correct. Does it sound like something you want to do?"

I nodded. "I trust you, and if you think it will be effective then I will try it."

"Good. You have had enough trauma for the day even admitting it to me. You have not told anyone else about the rape, have you?"

"No, I haven't. I almost told my two best friends, but I couldn't get it out."

"Would you consider pressing charges?"

"No."

"All right. I did not think that you would, and I will not try to convince you. I had to offer it, though."

I didn't smile, but I felt a bit brighter after she said this. She hadn't forgotten my personality and the things that were important to me. My pride was the thing that drove me to succeed. It was also the thing that wouldn't let me admit that someone had taken advantage of me sexually. I would never be able to testify in court.

"Thank you, Dr. Mays. For the offer and for understanding."

"When you go out to make appointments with Holly make at least four."

"Only four?"

Dr. Mays nodded. "You will know four sessions in if this treatment is working for you, and so will I. We can then assess our next steps."

Our next steps. The other thing I loved about Dr. Mays is that she was on this journey with me. I wasn't going to be alone.

"Okay. Thank you. I'm ready to be well."

"Asé. And it shall be."

There was power in Dr. Mays's words, so I believed. She would help me see this through.

Chapter 7

HAHNA

Sam picked up the leavings of our soul-food lunch as I checked the calendar on my laptop. We had these lunches at least once a week, and I loved them. It made me stop and reflect on everything good and perfect in my life while in the middle of my worst work crisis.

While Sam worked, he hummed, not even remotely aware that his easy and peaceful demeanor combined with his tight abs and sculpted arms made me want to abandon the rest of the working day and head home. I stopped looking at the computer and beheld my man in all his melanated greatness.

He looked up at me and grinned. My body immediately responded. I crossed my legs to calm the growing fire.

"You want dessert?" he asked.

And just like that I was ready to start pulling clothes off. And I was unashamed about it.

There was a knock on my office door. Shoot.

"Come in."

Sam chuckled at what I was sure sounded like pure disappointment in my tone. I wanted my dark chocolate treat.

Sylvia emerged from the other side of the door with a smile on her face. She enjoyed looking at Sam as much as I did, even though she was old enough to be both our mothers.

"Your one o'clock is here, Hahna."

"He's early," I said. "That's a good sign."

"That's what Corden said. He's already gone down to greet him. I think he's going to give him a tour while you wrap up with Sam."

"Perfect. Thank you, Sylvia. I'll be down in a few."

Sylvia looked at Sam. "Did you save me some of that lobster macaroni and cheese?"

"Save you some? I made you your own."

Sam retrieved the sealed container from the edge of my desk and handed it to Sylvia. She squealed and gave him a hug.

"Thank you, baby."

"I know whose good side to stay on around here," Sam said.

I laughed out loud. "Mine."

"And mine," Sylvia said. "He knows who will clear that calendar and free up his lady for a little afternoon delight."

"That's what I'm talking about," Sam said as he hugged Sylvia again.

"What you know about afternoon delights, Ms. Sylvia?" I asked.

"Baby, I know about morning, afternoon, and midnight delights. Don't play with me. Now you 'bout to have me repenting at prayer service."

Sylvia laughed and shook her head as she closed my office door.

"She's great," Sam said. "She reminds me of my mother and my aunt, Celestine. There is a common experience of older women of the African diaspora that makes them a comfort to me."

I closed the laptop and stood. Walked around the desk to touch what I'd been gazing upon. His breathing shallowed as I dragged my nails across his chest down to his lower abdominals where he placed his hand over mine.

"And what about the younger women of the African diaspora? Are we a comfort too?"

"You are my peace and my fire."

Sam pulled me into an embrace and placed soft kisses on my

neck. My favorite thing. I swooned, then thought about my visitor downstairs.

"Babe, can we pick up right here later on tonight?"

Sam released me, and I almost changed my mind.

"Yes. Your place or mine?" Sam asked.

I sighed when I thought about my houseguest. "Yours. Twila is staying with me right now."

"Is she remodeling?"

"No. Something's going on with her, and she's not sharing."

"Man problems? A stalker? She doesn't have to be afraid of that. I can . . ."

"No, no, I don't think it's anything like that. I've never seen her this afraid. She tried to tell me and Kimberly what it was, but she couldn't get it out."

Sam lifted his eyebrows. "This sounds serious. Do you need to stay with her? I mean we can be quiet in your bedroom."

"I can't be quiet with you."

"That will make it exciting. You trying to be quiet."

I thought about how Sam has helped me through every inhibition and found every button to push. He'd found hot spots I didn't know I had, and erogenous zones on top of erogenous zones. Every nerve ending in my body craved him.

There was nothing silent about this.

"I'm going to meet this lawyer who wants to rent office space from me, and I will meet you later, at home."

"You're renting out space? How did that come about?" Sam asked.

"Corden did the numbers. It makes sense. With our reduction of staff and clients, we're not using all this space, and we could use the steady cash flow."

"Smart. Corden's idea?"

"Absolutely."

"You're blessed to have him on your team."

"I am." I kissed Sam softly on the lips. "And I'm blessed to have you on my team as well."

I left the comfort of my man's arms to go and talk to my potential tenant. I hoped that the lawyer wasn't an arrogant prick, or worse, a sleazeball. This space had been powered by black girl magic, and I wasn't ready to share.

As I descended the stairs, Corden chatted with DeAndre Williams, Esquire. That was the signature in his email. A little pretentious if you asked me. I had a bet going with Corden that he probably attended an Ivy League law school. Those were the only guys I knew who put Esquire in their signature.

They both looked up at me and smiled. Mr. Esquire was easy on the eyes, that was for sure. I guess that would've been a bigger plus if I were single, or maybe an even bigger distraction. But since I had my own personal chocolate buffet still hanging out in my office, DeAndre Williams was just an attractive black brother.

"Mr. Williams," I said as I walked off the last step. "Corden gave you the tour?"

"He did." DeAndre extended his hand, and I shook. "It's a beautiful space. Where do I sign?"

I chuckled. "You don't need to talk to your other associates?"

"It's just me. I'm a one man show."

Corden looked at me with eyebrows raised. He wanted me to seal the deal immediately, but we hadn't spent enough time around this man yet. I needed to feel comfortable before giving him the keys to my queendom.

"Is there a gym nearby?" DeAndre asked. "I do like to work out in the mornings and it would probably be better if I choose a location close to the office instead of near my house."

DeAndre clearly used a gym daily. I could see his tight abdominal muscles through his skin-tight dress shirt. And his thighs were almost too bodacious for the slim-fit designer dress pants he wore.

"How far out are you?" I asked.

"Duluth."

"Yikes. That is far. There is a gym at the country club you passed to get inside the community. We get to use that for free. Corden will get you a pass."

"Do they have free weights?" DeAndre asked.

I laughed, and Corden laughed harder. The extent of my working out was swimming a few laps in my pool from time to time. I needed to do more, but I had my genetics to thank for my muscle tone.

"Doesn't Twila work out there?" Corden asked.

"She does. I'll ask her about the free weights."

DeAndre looked at me and then down at the phone in my left hand.

"Oh, you want me to call her now?"

"If you don't mind," DeAndre said. "I really want to close this deal today. This place is perfect. I can't wait to bring my clients here."

"What kind of law do you practice?" I asked.

"Entertainment law primarily, but I do take other types of cases from time to time. When it comes to my family, they think I can do everything—landlord/tenant, labor, and going to get Ray-Ray out of the county lock up."

I could tell that DeAndre was waiting for a laugh. I couldn't give him one.

"I have a cousin named Ray-Ray. He's never been to jail, though."

"Oh, I'm sorry. I didn't mean anything by that," DeAndre said. "Just a little joke."

"Can I talk with you for a second in your office, boss lady?" Corden asked me. "I want to make sure we have everything spelled out in the rental agreement. DeAndre do you mind waiting for us in your new office? We'll find out about those free weights too."

DeAndre beamed. "My new office. I love the sound of that."

"We'll be right down in a second," Corden said.

Corden glared at me all the way up the stairs. I didn't care about his attitude. I was just fine with this, until I thought about this man being up in my space every day.

Corden held the door for me as we walked into my office. Sam was finishing up with the lunch dishes.

"That was quick," Sam said. "You're already done with your meeting?"

"She's trying to scare off the tenant by acting crazy," Corden said. "That is what you're trying to do, right?"

"I don't know him, and he seems just a little too pumped to move in here."

"I did a background check on him. I checked all his social media. I even checked out some of his clients on his law website. He's got some A-list celebrity clients, Hahna. He's legit."

I rolled my eyes. "Is there a clause in the lease to cancel if we don't need his money anymore?"

"The first lease is for eight months," Corden said. "He pushed for a year, but I told him we might be looking to sell in that time. He was interested in being considered for the purchase."

"You told him I want to sell my property? I didn't tell you to say that."

"I had to explain your crazy lease terms."

I looked at Sam for help, and he was packing the final food items and dishes into the picnic basket.

"Sam."

Sam looked at me and shrugged. "I'm with Corden. You won't hear anything about selling, so this sounds like it's the best option. Corden has done his research."

I sighed and sat at my desk. Of course, they were both right. Corden had my approval to proceed, and he did what was best for The Data Whisperers.

"Are you sure you think I should rent to this guy?" I ask Sam. "He looks like a body builder."

"Muscles on top of muscles, huh?" Sam said with a hint of laughter in his voice.

"You don't care, do you?"

"I do not."

Corden laughed too hard. If I'd had something to throw at him, I would have.

"Come on and let's get this lease signed," I said.

"Can you ask Twila about the gym?" Corden asked.

I called Twila's phone number. She answered on the first ring.

"What's up?" she asked. "But make it quick, I'm on my way to the office. I've got a patient waiting."

"Hey girl. Do they have free weights at that gym you go to over here?"

Twila laughed out loud. "Why the hell you wanna know? You bout to start working out for the wedding? Trying to get some Angela Bassett arms?"

"Um, no. They bout to get whatever arms I already have. My new tenant wants to know."

I hated the way tenant sounded as it rolled off my tongue.

"Oh. Yes, they have everything. Is your new tenant a man?"

"Yes."

"He fine?"

"He's all right."

Both Corden and Sam smirked.

"I'm on speaker phone, aren't I?" Twila asked.

"Yep."

"You can tell me about your fine new tenant later. Find out if he's single and straight. Or bi, shit. And stop putting me on speaker phone. You know good and damn well I'm not speaker phone appropriate."

"Bye, girl."

I disconnected the call and both Corden and Sam hollered. I couldn't help but join them. It was good to hear Twila making jokes. I hoped that meant her therapy was already working.

"Come on, Corden. Let's go get this over with. We're land-lords now."

"You're the landlord, boss lady," Corden said. "I'm just your right-hand man."

Sam gathered all his picnic supplies and walked to the door with us.

"I'm proud of you babe," he said. "I know this was hard for you. I'll reward you later tonight."

"I'm right here," Corden said. "Right the hell here."

I kissed Sam again and followed Corden back downstairs to sign the lease. The proof that my success was waning. The evidence that I was failing and needed to go to Plan B. Why couldn't anyone understand why this was heartbreaking except for me?

DeAndre didn't need to get too comfortable in that office space. He wasn't going to be there long. The Data Whisperers were coming back—not with a whisper, but a roar.

Chapter 8

KIMBERLY

Kimberly squeezed Ron's hand tightly as they walked into Pappadeaux's. He squeezed back and kissed her cheek. Though she appreciated Ron's assurance, she didn't know why *she* was nervous. Meeting with Ron's ex-wife, Sabrina, shouldn't have bothered Kimberly at all. If anyone should've been nervous it was Sabrina. She was the one watching her ex-husband marry his longtime love.

"We should've taken her somewhere cheaper," Kimberly said in jest. "I bet she gonna order an appetizer and dessert."

Ron laughed. "And cocktails. Don't forget the cocktails."

"And she gonna add extra shrimp on her entrée."

They both stopped talking when they saw Sabrina sitting in the waiting area. She'd grown her hair out some and darkened it. She had an almost olive glow to her skin, either gotten on a beach vacation or by spending time baking in the sun. Sabrina stood to her feet and smiled at Kimberly and Ron. She looked like she wanted to hug them, but Kimberly held her arms firmly at her sides as she squeezed Ron's hand again.

There would be no hugs. This woman was not her friend.

And yet, Sabrina wasn't an enemy either. She existed in a weird space between friend and foe. She couldn't be trusted, but Kimberly had no choice but to have Sabrina in her orbit.

Kimberly gave a weak smile back. "Hi, Sabrina," she said.

"How's it going?" Ron asked as he gave Sabrina a smile as well.

Kimberly loved how Ron matched her energy. If she wasn't hugging, then he wasn't hugging. Even though he shared children with Sabrina, he was going to reserve a hug until Kimberly led the way.

The hostess signaled that she was ready to take them to a table. They were silent as they walked to the dining room. Perhaps the warmth that Sabrina had arrived at dinner with had been cooled.

Sabrina sat at the round table first. Kimberly and Ron sat next to one another directly across from Sabrina. The table was too big for the three of them, and the empty chairs on either side of Kimberly and Ron made it clear that they were on one team, and Sabrina another.

The waitress came to take their drink orders. She gave their little dinner party a curious look. Kimberly was sure they seemed strange.

"Would you like to order beverages this evening?" she asked. "The house white wine is on special. The whole bottle is only nine dollars."

"We'll have one of those," Ron said, "and I'll have a double of Maker's Mark."

The waitress nodded. "I'll be right out with your drinks."

Sabrina said, "You like white wine too? It's my favorite. We probably should've gotten two bottles."

"One is enough," Kimberly said. "We wouldn't want you to have trouble driving home."

"Oh, Ron can just take both of our drunk asses home, right?"

Kimberly's nostrils flared a little, but she was determined not to give Sabrina a reason to feel like a victim.

Sabrina opened her menu and scanned. Maybe she didn't want to know why Ron had asked her to come to dinner, but she couldn't have missed the big ring on Kimberly's finger.

"What are you guys going to eat?" Sabrina asked. "I'm thinking fried catfish."

Kimberly gave Ron a look and he nodded. It was time to introduce Sabrina to the big gray animal who'd joined them in the room. The one with the trunk and wrinkly skin.

"So, we asked you to come here tonight because we're getting married," Ron said.

Sabrina looked up from the menu with the fakest smile plastered on her face. "Congratulations, you two. That's awesome. Are you going to have a big wedding?"

Ron nodded. "Yes, in Jamaica. We want the girls to be a part of the ceremony."

She shifted in her seat. "I . . . I don't know about that. What will they think of you marrying someone?"

"What do they think of you and your husband?" Kimberly asked. The question had to sting because of the history, but Kimberly still felt it was valid.

"I've explained to them why their daddy lives somewhere else now, and they have accepted it. I just think the wedding is a whole different thing. Kids are so literal."

"I think we can all talk to them together and explain what's happening," Ron said. "But I want my family standing with me. That part is not up for debate. You're welcome to come to Jamaica as well."

Kimberly had a nervous moment where she thought Ron might invite Sabrina to stay in their vacation rental. They could share a Caribbean island, as long as they weren't under the same roof.

"Do you mind if I bring Frank?"

"That's a tough one, Sabrina."

"You two have been cordial over the years. Since you're getting married now, maybe it's time to let go of your anger toward him."

"My anger was never toward him," Ron said. "It was toward you. And you're right, I'm not angry about you leaving me anymore. You were making room."

"Wow," Sabrina's face reddened with embarrassment.

Kimberly bit the inside of her cheek to keep from laughing. Sabrina had brought Ron's harsh response on herself though.

She was audacious enough to sit in front of the new fiancée and suggest that Ron was still butt hurt over their breakup? That was bold.

"Look, I can't stop your man from getting on a plane, but he's not welcome at the ceremony. As the mother of my children who are in the wedding, you may attend."

"But I'm not really welcome, either."

Ron looked at Kimberly and smiled. "Kimberly, how do you feel about Sabrina and her husband coming to the wedding?"

Kimberly turned her gaze to Sabrina and gave her a slow smile. Sabrina seemed like a woman who wanted to be the center of attention. Even though she had a new husband and no longer wanted Ron, she wanted Ron to consider her feelings above all. Why would he do that?

"It doesn't matter to me who witnesses our joy."

Ron brought Kimberly's hand up to his mouth and kissed it. "Well, Sabrina, my future bride has spoken. You and Frank can come to the wedding."

"Why don't you come to the engagement party too?" Kimberly asked.

Sabrina squinted with suspicion, but Kimberly held her composed smile. She would never let this woman see her flustered at all.

"W-when is it?"

"Next Saturday, at the Bailey Wine Cellar. Eight o'clock. We'd love to have you."

"I'll see what Frank has on his calendar. Thank you for the invite."

Sabrina stared at Kimberly and Ron for a moment, with their own plastered-on smiles. Then, she grabbed her phone out of her purse. She scrolled through as if she'd gotten a text. Then, she looked back up at their still-smiling faces.

"I'm so sorry you guys. I have to go. Emergency."

"Everything all right with the girls?" Ron asked. "Do we need to go with you?"

"No. Nothing like that. The babysitter has to leave early. Hopefully, I'll see you two at the engagement party."

She stood and so did Ron. Kimberly kept sitting and grinning. Sabrina paused as if to hug Ron goodbye, but then seemed to think better of it. She rushed out of the restaurant and Ron sat again.

"We ain't have to do her like that," Ron said.

Kimberly and Ron both burst into laughter. Even though they had been extremely petty to Ron's ex, it felt good to Kimberly. She and her man were a team. And once they exchanged vows, two would become one.

"That was you. I was just an innocent bystander," Kimberly said.

"Eh, I know. She pissed me off acting like I was mad about her husband."

"Yes, that was something else. Why would she think that you're still angry?"

Ron scoffed. "I am not angry, but I want nothing to do with the guy. I don't consider him a stepfather to my kids. I call him the man who lives in the house with my children."

Kimberly was happy for the distraction of the waitress bringing the wine. She understood how Ron felt. Who wouldn't hold a grudge against the man who'd slept with his wife? But she didn't want Sabrina treating her like the woman who lived with her ex-husband. Kimberly wasn't all that concerned about being a stepmother to Sabrina's children, but she wanted Ron to feel like she was his partner in things concerning his daughters.

"So, how will this work when we're married?" Kimberly asked.

"How will what work?"

"I am trying to be cordial with Sabrina, for the sake of the babies."

"As long as Frank treats my children well, he has nothing to worry about. I don't have to be cordial with him."

"I know and I'm not suggesting that you should. I'm just saying it might be awkward for Sabrina if she and I are cool, and her husband is the enemy."

Ron took a swallow of his bourbon. "You care about things being awkward for Sabrina?"

"Hell naw. I just don't want her giving you any drama about seeing your children."

Ron shook his head and frowned. "She wouldn't do that." He set his glass on the table, punctuating his thought.

Kimberly wanted to trust Ron's judgment on this one, but she wasn't so sure about what Sabrina would or wouldn't do. Kimberly hoped the diamond ring on her finger didn't bring out another side of Sabrina. A side that might try to use those two beautiful girls as pawns.

"Well, it looks like we've got two extra guests for the wedding. She better not show her ass, because you know my line sisters are going to get her all the way together."

"I would pay money to watch Twila go upside her head. I'd record it on my phone so I could watch it over and over."

Ron laughed, but Kimberly didn't join him. She thought about Twila's demeanor at Hahna's house. There was something seriously wrong with their friend.

"You don't think that would be funny?" Ron asked.

"Babe, Twila is having problems. I don't know what, but she's moved in over Hahna's. She says she can't stay at home."

"Somebody bothering her? Me and the bruhs need to pull up?"

"I don't know, she won't say. But she hasn't been right since something happened at that damn night club. That Club Phenom."

"Oh, Traci and Abena's spot?"

"Yes. Twila was hurt there. I don't know how and by whom, but you know they have some kind of sex dungeon in that place. They offered to host our engagement party, and Twila looked like she'd seen a ghost."

"Are you assuming something happened there, or . . ."

"No, I just remember Twila telling me and Hahna that she never should've gone there. After that she started all her self-defense classes."

"Maybe one day she'll tell you the whole story."

Kimberly nodded. "Maybe. But I think she has to deal with it herself first."

Chapter 9

TWILA

I needed to do this. Had to follow Dr. Mays's instructions if I wanted to get to the other side of this damn thing. But, I kept thinking about how I'd seen him in my subdivision. He'd shattered me once, that night at Phenom. It was bullshit that he'd found the opportunity to shatter me again.

"Twila, what happened after you woke up in the room encased in glass?" Dr. Mays asked pulling my attention back to the conversation.

I wasn't sure if I could continue. In my mind, I always stopped the memory there. With his laughter.

"He started laughing."

"How did you feel? Were you in pain?"

I closed my eyes and breathed. Put myself back in that room with my attacker. In my mind I could hear his deep, grating laugh. I could almost feel his breath on my face. It smelled like wine.

"You are back in the room," Dr. Mays said. "Take me there with you."

"I couldn't move. He had laid my body on a chaise that was in the room. He knelt on the floor next to me. I was awake, but I couldn't move. Except my eyes. I looked around the room, at the people walking by the room. I tried to scream, but no sound came out of my mouth."

"You felt afraid then?"

"I felt angry that I couldn't do anything to him. That my body wouldn't cooperate."

My hands gripped the armrests of my chair so tightly that the skin across my knuckles stretched taut. I didn't want to relive this. My eyes shot open and I shook my head.

"Can we just stop here?" I asked. "Let's pick up here the next session."

"Breathe Twila," Dr. Mays said. "Facing this will help you get your power back. Take a moment, then try to continue."

I relaxed my hands and put them in my lap. I breathed. Relaxed but not completely.

"He started touching me. Tore my panties off from under my tutu. He licked my inner thigh. He said things that weren't true. That I was a slut, and that I wanted to be dominated, so he was going to take mastery of me."

My breaths became shallow again, and my heart raced. I picked up the glass of water next to me on the table. My hand trembled as I set it down again.

"After he said that to me, he put on a condom and straddled me. I couldn't move, so I memorized his face. His eyes were grey like a glacier. His hair was red, he had thick eyebrows, and thick eyelashes. If not for him raping me, I would've thought he was handsome."

"Did he look at your face too? Were you memorizing each other?" Dr. Mays asked.

"He barely looked at me. I kept trying to get him to make eye contact with me. I hoped that if he saw the tears he would stop and find another woman. There were plenty of women in the club who would've slept with him."

"You were crying."

I nodded. "Yes. I cried while he was on top of me. It was quick. Just a few strokes and he was done. His breath. The wine. It made my stomach turn, but I didn't vomit. I still can't smell that kind of wine without remembering."

"What kind of wine was it?"

"I'm not sure, but my friend was drinking Riesling the other day and her breath smelled like his."

"What happened next, Twila? After he raped you."

"When he finished . . . he seemed almost ashamed of himself. Like how a teenage boy might look if his mother walked in on him masturbating."

"Did he say anything else to you?"

"He touched my face, and said, 'You're pretty.' Then, he propped my head up on a pillow, kissed my forehead and turned off the spotlight in our room. When the light was off, the voyeurs didn't look in. It was a club rule. To give couples privacy."

"And then he left?" Dr. Mays asked.

I nodded. "He left the room, and I was there alone for what felt like a long time, but it was only a few minutes. Eventually, I could feel my limbs again. It felt like when your leg falls asleep from sitting on it wrong or something. When I could finally move, I got up. I stumbled out of there."

"Why did you not report it then? Do you think he could have been caught?"

"I felt like it was my fault."

"Twila . . ."

"No, wait, Dr. Mays. I know rape is never the victim's fault in that way. I just mean that I had no business being there. I go to church—not often anymore—but I do. That was a den of iniquity, and I'd gone there willingly. I don't even know what I was looking for by opening that door."

"So, you believe that this was some sort of punishment?"

"No. Reaping. I sowed by walking into that room. Looking at all those couples fornicate. I enjoyed it. It turned me on. Maybe . . . maybe that guy could tell that I was turned on. What if he really did think I wanted it?"

"Are you asking me to answer that question, Twila?"

I shook my head. Of course, I didn't want her to answer the question.

"I was just curious about it. I thought, I don't know, that I was missing out on something fun. That I was too much a prude and maybe that's why I didn't have a man."

Dr. Mays got up from her seat and sat on the couch next to me. "Twila," she said, "there was nothing you did to deserve being raped."

"But going into that room didn't feel right, though, now that I look back on it. Not in my spirit."

"Are you sure that feeling in your spirit is not a bit of Monday morning quarterbacking?"

"What do you mean?"

"You told me that you were turned on when you observed the couples involved in consensual sexual behaviors."

"I was."

"Well, take that at face value. Do not judge the experience based on what happened to you."

My eyes became slits, and I shook my head. "What are you trying to tell me? I don't understand. Are you telling me I should go back there?"

"Not at all. I am telling you not to view that experience through a crime and punishment lens. God did not punish you with rape, Twila."

"I don't know if that's what I'm saying. I mean, I know God didn't punish me, but maybe . . . maybe He allowed it to happen."

"If you had not been raped, would you have gone back?"

"I don't know. Maybe. But, I can't separate the room from the rape, so I don't know."

"Hopefully, when we are done with your treatment, you are able to separate the two."

Even if I did progress to that point, I wasn't going back to that room at Club Phenom. I've been to the club, but this was one thing I could say never about.

"I took my last boyfriend to the club, and he was jealous. He thought I was a regular visitor behind the red door."

"You still visit the club. Just not the room behind the red door."

"Correct."

Dr. Mays nodded and sucked her teeth absentmindedly. I usually loved when she made that sound, because she always came up with good ideas after. It was as if that sound got her thinking juices going, just like running did for me. But I didn't know if I wanted to hear any ideas, good or bad, about Club Phenom. I was still trying to unpack all of the day's revelations.

"I feel like I need to know who he is," I said, before Dr. Mays could tell me what she was thinking.

"Your attacker? And what would you do with that information?" Dr Mays asked.

"I don't know what I would do with the information."

"Would it make you feel empowered to secretly know something about him?"

"I think so."

"There is some power in knowing things, but there is also freedom in ignorance."

I scoffed. "This doesn't feel like bliss, though."

"I didn't say bliss. I said freedom. If you have this information, you might feel compelled to act on it. I think you should first focus on desensitizing your mind and spirit to the attack. Once that is neutralized, you can move forward."

"You're probably right."

"I am. You have done good work here today, Twila. You got through the entire event, and you did not fall apart."

"I feel heavy though."

Dr. Mays touched my hands and squeezed. "Soon, you will feel lighter."

"You know . . . I meant to come to you sooner about this, Dr. Mays. I don't know why I waited."

"You are here now."

I couldn't hide anything from Dr. Mays. None of my motives were safe from her all-seeing eyes. She saw right through me and prophesied my next move. When I got my attacker's information I was going to be compelled to act. That was the entire point.

Chapter 10

HAHNA

Why did I let Twila talk me into coming to the gym with her at five in the darn morning? I was not awake. I was barely alive. But here I was anyway, and I was supposed to spin.

"Stop looking like that," Twila said as we walked into the spin room.

"Like what?"

"Like somebody's holding you hostage."

"Somebody is holding me hostage. An exercise terrorist. I don't appreciate this."

Twila picked out her bike and jumped on effortlessly. I selected the one next to her and fiddled with some of the knobs. I had to adjust the seat height, the handlebars, how close the seat was to the handlebars, and the pedals.

"Girl what are you doing?" Twila said with a laugh. "Get your ass on the damn bike."

"Listen here. I'm not about to get injured, shoot."

"You are going to thank me when you're looking like a goddess at Kimberly's wedding," Twila said as I eased myself gingerly onto the seat.

"I'm fine just looking like a mere mortal. Why don't you go harass Kim? It's her wedding."

Twila started pedaling while I was still strapping my shoes in. I didn't care one bit about catching up to her.

"She always gets weird when we talk about weight loss. She acts like I can't relate."

"Well, you can't relate to her struggle."

"Girl, if you don't move your damn legs! You're on the damn bike. Stop stalling."

I scowled at Twila and slowly pumped my legs. It hurt from the start. "Are you happy?"

"No. But your muscles are."

They weren't. They were silently screaming.

"Back to Kim," I said. "Her weight loss journey is different from yours. So, I guess I understand why she acts weird about it."

"And maybe she doesn't plan on losing any weight. It's not like she has to. Ron loves her just the way she is."

"And that is the moral of this story," I said as I tried to swing one leg off the bike.

"If you don't get yo . . ."

My new tenant, DeAndre Williams, walked into the spin room and stopped Twila's mouth in the middle of the sentence. Good. His arms were enough to halt speech and thoughts. Those things were impressive, and the single tattoo, a cross on his bicep, was just the perfect amount of hood to go along with his chocolate.

"Good morning, Hahna," he said.

"Morning DeAndre. You spin?" I asked. "It's a good workout isn't it."

Twila made a sound that was a cross between a choke, a snort, and a laugh. She was such a hater.

I shoved a thumb in her direction. "This is my friend Twila Bennings. The gym rat. Twila, this my new tenant, DeAndre Williams. His law office is now on the first floor of my building."

Twila continued to pedal, but with a huge smile on her face. "Nice to meet you Mr. Williams. Am I going to get to see you every morning?"

DeAndre gave her that heart-arresting smile. Her pedaling slowed a little.

"If you're going to be here, that's motivation for me to get in gear. You work around here?"

"My orthodontics practice is about five minutes away."

"An orthodontist? So, I can have a sista take care of my pearly whites?"

Twila grinned. "I'll take care of you."

DeAndre bit his bottom lip, nodded and chuckled. Twila had no problem letting a brother know she was interested.

"Again, it was a blessing meeting you this morning, Ms. Bennings. I hope to see you again tomorrow, and the next day. Hahna, I'll see you in the office."

DeAndre swaggered down to a bike on the other end of the room. Twila's eyes followed him the entire way. Just as he turned to look at them, Twila started pedaling hard.

"Damn, damn, damn," Twila said.

"What? He's fine, he's single, and he's paid. You betta capitalize on all that electric attraction."

Twila sighed. "I can't. Not now. The timing is hella off. This therapy thing I'm doing is ripping some shit wide open."

I kept pedaling while I waited for her to continue. Twila was notoriously guarded about her therapy and trauma. If she was talking about it, I wasn't going to interrupt.

"Dr. Mays is working me. I mean, I'm doing the work, but she's taken me to the damn brink of everything I thought I knew."

"Like what?"

"She's challenged me on my faith view and my values. I feel like I'm having conflict with my damn self. Or the self I was when I was nineteen and in the youth choir and the self I am today."

"Conflict?"

"Yeah, mostly the things I've beat myself up about. I've always looked at things like if you put yourself out there, in the world, when you know you belong to God, then you're gonna have calamity."

I scrunched my eyebrows, but didn't respond, because that was *my* take on things. My grandmother always said a righteous person's steps are ordered by God. I wasn't perfect—no one was—but I tried to live mostly right.

"And maybe, just maybe, calamity isn't because of something I did. Shit, I don't deserve calamity."

"So, are you going to keep seeing her?" I asked.

"Yes, of course. Dr. Mays's methods are what I need."

"And that's the reason you can't follow up on DeAndre?"

She nodded as she sipped a bit of water from her hydro flask. "I'm not ready to focus on a man, or dating, or any of that. I need to focus on getting my power back and moving back to my home."

"Are you going to tell me what happened?"

Twila cocked her head to one side and frowned. "I was raped."

I stopped pedaling and got tangled up in the bike trying to get to Twila. I needed to hug her. I knew it was something like that. Kimberly and I had surmised rape as the worst-case scenario, mostly because neither of us wanted to accept that as a reality.

"Don't, Hahna. Don't react like that."

"What do you mean, don't react like that? I mean, what am I supposed to do?"

"Nothing except listen to me. This may be the reason why I never told you and Kimberly what happened."

"Because we react?"

"We all do. It's what we do for each other in our friendship, and I love y'all for it. I just didn't want y'all trying to get *me* to react."

"Has the statute of limitations passed?" I asked.

"Hahna."

"I'm sorry. When did it happen? Where?"

She shook her head. "I'm not ready for the details yet. I'm working through that in therapy. I might never be able to share that part of it."

"Okay."

"But, I will tell you that I saw him in my subdivision, and

that's why I'm at your house. If I can't see my way clear of going back, I'll sell the place."

"No, you love that townhouse."

"I do, but I'll walk away from it, before I feel powerless in my own home."

I eased my one tangled leg onto the floor. "You don't have to feel powerless. I know people . . ."

"No, Hahna. That's a reaction."

"I got you."

"Get back on the bike," Twila said. "You're not done, and you ain't slick."

I groaned and hoisted myself back up.

"Ten more minutes," Twila said. "You can do this."

"Okay, okay."

I pressed my legs down again, although they felt like gelatin. My muscles must have atrophied from sitting at a desk all day. At least Twila stood up to work on her patients.

"Twila?"

"What?"

"Why in the heck did you flirt so hard with that man if you weren't going to talk to him?" I asked.

"Girl, he was so fine I went into autopilot mode. I didn't even think until he walked away."

"He short circuited you, huh?"

"Took me to those primitive, primal urges, chile."

"Well, now he's gonna be looking for you every day. You started something."

Twila sighed. "I wish I hadn't," she said.

I didn't want to tell Twila this, but I didn't think her flirting with DeAndre was a short circuit. Perhaps her sharing with her therapist, and then me, about being raped had taken a weight from her. I think for a moment, Twila felt normal and did a natural thing—hit on a handsome man.

And I was going to pray that natural things continued to happen every morning in the spin room.

Chapter 11

KIMBERLY

The bridesmaid crew had turned the Bailey Wine Cellar into a blue, pink, and silver wonderland to celebrate the union of Kimberly and her Big Ron. A Gamma Phi Gamma to an Omega Phi Kappa. The sorority's colors were blue and pink, and the fraternity's colors were silver and blue. The sight of it made Kimberly beam. Ron stood next to her in the doorway and kissed her neck.

"This looks great," he said. "Your girls did all this? They can decorate for the wedding too."

"I'm having a professional decorate the castle."

"The castle?"

Kimberly glared at Ron. He was such a man's man, that she suspected he'd never look at the website links she sent him, or the link to her Pinterest page with bouquet arrangements. But he didn't have to let her know he didn't pay attention. He was supposed to fake that part.

"The stunning cliff side castle in Negril where we're exchanging vows."

Ron feigned understanding. "I knew what castle you were talking about. The one with the bathtub outside on the patio of the honeymoon suite. I plan on using that multiple times."

"What we gone do with that little plunge tub?"

"I'm gonna plunge my juicy wife right on in there."

Kimberly laughed. "You're nasty."

"You like it. You better be glad the guests are starting to arrive, or I'd take you back to our hotel room to give you a trial run."

Kimberly almost did wish they were back at their suite at the Marriot Marquis. She was worn out from managing the mass production of her hair products. A nap before this party would've helped. A party in her and Ron's honor meant that she had to be *on*. The last thing she wanted to do was tell and re-tell the story of how Ron proposed, or share her wedding plans. She just needed a pillow and a soft mattress.

"It's not too late to go back to the hotel," Kimberly said. "I'm so tired."

"Just a few hours and we can duck out of here, even if everyone else is still partying."

As guests started to crowd into the space, the DJ played the music Kimberly and Ron had loved in college. 90s R & B, Biggie, Pac, Little Kim. It was the soundtrack of their love story.

"I feel like stepping," Ron said. "Let me go find some of the frats."

Ron kissed Kimberly's neck and she felt the familiar tingle that she felt whenever he touched her. She'd hoped that he would stay near her so that they could receive congratulations together, but she also loved when the frat brothers got together.

Hahna walked over with her arms outstretched and Sam in tow. Kimberly took the warm embrace from one of her Maids of Honor and one from Sam as well.

"Hahna, are you working out?" Kimberly asked. "Your face looks slimmer."

"You noticed? I've lost four pounds thanks to Twila dragging me to the gym every day."

Kimberly lifted an eyebrow. They hadn't invited her to work out, and usually they had their weight loss missions together.

"She has me drinking green stuff in the mornings," Sam said. "I prefer bacon, but the green stuff is all right."

Kimberly laughed. "What's in the green stuff?"

"Plants and dirt. And I think I can taste banana."

Hahna hit his arm. "He is exaggerating. It does not have dirt in it. That's probably just the kale."

"Kale does taste like dirt," Kimberly said. "And kale chips taste like dried dirt."

Sam cracked up and gave Kimberly a high five. "I'm making shrimp and grits in the morning. You're welcome to join."

"He's such a diet killer," Hahna said. "I need to get this belly on flat for the wedding."

Kimberly pressed her lips together and nodded. So, they were trying to get fine for her wedding without including her? It wasn't like they weren't already going to look better in their dresses. It wasn't like they would have to wear the same kinds of corsets that felt like the jaws of life.

"Where's Twila?" Kimberly asked, wanting to not think about being overweight.

"She just texted me that she was looking for parking. There was a paid lot down the street."

LaShea, Kimberly's assistant, rushed over to Kimberly with a worried look on her face.

"What's wrong?" Kimberly asked as the young woman stood in front of her with wide eyes and flaring nostrils.

"Did you know that Ron's ex-wife was coming?"

Kimberly relaxed, but she could see why LaShea would think this was an issue. She placed a hand on the girl's shoulder, trying to calm her.

"It's okay. I knew she was coming. We invited her. Did she bring her husband with her?"

LaShea shook her head. "No, she brought two other white women with her. Maybe her friends?"

"Oh, I know this ho didn't bring her homegirls to your engagement party," Hahna said. "Let me text Twila and Debbie."

"Do not text them," Kimberly said. "It'll be fine."

Sabrina spotted Kimberly, waved, and started over with her friends behind her. All three of them had similar long hairstyles with big barrel curls. Sabrina's hair was deep brown, but the other two were shades of blonde. All three looked athletic and fit, and completely out of place. Guests turned heads, especially the women. The men did also, but less conspicuously.

Kimberly regretted inviting Sabrina into her space. She made eye contact with Ron, and he nodded. He crossed the room quickly, but not in time to make it to her before Sabrina. Hahna and Sam would have to do as protectors.

The women pranced up to Kimberly, edging Hahna and Sam to the outskirts of Kimberly's space bubble. Hahna frowned but didn't move farther away. One of the women was standing almost shoulder to shoulder with Hahna. Hahna didn't move.

Sabrina gave Kimberly a tiny hug that Kimberly barely returned.

"Glad you could make it," Kimberly said. "You brought friends?"

"Oh, I hope it's all right," Sabrina said. It wasn't. "We are on our way to a charity auction tonight, but I wanted to stop by first and congratulate you and Ronald."

"Ron!"

The voice was one of Sabrina's friends—the lighter blonde. Not the one damn near elbow-bumping Hahna, though. Ron gave her a weak smile. Kimberly winced as the woman hugged her man. It was way too much. Ron untangled himself quickly, though, so that was good.

"Hi Wendy. It's been a long time."

"Too long."

Ron held out his hand to shake the other friend's hand. It seemed like she was pretending not to see his hand. After being left hanging for a few seconds, Ron shrugged and dropped his hand.

"He's trying to shake your hand," Hahna said loudly, right in the girl's ear. Kimberly almost laughed at this, because the girl's face had to have Hahna's spittle on it they were standing so close. Not Hahna's fault though. All she'd done was stand her ground while someone tried to act like she was invisible.

"Thanks for coming, Sabrina, Nicole, and Wendy." Ron said.

"Of course, Ron. I wouldn't miss it," Sabrina said. Her words slurred as she spoke. She'd clearly already had a few glasses of wine. In fact, the whole crew looked a little drunk.

"Well help yourself to the food and beverages," Kimberly said. "There's a cookie and cupcake station for dessert. The cupcakes are divine."

"Can't do wine and cupcakes," Wendy said. "Don't want to be all bloated in this dress."

Nicole looked at Kimberly's not bloated, but fluffy belly and smirked. "I don't think bloating is a concern here," she said.

Nicole was the first to walk off to the buffet. That was probably a good thing, because Hahna looked about a half second away from yanking out Nicole's high-priced hair extensions. Sam had his hand around Hahna's waist. He looked ready to intervene if necessary.

Sabrina mouthed the word 'sorry' as she and her friends pranced away the same way they pranced in.

"What the hell?" Hahna asked, beating Kimberly to the punch. "Like that ho really came in here and didn't speak to neither one of y'all?"

Ron closed his eyes and sighed. "They were her bridesmaids when we got married. Not sure why she would bring them."

Hahna snatched her phone out of her purse and started texting.

"Don't text Twila," Kimberly said. "They said they were going to another event, so they'll be gone soon."

Hahna shook her head. "Too late. She and Debbie will be inside soon."

"Don't let her start nothing," Ron said. "We don't need any negativity."

Kimberly gave Ron a look that could've melted his nose hairs. Sabrina had started it by bringing her bridesmaids to their engagement party.

"Why would she bring those girls? They weren't invited, and they're not even friendly." Kimberly said. "If anything happened it would be Twila finishing what *she* started."

"Nicole's hated me since before we were even married, and they're her best friends. I guess Sabrina feels some kind of way about all this," Ron said. "But she should've stayed home."

"All what? Our marriage plans?"

Ron didn't get to respond to that question because Twila and Debbie marched into the party on a mission.

"Where's the ex?" Twila said instead of hello. Kimberly sighed and glared at Hahna. Hahna shrugged.

"She and her friends are across the room, but look," Kimberly said, "don't worry about it. She can feel however she wants to about me and Ron getting married, but she's not going to stop the show."

Ron led Kimberly away from her friends, although Kimberly didn't feel comfortable about leaving Twila unattended.

"I think if we just ignore them, they will leave," Ron whispered. "Sabrina's looking for attention for some reason."

For some reason? Kimberly knew the reason. Just like her little friend, Nicole, had scoffed at Kimberly's belly, Sabrina was trying to figure out how her ex-husband had chosen a plus-sized black woman to be her replacement.

"I don't know what she's looking for, but if she and her friends act up, I guarantee she's gonna find it."

Kimberly watched Abena and Traci walk in with their husbands. They'd apparently already been warned about Sabrina and her posse, because they walked straight over to Twila and Hahna. After a few words, they went and sat at the bridesmaid's table looking like a tribe of black girl warriors.

The men, including Sam, scurried to the buffet and brought wine and food.

"Looks like everything is going to be fine," Ron said. "Let's go say hi to some of our other friends. You've got colleagues here, right?"

"I do."

"Well, calm down and come on. No one will hold you accountable for anything Sabrina does."

Kimberly took Ron's outstretched hand and he smiled as he

laced his fingers through hers. She smiled back. That one little gesture calmed and centered her.

Samantha walked into the party, still wearing her office clothes. Kimberly waved at her and pointed over to the brides-maid's table. She rolled her eyes. Probably didn't want to sit with the other women, but there was nothing Kimberly could do about that. They were all her line sisters too. Kimberly just hoped that Samantha didn't do or say anything to add to the tension. The air in the room was already heavy enough.

Chapter 12

HAHNA

I couldn't believe Samantha walked into Kimberly's engagement party looking like she was going to a middle-of-the-day staff meeting at work. The kind of meeting she might've brought her second cup of coffee and a cookie to get through. Her clothes matched that kind of meeting—an ill-fitting suit and sensible heels. Even her hair said staff writer. A bun pulled to the nape of her neck and loosely held together with straight pins.

Samantha sat at our table but didn't say hello. Just sat on down and acted like none of us were there. She took out her phone and started scrolling.

"You can't speak?" Debbie asked.

Samantha ignored her, although I know she heard her. I wondered what her beef was with us. Maybe it was just the fact that she wanted to be the Maid of Honor. But it could've been something else.

"Samantha, have you met my boyfriend, Sam?" I asked.

Sam grinned. "I'm pleased to meet another sorority sister of Hahna's. Do you go by Sam for short? If so, we might have to do Sam one and Sam two for the wedding festivities."

"Or you could go by Hahna's Sam," I said. Sam kissed my neck, so I guess he preferred that choice. "Except, Samantha never goes by Sam. She and Kim used to have a thing in college about preferring people call them by their entire names."

"Yet, Kimberly fell back from that," Samantha said. "Pleased to meet you Sam."

"She did. When Ron started calling her Kimmie Kim it was over," Abena said. "They were so cute even back then. I'm so glad they found each other again."

Samantha went back to looking at her phone.

"You got somebody you need to call?" Debbie asked. "'Cause we're at a party and it's hella rude for you to be on your phone."

"Well, sis, sometimes remaining gainfully employed requires you to take time away from partying to handle your business."

Debbie scoffed and looked Samantha up and down. "What are you trying to say about me?" she asked. "I am gainfully employed."

"Gainfully might be questionable," Samantha said. "But yay you for being a taxpayer."

I looked at Twila for help with deescalating the minor drama, but she was watching them with spectator's eyes. All she needed was a bowl of popcorn.

"So, Samantha, as member of the bride tribe, we need to get you caught up to speed on a situation," I said.

"What situation?" she asked.

I tilted my head over in the direction of the drunken Sabrina and her two friends. "Ron's ex-wife and the bridesmaids from their wedding."

Even Samantha couldn't hold her dry expression on hearing that. She dropped her jaw as she looked over at the three women. They were flirting with a few of the frat brothers, even Sabrina, who was definitely married. I didn't know about the other two. To the guys' credit, none of them seemed to be flirting back.

"Why would she come to this?" Samantha asked the question all of us wanted the answer to.

"Why would Kimberly and Ron invite her?" Twila asked. "I know they're trying to have a decent relationship for Ron's kids, but this is too much."

"Ron had kids with her?" Abena asked.

"Yes, two pretty little girls. Twins," I replied. "They're in the wedding, so I can imagine they're inviting the mother since it's out of the country."

"Still," Abena said. "They didn't have to come to this."

I held my breath as Angela Cummings walked into the party. She was a colleague of Kimberly's at the law firm, before she'd launched CurlPop. But, Angela had also gone to college with us. She'd shown interest in Gamma Phi Gamma during rush week the year we pledged but hadn't made the line. It was awkward with her ever since, because she *made* it awkward. Like why would she wear a pink blouse and blue skirt? Our sorority colors.

Angela smiled when she saw us and came straight to our table. It was a twelve-seat table, so there were empty chairs, but I wished there weren't. Angela wasn't bad news, but she wasn't good news either. She was the little segment about the local zoo at the end of the broadcast. She was news that no one could use.

Angela sat at the table and hugged Samantha who was in the seat next to her. There was no one directly on the other side, so no additional hugs were given. Traci could've reached her, but when Angela sat, Traci twisted in her chair so that she gave Angela her back.

"Hey y'all," Angela said. "It's been a while since we've all hung out."

I lifted an eyebrow. We'd never all hung out.

"Yes, that would've been in college," Twila said. "So, hell yeah, it's been a while."

Neither Traci nor Abena introduced Angela to their husbands, and I had no reason to introduce her to Sam. But, I wasn't going to be rude.

"Sam, this is Angela. She went to school with us too."

"Another Gamma girl I see with the pink and blue," Sam said.

I jabbed him in the ribs with my elbow and he yelped. Definitely didn't want him to go down this conversation route.

"Not yet," Angela said. "I am hoping to get into an alumni chapter as a graduate."

"Oh, I just thought . . ."

"That she shouldn't be wearing our colors to a Gamma event especially if she wants to pledge?" Abena asked.

Sam shook his head. "No. I just thought that she was one of the crew. I apologize, Angela. I didn't mean to put you on the spot."

"No problem, you didn't mean anything by it," Angela said. "Plus, you're too handsome to offend me."

Sam gave her a confused glance. "Um . . . thanks," he said.

Abena's husband Kyle stood and stretched. "I'm going to go over to the DJ booth," he said. "They need help with the sounds. My brothas, y'all want to come with me and leave the ladies to whatever they talk about when we're not sitting there?"

Sam jumped up so fast I almost laughed. He must've been looking for an escape route. I guess I could've used one too. With Samantha and her bad attitude, and wannabe Angela, this table was getting on my nerves.

"So, are all you guys in the wedding?" Angela asked. "I think I'm going to try to come to Jamaica. I love a destination wedding."

"Yes, her line sisters are her bridesmaids," Debbie said.

A woman giggled loudly, and of course, we all looked in the direction of Sabrina and friends. Wendy's hand was placed squarely on Kyle's chest as she threw her head back and laughed about something.

Before I could intervene, Abena and Traci were already on their feet.

"Don't start anything," Samantha said. "Clearly, they've had too much to drink."

Abena ignored Samantha and marched over to the action with Traci and Twila following closely behind.

"You're not going too?" Samantha asked Debbie.

Debbie cleared her throat and shook her head. "Nah. I can't. I'm still on probation from the last time I had to beat a ho's ass."

Samantha scoffed and then looked at me. "I guess it's up to you then, Maid of Honor. Go get your sisters."

"They're your sisters too."

"Not since college."

I stared at Samantha for a moment, to give her time to take that back. She came through for me when I needed her, so I would've never called the sisterhood into question. But maybe she helped me for another reason. And I didn't miss the Maid of Honor shade either.

She was right, though. I was the only one left who would stop the crazy from unfolding. I dragged myself across the room, hoping that the whole thing would dissipate without my intervention.

"Listen, listen, listen, everybody," Sabrina said as I walked up. "I just wanna do a toast to Ronald and his future wife."

"You are not toasting anything up in here," Twila said.

Abena had already removed Wendy's hands from Kyle's chest, and had positioned herself between the two of them. Wendy smirked and sipped her glass of wine. Seemed like Sabrina wasn't the only one in her circle with a taste for chocolate.

Sam slid over from his place in the DJ booth and stood next to me. "Glad you came over," he whispered.

I walked over to Sabrina who was so liquored up that she couldn't stand still. She staggered left and right, with the biggest smile on her face. The friends she brought with her weren't real friends. My sisters would never have allowed me to make a fool of myself like this.

Sabrina gazed at me as I grabbed her free hand. "Is it time to toast?" she asked. "I have one."

"No, sweetie. We're not doing toasts tonight. They might do them at the wedding, you can save it until then."

Sabrina pouted a little, but then smiled again. "In Jamaica. Girls, you coming with me? These guys are taken, but there are plenty single Jamaicans!"

Neither of her friends responded. They both gave Sabrina a "bless her heart" expression.

Since they weren't going to help her, I gently pulled Sab-

rina's arm and started walking. She stumbled behind me slosh-
ing wine everywhere.

"Where are we going?" she asked. "My friends are back there."

I wanted to tell her that from the looks of things she didn't
have any friends, but I didn't want to be mean. I just wanted
her and her entourage gone.

"To the bathroom. You spilled a little wine on your dress. I'm
gonna help you dab it out."

"Oh, okay, good. 'Cause that's gonna stain."

"Mmm-hmmm . . ."

I made eye contact with Kimberly who had a look of horror
on her face. I gave her a little head shake. I had things under
control and was doing my Maid of Honor duty or whatever
Samantha had implied that I needed to do.

In the bathroom, I gave Sabrina a wet paper towel. She set
her glass of wine (what was left of it) on the sink and squinted
in the mirror trying to find the stain on her dress. She would've
been squinting all night, because there was no stain.

"Girl, there is nothing on your dress," I said.

"Wait, what? Then why did you give me this damn paper
towel?"

"Wipe your face, 'cause you're drunk."

Sabrina rolled her eyes, "I am fine. I'm not drunk."

"I hope one of your friends is driving, because you can't. I'll
take your keys."

"Wendy is driving, but I said I'm fine."

She started toward the bathroom door, but I blocked her.

"If you were fine, you wouldn't be out there embarrassing
yourself."

"I wasn't embarrassing myself."

"By trying to give a toast at your ex-husband's engagement
party? How do you think my friend Kimberly will feel about
that?"

Sabrina shrugged. "She shouldn't feel any way at all. I had
Ronald first, and I just want them to know they have my blessing and good wishes."

"They don't need your blessing."

Sabrina backed up a few steps until she bumped into the sink. Backed up like the power of my words pushed her.

"They do. Because I'm not going anywhere."

That sounded like a threat. "Excuse me?"

"Oh, I don't mean it that way. It's just that Ronald and I have children together. So, I'm always going to be there. It's better if we all get along."

"Getting along is one thing. You blessing their union is another thing," I said, insistent upon the fact that they didn't, nor should they have been seeking her approval.

"I get it," Sabrina said. "You're feeling protective of your friend. But trust me, if I wanted Ronald I would still have him. One of my biggest regrets is what I did to him when I cheated on him. I didn't think he'd survive it, honestly."

"He survived and clearly thrived."

"Yes, for his children. He couldn't leave his daughters or even his older son, Sean. Does Kimberly know about Sean?"

I didn't tell Sabrina how Kimberly knew about Sean. It wasn't her business that the reason Kimberly and Ron reunited was because she was on a date with his son.

"She knows everything that she needs to know about Ron and his life."

Sabrina took a new paper towel and wet it in the sink. She dabbed the corners of her eyes. Were those tears? I didn't know what she was crying about, but she could take her tears get on home.

"You should leave now," I said. "Please don't make me have you and your friends ejected from the party."

"I wouldn't give you the pleasure of doing that. We'll leave. I'll save my toast for the wedding."

Sabrina wasn't giving a toast at the wedding. If she was even in attendance, the bride tribe would take care of her. I would make sure of that.

Chapter 13

HAHNA

I loved when Sam stayed over at my house. He made a point not to stay more than two nights in a row, but I wished that he would just move in. What was the point of maintaining more than one household when we wanted to be together most of the time?

Sam unpacked his man bag one item at a time. It always had the same contents: t-shirt, socks, underwear, deodorant, toothbrush. He placed the clothes items in the drawer I thought of as his, and he walked his toiletries into the bathroom.

He noticed my staring on the way out of the bathroom. I didn't try to look away.

"What's up?" he asked. "What did I do?"

"Nothing. I'm just watching you be you. Can I do that?"

"You're weird," Sam chuckled. "But in a good way."

"You love my weird self, so I don't care."

He sat next to me on the bed and kissed me. "I do love you. What are you thinking about? The party?"

I was thinking about the party, but I was also trying to deal with what Twila had told me. I kept thinking about her revelation. I wondered when and where it happened. Who was the man who hurt her?

But I couldn't talk about that, not to Sam. That was sister business.

"The party was crazy. Ron needs to do something about his ex-wife. She's a whole problem."

Sam stretched out on the bed onto his stomach and propped his chin under his hands. I stretched out next to him. I wasn't tired, though. I wanted to talk.

"What is he supposed to do about her?" Sam asked. "I don't know that he could've done anything about her. She seemed determined to be seen."

"Why was she even invited in the first place? I bet it was a Kimberly thing. Inviting her is something she would do."

"Nothing necessarily wrong with that."

"Except that the chick basically said she's always going to be up in their mix because of her kids with Ron. She's not going to terrorize my friend. That's not happening."

"Yeah, Abena seemed pretty amped."

"Abena was about to beat the brakes off Sabrina's friend, Wendy. Sabrina ought to be thanking me for saving her behind."

Sam laughed at this, but I wasn't joking. Abena could've taken all of them, but the last thing we needed was a bridesmaid arrest.

"What was the deal about the girl, Angela? Y'all got really awkward when she came to the table. Did someone have beef with her back in college?"

I rolled my eyes not wanting to talk about Angela. She was not even worthy of conversation.

"No one has beef with her. She's just thirsty."

"Thirsty how? She seemed pretty friendly to me."

"I didn't say she wasn't friendly. She is. She just really wants to be a Gamma Phi Gamma."

"Why can't she be in the sorority?" Sam asked. "What does she have to do?"

What he was asking wasn't a secret. Anyone could see the base requirements to be a Gamma Phi Gamma sister on our national website. The part that was missing was the thing that was hard to quantify or even qualify. That little extra bit of something . . . special . . . wasn't something you could call out or see. It was just a thing you knew when you saw it, and Angela didn't have it. On paper she had all the qualifications. College degrees, portfolio with lots of service, and a strong desire to join were all great. But at the graduate level, a potential pledgee had to have a sponsor. An already crossed sister in the alumni chapter needed to write a letter of recommendation. I am almost one hundred percent sure that Angela couldn't find a Gamma Phi Gamma to sponsor her.

"She has to be a good fit for the organization," I said.

I could tell by Sam's frown that the answer wasn't sufficient, but I didn't know what he wanted to hear me say.

"And how does one become a good fit? Is there a brochure or something that she could read?"

"I mean she tried in undergrad. If she had been accepted, she would've been on our line."

Sam sat up in the bed. I didn't move, although he looked like he was going into full debate mode. I didn't want to debate about Gamma Phi Gamma. I just wanted Sam to take me to the mountaintop, so I could screech out beautiful high notes.

"Is there something wrong with her?"

"Oh, my goodness, Sam. We can't let everybody in."

Sam gave a grimace that made me think the mountaintop was farther and farther away. I wish I could change the topic like changing a television channel, but Sam had dug his heels in and wouldn't stop until he came away with an answer.

"But I mean, if she meets the qualifications, then shouldn't you let her in?"

"Even if she meets everything on the check list, she still may not get in."

"Why not?"

"A lot of reasons. We only have so many members on a line or in a chapter. If we've exceeded that then she can't be on the line. She might need service hours that don't have anything to do with her job. They have to be purely selfless."

"And if she has all that?"

"She needs a recommendation from a current Gamma Phi Gamma."

Sam laughed. "Wow. So, would you recommend her?"

"Probably not. I mean, we're not friends. I don't know anything about her. It should be someone close to her."

I could tell that Sam still didn't understand. He wasn't part of a black Greek letter organization, so he didn't get the pride that we have in what we do, and our standards.

"We have to have standards, or else it means nothing to be a Gamma Phi Gamma."

"What does it mean?"

I felt like Sam was mocking me, but I wasn't going to give him the pleasure of seeing me angry about this.

"It means you're part of a global sisterhood that serves God, our community, and our organization. It means that I'm a part of something greater than myself."

"An elite global sisterhood," Sam said.

"I don't think elite is a bad word or an insult. Yes, Gamma Phi Gamma is elite, and I'm proud to be in the number."

Elite was what I'd strived my whole life to be. I chose Spelman because it was the college of choice for elite black girls. It didn't matter that I was from Goldsboro, North Carolina. Well, it did to some people, and that was the whole point. Being accepted into Gamma Phi Gamma helped equalize my past and my upbringing. Before I had my own business, I led my networking spiel with, "I am a member of Gamma Phi Gamma." It was a name that opened doors.

"Why didn't you pledge a fraternity at North Carolina A & T?"

"Gang initiations weren't my thing."

I rolled my eyes. "No one was doing any gang initiations. Please stop exaggerating."

"No, some of the fraternities beat their pledges. I didn't investigate them all to see which one didn't beat everyone. I decided then that it wasn't for me."

There it was again. That self-righteous tone Sam took when it felt like he was judging me for something. He never came right out and said it, but it was something I felt in my spirit. There was a tone, and a look, and a silence. The silence that hung now in the room, because of me subduing my opinion in order to change whatever opinion Sam had formed.

Sam leaned over and kissed me behind my ear. I shivered. It was my favorite spot to receive his kisses. I dabbed expensive perfume there to entice him to leave his love touches behind.

"I mean, it seems like Ron and his fraternity brothers are cool, though," Sam said. "And I know being in your sorority means a lot to you."

Maybe Sam did notice that his unspoken opinions bothered me. Was he softening it so I wouldn't be mad or because he'd judged too harshly?

My phone buzzed on the dresser. I didn't want to move. I was on my way to the mountaintop. Neither one of us moved, so maybe Sam was thinking the same thing I was thinking. Whoever that was could wait.

Sam turned my face toward his. I closed my eyes as he kissed me deeply. My entire body melted under his touch.

The phone buzzed again. I ignored it again. Then I started to wonder who would be blowing up my phone this late. Twila was going out with Debbie, but it was nowhere near time for the club to close, and she had a key.

"Sam, babe, let me just see who that is. I won't even call them back if it isn't important."

I rolled out of the bed and Sam grunted. I felt the same way, but I wouldn't forgive myself if there was some emergency and I was unavailable.

I picked up the phone and looked at the missed calls. My aunt Sherrie in Shady Falls. If it was my auntie, it was one of two things. Somebody was dead or somebody was in jail. With our ghetto family and her cirrhosis-of-the-liver-having husband, it could've been either one.

"It's my aunt. Let me see what she wants, 'cause she's just gonna keep on calling back."

Sam gave a dismissive hand wave and closed his eyes. I'd

have to get creative to wake him up if I wanted to finish what we started. I was up for the challenge.

I took a few steps until I was out of the bedroom and then padded barefoot to the kitchen. I could get us a snack while I heard whatever amount of money Aunt Sherrie needed.

"Hello," Aunt Sherrie croaked into the phone.

"Hi auntie. Sorry I missed your call."

"You got a gentleman caller?"

I rolled my eyes. Aunt Sherrie was so nosy and wouldn't stop until she got all the details. I wasn't ready to share Sam with my family yet. Once Sam knew about my family, he couldn't un-know. Knowing was going to be a problem.

"I just didn't get to the phone fast enough. What's going on? It must be important for you to call me this late."

"Honey."

When Aunt Sherrie said 'honey' it was a whole statement of distress. Honey meant things were not the way they needed to be, and you were part of the help to get things back to Aunt Sherrie's normal.

"What's wrong?"

"It's your Uncle Joe. You need to get down here."

"What happened? Did he have a stroke? Heart attack? What happened?"

"Well, he had both."

"Oh lord. Is he okay?"

Aunt Sherrie went quiet, so that could only mean one thing. I felt my voice catch in my throat. Not my Uncle Joe. He taught me how to ride a bike and how to make my own pickles just like he did down at the Shady Falls pickle plant. He was Aunt Sherrie's husband, but he felt like my blood.

"His old nasty ass up and died."

The fury in Aunt Sherrie's voice made me wonder the circumstances of Uncle Joe's death. I'd never, in all forty years of them being married, heard Aunt Sherrie call Uncle Joe nasty. Not even when he was running around on her with a woman he worked with at the pickle plant.

"Aunt Sherrie, we don't speak ill of the dead now. Rest in peace, Uncle Joe."

"Anyway, I need you to come down here and help me bury his nasty ass."

If this wasn't my Uncle Joe we were talking about it might be funny that she just kept calling him nasty.

"Of course, I'll help, but I thought he had life insurance. Do you need me to come and help you sort through the papers?"

"Don't nothing need sorting. He stopped paying the premium on that policy, right about the time when he started seeing that heffa again."

"Oh, no, Uncle Joe. But, I'm sure he thought he'd have time to get it back, before . . . before something like this happened."

"I don't know what he thought. I just know he died over there at the Starlight Motel. The pickle ho the one called the ambulance."

I whispered *Lord have mercy* under my breath.

"Yeah," Aunt Sherrie continued. "I think he was back to taking those blue pills."

"Viagra?"

"Yep. I knew because that mess always dropped his blood pressure. He fell in the kitchen last week; said he wasn't feelin' too steady. It was that damn ding-a-ling pill."

The giggle came into my throat accidentally. I didn't mean to think any of this was funny, 'cause it was tragic. Uncle Joe didn't deserve to die. Even if he had a pickle ho.

"Will you come and help? I wouldn't need you to pay for the whole thing. I got a little bit stashed away for such a time as this."

"How much you got stashed?"

"About three hundred."

So, she needed me to pay for the whole thing.

"I'll send you the money, Auntie."

"You aren't going to come down? It would really do my heart good to see you. Your mama's too."

"Is she there yet?"

My mama lived in the next town over from Shady Falls, Goldsboro. If she wasn't there already, then surely she was on her way. I hadn't talked to her in two years. Not after what she'd done when my grandmother died. She'd stolen all of her nice things, pawned what she could, and kept the rest. By the time Aunt Sherrie had gotten there, everything was gone.

"Rochelle doesn't need her heart to feel good."

"Hahna, don't be like that. I understand her. She was desperate when Mama died. If I can forgive her, you can."

"Grandma managed to keep all of her jewelry even when she was sending me care packages at Spelman and paying any bills I had that fell short. She wasn't even cold in the ground before Rochelle started stealing."

My mother was only fifteen years older than me, so Aunt Sherrie and Grandma were my mother figures. I never could call Rochelle, Mama, or Mom. I tried, but it didn't ever sound right. I don't think she even liked it.

"Your mama's a different person now. She's gotten saved and she's running for the Lord."

The Lord must've been giving her lottery ticket money and a fifth of gin, because that's the only thing that got her running.

"I'll be there, Auntie. Will clear my schedule for the rest of the week."

"Good. And bring that fella you laying up with."

"Auntie."

"Don't Auntie me. Anybody who don't answer their aunt's calls in the middle of the night must got a man between their legs."

This time I couldn't contain my laughter. It rolled out and Aunt Sherrie joined right on in. I was glad I could make her forget her sorrows for a moment. 'Cause she didn't fool me one bit. I knew that even though Uncle Joe was a cheater, she loved him. She'd loved him her whole life. And I was going to help her bury one of the few male figures I'd had in my life.

"I'll see you in a day or so, Auntie. And I will bring my gentleman caller. His name is Sam."

"We'll be happy to meet him."

I took a bowl of grapes and two bottles of water back into the bedroom. Sam opened his eyes as I climbed into the bed.

"Everything all right?" he asked.

"No. My uncle died."

Saying the words to Sam made them feel more real than when Aunt Sherrie had told me. I sobbed a little as a flood of tears fell. Sam rubbed my back and kissed my neck. Even the good feelings that he brought didn't overcome my sudden sadness.

"Is he here in Georgia?"

"No, he and my aunt Sherrie live in Shady Falls, North Carolina."

"Did you know that's where Ron grew up?"

"I think I did. I lived in the next town over. Might as well have been another country, but it was only about thirty minutes away."

"Are you going to the funeral?" Sam asked.

"There won't be a funeral unless I do."

"Let me guess. You're paying for everything?"

"Yeah."

"Well, it's good that there's someone in the family that can pay."

Sam's comment didn't hit right for some reason, but I didn't have time to dissect that. It was time to grieve for Uncle Joe.

"That's true. I told them you're coming with me."

"To the funeral?"

"You will, won't you? I don't really like going home. There's so many things I'd like to forget about the way I grew up. This is going to bring it all back."

"Yes, of course I'll come, babe. You know I've got you."

I snuggled into Sam's arms and felt a different kind of warmth. The feeling of safety and security. I just hoped meeting my family wouldn't have Sam looking for his own safety net.

Chapter 14

TWILA

I didn't know why I let Debbie talk me into coming to Club Phenom. Traci and Abena had spent the whole night bragging about some huge NBA party they were having, and Debbie just *had* to go. I didn't care about finding a baller to fleece, so I was less motivated for the club—especially Phenom.

Typically, Debbie wasn't even the kind of chick who could get through the doors of Club Phenom. She didn't have the right number of zeroes in her bank account. Wasn't in the correct circles. Those years right after she dropped out of college would've disqualified her also. There weren't too many ex-strippers who had turned tricks that were allowed in Club Phenom.

The only thing qualifying Debbie was the fact that the place was owned by our line sisters. I would've felt some kind of way about that if I was Debbie. She didn't care.

We had a VIP booth in the upstairs portion of the club. VIP was almost a misnomer at Club Phenom, because everyone there was beyond that status in real life. But our booth gave us a view of the club from behind a glass partition. We could observe and not partake. Same as in the room behind the red door.

The door I didn't want to think about.

Traci swallowed the rest of her second shot of Hennessy and slammed the glass on the table. That glass slam meant she had something to get off her chest.

"Are we not going to talk about how disrespectful Big Ron's ex-wife and her friends were?" Traci asked. "I hope those hoes are not coming to the wedding."

"She probably is, since her daughters are in it, that will be her excuse. I certainly hope she doesn't bring her entourage," Abena said.

"And what the hell you think she wanted to say in that toast? She hit it first?" Traci was big mad when she said this, but I cracked up.

"She probably just wanted to tell everyone that she was okay with them getting together," I said when I stopped laughing. "Maybe she didn't want anyone to feel weird."

Abena shook her head. "Trying to make their upcoming wedding about her. Just like a damn Karen."

I lifted an eyebrow at Abena. I didn't like how recklessly my friends were labeling white women as Karens. It was the new Becky. Except Becky was the kind to sleep with all the black men, and Karen would call the police on the same ones. I didn't think Sabrina was either.

I tried to put myself in Sabrina's shoes. Ron was a good man—maybe even better than the man she left him for. She could've been remorseful about the way things turned out. Maybe she always thought that Ron would be there when she was ready to have him back.

I'd been there and done that. Not with a husband, but with more than one boo who was gone by the time I'd made up my mind.

"I don't think she's like that," I said to hostile glares. "We gotta remember who Big Ron is. He loved her. He had kids with her."

"And?" Debbie asked.

"And I think we ought to give her a break. Couldn't she just be a woman who fell in love with a man, divorced him, and is feeling uncomfortable about his moving on?" I asked.

Abena shrugged. "That's her fault, and maybe a conversation she needed to have offline with Ron. I do know this, my line sister will not be subject to her shenanigans again."

"Twila, you were the main one about to beat her tail," Traci said. "But now you want to give her a break?"

"I wanted to smack her friends. If she had left them at home, she probably wouldn't have felt the need to show out."

"You probably right," Debbie said. "I'm sure her friends were talking all kinds of trash in the car on the way to the party."

"Of course, they were," I said. "I think she had good intentions coming to the party, but she just went left at some point."

"Well she needs to ditch her friends before they get her ass beat," Traci said.

Abena nodded in agreement. "This bride squad rolls deep."

I took another long sip of wine. I couldn't judge them, because I had violent tendencies my damn self, and there's no way I wasn't jumping in if they were all in some sort of brawl.

"Y'all ain't 'bout to have me on *Straight from the A*," I said. "That girl be having all the business."

"That girl ain't gonna put you in her blog," Debbie said. "You ain't a celebrity."

"I'm celebrity adjacent. I have been invited to join the cast of several Atlanta reality shows." I said that as a brag, but was it really something to brag about? Once the words came out my mouth, I decided I wanted them back.

"Speaking of celebrities, which Twila is *not*, where are all the NBA players?" Debbie asked. "Y'all said it was gonna be hella ballers in here tonight. I saw two."

Abena laughed. "All you need is two and that makes it an NBA party."

"Well they both showed up with groupies. I need to meet somebody. Who in here is single?"

"There are plenty available men on the dance floor," Traci said. "You want to go down there?"

"Abena, you coming with me?" Debbie asked, knowing that me and Traci were not the type to go out on crowded dance floors.

"Let's go, but as soon as my feet start hurting, I'm done."

Debbie laughed. "You are such a grandma. You should've worn comfortable shoes."

"I just need another shot of Henny. That will make toes numb."

They left me and Traci in the VIP section, and neither of us felt upset about being left behind.

"How have you been?" Traci asked me. "Hahna let it slip that you've been staying at her house."

I rolled my eyes. Hahna and her big mouth.

"Girl, I just have a thing going on. Started therapy again. Nothing I can't handle."

Traci poked her lips out and lowered her eyebrows in irritation or anger, I couldn't tell which.

"Seriously, Twila? You haven't been to the club in more than a minute. You were a regular. We haven't seen you since you popped up with your last man. And it hadn't been awhile before that."

I'd kept the truth from Traci and Abena, but maybe they needed to know. What if the guy came back and raped someone else? Maybe he already had.

"Can I share something with you, and you not say anything? Not even to your husband or Abena?"

Traci narrowed her eyes at me. I knew this was asking a lot. Telling Traci anything was like an automatic three-person share. I didn't even think she tried to keep secrets.

"This must be something big if you're asking me not to tell them."

"It is. I haven't figured out how to deal with it yet, so I just don't want everyone up in my business."

Traci scooted closer to me at the table. That was good. I didn't want to have to speak too loudly.

"I'll keep your secret, Twila."

"Are you sure? 'Cause when I tell you why I haven't been at the club, you are going to want to immediately tell someone."

"I have you my sister."

"I was raped here, Traci. In the lifestyle room."

Traci's face was a mixture of disbelief, shock, and finally sympathy. I'm not surprised that the sympathy piece came last. She owned Club Phenom and prided herself on her safety protocols.

"How were you raped? We run background checks on everyone that we allow in here."

I nodded. "That's honestly why I'm telling you. I want to know who he is."

"Wait. When did this happen?" Traci asked.

"About two years ago. I haven't been right since."

"Is that when you started collecting weapons and shit?"

I nodded. "Yeah. I mean, I already had a gun, but the tasers, machetes, and switchblades that I have stashed all over are because of being attacked."

"Why do you want to know who it is? Are you going to press charges?"

I had no intentions of pressing charges, but the urgency in Traci's voice irritated me. Did she care more about the success of her precious club than she cared about me? I shouldn't be surprised.

"No, but would you support me if I did?"

Traci blew out a long stream of air. "You know if law enforcement knew what we did in here, we'd be shut down."

"I get it, but I still want to know who the guy is that raped me. He's moved into my subdivision, I think. I saw him a few weeks ago and I've been staying with Hahna ever since."

"You give me a description of the guy, and I can scan our files for who he might be. But, what do you plan to do with the information if you're not pressing charges?"

"I would be incriminating myself if I gave you details."

Traci nodded. "Do you need any help with that?"

"I might."

"Let me know. I don't appreciate my sacred space being desecrated."

I felt seen in that moment. She understood my need for revenge. Hahna and Kimberly would've both tried to stop me. They, like my therapist, would think this part was unhealthy. But the only way I could get my power back on this one, was to make sure that asshole paid for what he'd done to me.

I should have told my sister sooner.

Chapter 15

KIMBERLY

The suite at the Marriott Marquis was the size of a small apartment, but it felt tiny and the air heavy. Ron hadn't said a word since they'd gotten there. He'd done a fair amount of pacing back and forth, but no speaking. Kimberly sat on the couch with the television remote in her hand, and waited for him to break the silence, because this was his mess that needed fixing. She didn't have any toxic exes.

"I don't know why she showed up acting like that," Ron finally said. "We've had peace since the divorce. This just doesn't make any sense."

"Maybe her happy home isn't," Kimberly said. "Maybe seeing you with someone else made her wish she'd done things differently."

"Too late for that kind of thinking. It was too late for that when she decided to lay up with her ex. Cheating is a deal breaker for me, Kim. It might be my only one."

They agreed there. Cheating was on the top of Kimberly's deal breaker list, but it sure wasn't the only one. Not keeping ex-wives in order was slowly climbing the list of importance.

"Maybe it was just the alcohol. She was pretty lit. She showed up almost drunk and kept drinking non-stop at the party."

"Her friends were lit too. Wendy was pushing up on half the frats."

"Yeah, she exclusively dates wealthy black men, so she was in her element."

"Not Nicole, though? Is she single too?"

Ron shook his head. "Unless things have changed, she's engaged to the head of a private equity group. He's worth millions."

"What's her beef with you?"

Ron shrugged. "I have no idea. They all know that Sabrina cheated on me. So, I don't know what she could be angry about. I think she, like you, has an issue with interracial marriages, but she won't say it out loud because she's white."

"And I can say it out loud because I'm black?"

"You know it's different when you say it. It comes from a different place."

Kimberly pressed her lips together and frowned. Then she said, "I don't have an issue with interracial marriages. I have an issue with black men being married to white women."

Ron scoffed. "What does that mean?"

"It means that when people tell black women to keep their options open, I want to know with whom they mean. Because, my big, black ass has never been hit on or even approached by anyone but a brother. So, yeah, until the whole spectrum of men are out here checking for us, I have an issue with women who can have anyone snatching the few options we have."

"I see a lot of white men with black women lately."

"Doesn't change my experience, Ron. Or the experience of any of my friends."

Ron sighed. "How hard do I have to love you for you to get over this issue?"

"You love me well enough, Ron. But, I still have a gang of single sisters. It would be different if they didn't want to be married. Look at Twila. She's got it all, banging body, money, she's beautiful . . ."

"And crazy."

"Ron, why would you say that?"

Ron sat next to Kimberly on the couch. "I'm sorry. Not crazy, but unstable at times. That whole thing with the Instagram dude . . ."

Yes, the Marcus thing was crazy, but they'd made a sister pact to date the next man that asked them out. For Twila, it had been the insta-thot that cheated on her with one of the younger sorors. That wasn't her fault, and that didn't make her unstable.

Twila wasn't well, though, and it bothered Kimberly that no one was telling her what was going on with her. Did Hahna know something more than what she said? If she did, Kimberly would find out, because Hahna couldn't hold water, much less a secret.

"Let's not change the subject of tonight's narrative," Kimberly said. "Twila and Marcus have nothing to do with your ex-wife coming to our engagement party showing her entire ass."

"I will talk to her."

"You'll do no such thing. She owes me an apology, and I'm willing to speak with her. She doesn't have anything to say to you."

"I mean, she owes the both of us an apology."

"She does, but because I don't know what her intentions are towards you, she doesn't need to have an audience with you."

"But she will have an audience with me about other things."

"What other things?"

"Our children, Kimberly."

It was past time for them to have this conversation. The what-does-coparenting-look-like chat. They needed to be on one accord there, because Kimberly had a feeling that any break in their armor would give Sabrina hope or satisfaction or whatever it was that she needed when she came to the engagement party showing out.

"I'll be included in those conversations as well. She will have an audience with us about the twins."

"Only if she feels comfortable with that," Ron said.

Kimberly clenched her fists and stared straight ahead. She didn't need her protector to feel like he had to protect the feelings of any other woman. *Her* needs were first. Had to be. Or she wasn't going to be able to do this.

"Sabrina told me that she was happy to have a black woman as part of her children's parenting team. Do you not want me on the team, Ron?"

"Oh, well if Sabrina said that, we should be good."

"But if she hadn't said it. If she'd said, she didn't want me to have anything to do with the raising and discipline of her children, would you be okay with that?"

Ron sighed deeply and took Kimberly's hand. He'd been doing that a lot lately. Taking her hand trying to calm her feelings. But it wasn't going to work this time. Kimberly snatched her hand away.

"Would you be okay with that?" Kimberly asked again.

"If she did feel that way, I would have to take a diminished role in my daughter's lives. I don't want that. And you shouldn't want a man who would want that."

"So, we're lucky that Sabrina is okay with this, huh?"

"It's not all up to her, Kimmie Kim. It just makes it easier that she's on board with the coparenting. That's all."

Kimberly didn't like Ron's answer. It was a non-answer really. He was telling her that peace in her home and her marriage would hinge on the feelings of a woman who didn't seem to know what she wanted. What if she decided differently in the future?

"Ron, I'm going to set up a time to meet with Sabrina. I'm going to let her know that her behavior was unacceptable and help her come up with a plan moving forward."

"You're going to manage this situation?"

"Is that what I said? Do I sound like a manager?" Kimberly asked.

"You just sound like the woman I know well. The one who's such a boss that she expects people to move the way she wants."

"I don't have that expectation. Not of everyone."

"I bet your friends would agree with me. We just accept it, because you being a boss adds value to everyone's lives."

"And you don't think Sabrina will feel the same way?"

"I don't know. I think she will maybe buck against your expectations, especially in the only area where she maintains any leverage or control."

Kimberly let this sink in. No matter what Ron said, she had no plans on managing Sabrina. But she *did* have expectations that would be met, or Sabrina would find that Kimberly was a more than worthy opponent. If Sabrina wanted to maintain full physical and legal custody of her children, then she would comply. Ron was a great dad, and there was no reason an Atlanta judge wouldn't give him joint custody. Especially since there were two Gamma Phi Gamma judges in the family court system.

Kimberly wouldn't make that happen unless she had to, and that hinged on Sabrina's reaction to the expectations. And Kimberly only had two.

She expected Sabrina to dispose of any baggage she had related to her and Ron's divorce. And Kimberly expected Sabrina to respect any space Kimberly allowed her into. Kimberly wasn't going to spend her marriage being worried about Ron and Sabrina getting into some sort of entanglement. And she damn sure wasn't going to be embarrassed in front of her friends and Atlanta's society.

That wasn't too much to ask.

Chapter 16

TWILA

After telling Traci about my assault I felt lighter. Maybe because I had a plan of action, or maybe because it just felt good thinking about how to make that man pay. Traci had asked me to describe him, and we were going to meet later for her to show me a series of photographs from their background investigations.

The feeling of lightness allowed me to go hard at the gym. Hahna had already fallen off, but in her defense, she had to pack, so she could go see her country bumpkin ass family in Shady Falls, North Carolina. She'd told me about that place and her hometown Goldsboro. I had never decided that I didn't need to ever visit a place just based on description, but that one stoplight town with a pickle plant was the last place on earth I wanted to go.

And she was taking Sam too. Poor Sam.

I was doing my third set of lunges when DeAndre walked over into the floor exercise area of the gym. The man was fine, and he *knew* he was fine, which were the makings of a manwhore. He glanced over at me, smiled, and waved. I waved back, but I didn't smile. I didn't need a manwhore right now. Or ever. I was done with men with errant penises.

Why was he walking over to me? I didn't give him a come-hither gaze. If anything, I'd given him a go-thither glare. I rolled my eyes, not wanting an interaction. I just wanted to feel the burn and fantasize about revenge.

"I hate to interrupt your workout," DeAndre said, "but would you mind spotting me really quick? This place is a ghost town this early, and I have a few more heavy reps to do."

The audacity of DeAndre to walk up to me, looking and smelling like a slice of heaven and ask me to spot him. I mean, it was annoying, but yet I was following him over to his weight bench. I didn't make this decision, my coochie made this decision. I was sick of her ass too. Always getting me into shit I didn't want to deal with. I swore the ho had a mind of her own.

"I like that it's empty here in the early mornings," I said as I stood behind DeAndre. "That way I avoid all guys trying to hook up."

"No one here this early is on that, huh?" DeAndre asked.

"Nope. The guys here are usually serious as hell about their workouts. The women too."

I watched DeAndre's muscles glisten as he effortlessly did his first heavy set. He looked as if he was carved out of chocolate.

He sat up for his first rest period. "I think that a gym is a fine place to meet someone," he said. "You can tell a lot about a person by their dedication to fitness."

Except guys like him never tried to talk to the women who were really dedicated to fitness. The ones who were in full sweats because they weren't comfortable enough with their bodies to wear tight leggings and sports bras. They never talked to the women who had lost one hundred pounds and who had another hundred to go. The DeAndre type of guy wanted girls like me. I didn't judge them for it, but he was full of shit.

"Interesting."

He turned to face me, and I had to look away from the bulge in his shorts. But it was too late. His print was imprinted in my mind. Why was my coochie such a damn ho?

"What's interesting? I like to see someone set a goal for themselves and accomplish it. What's your goal?"

"Eight pack by the time of my friend's wedding."

"Eight pack? Whoa. That must be some dress you're wearing."

"We haven't even picked them yet, but I just want to look my best. I think weddings are a great place to meet guys."

DeAndre laughed. "It's a great place to meet guys who just wanna hook up."

"Any more than the gym?"

"You have a point."

DeAndre spun back around and hopped off the bench. He added more weight onto the bar.

His muscles strained harder on the second set. I could see the exertion in his face, and from the beads of sweat that popped out on his forehead. He heaved the bar back on the bench and exhaled. The scent of cinnamon wafted up to my nose. Maybe it was the dentist in me, but I loved a man with good oral hygiene. Funky breath was a complete turnoff. Unless it was a potential patient with deep pockets, because I would get a person together, but for a price.

"So, you're looking for a nice guy at the wedding?" DeAndre asked as he took his second rest period.

"I'm not looking, but I like to be prepared should anyone present himself."

"What if I presented myself this morning? You could take me to the wedding with you, and I'd only require a six-pack, not eight."

I narrowed my eyes at him but softened when I saw that he was joking. I offered him a chuckle.

"I don't know how I'd feel about your presentation this morning. You were a little lazy on that last set."

"I was not."

"You were. Watching a person work out can tell me a lot about their character. If you're lazy in the gym, you might be lazy in other venues."

DeAndre tossed his head back and laughed, and I almost fell

in love with the sound. It was so damn joyful, like he had no cares. And why would he? A muscular, chocolate lawyer in Atlanta? Life was a playground for him, and it looked like he wanted to pull me onto the merry-go-round with his fine ass. Ugh.

He hopped up and added more weight to the bar. I sure hoped I didn't have to pull this off him. I was strong but might have a bit of trouble with that heavy weight.

DeAndre did the last set. Went hard with it. He kicked that last set's ass. What was he trying to show me?

He slammed the bar back on the bench. "Never lazy. Not here nor in any other venue."

"I see. Well, enjoy the rest of your workout. It's been fun verbally sparring with you this morning."

"Are you about to leave?"

"Gonna grab a bite to eat at the smoothie bar, and then yeah, I'm out. I'll see you the next time."

DeAndre stood and stretched. Good God almighty, the man was blessed.

"Mind if I join you?"

I did mind, but I wasn't sure if my ho coochie was going to let me say that. She must've been putting out pheromones that gave DeAndre "all systems go" messages.

"Well . . ."

"I just want to get to know you in a safe setting. One protein shake, and that's it. I promise."

"I like kale smoothies."

"That doesn't surprise me. That is the choice of the bourgeoisie."

"Did you just call me bougie?"

"Yeah, I did. Am I wrong?"

I chuckled. "You're not wrong, and I didn't take it as an insult. I thought you were being very perceptive."

"I am that."

The bougie perception wasn't the thing that made my pulse quicken, though. It was the fact that he saw I needed to connect with him in a safe space. I was unsure if there was a man who could meet me where I was in my journey to wellness.

"Okay. We can have post-workout breakfast," I said. "But it isn't a date."

"Definitely not a date. We'd have to plan for that. I don't know enough about you to plan a successful date."

My only response to this was a smile. He was hitting all the right notes so far. But no need to think this would be anything past breakfast.

"I usually get dressed for work after my workout, and before my breakfast. Do you have time for me to do that?"

"I do the same. I'll meet you at the smoothie bar?"

"Yep. That works."

We both retreated to the men's and women's locker rooms. In the shower, I let my mind roam. I tried not to get hopeful on a first encounter with a man, but I couldn't help it. When the guy was the full package like DeAndre—career, body, and looks, there was always something to mess it up. Like he probably had baby mama drama, a crazy ex, or crazy exes. Or he was crazy his damn self.

But was it even fair for me to hope for perfection? I had more than a few issues. Maybe some of my shit was somebody's dealbreaker.

I got out of the shower and sprayed one of Kimberly's natural conditioners into my hair. If my girl did this right, she was going to be close to a billionaire. Her formulas were perfect.

I pulled on my snug blue slacks (what's the point of working out if I'm not showing my ass), and a button-down blouse. My lab coat didn't go on until I got into the office.

Since I was sure my locker room time had taken longer than DeAndre's, I power walked over to the smoothie bar. DeAndre was standing at the counter chatting with the college student who worked there. The pretty young college student who stared at DeAndre like she wanted him to take her to school.

DeAndre turned as I walked in. "Hey," he said, "what's your favorite smoothie?"

"Apple, banana, kale. Extra kale in case I don't want salad for lunch."

"Good choice. Gotta get those greens in. Is that what you want today?"

I chuckled. DeAndre was not typical. Most guys would've assumed that because I said that was my favorite that I wanted to have that from the menu. That was only correct about sixty percent of the time for me, because I always liked to mix things up. I craved change in all things.

"That is what I want today."

DeAndre turned to the college girl. "We'll have two of those. Add protein to mine."

"Gotta feed those abs, huh?" she asked.

I lifted my eyebrows and stifled a giggle. These young girls were bold as hell. Maybe that's why they were taking all the silver foxes.

We sat at a small table while we waited for our smoothies.

"You know I debated asking you to breakfast," DeAndre said. "Seems like asking someone out at the gym is kind of tired."

"Not tired, but expected," I said. "The gym is the hook up spot, and if not the gym, where?"

"I don't know. Online?"

"Ugh. I hate online dating. It is the worst."

"Yeah, I've tried it. Most of the women I connected with were totally different when we met."

"They looked different?"

"Well, yes, those filters are a beast."

I burst into laughter. It was true, but women weren't the only ones guilty of visual trickery.

"Not just the filters, though," I said. "What about these fake beards and the hatfishers?"

DeAndre joined my laughter. "Dudes just trying to catch up with y'all. But it wasn't just the looks. These women have travel, good credit, and no drama in their bios and yet they've only been to Miami, their credit is *not* good, and there is more than a little drama."

"Just lying, huh?"

"Yep."

"I wouldn't think a guy like you would need to resort to on-line dating though."

"You would think. But where are good places to meet a single, professional woman, over thirty-five? Think about it. Church, but I don't do the church thing consistently."

"Oh, you're like me. Easter, Christmas . . ."

"Sometimes Mother's Day, 'cause my mother is known to demand a brunch."

"Yours too?"

"Yes ma'am. But church and like, where else? The club? I did that in my twenties. I got a lot of ass, but not one relationship. Work? Not me. I work alone. Unless I have a random encounter with someone like you, the pickings are slim."

"Networking events?"

"Wait. Are you steering me away? 'Cause clearly I have settled in on this random encounter we're having right now."

I laughed. I wasn't trying to steer him away, but I didn't want to seem pressed for this encounter to turn into more. If it didn't, I would be cool with that.

"I'm also enjoying this. Didn't think I would, but I am."

"Really?"

I sighed. "I have a lot on my plate. Not quite focused on finding a nice guy."

"Are you saying that if I did ask you out on a real date that you'd turn me down?"

I knew this was coming, and dammit I hadn't decided yet. He was a damn black unicorn, so how could I say no?

"Could I ask you to hold that thought? Could you not ask me yet?"

His eyes widened with shock. I was sure no one had ever said anything like this to him before. He was used to getting yeses, and I was saying hold up a second.

"This is a first."

"I'm not surprised about that."

"Not the hold that thought part. I've had women tell me they were in the middle of a divorce or getting out a relationship, and could I give them a minute. I was never willing to do that."

"I see."

"It's a first that I'm okay with it."

"I'm worth a little pause?"

He nodded. "A strategic pause. And I think you might be worth it."

I smiled, marveling about how calm and safe I felt talking to this handsome stranger.

"I am."

Chapter 17

KIMBERLY

Kimberly arranged her office desk neatly and wiped away the crumbs from her morning muffin. She had an official meeting this morning, and it wasn't with a client. It was with Sabrina.

She'd decided to have the meeting at her office, because there was going to be nothing friendly about their chat. No coffee shop, no small talk, and no frivolities. Kimberly was about to gather Sabrina's edges and hand them to her in a little plastic bag.

LaShea, Kimberly's assistant, walked into the office, and Kimberly sat up straight at her desk and glared.

"How do I look?" Kimberly asked.

LaShea laughed. "Are you supposed to be looking mean or something?"

"I'm supposed to look like I will beat a bitch's ass."

LaShea cocked her head to one side and concentrated. She narrowed her eyes and then exhaled.

"There's something missing. I don't know what."

"Seriously, LaShea?"

"You just have an underlying friendliness to your face. You have resting friend face."

"Oh my god. I need resting and unresting bitch face."

"Nope. Maybe you can pull your hair back. Your hair all curly like that, has a bubbly personality of its own."

"I don't have time for all that. I'd have to wet my hair completely and reapply product to get it to go back."

LaShea shrugged. "Well, you don't look mean or scary. Maybe you should try a different approach."

Kimberly dropped her shoulders and sighed. "Like what? She disrespected our engagement party. I should be able to get her in order. Threaten her so bad that she won't come back looking for more."

"I think if you threaten her, she's gonna go crying to your fiancé about how mean you were to her. Then she might even try to tell him she doesn't feel comfortable with their kids around you."

Kimberly didn't put that past Sabrina at all. Sabrina was highly uncomfortable when Ron had first shown up with her. Ron had put his foot down then, but if Kimberly was aggressive with Sabrina, would that prove the point Sabrina was trying to make in the first place? That her instincts were right and that she didn't want her children around Kimberly? That couldn't happen. They'd made too much progress for that. But then Kimberly couldn't allow the disrespect to continue either.

"You might be right," Kimberly said to LaShea. "Let me think of a different way to approach this ho."

"Maybe don't think of her as a ho. That feels a little hostile."

"It does, doesn't it. Ugh. Okay. Send her in when she gets here."

"You'll do fine. Just think about Ron and the children when you're talking to her. You only care about his happiness, not hers. But his kids make him happy, right?"

"How are you so brilliant about this stuff?"

"Ummm . . . baby mama drama is my specialty. I believe I have a doctorate in it."

Kimberly laughed at LaShea, but the young lady wasn't exaggerating. The father of her son had three other children, and at least one of those relationships was toxic. One of the girls had come to their previous office cutting up. LaShea held her composure though and called the police. She'd told Kimberly she wasn't giving up her career over a hood chick who had nothing to lose.

Kimberly thought about calling Ron for advice, but he was almost no help. The things that he would say to Sabrina would only work for him.

LaShea sent Kimberly a text that said, *Incoming*.

Kimberly took a deep breath and sat up straight again. She ditched the scowl but stopped short of smiling.

There was a little tap on the door. A timid tap. Good. She needed to humble herself.

"Come on in."

Kimberly didn't stand to her feet or wave or give any pleasantry. Kimberly let her walk across that office without any encouragement.

"Hi, Kim. Oh, wait, do you ever go by Kim?"

"It's Kimberly."

"Sorry, Kimberly. How are you today?"

Sabrina was out of breath from talking, walking, and perhaps hyperventilating by the time she got to the open seat in front of Kimberly's desk.

"I'm doing well today, Sabrina. And you?" These were measured and peaceful words. No harsh edge to them, but no softened edge either.

"I'm just well . . ." She plopped into the chair. "I've been a mess since your engagement party."

She'd been a mess? Kimberly's eyes narrowed and her face tightened. Was this supposed to get her sympathy?

"Why have you been a mess?"

"I'm just so embarrassed. I didn't mean to do any of that. I was just so damned drunk."

"You did seem to be rather tipsy."

"I just started with a glass of wine to calm my nerves, but then I just kept going. My friends didn't stop me. I think they egged me on."

"You need new friends."

Perhaps Sabrina didn't know how to respond to that, because she simply blinked.

"You're right to be embarrassed," Kimberly said. "But I'm more concerned about how we don't extend that same kind of situation to the wedding. I'm not interested in that."

Sabrina wrung her hands as tears welled up in her eyes. "I totally agree. That's why I'm here today. I wanted you to know that I would never . . ."

"But you did."

"I mean, I wouldn't do it again," The tears started dropping. "Not at your wedding. Not at all."

Kimberly wished she could collect those tears in a cup and throw them in Sabrina's face. This was exactly what Kimberly expected this heffa to do. Start crying and act like the magic of her fairy tears was supposed to make all her anger disappear.

"So, you're not going to try and give a drunken toast at our wedding?"

"No, I promise."

"I'm curious. What were you even planning to say in the toast? Our friends and families were there."

"I just wanted to give my blessing. I mean in case anyone wondered whether or not I supported the union."

"Why would our friends and family care what you thought, Sabrina? That doesn't make any sense to me."

"Maybe they wouldn't care, but some of the people at that party were at our wedding. Some of the groomsmen were there. It overwhelmed me."

"So, then the toast wasn't about us at all. You were trying to feel not so overwhelmed."

Sabrina sighed. The tears were uncontrollable at that point, so it may have seemed insensitive that Kimberly hadn't offered a tissue. It mattered not to Kimberly.

"I couldn't help but remember our wedding day, and then how it had all gone terribly wrong. Ronald was so unrelenting with his lack of forgiveness."

This was starting to get uncomfortable. What was the purpose of rehashing that bit of trivia? Kimberly didn't care to hear about how their marriage had imploded. This child needed a therapist, or better friends.

"I don't really want to talk about all that," Kimberly said. "I just need you to agree to say nothing at our wedding, or I will have you escorted out by security."

Sabrina scoffed. Through her distress and sadness, she'd summoned enough energy to disdain the thought of being escorted out. Kimberly meant every word, though.

"You should talk to someone about all this," Sabrina said. "Ronald scared me that night. It was like the gentle giant that I knew . . ."

Oh no this ho did not say gentle giant.

". . . had turned into the incredible freaking hulk. I thought he was going to beat the hell out of me that night."

"You were afraid of Ron? I could never be afraid of him."

"Well you should be. He showed me a violent side that I never knew he had. He took one of our doors completely off the hinges and put several large holes in the walls of our home. The children were scared. He'd turned into a monster that night."

"Did he put his hands on you?" Kimberly asked, pretty sure she already knew the answer.

"No. He never did, but only because I got out of there. I took the children to my mother in Charlotte, and we stayed there until we had a plan."

Exactly what Kimberly thought. The Big Ron she knew would cut off his own arm before he hit a woman. He'd been raised by the same kind of southern black women that had raised her.

"And then?"

"Then what?"

"You're telling the story about the monster Ron became. It sounds like you were the monster. You slept with your ex-boyfriend . . ."

"My soulmate."

"Does that make it better?"

"Maybe not to you, but Ronald said knowing that made it easier to accept."

Sabrina had stopped crying and turned defensive. She stuck her chest out as it heaved up and down. This woman was a real piece of work.

"You slept with your ex, and then when you divorced Ron, you moved him in with Ron's children . . ."

"They're my children too."

"Of course. But you moved your new man under the same roof as a black man's daughters. I'm surprised Ron didn't try to get full custody of those girls."

She scoffed again, and clutched the handle of her Louis Vuitton handbag. Sabrina seemed annoyed, but Kimberly had given up trying to be nice to this delusional heffa.

"Ronald would never do that to me."

"To you? I don't think he gives a damn about you. I don't think he would do that to his daughters, though. Young ladies need their mothers."

This third scoff sounded almost like a chuckle. The real Sabrina was coming out. Contrite Sabrina was gone. Entitled Sabrina had arrived.

"You probably hope to God that he doesn't give a damn about me. Just know that you don't have to worry, because I'd never want Ronald back. Not after I saw the man he truly is. I was just warning you."

"Noted."

"And you don't have to worry about me saying anything at your wedding. The only reason I'm even attending is to make sure my children aren't mistreated."

"You should probably start making yourself comfortable with them being with us unattended by you. Because you won't be at every visit Ron has with his children once we're married."

"We'll determine what that situation looks like later. We will probably need to sit down for family counseling sessions to get all this sorted out. We may need to revisit Ronald's violence also."

Kimberly took these for exactly what they were. Threats. Finally, she stood.

"I think our conversation for today is done," Kimberly said. "LaShea will show you out of the building."

"You don't want to discuss this? Since you're calling the shots, now, I thought you'd want to have a say."

Kimberly's eye twitched. She wasn't unfamiliar with these tactics. Sabrina was throwing rocks, but as soon as something went down, she'd hide her hands. She'd cry, and tell the police she felt threatened by the fat black woman, and then Kimberly would be dragged out of her own building in cuffs.

Kimberly didn't give the ho an opening to do anything of the sort. She smiled.

"I'll be in touch about the girls' fittings for their dresses. Thank you for stopping by."

"That's it?"

"I got what I needed today. Your agreement not to say a word at my wedding. The rest of the conversation will be attended by the men."

"My husband won't come within ten feet of Ronald."

Smart man. Kimberly was sure Ron didn't have the same rules about hitting a man who'd slept with his wife that he had about not hitting women.

"Sounds like you need to work your magic there," Kimberly said. "Maybe turn on the waterworks like you did here. Maybe that'll help."

Sabrina stood and stormed out of Kimberly's office. As soon as she slammed the door, Kimberly burst into laughter. She didn't know if she'd made things better or worse, but getting her together sure made Kimberly feel better.

Kimberly was glad not to have this weight on her shoulders for the rest of the day. She was going to pick her wedding dress with her bridesmaids, and she needed all her peace for that outing. She had a feeling it was going to be a battle between the Maids of Honor and the one that thought she should be.

Chapter 18

HAHNA

I sat in the fancy bridal boutique, of course, the first to arrive, sipping my glass of expensive champagne. Samantha sat across from me, drinking her sparkling cider, and looking sour. She was a minister, so how was she so gruff all the time? Didn't the love of Jesus make a person joyful? It was supposed to. Joy was a fruit of the spirit. Sour was a fruit of something else.

"Did you have a good day today?" I asked, trying to be friendly.

"I broke what I thought was a good story, but it didn't have any teeth. So, no. I did not have a good day. I had a decidedly nothing day, but thank you for asking."

"Well, it's about to get better, because Kimberly is gonna say yes to the dress tonight."

"I see a lot of skinny girl selections in here, but not a good variety of plus sizes. Did you and Twila pick this place?"

"Yes, we did."

"Figures."

Samantha was not about to take a dump on our Maid of Honor planning. Not tonight. Twila and I did a good job with this one, and Samantha was about to eat her words. The next time she'd sprinkle honey on those mean judgments, 'cause this was going to taste like a rotten lemon going down.

"I did my research. This bridal boutique not only has the most extensive designer plus size collection in the country, but they also have the ability to customize anything she selects. Kimberly will find a dress here, and we're going to help."

"I'm going to sit back and look at Donny's Bridal's website while you guys try to squeeze Kimberly in these size eight dresses."

I shuddered. Donny's Bridal? Clearly, Samantha was unaware that our friend, the bride, was a multi-millionaire. She did not need to wear a dress that cost one hundred ninety-nine dollars. Our budget was under twenty thousand, with the ability to do more if necessary. This was going to be Kimberly's only wedding (because she and Ron were forever loves) so no way there was going to be any thrift shopping.

I sipped my champagne and decided not to give Samantha any more energy. I had enough to think about anyway before the others arrived.

Sam and I were leaving in the morning for Shady Falls, North Carolina. I wanted to fly, and he wanted a road trip, so we could talk for five hours. Sam loved deep, soul-searching conversations, but every time we had one, I was left feeling unsure of our relationship. With us, it always came back to my (supposed) love of money and material possessions. Maybe, this time, I'd be able to steer the conversation in another direction.

Twila showed up next. For the first time in weeks, she was all smiles. She plopped down in the empty chair next to me and kissed my cheek.

"Hey girl."

"Hey girl, hey," I said in our customary greeting. Out of the corner of my eye, I saw Samantha rolling *her* eyes. Ugh.

"Guess who I saw today?" Twila asked.

I was afraid to guess, but I assumed it was no one bad or scary, because she was smiling.

"Who?" I asked.

"Your tenant, DeAndre. I saw him at the gym."

I smiled. "Oh, did you keep flirting with him? I thought you were gonna take a bite out of him the last time you saw him."

"I didn't really flirt hard at all, but he asked me to spot him on the weight bench. I guess the conversation got so good that he wanted to have breakfast smoothies with me."

"A breakfast date?"

She shook her head. "We are specifically not calling that a date. He says he needs to know me better before he can properly plan a date."

"Did you exchange numbers?"

"No, but I followed him on Instagram, and he followed me back."

I shook my head. "Y'all worse than the kids. Gonna be sliding into DM's?"

"I won't," Twila said. "He's still coming around at the wrong time. I'm not ready to give a new relationship energy right now."

"But you're not ready to turn him all the way down."

"Girl, you saw him. I mean . . ."

"I get it."

I *did* get it, but it didn't keep me from worrying about my sister. Something had changed in Twila's demeanor, and I couldn't tell if it was the therapy or something else.

There was no time to ponder this any further, because Kimberly arrived and we had to spring into action. I jumped to my feet seconds before Samantha, who had no idea what was about to happen. Both Twila and I hugged Kim at the same time.

"Hey y'all," Kimberly said. "Sorry, I'm late. Traffic."

"You're good. We're the only ones here so far."

Kimberly blew a kiss at Samantha. "Thank you for being on time, girl. I think we only have what, two and a half hours?"

"That's right," Twila said. "And they had to squeeze you in for that. I knew we should've told those heffas to come at six o'clock."

"Come on, Kim," I said. "They've already set up your dressing room with some of your first selections."

Then, I looked over at Samantha. "When the rest of the girls get here, tell them Kimberly will be modeling each dress, so they can get their glass of champagne and relax."

Samantha eased back down in her seat as Twila, Kim, and I

went to the back of the store. We showed Kim to the full dressing room that was set up for her. We had her undergarments selected too, so that she would look her best in every one of the dresses.

Kimberly looked at two of the dresses. "These are size twenty-two. I wear a twenty. I might even be an eighteen by the time of the wedding."

"Don't even look at the size number," Twila said. "Wedding dresses run differently. It's based on how the dress is cut and your measurements. Some of these dresses have tighter bodices, so you'll need a bigger size in those. But then some are bigger in the hip area than you need. Trust me on this."

I listened to Twila explain and cajole Kimberly into putting on the first dress. I was still stuck on Kimberly trying to get down to size eighteen for her wedding. Did she want help on that journey? She hadn't mentioned it.

"Kim, you're trying to lose weight for the wedding?" I asked.

"Um . . . yes . . . not that you two care about it," Kim said.

Twila's eyes widened and her jaw went slack. She couldn't have been more surprised than I was.

"You always act weird when we talk to you about losing weight," Twila said. "You know I can put together a workout plan for you."

"I don't know about that," Kim said. "Your workout plans are killer."

"They kill fat."

"I don't act weird when you all talk to me about weight loss. You're the ones who get uncomfortable. You get all body positive and stuff."

I was confused. "So, we're not supposed to be positive?" I asked.

"It just doesn't hit right when girls with perfect bodies are telling the fat girl to love her rolls."

"You don't like us saying anything about weight?" Twila asked. "At all?"

"I haven't had one conversation with either one of you about it that wasn't awkward," Kimberly said. "Sorry. I'm just being honest."

"Okay, so we won't talk about it," I said. "But let's get into the first one of these dresses."

I wondered how long she'd been holding that in. How long had she been meaning to tell us that our constant refrains of *You go with your curvy self* or *Real women have curves* didn't come across how we wanted them to. I only wanted her to feel good about herself. I never meant to draw attention to the thing she didn't want to talk about.

I watched Twila fasten the back of the first dress. A strapless number with a corset and ribbon ties in the back. It was white silk with silver embroidery. I loved this one. It was my favorite of all the dresses we'd set aside for Kimberly.

"This is a twenty-two?" Kimberly asked. "It fits perfectly."

"I told you to trust me," Twila said. "I used your accurate measurements. I want you to pick a dress that needs the fewest alterations."

"Yeah, because if they have to reconstruct the whole dress it won't look the same," I added. "I love this dress on you, Kim. You look like a Disney queen."

"I love it too. I can't stop looking at myself in the mirror."

Twila smiled. "Good. Let's show the other bridesmaids."

I rushed out of the dressing room ahead of them to see who else had arrived. Luckily all the other bridesmaids were there, although they were all congregated on one side of the room, and Samantha was on the other.

"Hello, ladies. Glad everyone is here. Kimberly is coming out with the first dress. I like to call this one, Fairy Snow Queen," I said.

I caught Samantha's eye roll, and wanted to cuss her out. I was sick of her raining gloom and doom on everyone's good time. She could take that cloud she carried over her head out of the bridal shop. We didn't need her negativity.

"Did you give all the dresses nick names?" Abena said.

"No. Just the ones I really liked."

Traci, Abena, and Debbie laughed. Sour puss sipped spark-ling cider. But laughter and sipping both ceased when Kim-berly walked out of the dressing room and into the main area of the store. Those other sounds were replaced with squeals of delight. Even scowling Samantha broke a smile.

"That dress is stunning," Traci said. "I love the silver threads."

"Yeah, they make it look blingy," Debbie said. "This one is a winner."

"I really do love it," Kimberly said. "Thank you Hahna and Twila for setting this all up. I wouldn't have known where to begin."

"I have to apologize to Hahna," Samantha said. "I didn't think they'd be able to find anything for girls of our size in this store."

I acknowledged the apology with a tight head nod. I wasn't letting her off the hook that easily. She was going to have to suf-fer a little bit more.

"And there are plenty more. This was just the first dress," Twila said.

"We don't even need to keep looking, though," Traci said. "I can't imagine another dress looking more perfect."

Twila grinned. "You might be right, but we're going to look at them all. Settle in and have some more champagne and snacks."

I let Twila lead Kimberly back to the dressing room to try on the next gown. I sat down next to Debbie, because I had some other Maid of Honor duties I needed to accomplish before I left for my uncle's funeral.

"After we leave here, do you all mind coming back to my house for a meeting? I have to leave for my uncle's funeral in North Carolina, but we have some stuff we need to iron out as bridesmaids."

"What kind of stuff?" Samantha said. "I've already had a long day. I was hoping this was the end of it."

"You don't have to come if you can't make it. I'll email you what we discussed. In fact, I'll email everyone on the decisions made."

"What decisions?" Samantha asked.

"First we need to decide where we're purchasing our dresses."

"Oh, Donny's Bridal is having a ninety-nine-dollar sale," Samantha said. "I think we should just go with those."

Abena laughed out loud. "No ma'am. Not wearing one of those cheesy dresses. They don't fit well, and the fabric is just . . . no. Not doing it."

"Well, I hope y'all don't plan on spending thousands of dollars on a dress," Debbie said, with real concern in her voice. "I ain't got it like y'all."

"Thousands?" Samantha said. "This isn't our wedding, it's Kimberly's. The only one who needs to go all out is Kim."

I ignored this. We were absolutely going to go all out for our line sister's wedding. I already knew Debbie's situation and was planning to pick up the tab for her dress, because it was going to be a sight more than a hundred bucks.

"Well, it's not just the dress," Abena said. "We'll need to pay for a lot of other things. Makeup, hair, shoes, undergarments, and our plane tickets to Jamaica. So, if you need to budget, budget accordingly."

"Shit, I need a sponsor," Debbie said. "And I wish I was joking about that."

I tried making eye contact with Debbie to let her know I had her, but I couldn't get her to look at me.

"I don't care about makeup or hair," Samantha said. "I'm perfectly fine with how I look every day. Why do I need glamour? I'm not the one getting married."

"So, you're just going to be difficult the entire time, huh?" Traci asked. "It's our sister's wedding. We all need glamour. Some of us more than others."

"I'm not being difficult," Samantha said, "but we're not all wealthy. I'm not going broke for this wedding because y'all spend money like drug dealers."

I was about to respond when Kimberly and Twila walked out of the dressing room. This dress was a halter style with a big circle skirt. It was beautiful, but nowhere near as perfect as the first.

"What do you guys think?" Kimberly asked.

"I like the other one better," Debbie said. "Go with the bling."

"What do you think?" Samantha asked. "It doesn't matter how we feel. It's your wedding."

Oh my God! I wanted to scream at the top of my lungs, but I knew that wouldn't be appropriate behavior in the high-end boutique. Neither would pulling that fake bun off the nape of Samantha's neck.

"I value your opinions," Kimberly said. "Or I wouldn't have invited you here. Fashion isn't necessarily my forte."

"Well, I agree with Debbie," I said. "This is a gorgeous gown, but the first is still tops, in my opinion."

Everyone else agreed with chatters and head nods. Kimberly smiled and nodded.

"I need some of that champagne," Kimberly said. "I have a headache. Talked to Ron's ex-wife right before I came over here."

"Yes, you told me she was coming to your office," Samantha said. "Did you get her together like we discussed?"

Ooh. She just had to let us know that she'd been privy to information the rest of us didn't have. I think Samantha had worn out the grace I gave her for writing that article about my business.

"To be honest, I'm not quite sure how it went. She promised not to make a scene at the wedding, 'cause I told her I'd have her removed by security."

"She agreed?" I asked.

"She did, but I have a feeling problems with her will continue," Kimberly said. "Not just at the wedding but afterwards."

"You have us," Twila said. "We're your tribe. Don't worry about her."

"More importantly, she'll have her *husband*," Samantha said. "When she marries, she will cleave to her husband and not her tribe of single friends."

"Some of us are married too," Abena said. "And why do you think she wouldn't need her friends after she says I do?"

"I'm just resting on what the Word of God says," Samantha

said. "A marriage with Christ at the center just needs three cords. Husband, wife, and Jesus."

"Come on, let's go try on the next dress," I said.

I couldn't take a word, not a syllable, more of Samantha's self-righteousness.

Back in the dressing room, Kimberly said, "What is Samantha on this evening?"

"This evening?" I asked. "This has been every interaction. She was just arguing with everyone about everything. Bridesmaid's dresses, makeup, hair. Everything. It's almost like she's determined to make everyone miserable."

"All because I didn't ask her to be Maid of Honor," Kimberly said.

"Well, hurt or not, it's really shitty for her to act like this," Twila said. "I know we said the line sisters would always be our bridesmaids, but damn."

"This isn't just about Gamma Phi Gamma, though. She's one of my best friends," Kimberly said.

"Well, she's toxic as hell," Twila said. "Ain't nobody got time for that."

Kimberly shimmied out of the dress with our help. "Maybe you guys could help her feel a part of things. Could she have a job that's all her own?" Kimberly asked.

"It's up to you," I said. "It's your wedding."

"Okay. I'm going to ask her to plan the bridal shower. And we're going to show up for it and support it," Kimberly said.

"I guess," Twila said.

Kimberly sighed and pointed to the next dress.

"Listen, y'all know she and I are close. We've always been. The two big girls in the group of Gamma Phi Gamma cuties," Kimberly explained. "Out of all of us, this was probably her only chance to be a Maid of Honor. None of you would pick her."

"Well, you've made it easy for me when I get married," Hahna said. "Twila is the Maid and you will be the Matron of Honor."

"What makes you think you're getting married before me?" Twila said.

I cut my eyes at Twila and almost laughed. I would be surprised if Twila made it to the altar.

"A few things, but mostly the fact that I have a man who is completely in love with me," I said.

"Until he meets your country ratchet family," Twila said.

"Ugh, don't remind me," I said. "The champagne had helped me put that at the back of my mind."

Twila buttoned about ten small buttons on the back of the dress. Another beauty. It had a bit of bling in the way of glitter on the lace and tulle bottom.

Kimberly scrunched her nose together. "I don't like this one at all. I look like Glinda the good witch."

"Pretty appropriate, don't you think?" Twila asked. "You're out here granting Samantha's wishes and it sounds like you granted Sabrina some too."

"Don't get me started on that. She tried to make it seem like she was afraid of Ron during their divorce. Like he was going to beat her or something."

"Whatever," I said. "I don't believe that."

"Me either. But why would she try to sow discord between us?" Kimberly asked. "Because, of course, I'm going to have to say something to Ron about it. But what?"

"I wouldn't say shit about it," Twila said. "Ron is not a woman beater. That ho just doesn't want him to be happy."

"Agree," I said. "She can kick rocks."

"Y'all think so? I mean, we only knew Ron in college. Maybe things happened later that we didn't know about."

"This is exactly what that ho wanted you to think," Twila said.

"She wants to get rid of you, so that Ron will be there, available whenever she wants him back."

"Y'all are right. Help me out of this dress. I want to put the first one back on. That's the one I want to buy."

"My favorite one," I said.

"Are they gonna ring a bell or something? Take a picture?" Kimberly asked.

"Um no. It's not that kind of boutique. We can take a photo if you want," Twila said. "But I don't think we have a bell."

Kimberly burst into laughter. "Y'all are funny without even trying to be. This is why I trusted y'all to handle all this. Thank you."

We helped Kimberly back into the first dress and twisted her hair up in the back, giving her a wedding-like updo. She smiled at her reflection in the mirror.

"I love this dress so much," Kimberly said.

"Let's go announce to everyone that you've made a decision," I said, ready for the evening and Samantha's sour attitude to come to an end.

Kimberly touched the doorknob but stopped before turning it. "Can you guys not mention to anyone else what Sabrina said about Ron?" she asked. "I don't want anyone thinking poorly of him based on that."

"We've got your back," Twila said. "I'm the best at keeping secrets."

"We know," Kimberly said.

"I feel attacked," Twila said.

"I do as well, but just because I'm not the best at keeping secrets doesn't mean I won't keep this one," I said.

"I love y'all," Kimberly said. "And I don't care what Samantha says. I need y'all even after I get married."

She held her arms out for a group hug and both Twila and I obliged. I believed what Samantha said about a husband, wife, and Jesus. But sisters would always be waiting in the wings with a prayer, a word of advice, or maybe the ability to take the ex-wife to task when the current wife could not.

We were her tribe, and we'd be there for her. Just like we were going to be there for Twila through this sexual assault situation. I just had to figure out how to break it to Kimberly in the middle of planning for her wedding.

Chapter 19

TWILA

I had to pull Traci away from the rest of the bridesmaid crew who'd taken up Hahna on her offer for a post dress shopping meeting. I'm glad we'd convinced Kimberly that she didn't need to be there, because she would've noticed Traci and I stepping away.

In Hahna's guest bedroom, Traci pulled a folder out of her Birken bag. She handed it to me. I held it gingerly like it was a live bomb. I sat before I opened it.

"There are a couple of profiles in that folder. I was able to narrow it way down because we only have about two dozen white men in the approval files for the Lifestyle room. Only three that matched your description. If it's not one of them we're back to square one."

I lifted the corner of the folder and took a deep breath. I wouldn't leave this conversation the same. The power of knowledge was synonymous with the burden of knowledge. Even if I didn't take any actions, knowing would change my life.

"Do you want the information or not? I understand if you don't," Traci said. "I could take the contents of this folder and shred them."

"No. To hell with that. I need to move back to my damn

house. Do you know how maddening it is to have to hear Hahna and her man humping and bumping all night long?"

"They never go to his place?"

"Yeah, but I think it's like the size of a closet or something. I think Hahna said it was a tiny house."

"What the hell kinda pact did y'all make in St. Lucia? Kimberly found Ron, Hahna is with a struggling artist, and you got yourself a trap ho."

"We just wanted to throw away our dating rules. Or they did. I don't even know what I wanted out of it. Maybe, that's why I didn't find a man. Wait, I know what I wanted. To not have to get off with a dildo."

"That is a good reason to make a dating pact my sister."

I was glad Traci distracted me from the folder for a minute. But the weight of it in my hands reminded me. I thought about the handsome lawyer who was interested in me, and how I couldn't even think about pursuing anything other than social media interaction. I needed to do this. Had to get this whole thing behind me.

Before I lost the nerve, I opened the folder. The top photograph was absolutely not the guy. Face too long, and beard too sparse. I took that sheet out of the folder and set it on the bed. The next one was him.

"This is the mother fucker," I said. "Alexander fucking Adams." I read the name on the sheet over and over again. Alexander Adams. This was the name of the man who'd ruined my peace.

Traci sucked her teeth. "I thought it was him. I didn't have a good vibe about him, so we actually did an extended background investigation on him. Had him followed for about a week, but we weren't able to turn up anything."

"I bet I wasn't the first woman he raped."

"And won't be the last."

"I'm gonna make him regret the day he touched me," I said. "He'll think long and hard about messing with another woman."

"I stand at the ready to support you with whatever plan unfolds," Traci said.

"Thank you."

Trouble was, I hadn't given any thought to what that plan might be. I liked to think I was capable of violence, but I didn't know if I could be sure without facing the situation. What if I wasn't capable and ended up getting hurt again, or worse, what if I was over capable and went too far?

But the plan could come later. First was the knowing, and I had gotten that out of the way. I was lucky I had a session with Dr. Mays this week. Or, maybe Alexander Adams was lucky. But I had to talk to her about this, even though I'd decided against it at first.

Perhaps there was as much trauma in knowing my attacker's identity as there was in the actual attack. Maybe I'd have to relive this moment over and over again before the information was benign.

'Cause right now it was pretty malignant, like a cancer set to metastasize and ravage my entire world as I and everyone else knew it.

There was a light knock on the door and then it was opening. Hahna, of course. She looked at me and Traci with curiosity in her eyes. Then she looked at the folder in my hands and I could see even more questions forming.

"Are y'all coming back out here? We're just starting the conversation about dresses, and I could really use your support."

Traci stood first. "Yes, girl. Here we come."

I packed the folder away in my belongings all while Hahna watched. She wouldn't ask, but she wanted me to tell her what it was. It wasn't happening.

I linked arms with Hahna and pulled her out of the room. I closed the door behind us.

"Twila . . ."

I shook my head at Hahna, putting a period on the sentence she'd started. "No ma'am. Don't even ask."

"Why not? I won't say anything. Is it a surprise for the wedding? I want to know."

That was good. I'd let her think that, because it was a much

better narrative for positive Hahna than *I know who my attacker is
and I'm thinking of revenge.*

"It is a surprise, and since you can't hold water, I'm not
telling you."

"I promise I won't say anything."

"Nope. Last time I asked you to keep a secret, I heard my
business in the sorority group chat."

"That happened like one time."

I laughed. In college, she wasn't just leaky, Hahna was the
town crier. She might as well have entered the room yelling
Hear ye, hear ye.

"Okay, a few times, but I'm older now. Wiser."

"Girl, I am not telling you," I said. "Now who is giving you
problems about the dress?"

She sighed. "The broke people's party."

"Ooh. That particular constituency is pretty dogmatic with
their views."

"You ain't lying. Come on. I need the bougie constituency
to win."

We walked back into Hahna's family room and we sat on the
couch while Samantha was in the middle of a full-blown solilo-
quy. She stood in the center of the room, pointing and growl-
ing as she talked, like she was a pastor preaching to his board
members who hadn't paid tithes in a year.

"If I'm being honest, I can't afford a five-hundred-dollar
dress. Not and attend this wedding. This is too much. And now
y'all talking about spa treatments and onsite makeup artists
and hair stylists."

"I mean, I want all that stuff," Debbie said, "but I can't afford
it either. Maybe some of my rich sorors can sponsor me."

"Why don't we just pick a fabric and designer for the dresses,"
I said. "Then we can have a range of prices for the dresses. There's
a couple of websites that can help us with that."

Samantha, still standing in the middle of the room, dropped
the hand she was using to point. She tilted her head to one side
like she was sizing me up. I was ready for whatever she wanted
to throw my way.

"Whatever fabric you pick better have some stretch in it," Samantha said.

"I think you can trust that we know what to do for our plus-sized sisters too. We got Kim together for her bridal gown," I said.

"Exactly," Hahna said. "You're worrying about the wrong thing. We want everyone to look their best at Kim's wedding."

"But I see no one is saying anything about sponsoring me," Debbie said. "I wasn't joking."

And I wasn't responding to that bullshit. I was going to let Hahna deal with Debbie on that front. Debbie was always trying to make everyone feel bad about the fact that she dropped out of college and had a baby. That was not our fault she didn't recover and make better career choices, and I damn sure wasn't going to feel guilty about having shit just because she did not.

"Let's talk about that offline," Hahna said. "We'll figure something out."

I knew Hahna would fall for it, but despite her situation with her kids, Debbie did exactly what she wanted to do. She found men to sponsor trips and everything else. If none of us helped her pay for the wedding stuff, she would find a way, because there was no way she'd miss being a bridesmaid.

I guessed Samantha was either out of steam or felt double-teamed, so she had a seat on the couch across from us. She still didn't look happy.

"Okay y'all, I hate to bring this evening to a close, but I have to travel to my family in North Carolina tomorrow."

"Ooh, your country family?" Debbie asked. "Is your cousin Tennessee gonna be there?"

"Yes, but ugh. He's way too young for you," Hahna said with disgust in her tone.

Her cousin was too young for Debbie. He was only about twenty-five.

"He might be too young to be my man, but he ain't too old to break me off, 'cause he's fine. I just want to comfort the family," Debbie said.

Hahna rolled her eyes. "Anyway. I'm traveling tomorrow so I need to finish packing, rest, and get my mind right to deal with them. So, I will be sending out an email with a few website links for dresses for us to choose from. We'll need to make a decision over the next couple of weeks. Also, I will be providing a travel agent's phone number and website for us to start booking travel. I know the wedding isn't until the end of March, but it's already October."

I wanted to laugh at the facial expressions that Hahna got from Debbie and Samantha. Samantha wasn't going to accept our word for anything. I knew she was going back to Kimberly. So that was why she was giving Hahna a blank, straight-faced stare. Debbie smiled, damn near cheesing, because she knew Hahna was going to pick up the tab for everything.

I didn't laugh though, because Hahna was trying her best, and I was supposed to be helping. I was the co-MOH.

I hoped that Hahna wasn't going to get too tired about doing the heavy lifting on the wedding, because I needed my energy. I couldn't focus on dress fabrics when I needed to focus on punishing Alexander Adams for his crimes.

I couldn't walk down the aisle and chew Big Red at the same time. But Hahna would have my full attention once I'd finished my unfinished business.

Chapter 20

KIMBERLY

Kimberly sat at the edge of Ron's bed fully dressed. She was too nervous to go get in the shower and put on her nightgown until she'd talked to Ron about her meeting with Sabrina. Kimberly was wrong to meet with Ron's ex-wife without him. She should've known better, but she just had to put her foot down and get the woman together. She'd done no such thing. Whether she'd known it or not, Sabrina had left that conversation with the upper hand. She'd managed to sow seeds of doubt in Kimberly's very fertile mind.

"Kimmie Kim, you want the shower first?" Ron asked from the bathroom.

"Um . . . if you want to go first, I can wait."

Ron walked out of the bathroom shirtless, showing his still-fit frame. Kimberly's first thought was to reach out and touch him. Anytime she saw his bare, chocolate skin, she wanted to feel him beneath her fingers.

"Is there something wrong?" Ron asked, probably wondering why Kimberly's hands weren't already touching him.

"I don't know."

"You don't know? Did something happen? Did you not find your dress?"

"It's not that," Kimberly said. "I found the perfect dress. Or I should say Twila and Hahna found the perfect dress. They are the real MVPs on that front. I would've never known where to look if not for them."

"So, what's bothering you then?" Ron asked.

Kimberly sighed, and Ron got a look of recognition on his face.

"Oh, I forgot," Ron said. "You were talking to Sabrina today. How did that go?"

"It went horribly," Kimberly said. She surprised herself when the tears fell from her eyes. She didn't think she was that broken up about it, but maybe she was.

"Why? Did she say she wanted to give a toast at the wedding?"

"No. She promised she wouldn't do that, and she apologized for being weird at the engagement party," Kimberly pulled herself together and stopped the tears. "The apology was crazy though, because she felt some kind of way that a lot of the people at our engagement party were at your wedding."

"I have the same friends as I did back then. I don't know what she wants me to do about that."

"She said she was overwhelmed by that. Do you think she feels judged by your friends because she cheated?"

"My friends didn't know about that."

"She was exaggerating then. No one cared about her at the party."

"And that might have been the issue," Ron said. "She was used to being the center of attention. She played second fiddle to you at our party."

"If she was going to feel that way she shouldn't have come."

"Agreed," Ron said. "But that doesn't sound too awful, Kimmie Kim. What made you cry?"

Kimberly closed her eyes and inhaled deeply. She held the breath for a moment, and exhaled slowly, trying to center herself. Was asking Ron about Sabrina's wild and outlandish claims a way of somehow taking Sabrina's side?

"She said that the two of you had an argument that scared her. She thought you were going to put your hands on her, and she was frightened of you forever after that."

"I know exactly the argument she's referring to," Ron said, "but she is completely exaggerating. I never threatened to hit her."

"You put holes in the wall?"

"Yeah, but I never would've hit her," Ron said. "You know I don't do that."

Kimberly nodded and tried to imagine Ron punching a hole in the wall. She'd never seen him *that* angry. Should they be getting married if she hadn't seen his full range of emotions?

"Kimmie. She hurt me badly. She cheated on me and then said she wasn't sure if she ever loved me in the first place. But still I never and would never hurt a woman or children. I can't believe she told you that."

"She said she was warning me."

"You're not Sabrina. And our love is different."

"How is it different? How do I know I won't do something to hurt you?"

"One way it's different is because there is reciprocity. I always felt like I was giving too much away when I was with Sabrina. Things were never quite the way I wanted."

"We're more of a team?"

"We are. Nothing about us is hard."

But what if things became hard? Kimberly bet Sabrina never thought things would deteriorate the way they did.

"Don't let her get in your head," Ron said. "For some reason she doesn't want to see me happy."

"Maybe she isn't happy herself," Kimberly said. "If that's the case she's more dangerous."

"If she ever does anything to try and keep me from my children, I swear, she's going to regret it."

"And by regret it, you mean we will go through the legal system and fight for joint custody?"

Ron stared at Kimberly. His breathing was even and measured, as if he was trying to calm himself. Had she angered him? Was this the beginning of what Sabrina had experienced?

"Kimberly. Don't let her get in your head. I'm not a violent man."

"I know."

Kimberly thought this wasn't the best time to tell Ron she'd kinda threatened Sabrina with legal action. She'd tell him that later when he seemed calmer, or at least not on the verge of anger.

"She's not in my head, baby," Kimberly said. "I just wanted you to know what we talked about."

"Well, I do believe that some people are just with the wrong person. That's what happened with me and Sabrina. Being with the wrong person can bring out the worst side of you," Ron said.

"That's true."

"Kimmie Kim, you bring out the best in me. I am the absolute best version of myself when I'm with you."

Ron took Kimberly in his arms and covered her face and neck with kisses. He was so gentle and kind. Ron made her feel nothing but loved.

"You don't just make me the best version of myself," Kimberly said. "This is a self I didn't know I had."

"What do you mean?"

"I didn't believe that anyone would ever sweep me off my feet, like in the romance novels. I didn't think that was for me."

"If not for you, then who?"

Kimberly looked up at Ron and basked in his love for a moment. Maybe she shouldn't tell him who she meant. It could remind him that if he wanted, he could have one of those vixen-bodied women who always seemed to win.

"I don't know. Women who look like Twila and Hahna, I guess."

"And look who's getting married first."

Kimberly laughed and Ron joined her. "I want my girls happy too."

"I know you do. I'm just saying, love doesn't have a shape. It's about two souls connecting. With you my soul is fed."

Kimberly snuggled into Ron's arms and allowed her body to melt into his. His words of affirmation had uprooted the seeds that Sabrina had planted. Kimberly chose to trust her instincts, and they told her that she'd never felt safer with a man than she did with Ron. Her heart, body, and mind felt safe. And like Ron, she believed that they connected at the soul level.

Kimberly would be crazy to let Sabrina steal her joy about the best and only real love she'd ever had. And nobody had ever called Kimberly crazy. She was the grounded friend. The crazy title, unfortunately, belonged to Twila. Kimberly sent up a quick prayer that Dr. Mays was doing everything possible to fix their friend.

Chapter 21

TWILA

I didn't like morning appointments with Dr. Mays because I was not a morning person. After my workout, I tried not to have a conversation until I'd consumed a copious amount of coffee. Early appointments for my patients meant that they had a dental emergency. I didn't do morning thought well. I had brain fog like a mug. That was probably why DeAndre kept tricking me into conversations at the gym.

He was on my mind as I sat across from Dr. Mays. We'd shared breakfast again, and I really enjoyed his company. I must've been hormonal because I didn't just want to take him up on his offer of a date. I wanted to take him to bed. I didn't feel whorish or apologetic about it either. I resisted the urge though—on the date and the bedroom activity.

"Are you ready to do your work today?" Dr. Mays asked, breaking through my thoughts about DeAndre.

"I am."

I recounted the rape again for Dr. Mays. This time powering through without displaying any emotions. I felt emotions, mostly rage, and a little shame, but I didn't feel like crying or hyperventilating. It felt like progress.

"Very good," Dr. Mays said. "Is there any reason why you rushed through it?"

I shrugged. "I didn't want to spend my whole hour on that. I have other things to talk about."

"I understand that," Dr. Mays said with a smile, "but I want you to experience the trauma until it cannot paralyze you anymore. If you are rushing through, you are not experiencing it here with me."

Dr. Mays might have been right within the rules of this particular therapy, but for real, I experienced that shit every day. Every time I woke up in Hahna's house, I remembered the reason why I wasn't in my own house.

"I hear you. Next time I'll take my time recounting the worst thing that ever happened to me."

"It is not about being masochistic and enjoying the pain. It is about becoming numb to it, Twila. It is about not letting it affect your life."

"Understood."

"So, what else did you want to talk to me about?"

"Good news or not so good news first?" I asked.

"Hmmmm . . . I never know how to answer that," Dr. Mays said. "Sometimes I think hearing the bad news first is best, because the good news will take the bad taste out of my mouth. But sometimes, if I think the news is bad enough, I do not want to hear it at all, and especially not first."

"So, what do you choose?"

"You choose for me," Dr. Mays said. "It is your news."

"I'll choose the good news first, then. I met a guy."

"Have you had problems meeting guys?"

I sighed. "No, not really. But, I met a decent guy and that's something different. He's a lawyer, he's fine as hell, he works out, and he's not intimidated by me."

"That is good news, then."

"The only downside is that I can't get into a relationship while I'm doing this work, right? It isn't smart."

"I would not say you cannot get into a relationship, but you need to be transparent if you choose to do that."

"Don't you think a man would be scared off by hearing a woman is in therapy?" I asked.

"Would you be scared off by a man seeing a therapist?"

"No, I don't think so. I mean, I'd want to know what he was working on, I guess. I'd probably applaud him for taking care of his mental health, to be honest."

"If this man you have met is a good prospect then he will feel the same way."

"So, you're saying I should go for it?"

"That choice would be yours. Just do not let therapy hinder you from that choice. Mental health care is an ongoing pursuit. If therapy works for you, then you will probably find times later in your life where you will seek a therapist. A partner should know that about you."

"Interesting. I may tell him. Or at least see what he thinks about therapy."

"Very good. Let me know how that goes."

"I will. Do you want the not-so-good news now?"

Dr. Mays sighed, but nodded. "Go ahead."

"I found out the identity of my attacker."

Dr. Mays gasped. "I am sorry. I was not expecting that."

"My sorority sister owns the nightclub where it happened. It's an elite club that you have to apply to be a member."

"And you told her about the rape?"

"Yes."

"What will you do now? What are your next steps?" Dr. Mays asked.

"I don't know. I think that's why I'm telling you now. Maybe I want you to talk me out of my next steps."

"Well, you decided to go down the path of knowing who your attacker is. I thought I had advised against that, or at least strongly cautioned against it."

"You did, but I don't think you understood how much not knowing tormented me. I felt powerless not knowing. That is the opposite of where I'm trying to be."

"Is knowing enough, though?"

"That's the part I need help with. I want to confront him. Tell him that I know who he is, and make him feel the same discomfort I've felt with him being in my space."

"Mental and emotional discomfort, but not physical discomfort?"

I knew Dr. Mays was asking me if I planned to hurt the man. I also knew that whatever I told my psychiatrist would be confidential, and that even if I committed a crime, she could never be compelled to testify against me.

"I honestly don't know. I'd like to think I could hurt him—even physically. I have all of these weapons in my house, and I tell myself that I would use them if necessary, but I've never had to use them."

"It is quite all right that you may not be able to cause another human pain. There is nothing wrong with not being wired to hurt people."

"But the next steps I've imagined are me hurting him. I couldn't hurt him the way he hurt me, though."

"Are you saying you could not rape him?"

"Yes. That's what I mean. It's sick."

"Any kind of physical torture of a helpless human being requires some level of depravity."

She just spat that last sentence into the atmosphere and the words hung there. I wasn't ready to face what she said, but her meaning was clear. If I hurt my attacker, I was as depraved as he was.

"It sounds like you don't think I should do this."

"I do not believe you will get the peace and empowerment you seek this way."

"You're telling me not to do it, then?"

"I do not make choices for you, Twila. This is your work."

It was my work, and it was my revenge. And Dr. Mays was right. It was one hundred percent my choice on what to do with the information.

I just wished I knew what that choice was going to be.

Chapter 22

HAHNA

On the entire drive to North Carolina, I wondered if I should warn Sam about my family. Several times, I almost started the conversation to let him know they were nothing like me. I could tell he was nervous about meeting them, but he need not be.

"So, this is your uncle on your mother's side or your father's side?" Sam asked as we passed the WELCOME TO NORTH CAROLINA sign.

"Uncle Joe was Aunt Sherrie's husband, and Aunt Sherrie is my mother's sister."

"I see. Do they have any children?"

"No. I spent enough time over their house that they treated me like a daughter."

"Who else am I going to meet? Your father? Siblings? Cousins?"

I felt a headache starting right behind my left eye. I hated talking about my complicated family tree. But, I guess if I'm going to be with Sam for the foreseeable future that I should probably tell him the basics at least.

"I haven't seen my father in twenty years," I said. "So, if he comes to this funeral I would be surprised."

"Why haven't you seen him? Or is that too personal?"

"No, not too personal. He got remarried, moved to Alabama and acted like we never existed. I don't even know if he told his new wife he even has a daughter."

"He and your mother must've had a strained relationship," Sam said.

This made me laugh. Strained was the mildest word that could be used to describe the relationship between my two parents. But even though my father was the one who'd disappeared, I didn't blame him for that. Rochelle wasn't someone a man, or anyone for that matter, could stay around. She didn't allow people to show her love without somehow throwing it back in their faces.

"But your mother should be here, right?"

"We'll see. She and Aunt Sherrie are close-ish. I don't have siblings. My mother's first cousin Yolanda and her kids may be there too. They live in Shady Falls and all work at the pickle plant."

"Everybody works at the pickle plant?"

"Pretty much. I think one of my younger cousins is a letter carrier, but the pickle plant employs that entire town. You've seen Shady Falls pickles in the grocery store."

Sam nodded. "Those are some good pickles. The relish too."

"Mmm-hmm. My mama called herself getting away from the pickles and Shady Falls when she was sixteen. She ran off with some man to Goldsboro."

"She ran off to the next town?"

I laughed. "Exactly. She ain't even run far enough away."

"It was a start, I guess. New scenery."

"Except the new scenery looked exactly like the old scenery. She ended up working at the grocery store instead of the pickle plant and she met my father at a pinochle game at someone's after-hours spot."

Sam chuckled. "It sounds like your family will give me good material for my next book."

"You will have material enough for ten books."

I pulled off at the exit for Shady Falls, and felt my anxiety heighten. Dealing with my mother was never fun, and Aunt

Sherrie was sure to be a mess. At least we were staying at a hotel instead of at Aunt Sherrie's five room house.

After driving a few miles, I turned onto an unmarked dirt road. Sam's eyebrows shot up.

"Are you sure this is the road? There's no sign," Sam said.

I laughed. "This town has a total of two stop lights. The main roads have street signs, but this isn't a main road."

It was an ongoing joke of Shady Falls residents that they were one step above a one stoplight town. But the joke was on them, because there wasn't much more than that extra traffic light. There was a library, a movie theater, a diner, five churches, and a couple of hardware stores. And of course, the dreaded pickle plant.

"I swear I couldn't wait to leave here," I said. "I was so happy to go to Spelman. The entire community helped me go, too."

"I bet your mother was proud."

I nodded. "She was. She bragged to everybody here and in Goldsboro."

"She ever think about moving to Atlanta to be closer to you?"

"I don't know if I've ever asked her that. I send her money every month, but I was much closer to my grandmother than I am to her."

"I'm looking forward to meeting her."

I laughed. Rochelle was definitely going to like Sam. He was tall, dark, and fine. She was probably going to flirt with him and embarrass the hell out of me.

At Aunt Sherrie's house, there were about six cars, meaning we'd gotten there with the rest of the family and well-wishers. This was a good thing, because all the focus wouldn't be on us.

My cousin Tennessee was on the front porch smoking a joint. Someone must've stressed him out inside, because he wouldn't be smoking at Aunt Sherrie's house otherwise. Aunt Sherrie was a church mother, head usher, and on the nurse's guild at the Apostolic Holiness Church.

"Uh-oh," I said as I parked behind three cars at the edge of the front yard.

"What's wrong?"

"My cousin is smoking weed. Must be drama happening inside."

"Maybe he just wanted some weed."

"Nah. Aunt Sherrie calls weed the devil's cigarette."

Sam burst into laughter. "Well, what are regular cigarettes?"

"She didn't like those either, but she used to be Baptist before she got saved for real, and Uncle Joe wouldn't give them up. He said if Jesus liked him at the Baptist church when he was smoking then he ought to still like him at the Apostolic church."

Sam had disintegrated into full-blown laughter with tears, snorts and knee-slapping.

"Pull yourself together," I said trying to contain my own laughter. "My uncle died. We can't go in there giggling."

"Okay. Okay. Tell me how your uncle died. That will help me get the laughs out of my system."

"No, it won't."

"What? Why?"

"'Cause he had a heart attack while he was screwing his mistress, the pickle ho."

Sam's whole body shook with laughter, and I just sat there biting my bottom lip. I knew we both had to stop, and I also knew the pickle ho story would make Sam laugh harder. Maybe, I just wanted to take away some of the anxiety I felt coming here. Laughter helped with that.

Tennessee walked up to the car, with the still-lit joint hanging from his lips. I lowered the tinted window so he could see inside. He smiled when he saw it was me.

"Big cuz!" Tennessee said. "Get on out the car so I can hug you. Let me not drop no ashes on this whip."

Tennessee put his joint out as I opened the door. He hugged me tightly and swung me in a circle. It's funny how much he and his sisters loved me since I was gone off to school before they were even born. They knew me as their rich cousin in Atlanta. The one who came down on holidays with expensive presents, and who paid college tuitions, and who kept family members from being evicted. Oh, and the one who paid for funerals.

I loved them too, though. Especially the youngest of those three, Dakota. She was a lot like I was, except she didn't make it to college.

"Are Dakota and Indiana here?" I asked.

"Dakota is. Indiana off chasing behind one of those baby daddies. You know how it go."

"Yeah."

"This yo dude?"

Sam had gotten out on his side of the car and held up one hand to wave at Tennessee.

"I'm Sam. Yeah, I'm her dude."

Tennessee laughed and walked around the car to hug Sam too. Tennessee had put on weight since the last time I saw him, but he was still tall and still handsome. Cousin Yolanda was always hailed as the pretty one of the family and both Dakota and Tennessee had her looks.

"Ooh, he that shiny dark," Tennessee said after hugging Sam. "You African or something? Big cuz done found an African prince."

Sam cracked up. "I'm Haitian, but I was born in Florida. Also, not a prince."

"Well, my cousin is a queen, so she need more than a prince anyway, ya dig?"

"I dig."

Tennessee patted Sam on the back. I guess that showed his approval. Sam seemed to be enjoying himself already, so maybe this wasn't such a bad idea.

"Y'all got here just in time for dinner. My mama cooked, so you know we bout to grub."

My stomach growled in anticipation of Cousin Yolanda's food. She was the designated holiday meal preparation person. No one ever thought about trying to make cornbread dressing, macaroni and cheese, candied yams, potato salad, or greens if Yolanda was cooking. If they did, their little contribution would sit on the table untouched, or worse, consumed by the folks who showed up late after all the good food was already gone.

"Come on," I said. "My cousin Yolanda could give your Papa Michel a run for his money."

Sam grinned. "She must put both her feet in the greens."

Tennessee stuck his chest out. "My mama cook her ass off."

"I thought the eating happened after the funeral," Sam said. "Or that's how my family does it."

"In our family, we start eating as soon as they get news of the person dying," Tennessee said. "I think 'cause cooking gives everybody something to do, and food makes everyone feel better."

I remembered how much food we had when my grandmother passed. My aunts and cousins cooked for days, and then the church cooked too. We ate until we damn near burst, so much that we weren't paying attention to Rochelle's shenanigans. I didn't know if I could ever forgive her for pawning my grandmother's pearls. I remembered being a little girl and looking up at the shiny beads and touching them in the little special pouch where grandma kept them. Those pearls were her most prized possession. The only real piece of jewelry she owned (only because she wouldn't let me buy her more), and she wore them every Sunday to church. She always said Jesus deserved her very best, and she gave it to Him.

"Is Rochelle here?" I asked.

Tennessee nodded. "Yeah, she here."

I didn't like the way he said that. "She showing her ass?" I asked.

"A little. That's why I'm out here. She was tripping about my girlfriend 'cause she white."

I shook my head. "You left your girl in there with them?"

"Naw, she had a friend come and get her. Jayden a good girl. She not gone act up around the family, so she left."

I felt my nostrils flare a little. I wasn't in the mood for my mama if she was showing her ass. Because that meant she was drinking. And if she'd already started, she wasn't going to stop until she passed out on Aunt Sherrie's couch.

"Rochelle drunk?" I asked to confirm my suspicions.

"On the way. Not there yet," Tennessee said. "She'll be cool though. She trying to keep Sherrie together."

Hearing this took away all the mirth and joy I felt in the car with Sam. This was the family that I expected. This was the Rochelle I expected.

"Come on, then," I said. "Let's do this."

"For Cousin Joe," Tennessee said.

"Yep, for Uncle Joe."

What had started as a cheerful trio walked into Auntie Sherrie's house a bit deflated. I still plastered a smile on my face, because I knew my aunt needed to see that. I could smell the food from the first step, and my stomach growled louder.

"Yolanda made those yeast rolls, didn't she?" I asked.

"Sure did. Six dozen. I had to help her last night," Tennessee said.

"God bless you," Sam said.

My cousin laughed. "When my mama starts in the kitchen, if you're home, you're helping."

I knew that Sam and Tennessee were being polite by letting me walk up the stairs first, but I didn't want everyone to stop and look at me when I walked in the door. With all the worrying about how Sam might react to my family, I forgot to mentally prepare myself.

I pushed open the front door to Aunt Sherrie's house and it was like I'd just stepped through a time machine portal. As the heat from the non-air-conditioned house hit my face, twenty-five years melted away.

The first person I laid eyes on was my mother. Rochelle was sitting on the couch facing the door, drink in hand and legs spread wide open to where I could see her pink underwear. I cringed and sighed. There was a reason why I only showed up for weddings and funerals these days. It used to be the holidays too, but I stopped when everyone started acting like my regular gifts of sweaters and scarves were cheap.

My mother jumped up and cackled when she saw me. "Looka here, everybody. It's Ms. A-T-L," she said.

She wobbled over to hug me with her arms outstretched, spilling what looked like her drink of choice, a vodka cranberry. I let her hug me, but I barely hugged back. The drunken version of my mother was more irritating than the sober version.

I unentangled myself from her when it became too much and went to my Aunt Sherrie. The hug I gave her was real, and so were the kisses I showered onto her face. Next, I hugged Cousin Yolanda, who was as pretty as ever.

"This your gentleman caller?" Auntie Sherrie asked.

I had momentarily forgotten about Sam, still standing at the door with Tennessee. I turned to him and smiled.

"Yes, everyone, this is Sam. Sam this is everyone."

Laughter erupted in the room. Probably because I didn't even know everyone in here. There was a man posted up next to Cousin Yolanda that I'd never seen, and a whole bunch of folks that probably worked at the pickle factory.

"She done brought her man to meet us?" Rochelle asked. "Well, lemme get a look at you. Must be special, 'cause she ain't never brought nobody home."

Rochelle wobbled over to Sam and he gave her a chaste hug. She laughed.

"I ain't gone bite ya," she said.

Sam gave a fake smile. "Pleased to meet you, ma'am."

"Ma'am! Oh, he got good manners," Rochelle said.

"Rochelle, leave that young man alone and sit on down," Yolanda said. "Deacon Jones 'bout to bless the food."

I rushed over to Sam and found a place for us at one of the eight or nine card tables erected in Auntie Sherrie's living room/dining room. It was really one room that was separated only by the back of the sofa. We were packed tightly, and it was stifling hot, but that part I expected.

Deacon Jones waited until we were settled in before he started to pray. He sat his hands right on top of his belly until we stopped moving chairs and stepping over people. That's because his prayers were a big production, and he wanted everyone to hear them. I just wished he'd hurry. I was hungry, and once folks started eating, no one would be worried about me or Sam.

"Dear Lord, our Father God in heaven," Deacon Jones said

in his loud, booming, behind-the-pulpit voice, "we want to thank you for bringing us all here today. Even though, we are here to celebrate the life of our dearly departed friend, husband, and family member, Joe. Lord, please allow us to remember all of the good times we shared with Joe. He wasn't a perfect man, but he was a good man. And that is what we choose to remember about him."

I glanced at Auntie Sherrie who rocked back and forth in her seat. I couldn't tell if she was sad or angry, or if Deacon Jones's prayer brought up good memories or a reminder of how Uncle Joe had died in the throes of passion with another woman. Rochelle had one hand on her back and her drink in the other. Couldn't even set down the liquor during a prayer.

"We are here to encourage our sister Sherrie," Deacon Jones continued. "To let her know that while you, oh God, will the send the Comforter, we will also stand in the gap. Lord, help her know we're holding her up. We are here for her in her time of need and sorrow, like she been for so many of us. We ask all of this in the name of Jesus we pray. Amen."

Before he even got the last syllable out good, folks swarmed the table with the food. Sam rose from his seat, but I pulled him back down.

"We're not eating?" he whispered.

"Yes. But wait. I always wait until the first round is done."

Sam relaxed in his seat. "Is that wise? These folks look hungry."

"Yolanda cooked enough to feed a whole congregation. We're good."

Tennessee and Dakota sat across the table from us. Looking at Dakota's butterscotch complexion and curly hair was like looking into a mirror.

"My twin little cousin," I said as I leaned across the table to hug her.

"We missed you, Hahna. Why you stop coming down for Christmas?" Dakota asked.

I nodded toward Rochelle who was standing in the food line dancing. Shaking her hips that needed to be contained in a girdle.

"Yeah, well, we need you," Dakota said. "Hi, Sam. I'm Dakota."

Sam smiled. "Nice to meet you."

"She's right, you know," Tennessee said. "When you come around big cuz, you make the rest of us think we can do something outside of here."

"You don't need me for that. Both of you are hella smart. You can get out of this town anytime you want."

Cousin Yolanda sat down at the table next to us with a handsome man I hadn't seen at any of my holiday visits.

"Hahna baby, we met your gentleman caller, so I want you to meet mine. This is Danny Bailey. Danny, this is our rich Atlanta cousin. She does something with computers, not sure what, but she's running thangs in Atlanta."

Danny waved, since he wasn't close enough to shake hands or hug. "It's good to meet you both, rich Atlanta cousin, and her gentleman caller, Sam."

"So, Sam," Yolanda said, "tell me about yourself. How in the world did you land Hahna?"

Sam smiled and looked at me. I nodded giving him my silent permission to tell the story of how we met.

"I met her at a book signing. Our favorite author."

I shook my head. "I have a new favorite author now, though. Sam is a writer."

"Oh, really?" Yolanda asked. "What's your last name Sam? Or do you have a pen name? I own a bookstore in town."

Now this was news. Since when did Cousin Yolanda own a bookstore?

"It's Sam Valcourt," Sam said.

The way Cousin Yolanda squealed, it was like Sam had said his name was Jay-Z. Although, Jay-Z probably wouldn't impress Cousin Yolanda. It would have to be somebody like Teddy Pendergrass or Al Green.

"The ladies at our store's book club love your books," Danny said.

Our bookstore? Oh, Cousin Yolanda found her a man that partnered with her and bought a bookstore. I wanted to high five her and shout, *Go 'head Cousin Yolanda.* She was another one who deserved all the good things. She had kissed every kind of amphibian in the Shady Falls creek—frog, toad, lizard, etc. Sounded like she'd found a good one.

"Sheila, come over here," Yolanda called across the room.

Sheila, who had a plate loaded down with more food than one person could eat in a sitting, shuffled over to where they were sitting.

"Girl, this better be good," Sheila said. "Don't keep a big girl from her food, now."

"Sheila, put your plate down on this table 'cause I don't want you to drop it when I tell you this," Yolanda said.

Sheila gave Yolanda a suspicious look but set the plate down anyway.

"My little cousin's man here, is Sam Valcourt."

Sheila's eyes lit up. "Sam Valcourt, the author?"

"Yes, I am he," Sam said. He stood to his feet when Sheila started to do a little shuffle dance that looked part like the Electric Slide, but also like a Holy Ghost shout.

"I wish I had known you was coming, I shole woulda brought my books for you to sign."

"How long are y'all gonna be here?" Yolanda asked. "You staying til the funeral, right?"

I nodded. "Yes. We'll probably leave the day after."

"Oh, well, maybe we can pull together an emergency book club meet and greet," Danny said. "It wouldn't be much but some refreshments and some avid readers."

"Two of my favorite things," Sam said.

I beamed with pride at how my family and extended family were making such a fuss over Sam. He seemed to enjoy it too, which made me feel even better about bringing him home with me.

"You shoulda led with the fact you a book writer," Tennessee said. "We need to talk about how I can get put on to that game. I heard it's good money in book writing."

Sam blinked a couple times but didn't miss a step. "What kind of books do you want to write?"

"Something real. Something street," Tennessee said. "Probably about the life of an up and coming emcee and his country-bumpkin ass family."

"Watch your language," Cousin Yolanda said. "We got the church folks over here."

"Them church folk know I cuss, and they be cussing too at home," Tennessee said. "Anyway, Sam, we definitely need to talk before you leave."

"If anybody needs to write a book, it's me," Rochelle said.

I'd watched her walk up to our conversation, but I'd hoped she would just observe and move on. I had never even seen her holding a book, much less reading one, but now she needed to write one.

"And what would you like to write about?"

Rochelle looked at me and scoffed. "Probably something like that movie *Imitation of Life*. The one where the ungrateful ass daughter left town and tried to act like her mama ain't exist. Mine would be different though. The mama wouldn't die, she'd go to Atlanta and show up at one of her daughter's fancy parties and make her daughter talk to her."

I knew she was baiting me for an argument with her drunk ass. I refused to give it to her.

"Go on and eat your dinner," Yolanda said, "so those carbs can soak up some of that vodka. You talking crazy, Rochelle."

"Mmm-hmmm. Y'all know that'll be a good book. A best-seller."

"Go on now," Yolanda said.

"You'd think nobody raised her ass," Rochelle said. "Look at her. Ain't even got up to make her man's plate. She know better than that. Probably why she forty-two and just barely keep a man."

Sam opened his mouth, but I touched his knee and shook my head. I had learned never to engage with her when she was drunk. My grandmother taught me that. She always told me to let her make a fool of herself, all by herself.

In fact, the whole room was silent. I remembered being embarrassed about her over the years, but I was done with that. Everyone in this room knew her except Sam. She hadn't changed.

And no, she hadn't raised me. My grandmother had, because she could barely get up in the morning most days from drinking herself into a stupor the night before.

"You know, I think I'm going to fix Hahna a plate. I'm here to help her grieve the loss of her favorite uncle," Sam said. "Tennessee, you want to point me to the food?"

Tennessee hopped up like the ride or die cousin that he was and showed Sam to the food. I cocked my head to one side and waited to see what Rochelle had to say to that.

"Humph," she said, and walked over to her seat, sat down and started eating.

"Well, I guess he shut her up," Yolanda whispered.

None of us laughed out loud, but there was definitely a shared moment of glee. That's what Rochelle got for showing her ass. Sam was perfection, and I was going to reward him for coming to my rescue when we got to the hotel later on.

I hoped that this was enough, and that Rochelle would simmer down for the rest of the week. I didn't need her to ruin Uncle Joe's funeral, and neither did Auntie Sherrie.

Chapter 23

KIMBERLY

Kimberly had asked Samantha to meet her at the flower shop without the rest of the bridesmaids to ask her to host the bridal shower. She was late though, and Kimberly only had an hour and a half before she had to meet with a supplier that wanted to buy in bulk at a discount. She wished she didn't have that meeting to go to, but she hadn't hired anyone to handle these kinds of things yet. Kimberly was thrilled beyond belief that her business had gone from her garage to a warehouse overnight, but she hadn't quite caught up.

Kimberly pulled her phone out of her purse to call Samantha, but just as she was about to press send, Samantha rushed into the store, out of breath.

"I'm so sorry I'm late, Kim. There was an accident on 285."

Kim placed her phone back in her purse and hugged Samantha. "I understand. It's fine."

"Where's everyone else? They all late too?"

"Oh, I only asked you to come. It's just going to be us."

"Really? What's that about?"

Kimberly wasn't surprised that Samantha was suspicious. She was a reporter, so it was her job to ask questions. But it was more than her job, Samantha just always needed all the answers.

"Can't I just want to spend some time with just you?"

"Yes, but we haven't done that in a long time. Definitely not since you started planning this wedding."

"That's partially my fault."

"You haven't been at any women's ministry events, but I didn't think you would. You're so busy these days with the wedding and the business."

"Life is crazy right now, but in a good way. But I have been missing my prayer partner."

"Same."

Kimberly pointed to pink begonias in a cluster. "What do you think of these? I know I want the bouquet to be mostly pink with a few white and blue flowers. The accents will be silver."

"Those are pretty, but how many of these would you need for a bouquet? That sounds pricey."

"Well, I wouldn't just use these. I would mix in some pink roses and calla lilies. They told me they could dye some flowers deep blue for me, to match the men."

"And they'll ship them to Jamaica?"

I nodded. "Yep. I've used this florist for years. They did recommend someone in Negril for me, though. You think I should go with a local florist?"

Kimberly shrugged. "I guess that's up to you. If it was me, I'd go up to the craft store and make silk flower bouquets and call it a day."

Kimberly wrinkled her nose at the thought of fake flowers for her wedding. She'd seen some beautiful silk flower bouquets in her wedding shopping, but she could afford to have the real thing and she was going to have them.

"I love real flowers. I've always dreamed of having a wedding reception with flowers everywhere."

"I've never dreamed of a wedding at all," Samantha said.

"Well, I dreamed of the wedding, but had no idea if the husband would ever be there. So, I get it."

"I'm happy for you, though."

Kimberly moved to the section of the store with roses while trying to process Samantha's words. Was her bad attitude about all the wedding plans really about the Maid of Honor duties, or was there a deeper issue that she hadn't talked about?

"I wanted to ask you to host my bridal shower," Kimberly said when Samantha caught up. "Do you want to do that?"

Samantha laughed. "I don't think the rest of your bridesmaids would be satisfied with anything I plan."

"What? Why do you say that?"

"If it's not over the top expensive or worldly they don't want it."

"I'm asking you, because I want to have a bridal shower where all my sisters in Christ will be able to come and celebrate. They can't come to the wedding, so . . ."

"Why can't they come?"

"I mean, some will, of course. Most folks don't just up and travel to Jamaica for someone's wedding."

"Well," Samantha said, "I know quite a few of the ladies are planning to come. They've found a hotel and everything. Gonna make it kind of like a singles' retreat."

This made Kimberly smile. It did feel sometimes that she was consumed with Gamma Phi Gamma business and primarily the lives of Hahna and Twila. They took a lot of energy and work, and Kimberly wouldn't trade it for anything. But it was also good to have her friends that were simply uplifting. They prayed for her business and her love life, as much as Hahna and Twila. Sometimes their prayers were more persistent.

"I'm glad they're coming. We can celebrate at the bridal shower too, though."

"I'll do it if you want me to, I just don't want to hear anything from Twila and Hahna about how it's not good enough. If this is my contribution to the wedding, it's not going to be what they want."

"This is not your only contribution to the wedding."

"It feels a little bit that way. Every idea I give is shot down immediately."

"I think it's partially in your delivery, though."

Samantha frowned. "What do you mean by that?"

"I'm saying this in love. The energy you bring is sometimes a little judgmental and contentious."

"Wow. Really? Is that what Twila and Hahna say?"

"This has nothing to do with anything they've said. This is just my observation."

"I can't help it if my Christianity makes them feel judged."

Kimberly had known Samantha was going to be defensive about this topic. It was why she'd waited so long to broach the subject. But now, Samantha's judgmental attitude was becoming toxic to their sister circle.

"It's not your Christianity. Christ is love. Sometimes you have to love people where they are. You can do this without condemning everyone all the time."

"Do you feel condemned when we talk?"

Kimberly pressed her lips tightly together. Answering this question would be complicated. In truth, she didn't feel condemned when talking to Samantha, but it was only because Kimberly censored the things she told Samantha. When she went out on the date with Shawn and then found out Ron was his daddy? That was not a story Samantha was getting. When Ron peeled her out of her Spanx and kissed and touched every part of her body? Nope. Hadn't told her that either. Kimberly hadn't wanted to hear about how God would sustain her until she married her husband.

"I don't tell you certain things, because I think I would feel condemned," Kimberly finally said.

"That's not me condemning you. That's the Holy Ghost that lives on the inside of you."

"Samantha, that's exactly what I'm talking about."

"Well, I'm not going to stop lifting Jesus up just so you can feel better in your sin."

Kimberly had known the conversation would be pointless. Mostly because Samantha didn't care how she made anyone feel when it came to Jesus.

"You know . . . you always talk about lifting Jesus up, but sis, you don't sound anything like Jesus," Kimberly said.

"I can't believe you're saying this to me. I thought . . .

I thought we had a connection that you didn't have with the others."

"We do."

"No, we don't. You're just like them. They're just more honest about who they are."

Kimberly's jaw dropped. "Did you just call me a hypocrite?"

"I'm just telling the truth. Why don't you just go ahead on and be like them? Go have strippers at your bachelorette party and everything else. Keep playing with God."

Samantha turned and walked out of the flower shop, leaving Kimberly wondering what came next with their friendship, her bridal shower, and their sisterhood. And for the first time in a very long time, Kimberly didn't want to run to Twila and Hahna for help. If this issue was going to be resolved with Samantha, it was going to have to be another way.

Chapter 24

TWILA

I decided to accept DeAndre's offer for a date for a couple reasons. One, because I needed to get my mind off Alexander Adams. Thoughts of what I should do with that information were consuming my brain, but I still hadn't made a decision on my next steps. Two, because I was curious about what Dr. Mays told me to ask DeAndre. If he was averse to therapy, then I could probably nip this entire thing in the bud.

I wasn't even sure if it was a thing. We'd worked out together a few times. Had a few breakfast smoothies and a few conversations. We followed each other on social media. Did that mean we were moving towards a thing?

He'd picked Top Golf for our date, and I chose to meet him there, even though I trusted him. I just felt some kind of way about having him pick me up from Hahna's house. It wasn't his business that I wasn't living at home, nor was it his business to know where Hahna lived. Plus, if things went left, I could have Kimberly bail me out with an emergency call.

I watched him as he examined the golf clubs for his first turn. He didn't look like he knew what he was doing, but he was fine as hell in his ignorance. Those snug jeans and fitted shirt showed off his perfect body, and I appreciated him for accentuating the positive. Women, well this woman, liked eye candy too. He took his shot and made a horrible score. I covered my mouth with my hand as he came back to the table.

"Have you done this before?" I asked as he sat and looked at the menu.

"I have not."

"So, why did you invite me here?"

"It seems like the kind of place you might like. A lot of people, good drinks, and a physical activity."

His perceptiveness pleased me. "You are correct. If you would've asked me where I wanted to go, I probably would've said a place like this."

"Well, I'm glad you trusted me."

His lips mesmerized me as he spoke, so I looked down at the menu. "I think I want a big drink with lots of alcohol in it."

"Long week?"

"Yes. I had some really tough cases. A reality TV star that got a little money and decided to get a mouth full of implants. Her teeth were almost completely rotten and crumbling. She'd been wearing grills and cheap veneers. I earned every bit of my money on her."

"Yikes. Grills are still in?"

"I guess."

We used the little computer on the table to order our food and drinks, and it was my turn to take a golf club swing. I didn't fare much better than DeAndre, but he laughed at me. Okay, with me, 'cause I cracked up too.

I sat back down at the table. "How was your week?" I asked. "I bet we share some clients."

"We might. And if not, we can sure refer business to each other. I'm always open to take on another client," DeAndre said.

"I'll send you some. My patients range from classy, bougie, ratchet, to savage."

We both laughed at this. It felt good to laugh and just feel light. That's what DeAndre brought me. Levity.

"My week was a little crazy," DeAndre said. "I've been working late every night except tonight."

"I know what that feels like. Lately, I've been trying to give myself more time for self-care."

"That is very important. When I was corporate, I used to take days off for mental health breaks. It's harder to do that now that I'm working for myself."

"Isn't that the crazy part? When you're a boss, you have to grind harder than when you work for someone else."

DeAndre nodded in agreement. "Nothing but truth. What do you do for self-care? Let me guess, long baths, expensive sushi, wine . . ."

"All that. And therapy."

I waited for DeAndre's composure to crack. It didn't.

"I went to therapy after law school. Put myself under so much pressure to get with the right firm, and then I didn't get hired where I wanted to get hired. Had a bit of a breakdown."

Wow. I did not expect that at all. I felt myself warm to the idea of dating him for real and it scared me a little, but not enough to make me cut and run. I could imagine seeing this through.

"And it helped you didn't it?"

"I wouldn't be where I am today had I not handled my mental health. I support you in taking care of yours."

He was legit sitting there sounding absolutely perfect and I didn't know what to make of it. I just stared at him in disbelief.

"What?" he asked.

"Okay, I'm gonna keep it all the way real with you for a minute. I just dealt with a dude a few months ago who was crazy, broke, and he cheated on me."

"A fuckboy."

"Pretty much. And I'm really not in the mental headspace to deal with that shit right now. So, if you're on some bullshit, just do us both a favor and ghost me."

DeAndre sat back in his seat and folded his arms across his chest. "Why do you think I'm on some bullshit?"

"'Cause why are you single? For real? You are forty-two, a lawyer, no kids, fine as hell . . ."

"Thank you."

"Dude. Cut the games. Why the hell are you single? Why aren't you someone's husband?"

"Why aren't you someone's wife?"

I shook my head and looked around for the waitress to bring my drink, because I needed a sip of it at that exact moment.

"I'm not someone's wife, because women like me are every damn where. You? You are a unicorn."

As if on cue, in the waitress delivered both drinks and appetizers to the table. I was grateful for it, because I needed to breathe for a second. This was not first date conversation. At all. But, shit, I was still in rule-breaking mode.

DeAndre took a swig of his drink. Bourbon. Neat. He even picked a perfect man's man drink. It was like somebody gave him the playbook and he didn't even care that I knew he cheated.

"I am a serial monogamist. At forty-two, I've had five relationships. I dated one girl in high school. Met her over the summer before freshman year and dated her until she decided she didn't want a long-distance relationship in college."

"You had one girlfriend in high school."

"I did. I found out later that she talked to a couple different guys, but I only wanted her. Lost my virginity to her and would've married her."

"College?"

"I spent the first two years of undergrad heartbroken over my high school love."

"I know you're lying to me."

"I'm not. Met a girl junior year. We dated for two years, and she met an NFL player at an internship. I couldn't compete with that. I was poor."

"By the time you graduated undergrad you'd had two girlfriends. Ever."

"I went on a few dates in college, but I didn't sleep with anyone. Graduated college and had only ever been with two girls."

"You might be a unicorn, the abominable snowman, and bigfoot wrapped into one."

"Well, you're going to like this part. I decided that in law school I was gonna be like all the other dudes. A hitter and quitter."

I nodded. "Good, now let's get to the real part of the story."

"I ended up falling for the first girl I fell in bed with. We dated for three years."

"Okay, that was number three. Where'd you meet number four?"

DeAndre laughed. "I can't believe I'm going through my entire dating history with you on our first date."

"We are clearly atypical. We've talked about therapy and now we're onto your unlikely dating habits. Have you had your testosterone levels checked?"

"Whoa."

"I'm kidding. Tell me about number four."

"This was the one that broke me for a while. I was right out of therapy. My first real job. I slept with one of the partners' wives for five years."

My jaw dropped. "Oh shit!"

"I'm not proud of this. You're actually the first person I've ever told this story to. I was determined to take this to the grave."

"This level of transparency has got to be the most refreshing thing I've ever experienced," I said. "Please don't stop. It's like having sex on the first date, but better. Like we're getting completely naked."

"So, sex is off the table tonight?"

I threw my head back and hollered. I wasn't going to tell him, but I felt like nothing was off the table.

"How in the hell did you end up sleeping with one of the partners' wives."

"I met her at a company party. She and I were the only ones not engaged in conversations with others, so we started talking. She was approaching fifty, but still fine as hell. She propositioned me."

"Was she white?"

"Does that matter to the story?"

I shrugged. "Not really, but it adds context. Makes it richer."

"Well, yes, she was white. Had red hair like Peggy Bundy. You know, I always had a crush on her. I wondered why Al Bundy wouldn't want a wife who was begging for sex and had a rack like that."

Oh, he tickled me. I don't know if it was the levity or the honesty, or maybe that his unbelievable story made mine feel somewhat tame in comparison.

"So, you got entangled with Peg Bundy."

"For five years. I was stupid. Thought she was going to leave her husband for me. She never had any intentions of doing that."

"He was a partner, right?"

"Yes."

"Chile . . ."

"I know. I was young. I thought we connected."

"Oh, y'all connected."

DeAndre laughed and finished off his bourbon. "That was number four."

"How old were you when you were done with her?"

"Thirty."

"So, you're telling me in twelve years, you've only slept with one other woman?"

He shook his head. "No. I had one more relationship that I got out of a year ago. But it lasted for three years. Before her, I had a couple of flings."

"And why did number five go south?"

"This one hurt pretty bad actually. I thought about going to therapy again after we broke things off."

"Yikes."

"Yeah, she just didn't believe in monogamy. She wanted to, every now and then, have a fling with another dude."

"An ex-boyfriend?"

DeAndre shrugged. "She cheated on me three times that I knew of. One was an ex. One was a co-worker. One was a guy she met in a club. Those are the three she told me about."

"Why in the hell did you stay?"

"Because I thought I could deal with it. She told me I could hook up with other women if I wanted. It seemed like a man's dream."

"But it wasn't."

"It was not. Well, it was a nightmare."

"And you've been single since you broke up with her?"

"Yes, but I didn't break up with her. She broke up with me."

"Really?"

"Yeah, she turned me out. She did things to me I never had done before."

I wrapped my arms around my stomach to keep from laughing. Because this wasn't funny, but for some reason all of it tickled me.

"She turned you out, huh?"

"Yep."

"Your freak number was like four and hers was a million."

"Accurate."

I lost it, and the laughter rippled out. Tears poured out of my eyes and my whole body participated in the laughter.

"You laughing at me? Wow."

"It's the way you're telling the stories, DeAndre. Only a man could tell these stories like this. If these things happened to a woman, I'd be praying for her."

"But you don't want to pray for me?"

"I just feel like, none of this stuff had to happen to you. Men always have options."

I stopped mid-laugh when I heard a familiar voice. The voice interrupted my mirth. It was Hahna's assistant, Corden. He was with a group of people a few golf bays down. When I realized what I was looking at, my lips formed an 'o' and I stared for a moment.

"What's wrong?" DeAndre asked.

"That's Hahna's assistant. He's with a group of gay guys."

DeAndre shrugged. "So?"

"So . . . since when was Corden gay? He's engaged. To a woman."

"Are you serious? I thought he was gay from when he opened the door at The Data Whisperers building."

My light feeling left me and my mood dropped like it had a concrete block chained to it, and it was on its way to the bottom of the ocean. *This* was why men couldn't be trusted. They cheated, they lied, they were closeted, and sometimes, they raped.

"Well, we're making an assumption that he's gay," DeAndre said. "Just because he's got gay friends doesn't mean he's gay."

"You have gay friends?"

"Yeah, I do."

"But riddle me this. Would you go out with a whole group of gay men? In Atlanta?"

DeAndre ate a few French fries. He knew there was only one answer to this question that did not prove the point he was trying to make.

"Nah, I wouldn't."

"I know you wouldn't."

"But you could go out with a group of lesbian women?"

"I mean, I could, and no one would assume I was a lesbian. I think most men don't want to accept that any woman truly doesn't want a penis."

DeAndre laughed. "You're right."

"I know it. But, back to Corden's ass. How in the hell is he still in the closet? It's 2021. He doesn't need to still hide it."

"I don't know. That's crazy."

"Should I go and speak to him?" I ask. "Or would that be awkward?"

"Yeah, don't. It'll be more awkward for Hahna than anything. Then, he'll feel like he has to come out to her."

"Well, he's out in public. Maybe he wants someone to see him. Maybe he wants to be outed."

I wondered if this was the truth. I didn't want to dissect it at the table, though. I wasn't sure if I wanted to dissect it at all. It wasn't my business. Shoot, my business was sitting in front of me.

"How about you? You're a damn unicorn too," DeAndre said. "No kids, business owner, in shape. Most of the time I meet a woman with no kids, and is in shape, but she's broke or with bad credit. Or in shape, got her money together, and has three kids. Never all of the above."

"And you want all of the above."

"I mean, well, yes."

"Younger women might have all of this."

"Yes, but then they're immature, or want to party. I went out with a girl in her twenties once. It was terrible. Even the sex was bad."

"'Cause you was used to entangling with older women."

"How are we back on me?" DeAndre said. "We're talking about you."

"Okay, I owe you some realness. I am just horrible at picking guys. I haven't been in a relationship where the guy was faithful. Never. I've had great sex, guys who splurged on me, and guys who seemed like they had it all together. They all cheated on me."

That sounded pretty sad, but it was the truth. I had been cheated on so many times I'd lost count. I once had a guy who was married, and cheating with me, and another girl.

"That's enough to put a person in therapy. Maybe could impact your self-esteem," DeAndre said.

"Oh, that's not why I'm in therapy. I was . . . um . . . assaulted."

DeAndre took in a sharp breath and nodded. And like that our transparency turned into a brick wall.

"I was sexually assaulted. In a swinger's club."

DeAndre reached for the bourbon glass. It was empty, so he drank his water. I knew that was a lot. I hoped it didn't make everything come to a screeching halt.

"Which club?" he asked after guzzling his water.

"Why? Are you a swinger?"

"No, not at all. I applied to get into this exclusive club— Phenom. They turned me down."

I chuckled. "That's the one. I can get you in if you want. My sorority sister is the owner."

"I heard that they had a swinger's room. I just wanted to be accepted for my law practice. I thought I'd meet people there that could probably use my services. Entertainment law, and maybe a touch of my criminal defense background."

"You will meet people there who need both of those."

"I'll let you know if I decide I'm still interested. It's disheartening to hear you were assaulted there, as careful as they are about accepting members."

"I know. My sorority sister is livid. If this wasn't Atlanta, I'd probably want to press charges."

"You don't?"

"I don't want it to be documented anywhere. Atlanta court records are fodder for bloggers."

"But you're not a celebrity."

"I'm celebrity adjacent. I'm just interesting enough for a slow news day. I can see the headline now. *Atlanta Dentist to the Stars Makes a Freaky Tape at Club Phenom.*"

"You made a tape?"

"No, but they don't care about the truth in the headlines. It's click bait."

"You don't have to tell me. So many of my clients are trying to sue bloggers for libel. All they have to do is put one disclaimer in the article or say allegedly."

"And the case has no water."

"None."

DeAndre pressed another drink order into the machine. "Do you want another drink?"

"Yes. I'll take the same thing."

"That's a lot of liquor. Are you going to be okay to drive?"

I laughed. "We'll make sure to stay and keep talking until I'm sober."

"Or we'll keep drinking and I'll get us both a car service."

"That works too."

"Are we going to have a second date?" I asked. "Because this is a lot for the first time out."

"If you'd like to have a second date, and a third, and a fourth, I'm down. You haven't said anything to scare me off."

"Do you think I was trying to scare you off?"

One side of DeAndre's mouth teased a smile. "I think so, but I'm not afraid of this."

DeAndre checked all the boxes. He was everything I was looking for, down to the blunt honesty. So why couldn't I relax and just agree to explore?

It was because, like a unicorn, a man like DeAndre was a mythical creature. He was sitting in front of me, but I had decades of dating experience that told me men like him didn't exist. Not in real life. It was hard to get my hopes up, when in a few seconds, he was probably going to disintegrate right in front of me. Or worse, turn into the frog hiding underneath the façade.

But yes, I was going to go on dates two through one thousand if he asked. He had me at serial monogamist.

Chapter 25

HAHNA

Even though Uncle Joe was a cheater, Auntie Sherrie had spared none of my expense for his funeral. His silver casket gleamed at the front of the church. It looked more costly than anything in the building. I remembered the hard pews from all the times my grandmother and aunt had dragged me to Sunday School, revivals, conferences, and Sunday evening services. There were always snacks and pieces of candy slipped to me in a tissue, but the pews still hurt my bottom.

I rifled through my purse for a mint, and a tissue, to keep my mind busy. I'd already looked at Uncle Joe in the casket. I couldn't look again. Auntie Sherrie's friends all said that they'd done a good job on the body. I didn't comment on that, because I didn't agree.

I didn't know if Auntie Sherrie had gotten up early praying, put a little brown liquor in her coffee, or if she'd taken a hit of one of Tennessee's joints, but she was surprisingly calm. She sat on the front pew, flanked by Rochelle and Cousin Yolanda.

Sam sat next to me with his arm around my shoulders. It felt good to have someone with me, unlike at my grandmother's funeral where I felt alone and without any support. Sam kissed my forehead and gave me a little squeeze as the preacher ascended to the pulpit.

"Dearly beloved," old Pastor Remington said in his scratchy voice, "we are gathered here today to celebrate the life of our brother Deacon Joe Davis. After we open with prayer, we will have an A and B selection by the choir, remarks by the family and friends—no more than two minutes per person please— and I will return to do the eulogy. Following the eulogy we will have a solo, and a prayer, and the family will follow the processional to the gravesite. After the burial, the family will return here for the repast."

Pastor Remington had done the program like we were at a men's conference where Uncle Joe was the keynote speaker or the special guest. It all felt regimented and planned. I wondered at what point in the service someone was supposed to fall out crying in the aisle. Or when someone was supposed to stand in front of the casket saying *Why oh Lord. Take me instead.* There didn't seem to be time allotted for those.

I blinked slowly and stared at the members of the church who'd I'd known since I was little. I was the success story they told their children and grandchildren about. My Chanel suit, matching handbag, and shoes probably cost more than everyone's outfit in the room combined. Still, being in the room with all the people from my past filled me with a sense of dread.

What if somehow, I got trapped here in Shady Falls? What if time went in reverse and I had to stay here in Auntie Sherrie's house? I squeezed Sam's hand tightly. Maybe we wouldn't spend the night at all. We could get on the road after the repast. Shoot, before. I didn't need any lukewarm fried chicken and spaghetti.

I listened to selection A and B from the choir. Just like when I was a girl, the choir only had about two good singers and the rest of the folk standing up there didn't need to have a microphone in front of them. But as long as Aunt Sherrie rocked back and forth with one hand up, it was fine. She was the one who'd lost the love of her life, and this was what she needed.

In the back of the church there was a commotion that made me and Sam turn in our seats. There was a woman dressed in black wearing a pill box hat with a veil over her face. By the way folk in the church were murmuring and sucking their teeth, I knew this could only be one person.

"Is this the pickle ho?" Sam whispered.

"Must be," I whispered back.

As she staggered up the center aisle of the church, I decided that my uncle's mistress had lost her mind. The closer she got to the front, the more I could hear her low moans. It sounded like she was in physical pain. I almost felt bad for her. She'd lost someone too—even if he was someone she wasn't supposed to have.

When she passed our aisle, I was amazed and astonished by the size of her behind. No wonder my uncle was under her spell. I had never seen a behind that big in real life. Each perfectly formed gelatinous globe jiggled against the constraints of whatever shapewear she had on under her dress. I had heard men describe a 'shelf booty' where one could comfortably sit an item like a glass or a bowl. The mistress's booty was shelf enough to hold a whole set of World Book Encyclopedias.

Deacon Jones was at the microphone. "Joe was more than my brother in Christ. He was my blood brother. We worked together thirty years at the pickle plant, and I can always say that Joe had my back," he said.

Deacon Jones stopped for a moment when he saw Uncle Joe's mistress in the center aisle. He shook his head and looked down at his notes. Maybe he'd find something in there to cast out a ho spirit, because this woman needed to leave. It wasn't the time or place for her to make her presence known.

Aunt Sherrie turned around in her seat and saw the mistress. Aunt Sherrie's eyes widened, and she shot up from her seat. Rochelle tried to pull her back down, but it was too late. Yolanda sighed and stood to her feet too.

"Who let this Jezebel in the church?" Aunt Sherrie said loudly.

Decorum was out the window, and this was about to go from a celebration of life to a viral video online. Some of my younger cousins already had their phones out.

"I j-just wanna see him. I wanna pay my respects," the mistress said.

"Isn't it enough that you killed my husband with whatever demonic spirits you carrying between your legs?" Aunt Sherrie said. "Now you're here to rub it in?"

"I didn't kill him. I tried to save his life."

One of the church nurses sprang into action and was at the mistress's side. Rochelle finally got Sherrie to sit again. Both Yolanda and Rochelle flanked Aunt Sherrie, but this time closer. She couldn't move without alerting at least one of them.

As the nurse led the mistress to Uncle Joe's still open casket, I wondered why they hadn't closed it before the service started. It was usually done that way. The family saw the body and then they closed the casket. Maybe someone had known that the pickle ho was coming.

She stopped in front of the casket and quietly wept. It felt strange that Uncle Joe's mistress was in the church after the prayer and A and B selections had gone forth. It kind of reminded folks that if they believed even half of what Pastor Remington said during Bible Study, then Uncle Joe might not be basking in heaven's glory. On account of the adultery and all.

"That's long enough!" Aunt Sherrie said.

A couple of chuckles and uncomfortable murmurs sprinkled across the sanctuary. Aunt Sherrie was right though. This attention-seeking heffa had showed up in the middle of service, jiggling her behind everywhere, weeping and crying to look in the casket at another woman's husband. She should be glad no one had jumped on her. My cousin Indiana was always ready for a good brawl. Her siblings flanked her just like Aunt Sherrie was being flanked, probably to keep her from making a scene.

The nurse who walked the mistress up to the front of the church, politely led the crying heffa away. To the rear of the church. She sat in her pew and wailed. It was troubling that she did this. She wasn't family. Why didn't she leave? Why didn't someone make her leave?

I was gonna make her leave.

I stood, and Sam got a look of terror on his face. Luckily, I didn't have someone flanking me, and Sam didn't move fast enough to keep me from walking into the aisle. He did get up and follow me though.

The service continued even with her wailing. It had to. We had an appointment at the gravesite, and we couldn't be late for that. They had to finish in a timely manner. Or decently and in order as Pastor Remington would say.

I stopped at the pew in front of the mistress and sat. Sam sat down next to me. I turned all the way around in my seat, like the bad little kid that stared at you all service until you crossed your eyes at him.

"What's your name?" I asked in a low tone, right above a whisper, but not loud enough to be disruptive.

"Melinda."

"Well, Melinda, you need to go."

"Who are you?"

"I'm Joe's niece, Hahna."

Melinda scoffed and rolled her eyes. "Oh, you the rich one everybody always talking about, huh? You paid for that casket? 'cause I know Sherrie ain't have no money for all this."

I rose up to my knees ready to spring on her, and Sam pulled me back down into my seat. I gave him a short glare and then turned my attention back to Melinda.

"I did pay for all this, 'cause Uncle Joe didn't leave any life insurance. You can stop all your hollering, 'cause he ain't leave you nothing either. Move on to the next one."

She touched her belly. "He left me something. Someone. And when this baby gets here, we gone get a social security check. We gone be all right."

I damn near threw up in my mouth. Uncle Joe was sixty-eight years old. She had to be my age. Why in the hell would she brag about this pregnancy?

"You gone be all right with a whole six or seven hundred dollars a month?"

"Yep. Shole will."

She had better hope Auntie Sherrie and Indiana didn't beat her whole gigantic ass when this news got out.

"Do you need help to your car?" Sam asked Melinda.

She gave Sam a shocked look. She was probably used to men being on her side. With all that junk in her trunk, she would have been hard pressed to find a man that would be her enemy.

"Help?"

"Yes, we can walk you out," Sam said.

"We?"

This part almost made me laugh. Did she think my man was about to walk her ole man stealing behind out of the church without me? We could all walk out. Together.

"Well, I want to hear the eulogy," Melinda whined.

This last thing she said was too loud, and people started turning around in their seats. Including my Aunt Sherrie, who seemed furious that she was still in the church.

"You're upsetting everyone by being here, so you're leaving, whether you want to or not," I said. "We're being nice, and we don't have to."

"Get that Jezebel outta here," Aunt Sherrie screamed at the top of her lungs.

I stood up. "Let's go. Unless you feel like tussling with me with your meal ticket in your belly."

"You threatenin' my baby?"

"I'm saying get up, and let's go."

Sam stood too, and walked to the end of Melinda's pew. "It'll be okay, Melinda. Come on, we'll walk you out."

I guess Sam did sound a bit (a lot) more sympathetic than I did. She rose to her feet and Sam held his hand out in the direction of the door looking like a properly trained Shady Falls church usher.

She stumbled out of the aisle, and Sam helped to steady her, but then quickly removed his hand. He wasn't escorting her out, just showing her the door. Sam was so brilliant and perceptive. I loved this man.

We followed Melinda as she walked across the gravel parking lot to her car. A couple of times, I thought those little rocks were going to trip her up in those five-inch heels, but she made it to her little 1990's era Honda.

She unlocked her car door then turned to face me and Sam.

"No matter what y'all think," she said, "me and Joe was in love. He was gonna leave Sherrie as soon as we had our baby. She never gave him any kids, and he always wanted one. She's a barren woman. Just mad 'cause my body is young and fertile."

I closed my eyes and swooned from the sun beating down on me. Or maybe it was because I'd skipped breakfast.

"Girl, if you don't carry yo ass on," I said.

She probably saw that it was a good idea for her to do exactly as I said. So, she carried her ass on.

"You cussed on the church grounds," Sam said as she peeled out of the parking lot.

"The Lord understands. He helped me to not cuss her out inside the church."

Sam chuckled and put his arm around me. "Your Aunt Sherrie is going to be devastated when she finds out about the baby."

"Please. They better give that baby a paternity test before they cut a check. My uncle was taking Viagra. That's the reason why he had a heart attack."

"I don't know. Sounds like the swimmers are still swimming to me."

If this was my uncle's baby, Sam was right. Aunt Sherrie was going to not just be devastated, but she was going to be embarrassed in front of her family and friends.

"Why would Uncle Joe do this to her? What makes a man hurt his wife that way?"

"Did you see her booty?"

I hit Sam's arm and he laughed. "I knew you were looking at that big thang."

"There is such a thing as too much booty, and that was it," Sam said. "I'll take your little donk any day."

"My booty is not little."

"Compared to that it is."

We started walking back to the church. I wished we could get in our car and just leave, but since this woman showed up to the funeral, I needed to stay around a little while longer. Aunt Sherrie was going to need reinforcements at the repast.

Chapter 26

HAHNA

The church hosted the repast for Uncle Joe's funeral, although I wished it was back at Auntie Sherrie's house. At the church, there were a dining room full of well-wishers. Some of them didn't even know or care about Uncle Joe. They just wanted to get some of that fried chicken and macaroni and cheese that Cousin Yolanda made. Or Deacon Jones's peach cobbler.

We sat at the table with Aunt Sherrie, but I was glad Sam was at my side. I was still numb from the funeral. Watching them lower the casket into the ground was hard. Especially with Aunt Sherrie falling apart.

Rochelle sat at the table across from me and Sam. I didn't feel like looking at her but moving would make me look bad and give Rochelle a reason to show her behind in the church banquet hall. Not that she needed a reason.

"Sherrie, it was a nice service," Rochelle said. "Joe woulda been happy at all the folks that came out."

"Mmm-hmmm. Even his ho came out."

I cleared my throat and looked at the table. Sam looked around as if he was surveying the room. Why would Rochelle mention the service? It was a nightmare with Melinda wailing and jiggling all over the sanctuary.

"She was just paying her respects, I guess. She knew her place," Rochelle said. "She didn't try to sit with the family."

"She ain't family, so why would she?" Aunt Sherrie asked.

"I'm just saying. Some of 'em think they got the right to," Rochelle said. "Especially if they got a child by the man."

I exchanged glances with Sam. Did Rochelle know about Melinda saying she was pregnant? I wondered how many other people she'd told that story. If it was more than one, Aunt Sherrie would hear about it soon. I hoped it was when I was already on the way home. I had already been down there more than my typical number of days in Shady Falls.

Tennessee and Indiana sat down next to Rochelle.

"Indiana did you bring your babies?" I asked. I didn't really care whether she'd brought her children or not. I just wanted to change the subject from Melinda.

"Everybody knows you don't bring kids to a funeral. A spirit could get on them." Indiana said.

"A spirit?" Sam asked.

"Yeah, spirits like funerals," Rochelle said, "not even just the spirit of the person who died. Sometimes other spirits come out too. Like a party."

"Oh, I see," Sam said.

"Where you from?" Rochelle asked. "I thought all black folk knew about that."

"I'm from Florida. Haitian. And I know all about spirits. Our whole family participated in the funeral when someone died."

Rochelle's eyebrows went up. "Haitian? Oh, you practice that voodoo. Lord, let me plead the blood of Jesus."

Sam's nostrils flared, and I squeezed his hand under the table. She was baiting him because she knew she couldn't get to me.

"I'm actually Catholic, but not practicing," Sam said.

"Catholic? That's even worse."

"How is that worse, Cousin Rochelle?" Tennessee asked. "Catholics believe in Jesus."

"Yeah, but they put Mary on top like she over the whole thing."

"Is that true, Sam?" Indiana asked, with a truly curious look on her face. She probably wanted to know for real.

"That's not quite how it goes, but like I said, I'm not a practicing Catholic, so I'm really not one hundred percent sure," Sam said.

"It's demonic," Rochelle said. "We might have to come up to that big mansion in Atlanta and cast spirits out. But I guess we gotta be invited first."

I knew it was going to go to this at some point. I've never invited my family to Atlanta. They've suggested that I should host the holidays or a family reunion, but I've always declined. It didn't feel weird to me that the woman who gave birth to me had never been to my house. She wasn't a part of my life.

"I been wanting to come through to the A," Tennessee said. "I want to get my music off the ground. You got a mansion cuz? Maybe me and my girl can stay in a spare bedroom until things take off."

"Call me after all this is over. We can chop it up," I said, knowing I was lying through my teeth. I wasn't chopping anything up and Tennessee wasn't moving into my house. Period.

Rochelle cackled. "What make you think she gone let you come up there? I could be living on the street and she wouldn't even let me come up there."

"I wouldn't let you be out on the street," I said.

This was true. I wouldn't let any of my family be homeless. But that was different than them moving into my space with me. I could buy one of these little Shady Falls houses for less than the amount that I got in interest on my smallest money market account. They'd be taken care of, but just away from me.

The young people that were part of the hospitality ministry at the church started bringing paper plates full of food to the family table. Good. Something to take their attention off me.

"Hey, can you put two pieces of chicken on mine?" Tennessee said, real sweet, to one of the girls as she handed Aunt Sherrie a plate. The girl nodded and smiled at him. He was probably gonna have a pile of chicken and macaroni and cheese. Church girls flirted with food.

All of our plates were full, but like Tennessee's, Sam's plate had extra chicken. Sam's punch cup was filled to the rim too when everyone else's was only three quarters of the way.

"Somebody's got a crush on you," I whispered as Sam sipped from his red Solo cup. "She gave you extra punch."

"She doesn't see I'm taken by the baddest chick in here?" he whispered back and kissed me on the cheek.

Rochelle glared at me with pure hatred and envy on her face. How could a mother be mad that her daughter was doing well? Especially when that daughter paid bills and took care of everyone's shortfalls.

I knew part of it was my relationship with my grandmother. My mother was the wild child and the outcast, but my grandmother had spoiled me rotten. Instead of reveling in the fact that her child was loved, Rochelle was hateful and jealous.

"Y'all look real cozy together. If y'all gonna have a baby, you better hurry up. She's getting long in the tooth."

"Okay, you know what? I'm sick of you taking digs at us. Find something else to focus on, because I'm over it," I said. Sam rubbed my back trying to calm me down, but she was getting on my nerves.

"See how disrespectful she is?" Rochelle said to anyone who was listening. "You would think that I wasn't the one who gave birth to her. You would think it's the other way around."

Fortunately, no one really fooled with Rochelle, so she had no allies at the gathering. Folks just shook their heads and went on with eating their food.

"Let's not show out at the church now," Aunt Sherrie said. "We can talk about this later on back at home."

"I'm not showing out," Rochelle said. "I ain't cussed nobody and I ain't said nothing that wasn't true."

"All right. And we all heard you, so you can be quiet now," Cousin Yolanda said as she finally brought her plate to the table to eat with the family. She was still wearing her little white plastic apron from the kitchen.

Rochelle rolled her eyes at Yolanda, but she quieted. Even

though Yolanda was the youngest of the three sister-cousins, she always seemed to have the level head and be in charge.

"Sam, thank you for coming out to our little book discussion last night. It was such a treat for them to meet an author in real life. Not too many authors come down to Shady Falls."

"It was my pleasure. I was surprised at all the questions they had. I really enjoyed the dialogue. If I go on a book tour with my next release, I'll make sure to put Shady Falls on the list. We can have a book party."

"When my book comes out, we can tour together," Tennessee said. "We can call it the Hot Boys of Literature."

"Sounds good. I'm down with it," Sam said.

Sam sounded so much more convincing and friendly than I did, but maybe he was being truthful.

"He ain't gone go on tour with you, just like Hahna ain't gonna come let you live in her mansion," Rochelle said. "You believe that, you dumber than you look."

That was it, I was done. Not going to let her continue to insult me in my face and act like I had to take it, just because she laid down with somebody and got up pregnant. She wasn't a mother to me, so nothing she said made me feel guilty. It just made me want to fight.

I got up from the table, and Sam followed suit. We scooted behind the chairs at the long table to say goodbye to Aunt Sherrie.

"Auntie Sherrie, I love you," I said. "Let me know what you need. Sam and I are gonna get on the road. I need to get back to Atlanta."

"Aw, baby, I thought you were coming back by the house," Auntie Sherrie said as she hugged me.

"I don't think that's a good idea. Rochelle is already acting up. Once she gets back to the house and starts drinking, it's gonna be worse."

"I hate to say it, but you're right. Safe travels, and call me when you get in."

I made the rounds hugging everyone, and so did Sam. I did not want to hug Rochelle, but that would've given her another reason to start hollering and to point out how disrespectful her forty-one-year-old daughter was.

"All right, Rochelle, we're leaving." I extended my arms for a hug, and Rochelle looked at me like I was crazy.

"So, you ain't gonna give me no money or nothing? You came down here and paid for this big ass funeral . . ."

She must've forgotten we were still at church, because the cussing had begun.

". . . and paying everybody else damn bills, and then make me gotta beg you for something."

"You ain't gotta beg me for nothing," I said, as I let my arms fall to my waist. She didn't want a hug anyway. She wanted cash.

Sam finished his hugs of my other family members and friends, and came and stood behind me.

"It was nice meeting you, Ms. Rochelle. Looking forward to the next time."

From her seat, Rochelle looked Sam up and down and said nothing. She gave both of us her back and went back to eating her food. Well, whatever. If she was done, I was done.

It always made me sad to see other families that were close knit, but this was my motivation to do well in life. It was also why my sorority sisters were my family, and now Sam. Now that my grandmother was in heaven, they were all I needed.

I just hoped that seeing this level of dysfunction wouldn't make Sam question our future.

Chapter 27

HAHNA

I was so happy to be on the road home I didn't know what to do. I loved my family, but the doses needed to be extremely small. And my mama showing her ass at the repast was enough to keep me from visiting for the next three or four years. I was embarrassed that all that happened in front of Sam, though.

"I think you left tire marks in the hotel parking lot," Sam said as I pulled onto the main road.

I laughed. "I don't care. I need to get back to civilization."

"Yes, I feel you. Do you think your aunt's going to be okay?"

"She'll be fine. Their house is paid off, and she's got her own pension from the pickle plant. She'll get whatever Uncle Joe was going to get for working there his whole life."

"She might have to share it with Melinda."

"That girl too stupid to even ask for it. She so country ghetto that she doesn't even know what a pension is."

"It's crazy the information people are lacking."

"Yes, it is."

My family and everyone else in Shady Falls was just content to only have enough to maybe buy a trailer to put on an empty lot and a nice car—a Lincoln or a Cadillac. The idea of building wealth was foreign to them. The amount of money I had in my portfolio was unfathomable. I was sure that my family, when counting and calculating how much money I had, didn't even come close to the correct amount.

"Hahna, I get it."

I lifted my eyebrow like it was a question mark. "You get what?"

"Why you're so obsessed with obtaining and keeping wealth."

I nodded. "I don't want to seem obsessed, but it is very important to me. I never want to end up back in Shady Falls."

"And I don't think you ever will. You're too driven, and too brilliant. You being a success isn't a fluke."

I thought about how The Data Whisperers was struggling to get clients again, and how we were a shadow of our former selves. Corden and Sylvia were still hanging in there, but they both deserved to work for a booming company with clients. That's what they signed up for.

"It may not have been a fluke, but what if it was like lightning? Who knows if I can strike again? I need to rebuild, but I'm not even sure how I start."

"How did you do it from the very beginning?"

"Relationship building and being able to offer a product that no one else could provide. Corden and I have some of the most innovative models for data analytics in the industry. Before all this happened, I got offered partnerships at consulting firms at least once a month. Now, it's crickets."

"Well, you've not lost your innovation or ability to build relationships."

"That's true."

"So, rebuilding is just going to take time. It might take a little longer than it took in the beginning."

"Yeah, because we've got to overcome our negative press."

"Exactly. But once you get one big company to use your services, all will be forgiven."

"I've pretty much expired my rolodex. I have reached out to everybody I know, and everybody I thought I knew."

"It's Atlanta. Why don't you host a party?"

"Yes! I'm going to have a Christmas networking party."

"A really lit party with no expenses spared. I'm talking open bars in more than one place in the house and fancy catering."

Both my eyebrows shot up and my jaw went completely slack. Sam talking about spending money? Now this was a new thing.

"You know how much money that kind of party costs?"

"I do. But this is a business expense. You have to let Atlanta know that you aren't down and out, and that you haven't missed a beat. Atlantans are the biggest fake it til you make it folk in the country."

"You're saying pretend like I'm doing well?"

"Pretend you're doing better than well. Give them what they want. A picture of success. They'll want a piece of that action."

"You sure you don't want to come be a strategist for The Data Whisperers?"

Sam laughed. "I would, but I don't think I'm going to have time."

"Why not?"

"I got a ridiculous offer for the follow up to *Repetition for Emphasis*, and a movie deal for both books."

"Are you freaking serious? When did this happen? Why didn't you tell me?"

Sam laughed while I peppered him with questions. How long had he been holding this information?

"I meant to tell you before we left for North Carolina, but it never seemed to be the right time."

"Why did you need to find the right time? This is good news. Every time is the right time."

"Honestly? I didn't think you'd be excited."

"Why wouldn't I be excited?"

"It's not a multi-million-dollar deal. It's only six figures. More than I thought I'd ever pull on a deal."

"Babe. I apologize if I haven't seemed supportive of your career. I understand that you have to start somewhere. This sounds like a hell of a start."

"It is, but I'm also a realist. This may be the only time I ever see six figures. I may never see more than that. Would that be good enough for you?"

"You are enough for me. I know you don't believe it when I say that, because you've seen me on the paper chase since we've been together."

"I understand why, now."

"Yes, and although I never want to end up in poverty again, I also don't want to be alone. We are good, and this is incredible news. I can't wait to brag about you."

"You gone tell your friends."

I did a little hand dance with the steering wheel. "I sure am. And they gonna be jealous. My man boutta do some movies."

Sam took one of my hands and squeezed. "I am so happy you're happy about this."

"While we're talking about happy things, I want to ask you something and just see where your head is on the topic."

"Okay . . ."

"You stay at my house like four days out of the week. Why don't you just move in and make some passive income on your place."

"Rent out my bachelor pad?"

"Yeah. What do you think?"

"Yes, I'd like that. Do you think I can turn one of those small bedrooms into a writing room?"

"Absolutely, and you don't have to ask me like that. When you move in, it's going to be our house."

Sam had a skeptical look on his face.

"You don't believe me?" I asked.

"I believe that you believe it. But, it's your house, babe."

"So, you want me to move in with you?" I asked. "Because I don't want you to feel like that. If you wake up and want to paint a wall, or change furniture or anything, I want you to feel free."

"Okay."

"Sam. You still sound like you don't believe me."

"Maybe when we get married, we can find a house together."

I swallowed hard. Was that a proposal? A pregame to the proposal? Was he putting that out there to see what my reaction might be? Because without question, I wanted forever.

"You okay, babe?" he asked. His voice sounded lighthearted like he was tickled at my anxiety.

"*When* we get married?" I asked. "I don't recall us talking about marriage."

"It's a natural culmination of things, don't you think?"

"Is this a proposal?"

"No, I don't think so. It's more like strategic planning."

I burst into laughter. Sam was teasing me, but he'd opened his mouth and said the m word. Now it was out in the atmosphere waiting to be acted upon.

"Should I start strategically planning a wedding?"

"Ooh, like this thing Kimberly and Ron are doing? He sounds stressed, so maybe not."

"He sounds stressed? What is he stressed about? He's not doing any of the work. We're doing it all. All he has to do is get on a plane, put on a tux and show up."

Sam shrugged. "Maybe I'm wrong. Maybe he's not stressed."

"Unh-uh. Nope. You're just trying to cover for him now. Spill it."

Sam laughed. "Only if you don't say anything to Kimberly."

"Okay, I won't say anything to Kimberly."

"Or Twila. Or any of the other sorority sisters."

Dammit. He got me on that one. If it was juicy enough, I absolutely would've told Twila.

"Oh, shoot. Okay. I won't say anything."

"I don't have all the details. It's something about his ex-wife and having his daughters in the wedding. I think his ex-wife might be giving him grief."

"Really? I thought she talked to Kimberly and they'd hashed things out."

"I don't know if Kimberly is privy to the conversations with Ron and his ex-wife."

I shook my head and glared at the road in front of me. I knew that heffa wasn't done with her shenanigans. She was working both sides. Putting a bad bug in Kimberly's ear about a so-called violent Ron and bothering Ron about the girls being in the wedding.

We were not going to let this heffa ruin Kimberly's wedding and her chance at joy. The bride tribe was going to mount a defensive, and she was gonna learn not to mess with a sister of Gamma Phi Gamma.

And Sam wasn't slick. He'd deftly changed the conversation from the natural culmination of things to Kimberly and Ron. I would wait for the proposal before I started planning for an actual wedding.

The first step was going to be getting Twila back to her own home, so that my man could move in.

Chapter 28

TWILA

I'd been sitting in a parked car, dressed in all black, in front of the townhouse where I'd seen Alexander Adams, since six o'clock in the morning. Waiting for him to emerge. I had no idea what I'd do if and when he emerged, but I waited, nonetheless.

I'd done some research. Alexander did own a home in this subdivision—with Fatima Adams. I assumed that was his wife. He dared to have a regular ass suburban life when he liked to rape women in sex clubs? I wanted to disrupt his normal life, like he'd disrupted mine.

I imagined doing physical harm to him. Even as I sat in the car, I had a taser in my purse. It felt like whatever I did to him needed to include the taser. I needed to render him helpless like he'd rendered me helpless.

Me just showing up at his home might not have been a good idea, though. It was Sunday morning. People slept in on Sundays. It could be hours before anyone came out of the brownstone. Or what if he wasn't home at all? He could've been out for the weekend, looking for another woman to assault. I hated that he was free to do whatever the fuck he wanted while I was trapped.

I dozed off for a little while. Didn't realize it until my head snapped upright. I needed to not sleep out here. What if Alexander came out, saw and recognized me? Or worse, didn't recognize me and treated me like a new victim?

The anxiety started to get the best of me, and I almost gave up. I would come back another day after staking him out more thoroughly. Maybe a weekday like when I'd seen him before, on his way to work.

Then, the front door to the brownstone opened. I sat up in my seat, adjusted my shades to make sure my face was covered well. I could barely recognize myself with my slicked back pony-tail and black lipstick.

The first person out the door was a little girl. She was cute. She had light brown skin and bright red hair. She wore a sun-dress and sandals and held a little bible in her hand. The kind they gave the kids in Sunday school.

Next was a beautiful black woman. The way she grabbed the little girl's hand I assumed she was her mother. The little girl's red hair made me think that Alexander was her father.

The little girl and the woman walked down the stairs and headed to a car parked in front of the brownstone. They had a garage, but the car was parked on the street. Maybe it was full of workout equipment or junk that they had put away never to think about again.

Finally, Alexander emerged from the brownstone. He was wearing a suit and had trimmed his beard down from the last time I saw him. The trimmed beard made him look more like how he did on the night he raped me. It was unmistakable that he was the man who'd hurt me.

Even though I knew I couldn't attack him in front of the woman and child, I wrapped my hands around my taser. That along with deep breaths made me feel calmer.

In Alexander's hands was also a bible. He was a damn rapist going to church on Sunday morning with his family. I won-dered if he'd repented for his sins.

Jesus might've forgiven him, but I never would.

I hadn't intended on following them, but now I had to. Church was a safe place for people, and he was a demon.

I waited a few moments after they pulled away from the curb, and I whipped my car around in a U-turn to follow them. I stayed just far enough behind them, that they probably wouldn't notice me. I was in a nondescript car anyway. A blue Honda Civic that I'd rented just for the purpose of stalking a rapist.

We weren't driving long. They pulled into the parking lot of New Mercies Worship Center. It was one of the newer suburban megachurches in the area. I didn't know anyone who went there, so it was probably full of Atlanta implants. I wondered if he was an implant, or if he just wanted to fade in amongst folk who wouldn't recognize him.

I wasn't dressed for church, so I couldn't go in. I'd be noticed and remembered in this all-black outfit. The prayer team would've probably swarmed me and taken my information down. I looked like I needed Jesus, salvation, and maybe even to have a few demons cast out.

Little did they know they had one of Satan's own sitting in their pews.

This knowledge, of where the demon came to worship, added to my cache on Alexander. Also, the fact that he seemed to have a wife and little girl. These facts didn't help me formulate a plan, but it made me feel more at ease.

Alexander might've done the unthinkable to me, but he had vulnerabilities too. It made him seem less threatening to my existence. Anyone who had a child and went to church on Sunday morning could be touched and be made to feel pain.

He should not have hurt me. Because now I was gathering a sufficient amount of tools to reciprocate.

Chapter 29

KIMBERLY

Kimberly and Ron had decided to bring a caterer from Atlanta to Jamaica to cater their wedding reception. Well, Kimberly had decided, and Ron hadn't objected, which was the same as agreeing in Kimberly's opinion. They were going to choose the caterer together, though, so after church on Sunday morning they were having brunch/lunch prepared by one of the potential caterers.

Chef Tam had a small café right in the heart of Atlanta. Kimberly had eaten there before, but Ron had not. He was going to be pleasantly surprised. In Kimberly's mind she was the top selection, but Ron had a frat brother he wanted to try out as well.

"Y'all looking good and blessed," Tam said as we walked into the cute and cozy café. "I hope y'all hungry too."

Ron patted his stomach. "My stomach is about to start eating my back. That's how hungry I am."

Tam laughed. "Well we better get you something good, chile. Sit on down, and let's get this party started."

Tam sashayed off to the kitchen, and I clapped my hands. I was ready for all these yummy vittles too.

"Did you look at the pictures of the flower girl dresses I sent you for Carly and Kayla? We should make a decision about that."

"Yes, they were nice. Was that African print?"

"Sure was. It'll go perfectly with our Afrocentric theme and all the customs."

"I thought so. Sabrina asked and I wasn't sure."

Kimberly slowly tilted her head to one side. When was Ron having conversations with Sabrina about their wedding? Seemed like after what Kimberly told him he shouldn't be speaking to Sabrina at all.

"When did you see her?"

"We met up in Charlotte a few days ago. I had to check on one of my properties. Plumbing issues. And she was visiting her mother with the kids. The girls wanted ice cream."

Kimberly created the scene in her mind. Ron, Sabrina and their two children looking like a happy interracial family at the ice cream shop?

"You didn't mention you saw her."

"I just did."

Also, this little meetup had happened right after Kimberly had shared the "violent Ron" scenario. Ron had gone to North Carolina that morning. How was he able to sit down with her and break bread after she'd just tried to ruin his relationship?

"I don't know how I feel about you seeing her without me being there. Especially since she tried to make me think I was about to be a domestic violence victim."

Ron sighed and stroked his goatee. "I know. I needed to talk to her about that though, because I thought we were in a good place. I didn't understand why she was bringing that up again."

"I don't trust her. If she would make up a story like that on you, what might she do now that you're going to marry someone else?"

"She didn't really lie. She just gave you her perception of the events. She really *was* afraid. I just know she didn't have a reason to be."

Kimberly narrowed her eyes with confusion. It sounded like Ron was defending Sabrina. Something didn't sit right about that.

"So, you don't have a problem with her telling me that?"

"Of course, I do. But she insists that she was just trying to give you information that she hadn't had when we got married. I don't like it, but I don't think she did it to hurt anyone."

"Why are you, all of a sudden, sympathetic toward her?"

"She told me about how she felt at the engagement party, and to be honest it was a little surreal for me too. It was part of the reason why I didn't want a wedding to begin with."

"Well, if you both are going to be uncomfortable, maybe we need to tell her to stay her ass at home and not come to Jamaica."

Ron nodded. "I thought about that, and I think you're right. But, if we want her to stay home, I think you're going to have to make her feel more comfortable."

"Bullshit. She knows I'm not going to do anything to your children."

"She suggested that the three of us go to family counseling prior to the wedding. I think it's a good idea. What do you think?"

Kimberly thought her head might literally explode. But how would it seem to Ron if she was against doing something that would put the mother of his children at ease? Certainly, he wanted to bring them to their home once they were married.

It was the matter of control that bothered Kimberly. It seemed that Sabrina wanted to establish a level of control in their marriage. Like she just couldn't get over the fact that Ron had moved on from her.

"She mentioned that when she came to my office to fake apologize."

"Fake apologize?"

"Yes. Now that I'm listening to you, I don't believe she was remorseful about her actions at all. I think she's a narcissist."

Ron's eyes widened in surprise, but he didn't say anything, because the server stood in front of them with serving trays of appetizers. There were miniature skewers with coconut shrimp, pineapple and ham chunks, little BLT biscuits with a tiny piece of fried green tomato, miniature lobster rolls, and cornbread cupcakes garnished with fried chicken nuggets and mashed potatoes. Kimberly's stomach growled as the aromas wafted to her nose.

Ron piled items onto his plate and took bites of everything. The chewing and little grunts of pleasure took the place of conversation for a moment. That was good, because they needed a timeout.

Ron took a deep breath and swallowed a huge swig of sweet tea. He patted his stomach.

"Am I supposed to try more food after this?" he asked.

"Yes. You should've paced yourself. We've got soup, salad, main course, and dessert left."

"Well, it's a good thing I packed my extra stomach."

"I didn't. I'm trying to lose a few pounds for the wedding."

"Why do you think you need to do that? You look beautiful to me."

Kimberly gave Ron a tiny smile. She loved when he validated her and made her feel beautiful in her own skin. But losing a few pounds for the wedding didn't have anything to do with him. She was even more determined since his ex-wife was trying to insert herself in their lives. Couldn't have her man comparing what he used to have to what he currently had.

"Thank you, baby," she said.

"There may be some truth to what you say about Sabrina, although I wouldn't go as far as calling her narcissistic. She's just self-centered."

"Selfish."

"Agree. Except she isn't that way when it comes to the girls. She thought the dresses were pretty."

"What were her exact words when you showed her the picture?"

Ron laughed. "She said, 'Oh how ethnic. Will there be drums too?' "

"Now see."

"That's not funny to you? I found it to be hilarious. She knows absolutely nothing about African culture. When she saw the print on the dresses her mind went to all she knows about Africa—drums."

"This is why I get bothered when brothers procreate with white women. She's raising two young black women."

"We're raising them."

"Yes, but women get a lot of their identity and ways from their mother. It's simple observation. She's going to raise two white women in black women's bodies, and it's going to be difficult for them to connect with other black women."

"They're lucky they have you now. Their stepmother will show them how to be strong black women."

"Right. Sabrina can't teach them to be strong, because strength is optional for white women. They can wait to be rescued when they're in trouble. Damsels in distress. A black woman has to get up and save her damn self."

"Baby, you're almost hyperventilating," Ron said. "Calm down. Your black knight in shining armor is here now."

He took both her hands and kissed them.

"Whenever you need rescuing, I got you."

Kimberly trembled and looked up at Ron. She knew he would do just that, because that was the kind of man he was. But Ron needed to understand that he was Kimberly's knight only, and not Sabrina's. She wasn't going to share her man or her life with Ron's ex-wife.

And by the time they got on that plane to go to Jamaica, Sabrina was going to know her place, and stay in it.

Chapter 30

HAHNA

Twila had suggested a green smoothie diet, to jumpstart my weight loss for the wedding, and my goofy self had listened to her. I took celery, kale, avocado, green apple slices, and cilantro out of my refrigerator and stared at them on the counter. I imagined how disgusting this was going to taste when I put it all in the blender.

"Where's the banana and or pineapple," Twila said as she walked into the kitchen and surveyed the ingredients for our liquid breakfast.

"Ooh, I knew I was forgetting something."

"Yeah, with all those vegetables, you need something sweet to balance it out."

I grabbed a banana from the pantry, but I'd forgotten to pick up a pineapple from the grocery store. The banana was going to have to be good enough.

"Tell me why we're doing this again," I said.

"So, we can be snatched in Jamaica."

"You're already snatched. Can I just be tucked in? I can tuck this little gut into a girdle."

Twila shook her head. "You are not gonna go out like that. Stop being lazy and a quitter. You don't even have much weight to lose. Ten pounds would do wonders for your figure."

I rolled my eyes and plugged in the blender. Twila started cutting the vegetables into little pieces.

"While you were at your uncle's funeral, I went on a date," Twila said.

"With DeAndre?" I asked. "He seems like a decent dude. Was he cool?"

"Yeah, we laughed a lot. He took me to Top Golf. I learned his whole dating history on the first date."

"How long were y'all out?"

"He's only seriously dated five people, so it didn't take a long time."

"Can you see yourself being number six?" I asked.

"Yes. He supported me being in therapy. I loved that."

"You told him you were in therapy? Did you tell him about the rape?"

Twila seemed too smart at me saying the word rape as if I'd pinched her. If it bothered her, I wouldn't say it again.

"I did, and it didn't bother him at all."

"Well, all right. He might be a keeper then."

Twila nodded. "I really like him. Even though the timing is bad."

"Did you give him some?"

"No, but I wasn't against it. He didn't make the move, so I didn't either."

"Even better."

Twila's face scrunched into a grimace. "How is that better? What if I wanted to get some?"

We both laughed at this. If she wanted to have sex, she would've asked, and then we'd be having a different conversation about how DeAndre had either put it down or hadn't put it down.

"Guess who I saw?" Twila asked.

"I have no idea who you saw out of all the people in Atlanta."

"Your boy, Corden."

"Oh, was he out with his fiancée?"

Twila shook her head. The grin on her face let me know she had some tea to spill, but I didn't know if I wanted to sip it.

"He was out with another girl?" I asked. "Oh, my goodness. I hope Corden isn't cheating on Symone. They have a little girl."

"He wasn't out with a girl."

"Okay, then what are you trying to tell me? He was out with a man?"

"Men. He was out with a whole group of men."

"So what?"

"They were all gay. He was with a crew of very flamboyant and boisterous queens."

"And so that means what? That he's gay? Y'all gone leave that man alone."

"I don't care if he's gay. You know good and damn well I'm an ally. I just wonder why if he's gay he doesn't just live his life. I don't like when gay men are with unsuspecting women."

"Well, that's his business."

People had been trying to tell me Corden was gay for years. I rejected the conversation every time, for the same reasons. I didn't care what Corden did with his penis as long as he gave me good business advice. Last time I checked, Corden was still good at his job, and was still advising me like the champ that he'd always been.

"You don't mind if one of your staff members is deceitful?" Twila asked. "'Cause this goes to his character."

"I don't know that he's being deceitful to anyone. You're assuming he's gay based on what you saw, and that was flimsy evidence."

"It was pretty substantial evidence, but okay. I can see you don't want to deal with this."

"Don't need to deal with it is more like it."

"Okay."

Twila took all of the smoothie ingredients and dumped them into the blender with crushed ice. Somehow, I didn't think this was going to satisfy my hunger, and I was sure it was going to taste like dirt.

Twila pressed a button on the blender to stop the whipping, grinding and chopping. I handed her two glasses and she poured the vomit colored smoothie into two glasses.

"Bon appetit," she said as she took a long swallow.

I waited to see how her face looked after drinking. She smiled.

"It's good. Try it."

I closed my eyes and swallowed a mouthful. Surprisingly, it wasn't as bad as I thought it would be. I could definitely taste the vegetables, but it the banana helped. Perhaps I could get through one whole day, but I was gonna need a piece of chicken soon.

"How's your Aunt Sherrie?" Twila asked.

"You already know that whole damn thing was a circus."

Twila laughed and shook her head. "Girl, your cousin was live streaming on Instagram and Facebook the whole time. I can't believe the mistress showed up at the damn funeral."

"I know. Me and Sam kicked her out. Or, I should say, we nicely escorted her ass out. She was sitting in the back of the church crying and wailing."

"Oh, so he really showed up with the boyfriend activities, huh? Go head, Sam."

"Yeah. He said after he met my broke and raggedy ass family, he finally understands why I am the way I am."

"What? Bougie for no reason?"

"I am not that."

"You are, but it's not a judgment. I am too," Twila said with a laugh.

"We really connected, though. I asked him to move in so that he can rent out his place."

"Oh, snap. Y'all moving up to the shacking up level."

"Don't say it like that. We have decided to cohabitate."

Twila shrugged. "No matter how pretty you say it, it means the same thing. Two unmarried people living together equals shacking."

"Damn, Twila. You're just being a real joy snatcher, aren't you?"

"I'm happy for you. Does Sam moving in mean you want me to pack my shit and get out?"

"Not necessarily, but how is the therapy going?"

"I know who the guy is. Followed him and his family to church."

"The rapist? What? How?"

"Traci gave me his info. He owns the brownstone in my subdivision. Has a wife and a daughter, I think. The little girl had his red hair."

"Why did you follow him?"

"Shit, I don't know. I was sitting there in the car watching his place and it just seemed the right thing to do."

"And now what?"

"I think I may have to move. I can't live there if he's going to live there. I can't see his ass on my morning jog. I can't watch him walking his damn dog or playing with his kid in the park. It's too much."

"I don't see why you can't just press charges. The statute of limitations on rape is fifteen years in Georgia."

"Come on, Hahna. Let's walk that all the way out shall we? I was in a swingers' room at a club, where pretty much everyone was engaged in sex acts. Even if he admits to having sex with me, he will say it was consensual."

"I mean you haven't given me details about the event. I just don't see why he should get away with it."

"He tased me. He used a condom. There was no proof of what happened to me, even then. It's been two years. There's definitely no proof now."

"Doesn't Traci have cameras all over that club?"

"Yes, but all that shows is that he and I both went into the room. There are no cameras inside."

"Seems like they want people to get raped, then."

"No. They do a background check on their people," Twila explained. "Plenty of perfectly normal folks get rejected. He slipped through the cracks."

"So, he gets to have control over your life? You have to move to another house because of a rapist?"

"Hahna, I know. It pisses me off too. I just haven't decided how to handle it without having my business in the entertainment blogs and destroying our line sisters' nightclub. You don't think this would be bad press for them?"

"Who cares about that?"

"I do. I can't ruin Traci's club in dealing with this. Just let me . . . let me figure it out on my own. And don't say anything to Kimberly."

"You still haven't told her? She knows something is going on with you."

"I know. I'm gonna tell her. I didn't want to weigh her down while she's planning a whole life with Big Ron. She's got enough on her plate."

"She would want to know this."

"I know it."

"So, tell her. Maybe not all of it. But some, so she can stop worrying about you."

"You're right. I will."

Kimberly might be able to stop worrying with whatever little snippet Twila was going to share, but that wasn't going to help me. I was full blown terrified about what was happening to my sister—mentally and emotionally. I hoped that DeAndre was someone who would lift her up and not drag her down even farther.

I hoped he was perfect.

Chapter 31

TWILA

I looked at the time on my phone and up at the restaurant door. I'd abandoned the green smoothie diet already and sat in my favorite sushi restaurant ready to fill my belly with smoked salmon and shrimp tempura. I'd also called DeAndre and asked him to join me. He'd said he had a client but would try to reschedule.

I was about to pour a second glass of wine from the bottle I ordered when he walked through the door, still wearing his suit and tie for work. The sense of urgency on his face made me smile. I'd called and he *had* to get here for me.

He sat at the table in front of me. Something was different about his face. What was it?

"You're wearing glasses," I said.

He reached up and touched them. "I forgot to take them off. They're my computer glasses. I wear them to keep from tiring my eyes out from reading documents on the screen all day."

"They look good on you. You look like a chocolate Clark Kent."

"Not Clark Kent. Superman was getting all the hoes and poor Clark wasn't getting no play."

"Except they were the same person. So . . ."

"Sometimes a dude wants the girl to like the regular side of him. You know?"

"You mean, you'd rather have me drool over the computer glasses than how much you can bench press?"

"Exactly. But on the real, I'll take either. Drooling is good either way."

"You got plenty women drooling over you, DeAndre. Stop acting like you don't."

"None like you, Ms. Twila. None like you."

I bit my bottom lip to keep it from quivering. "Do you like sushi? What's your favorite?"

"We talking about the menu now? Conversation getting too hot?" DeAndre asked with a smile.

"Maybe. Yeah. So, tell me what kind of sushi you like."

"Mostly anything with salmon will do it for me. You want to order for both of us?"

I smiled. "Yes. This place is my favorite. Their sushi is incredible."

I plucked the little sushi order form and pencil out of its cradle on the table. I placed little x's next to all of the rolls I wanted us to try. There was way too much food on the order for us to finish here, but maybe we could finish it later.

"You made this sushi dinner sound like an emergency," DeAndre said. "Is everything okay? Or did you just want to see me?"

"It is an emergency. I woke up this morning thinking about you. About our date. I think I even dreamed about you, but I couldn't remember once the brain fog cleared."

"Humph. That does sound like an emergency. I looked for you at the gym and was kinda disappointed that you weren't there."

"I had a seven o'clock appointment this morning. Actor with an early flight. Her veneers had loosened on the bottom."

DeAndre poured himself a glass of wine and took a sip of it.

"That's good," he said.

"I know. I was on my way to killing the whole thing if you hadn't showed up."

"There's no way I wouldn't show up. I feel so lucky that I met you. I was tripping this morning thinking I said or did something to mess it up. I was kicking myself for telling you about all my failed relationships."

I marveled about how someone as fine as DeAndre could feel insecure about messing up a first date. I mean I got it that good men *and* women were far and few between, but he had nothing to worry about. Not with me.

"No, that was great. It felt like you really wanted me to know you."

"I did. I want to know you too, but I can tell that you don't want to move too quickly."

"Moving quickly doesn't bother me like it used to. Sometimes you just know. It's not like we're in our twenties."

"Word."

I held the sushi order form up for our server to see that I'd made our selections. She came over, took the paper from me and gave a little bow before she backed away from the table.

"Their ramen is good too, if you'd like some," I said.

"I'd only eat ramen for lunch, not dinner. The liquid and noodles leave me a little bloated afterwards. I especially wouldn't eat that on a date."

"Not if you wanted to get some action later?"

DeAndre laughed. "Exactly right. Always have to leave my options open for that."

"I have a funny story about that."

"Please tell."

"So, I was on a date with this guy. He was so hot, and we had made out a couple of times. I was ready to take it to the next level."

"I like this story already," DeAndre said.

"Well, we went out and I had an ice cream sundae. I was young and at the time I had no idea that my body had decided to become lactose intolerant."

"Oh shit."

"Exactly. We got back to his place, and he started kissing on me and I was getting into it. Kissing him back."

"You're building the dread here. All I can think about is that ice cream you ate."

"Right. My stomach started bubbling like crazy."

"Please tell me you made it to the bathroom."

"I did, but barely. When I tell you, my ass exploded on this man's toilet."

DeAndre burst into laughter. "Oh my god. Was it loud?"

"Sounded like a machine gun."

DeAndre had tears in his eyes from laughing so hard. "W-what did you do when you came back out?"

"Wait! First, I didn't want to leave his whole situation splashed and splattered, so I was looking all over the bathroom for cleaning supplies."

"He ain't have none."

"I mean not a one! Then I panicked and started wondering if the toilet had ever been cleaned and what had I sat my ass down on in the first place."

"At this point, nobody's getting none."

"Hell naw. That explosion required me to sit in a bathtub or hot shower for an hour before I'd feel comfortable."

"So, what did you do? Did you come out of the bathroom?"

"Not for a long, long time. I kept flushing trying to get rid of some of the splatters."

DeAndre howled so loudly that other patrons started looking at us. I giggled at how tickled he was.

"I was legit contemplating my life choices in there," I continued. "Then, he knocked on the door."

"W-what did you say?"

Now, I was laughing as hard as he was. I couldn't help it.

"I was like, w-who is it?"

We deteriorated into uncontrollable and loud laughter. We both had tears pouring down our faces. DeAndre took his glasses off and set them on the table, so he could wipe his face with the cloth napkin.

"He just stood outside the door for a few minutes, and I didn't say anything else," I continued. "After a while I heard him in another room on his telephone. He sounded like he was talking to another girl."

"I guess he just decided that yo ass wasn't shit. Or was shit?" DeAndre laughed some more.

"Listen. I opened that door so quietly, grabbed my purse, and snuck out of his apartment."

"How did you get home."

"I. Walked."

DeAndre tried to calm himself down by drinking more wine. His laughter quieted to a chuckle or two between breaths.

"He never called me again. I didn't call him either," I said. "He was fine too. Oh well, it was ruined."

"Twila, I'm not sure that was an appropriate dinner story, but I needed that laugh."

"I am never appropriate. And I do mean never. I think that might be one of my tragic flaws."

"One of them?"

"Yeah. The other one is I'm always finding broken things and turning them into a project. Friends, men . . ."

"Teeth. You fix people's mouths."

"Exactly."

"I think our biggest flaws are only flaws when they're taken out of context."

"The last dude I dated was broken, and I'll tell you what, it was definitely the wrong context. My friends had to come move him out of my house when he decided he was going to lay up with a chick in my bedroom."

"He couldn't even take the girl to his own crib?"

"Man, what crib?"

"Oh, yeah he was broken broken."

"Mmm hmmm."

"I already told you my biggest flaw. My serial monogamy. It's only a flaw with the wrong person. That's why I still believe in falling in love."

I smiled at him. "I want to believe in it. My two best friends seem to have found it."

"You will too."

"You're sure about that?"

"You're too perfect not to."

"Thank you."

I rested back in my chair and gazed at this man. I knew he wasn't a mirage because other people could see and hear him too, but he damn near seemed like one. The pieces had never fallen together for me this way, and it scared me.

DeAndre slid his glasses back onto his face. Superman became Clark Kent again. He was still fine. I wanted to sex them both.

We both felt the pheromone rush or chemistry or whatever because we'd taken the sushi to go. DeAndre offered to drive and bring me to pick up my car later, but I told him I was fine to follow him back to his place. I really needed to make a phone call first.

I called Hahna first. She answered on the first ring.

"Twila? You had me worried. You coming home tonight?"

"Maybe. Hold on. Let me get Kimberly on the line too."

Kimberly took a few rings to answer. I hoped she wasn't laid up with Ron. Who was I kidding, she probably was.

"This better be good heffa," Kimberly said as she answered the phone. She sounded out of breath.

"It is. Take a water break and tell Ron you be right back with your nasty self."

"Girl!"

"Hold on. Let me click Hahna on."

"Both of y'all there?" I asked.

"Yes, I'm here," Hahna said.

Kimberly sucked her teeth. "Hurry up."

I laughed. "Okay, girl. I'm gone let you get back to that python you over there wrangling, 'cause I think I'm bout to wrangle one of my own."

"Who? DeAndre?" Hahna asked.

"Yep."

"Ooh, that fine ass lawyer that works in Hahna's building? I didn't know you were seeing him."

"That's 'cause you been missing in action. Picking out flowers and shit," I said. "He's incredible y'all, and I need some."

"Do you have condoms?" Hahna asked.

"Yeah, I picked up some on the way to the restaurant."

"A prepared ho. I love it," Kimberly said.

"Anyway. Neither one of y'all gonna try to talk me out of it?" There was silence on the line.

"Hello?" I called.

"Do you want to be talked out of it?" Hahna asked. "Because I wouldn't. His abdominals are crazy."

"Girl, I can't wait to lick them."

"I mean, I can't really, in good conscience tell you not to get yours," Kimberly said. "Not when I'm over here sweating out this good silk press."

"Well, I just wanted y'all to know where I am. Hahna did a background check on him, so I'm not worried."

"Yeah. Have fun. If you want to be talked out of it, we can get Samantha on the line."

I laughed. "I think I have a bad connection. Must be bad reception over here . . ."

I disconnected the call and kept laughing. It seemed like it was taking forever to get to Duluth, so I turned on music. Then, my phone buzzed. It was DeAndre. I put him on the Bluetooth speaker.

"Hey, I just wanted to hear your voice some more," he said.

"I thought I just talked your ear off."

"You didn't. Your voice is sexy. Your laugh is too."

I responded to that with a laugh. "I don't know if anyone has ever said that to me. My laugh is super loud."

"It's sexy, because you sound like you're really having fun. It's a *I don't give a fuck* laugh."

"I can see that."

"We'll be at my house in a couple minutes, and I want you to know a few things."

Something about how he said this raised alarm.

"What?" I asked.

"I have a full bathroom downstairs and upstairs. Both have full cleaning supplies under the sink. There's also towels and body wash if you should have an unfortunate occurrence. I don't care if your ass explodes. I still want you."

I hollered. "My ass is just fine, thank you."

"Also, I don't want you to feel like it's a foregone conclusion that we're going to have sex. If you change your mind at any time, I'm fine with waiting. Just let me know you're not feeling it, and we can stop."

"You trying to talk me out of it?"

"Not at all. You're worth it, tonight or the next night."

And that was the sexiest thing he could say to me. Again, he was perfect without even trying. I wished I could've met him earlier in life. The flawed version of him. Because he hadn't started out perfect. A man who knew exactly what to say and do had made his share of mistakes. But so had I.

One thing he clearly had done right was purchase real estate. I gasped with appreciation at the mini mansion we pulled up to. He opened his three-car garage and parked his car. There was a spot available for me, and another spot that held a Lamborghini. I knew he was a lawyer and that he did well, but Atlanta had so many smoke and mirrors folk, it was hard to know who really had a buck and who didn't.

DeAndre had the house, the cars and the private practice complete with clients. He was much more than smoke and mirrors.

"Dammit, I bet he has a little penis," I said to the inside of my car.

That had to be it. A man with all of this, and who loved love, and who looked the way DeAndre looked would be locked down by somebody. He wouldn't have made it to his forties without being married and without a woman popping out his pretty little chocolate babies.

Well, if nothing else, this would be a good story to tell on a girl's night over wine and popcorn.

DeAndre closed the garage doors, and I took my spend the night bag out of the trunk while he grabbed the sushi. He looked at the bag and laughed.

"Oh, you're prepared, huh?"

"Not prepared as much as hopeful."

"You didn't have to be hopeful. All you had to do was say the word."

DeAndre pulled me close to him with his free arm. He bent down as I stood on my tiptoes. His lips were warm and soft, and his breath still tasted like wine. His kiss was intoxicating and the swell that I felt in his pants wasn't small. It felt just right. I wanted to stroke it to make sure, but I restrained myself. Hungrily kissed him back instead. His groan told me he was as famished as I was.

He held my hand as he led me inside. The first thing I noticed was that it smelled clean. Like essential oils and cleaning supplies. I felt myself relax. Had I found a man obsessed with a clean house like I was? Oh, my goodness. I could've proposed to him that night.

He turned on a light and the house was immaculate. I shuddered.

"Your house is so . . . so clean," I said. "Let me touch you. You can't be real."

DeAndre laughed. "I like things neat, but I'm not this good. The housekeeper was here today."

"Even better."

I pulled his face to mine and kissed him again. I had to keep the physical connection before he floated away like the mirage that he had to be.

He set the bag on a table, so that he could pull me closer with both his hands. He gripped my waist in a way that felt gentle yet assertive at the same time. I wanted to feel his fingers on my skin, and not through fabric. Suddenly, I felt impatient for the full meal and this felt like an appetizer.

"May I use your bathroom?"

"Yes, it's right down that hall. First door on the right."

I took care of my business in the bathroom including freshening up and changing my panties. I swapped out the regular all-day long bikini briefs for a red thong that matched the red bra I was wearing.

I left the bag in the bathroom and walked back into the dining room where DeAndre had dinner on plates. One place setting was at the head of the table and the other at the seat to right of it. He'd even taken out chopsticks.

"Hungry? I popped a piece in my mouth while I was setting up," DeAndre said. "It's so good."

"I am starving."

I sat down at the place he'd set for me, and he sat too. We ate in silence.

"Why does it always get awkward when you know at some point in the evening, you're going to have sex for the first time?" I asked. "We were about to get kicked out of the restaurant for laughing, but now we're silent."

"I think because you get turned on, and you start fantasizing about how good it's going to be, and then you let your mind create a bunch of scenarios of what could go wrong."

"That is exactly right."

"So, stop thinking about it and enjoy the sushi and the wine."

I took in a deep breath and let it out. "You're right. I know I mentioned this already, but I love when a man has a clean house. I can't tell you how many times a guy invited me back to his crib and it looked like a tornado went through the place."

"I wonder why they weren't embarrassed. My mother used to tell me and my sister the same thing. Nobody wants to be with someone with a nasty house."

"You have a sister. Is she older or younger?"

"She's two years older. Always bossed me around, especially after our mother died."

I didn't ask about his father in case that was a bad memory. Didn't want to spoil the mood.

"You have any siblings?" DeAndre asked. "Family?"

"Only child. Mom and Dad live in Birmingham. But I definitely get my cleaning frenzies from my mom."

DeAndre smiled and leaned toward me. "Come closer," he said. "Bring your face to mine."

When I did, DeAndre kissed me again. I leaned back up and sipped my wine.

"You had enough to eat? You wanna watch a movie?" DeAndre asked.

"Oh, a little Netflix and chill," I asked.

"Better than that."

DeAndre grabbed the wine bottle and both our glasses. I followed him down the same hallway where the bathroom was. At the end there were a set of double doors.

He opened the doors to a theater room with a huge screen and several big cushy looking chairs.

"A theater? Oh, you're taking let's stay inside to another level."

"Absolutely."

DeAndre led me to the middle row of seats. "There's clean blankets in the little cube right there," he said.

I sat down and immediately the seat started to recline. DeAndre laughed.

"You must be sitting on the remote," he said.

I reached around beneath me and I was indeed sitting on the remote. For a second, I thought the chair had gone into autopilot. Get that ass mode.

"I'd like to get out of this suit and tie. Can you give me a few minutes?" DeAndre asked.

"Take more than a few. I'm patient."

DeAndre leaned down and put a soft kiss on my lips. "I'm not."

I rested my eyes for a for what felt like a few minutes, but it must've been more than that because DeAndre was back and wearing a t-shirt and gray sweats. Perfect. Easy access.

"What movie would you like to watch?" DeAndre asked.

"What's your favorite?"

"I'm sure you don't want to watch my favorite. It's an old karate movie with subtitles."

"Ew."

"What about *Love and Basketball?*"

"Now you're talking."

A movie that I could probably recite by heart, which was fine, because I didn't too much plan on watching it. DeAndre pressed through several menus with his remote until he had the movie playing on the screen. Then, he came and sat down next to me.

DeAndre pushed up the armrest that was between us, turning the two recliners into a love seat. I scooted in closer to him. He smelled good, like expensive cologne and wine.

I was never self-conscious about wearing hair weave, but I was glad that I was wearing my natural hair, because DeAndre started rubbing at my temples and kept going until he was giving me a full scalp massage. It felt so good and relaxing.

"You're going to put me to sleep doing that," I said. "It feels good."

"I don't want you sleeping though."

He positioned my body so that I was lying across the recliner. He knelt on the floor in front of me. I couldn't see the movie that way, but I didn't care.

He cradled the back of my head in one of his hands and kissed me deeply. His full lips totally enveloped mine. Who needed oxygen?

His other hand rested under my blouse. He reached inside my bra and freed both my breasts. Stroked the nipples and had them stand at attention. I felt warmth and moisture that soaked through the thong.

When DeAndre unbuttoned my blouse and lowered his soft lips down to my right nipple, I arched my back with pleasure. It had been too long since I'd been touched like this. I reached up to hold his face, and DeAndre took my bottom lip in mouth as he slid his hand under my skirt and between my thighs. When he removed his hand, his fingers were moist. He sucked his fingers and kissed me again. I could taste myself on his lips, mixed with red wine.

Next, he eased my panties down and savored me like I was a

delicacy. His tongue caressed and stroked every inch and fold of me. I wanted to cry from how good it felt. My whole body throbbed with pleasure as I neared orgasm. DeAndre seemed to know I was at the edge, because he eased up and stopped stroking.

He brought his lips back to my lips and nipples, but my breasts were so sensitive that I nearly climaxed from that touch. When the throbbing subsided, DeAndre went back to tasting, licking, and stroking. He brought me to the edge again and rested again.

My breathing was ragged, and I felt frustrated. I wanted that orgasm more than anything. My eyes were wet. It felt so good that he brought tears to my eyes.

"You ready now?" DeAndre whispered.

I couldn't formulate words, so I simply nodded.

This time, with the licking and stroking, DeAndre plunged two fingers inside my opening. He pressed his thumb on my anal opening and stroked there too. I thought I would explode from how amazing it felt.

When I started throbbing this time, DeAndre didn't stop. When my hips rose and fell to meet his thrusting fingers he didn't stop. When my body trembled and shook, he kept licking, sucking, thrusting and rubbing. He kept going until my hips stopped rising and falling and my body went limp.

"Did you come?" he asked.

I chuckled as he kissed me. I had never had an orgasm like that. Not even the kind I'd self-inflicted with my best battery-operated toys.

"That was amazing," I whispered.

"We're just getting started."

DeAndre lifted my legs and sat on the recliner under them. He pulled his sweatpants down some and unleashed his member. My goodness, I was wrong, wrong, wrong, about the size.

I had to lean to look at it up close. It was perfect. The right length and width. It was rigid and the skin was taut enough to show the veins. I wrapped one hand around it and slid my warm mouth over the head. It throbbed under my touch.

DeAndre tapped me and pulled me up. He put on a condom and lifted me into his lap.

"Is it okay if I penetrate you now?"

"Please do."

DeAndre held me like I weighed nothing and positioned my body so that he could slide into my still warm and moist opening. The fit was snug, but every one of my nerve endings celebrated.

Each one of his hands cupped my butt cheeks as he lifted me up and down. Slowly at first, and then gaining speed. I arched my back and helped him lift me by using my legs and knees for leverage. He moaned with pleasure until we both climaxed together.

I climbed off DeAndre and collapsed to the other side of the love seat. Both of us were spent.

"That was just . . . perfect," I said.

"It was. That was round one, though," DeAndre said. "It has been awhile for me, or I would have made you climax another way. I don't think I would've lasted long enough inside of you."

I laughed. "You know you're too honest, DeAndre. Most men would've kept that to themselves."

"No shame here. There's plenty more where that came from. I'm going to make you orgasm every way I know how, and then I hope to learn some new ways."

This man was like every nineties R&B song lyric I'd ever sang and every romance novel I'd ever read. And he was ready for a relationship. That's all he wanted. The only one who could mess this up was me.

I had to get well, and soon, because I didn't want to miss this opportunity to have the kind of love folks sing and read about.

But in order to move on, I needed to finish my unfinished business with Alexander Adams.

Chapter 32

HAHNA

I looked at my calendar and frowned. Usually this level of irritation came from being overbooked with back to back meetings, but it was the opposite. How, on a Tuesday, could I not have any client meetings scheduled? This Christmas networking event was important, and I needed Corden's help to pull it off.

I texted Corden, summoning him, and he was at my office door in less than a minute. He was always at the ready.

Corden plopped down in the chair in front of my desk, unwrapped a chocolate kiss from my candy dish, and popped it in his mouth.

"What is this bright idea, boss?" He asked between chews.

"Sam recommended that we have a bomb ass networking Christmas party. Where we kind of reintroduce ourselves to Atlanta."

"Wait a minute. Sam wants to spend money?"

I laughed and threw a balled-up piece of paper at Corden. "Yes, he does. Or he thinks we should. I agree it's an investment."

Corden nodded slowly and narrowed his eyes as if he were envisioning the party in his mind.

"I can see this. If we do it, this party has to be glam. No cutting corners. We can't let everyone think we're struggling. You know how black people are."

"That's what Sam said. I also think we need to diversify more. Invite some businesses that we haven't thought about reaching out to before."

"Yes, and with the invitation to the party there should be a proposal on our services with examples and testimonials."

"How many new engagements do you think we could manage? The two of us, I mean."

"We can worry about that when it's actually an issue," Corden said. "Because we've been in the trenches before. This ain't new."

"Yeah, but not while planning one of my best friend's wedding and moving a boyfriend into my house."

Corden looked shocked. "Tell me more."

"Not much to tell. I think it's just a natural progression. Sam's always staying over, and you know how I am about making money. He should be renting out his loft."

"His tiny house?" Corden laughed at his own joke, but I just shook my head.

"It's not that small."

"Naw, naw. You said it was like one of those tiny houses on TV. You said this negro had a wine cabinet built in the floorboards."

"He does! I actually like that feature."

"What you gonna do about your houseguest though?"

"Twila? I don't know. She doesn't seem ready to leave yet, and it'll feel crowded I think if she stays after Sam moves in."

"It'll be a ghetto ass *Three's Company.*"

"How? When there's not an ounce of ghetto between us."

"Excuse me. I forgot I was talking about the glorious ladies of Gamma Phi Gamma."

"Exactly."

I did the Gamma Phi Gamma hand gesture and call, drawing more laughter from Corden.

"Speaking of my houseguest, Twila told me she ran into you at Top Golf."

"She did? Maybe she saw me there, but she didn't speak."

"She didn't mention that she hadn't spoken to you, but she did say who you were with."

Corden sat back in his seat and folder his arms across his chest. "Mmm hmmm . . ."

"What?"

"I'm waiting for the rest of it. What you clearly want to ask me, because you started this conversation."

I wished I hadn't brought it up. I'd let Twila get to me talking about Corden being closeted said something about his character. Well, what did asking him about it say about my character? That I'm nosy? I didn't want him to think I was nosy.

"There's nothing else. She just mentioned that she'd seen you."

"Since I know exactly who I was with at Top Golf, I can imagine how the story went when she told you she saw me."

"You know what, never mind. Let's talk about this networking party we're going to plan."

"Ask the question, Hahna."

"Okay, okay. She said you were with a bunch of gay dudes, and she thought maybe you're gay."

Corden smiled, but it was a creepy smile that I couldn't read. He seemed to be taking pleasure in me being uncomfortable. He was the one with secrets. He should be uncomfortable, not me.

"I'm not gay."

"See, I knew you weren't gay. I'm sorry I even asked you this. It's not like it was my business anyway . . ."

"I'm bisexual."

I blinked rapidly, trying to make my brain comprehend what Corden had said. His arms were still crossed against his chest and he was still smiling.

"Symone is going to be devastated if she finds out."

"She knows."

"She knows?"

"Yes, I don't hide these details from people I'm having sex with."

My head was swimming. I couldn't believe that Corden's sweet little fiancée with the cute shape and the pretty face would accept a man who slept with men and women.

"And she's okay with it? She isn't concerned with catching something?"

"She's not going to catch anything, because I'm monogamous. Just because I'm attracted to men doesn't mean I'm sleeping with men. I'm only with her. Y'all single women with straight black men are probably more in danger of catching something than Symone is."

As soon as the question was out of my mouth, I wished I could gobble it back up. My question assumed that Corden was engaging in unsafe sex practices. I had to check myself for a second. I guess I did kind of equate bisexuality with promiscuity. The two weren't mutually exclusive.

"I'm sorry, Corden. My question was out of pocket."

He shook his head and sighed. "I guess I just thought you knew, and that you never said anything because you supported me."

"I do support you."

"As soon as you knew, you started judging. You did your church thing. Even though you're fornicating and talking about moving your man in your house, because I'm bisexual you made me a liar and a cheater in the same breath."

He wasn't lying either. I had done exactly that. And it was crazy too, the church thing. I was living outside of plenty of the tenets of my faith and I always prayed for forgiveness. My expectation was that God would forgive me where I fell short. I hadn't extended that grace to Corden, and I'd accused him of more than he'd even done.

My eyes filled with tears that I didn't want to fall, because for some reason I thought Corden wouldn't give a damn about them.

"It was momentary, and it was dead ass wrong. I'm so sorry. Will you accept my apology?"

"Yes, but only because I know you care about me as a person. The issue you and most black women have is deeper than one apology though."

"What do you mean?"

"How far do I want to go with this?" Corden posed the question to himself. "I guess I'm gonna go all the way there for a minute, because you've caught me at a real moment, and I have time."

"Okay . . ."

"The reason why a lot of y'all are single is because you're looking for a specific brand of masculinity."

"What?"

"I love women and I treat Symone like the queen that she is. I can't help that I'm also attracted to men, just like while you're out with Sam you might see another dude that looks good to you."

"It's different though, Corden."

"How is it different?"

"Because personally, I would feel like a man who likes men could never be satisfied with me. There would always be something missing."

"That is such a false premise. I bet right now if I asked Sam what he thought about Serena Williams's ass he would drool like ninety percent of the brothers I know."

"And?"

"Your miniature ass does not compare."

"I beg your pardon. I got cake."

"Ummmm . . . you got a cupcake."

"You're a damn hater."

Corden laughed. "I'm not. I'm just saying that satisfaction is more than attraction. I'm satisfied with Symone. Will love her for the rest of my life if she lets me."

"Then why would you be hanging out with a group of gay men? That would be like Sam going out with a bunch of big booty women."

"No. Those guys were my friends. I'd never slept with any of them. And I'm not attracted to any of them. They were celebrating an engagement."

"Symone wasn't invited?"

"She didn't want to come. She, unlike you and Twila, does not think that I'm going to fall into bed with a man because I go to Top Golf with him."

"I don't think that."

"But you couldn't date a bisexual man."

"I don't think I could. No."

"And that's why most of them are closeted. You've probably been with one before, especially in Atlanta."

"Bullshit."

"I heard your boy Torian . . ."

I covered my ears and hummed loudly. This was not information I wanted to consume. Ever. Whatever little secret he had about Torian, he could keep it.

Corden shook his head and smiled. I saw his lips stop moving, so I uncovered my ears and crossed my arms under my boobs like a hug.

"Let me know if you want me to do any research on Sam. The streets know everything."

"You can kick rocks until your toes bleed Corden. Keep your intel to yourself."

"How can you say what you'd never do, and you don't even want to know the facts?"

I looked at the door to my office and nodded my head in that direction. Corden burst into laughter.

"You kicking me out your office? I thought we had a Christmas party to plan."

"Out."

Corden got out of his seat and started shuffle dancing to the door. He hummed *Deck the Halls*.

"Corden . . ."

He threw his head back and belted, "Don we now our GAY apparel."

"Get. Out."

Still laughing, Corden closed my office door as he left. I could hear him still singing in the hallway. Maybe having this conversation with me had removed a weight he was carrying. Looks like I was the only one he was close to that had no clue.

And that was wrong. I did have a clue. I *knew.* Just like everybody else, I could feel that Corden was different in some ways. He felt more like one of my sister friends than my brother.

I wondered if Symone was really happy. Corden said he was monogamous, but he was still a man. Men were monogamous until they fell into an entanglement with someone else.

What would Symone do if Corden cheated on her with a man? Would it be the same as if it were a woman?

Luckily, I didn't have to lose a second of sleep over that situation. I just tucked the information into the back of my mind in case Symone needed my help in the future. Knowing that Corden was attracted to men had nothing to do with the magic he worked for The Data Whisperers.

But now did I have to give him side eye and make sure he wasn't looking at *my* man?

Chapter 33

KIMBERLY

Kimberly looked at the text in her cell phone from Samantha as she waited for Hahna and Twila at the soul food restaurant they'd loved in college.

I can't participate in the wedding. Sorry. I still love you though, sister.

Kimberly had hoped that Samantha's anger would've dissipated after time had passed, and she'd had time to reflect on her words. Kimberly certainly wasn't angry anymore, although she'd been more shocked by Samantha's words than angry.

Now though, Samantha had officially dropped out of the wedding, and Kimberly didn't know what to do. They were line sisters. They'd all pledged to stand up for each other at weddings, funerals, and the birth of children.

Had all of that changed now? Had they drifted so far apart after college that their sisterhood was forever damaged? Maybe line sister didn't have to mean friend when the sisters were in their forties.

Twila showed up first. Kimberly noticed that she looked to be in better spirits than she had in recent weeks. Kimberly stood up to hug her, even though there wasn't much room in the aisles of the tightly packed restaurant.

"I need some smothered chicken today," Twila said. "Sweet tea, and macaroni and cheese."

"I thought you were eating clean this week."

"Man, me and Hahna had those green smoothies for like two days before we gave up on that. I need some real food."

"I don't know why y'all doing all that anyway," Kimberly said. "Y'all already look perfect."

"We all look good, but I definitely am not perfect," Twila said. "I want my body to look like somebody photoshopped me in every photo."

Kimberly laughed out loud. "I'm in no danger of that happening to me."

"Kim, you can get here, you just don't want it bad enough."

"You're right, I don't."

"Well, you're beautiful either way. I know that gets on your nerves when we say it, but I mean it. You're one of the most gorgeous women I know."

"Okay, now you're laying it on thick. What's going on with you?" Kimberly asked. "Your therapist prescribe you some good meds?"

Twila shook her head. "Nope. I'm just feeling a little better about things. Have you ever heard of cognitive behavior therapy?"

"No, what is that?"

"It's what my therapist has me doing. Reliving the trauma that happened to me over and over again until it doesn't impact me anymore."

"What the hell happened to you that you have to do that?" Kimberly asked, hoping that this time Twila would tell her the truth.

"I was raped."

"What? Oh, my goodness when?" Kimberly took Twila's hand and squeezed.

"Two years ago. At Club Phenom."

"That's why you started taking the self-defense classes? The weapons?"

Twila nodded. "Yeah, I needed to feel safe."

"What made you start therapy now, though? Why not right after it happened?"

Twila gave Kimberly a half smile. "See, this is why I took so long to tell you. You get all down in the nitty gritty of the details."

"Well, girl, you know I need the whole scoop."

"He lives in my subdivision. I saw him one day when I was running, and I almost went into a full-blown depression. It's why I moved in with Hahna."

"Shit. What are we going to do?"

"For now, nothing. I have the guy's identity, and I'm working through it."

"We need a plan, though."

"We don't. You're planning a wedding, Hahna's planning a comeback. We don't need a plan for this."

Kimberly picked up the menu on the table and flipped it over twice. She didn't even need a menu, because she knew this one by heart. It wasn't in her character to not get to work resolving a problem.

Hahna rushed into the restaurant with her curls flying and cheeks flushed. She looked like she'd been crying.

"What's wrong?" Kimberly said instead of extending a greeting.

"Nothing is wrong with me. Well, maybe everything is wrong," Hahna said. She hugged Kimberly and Twila and plopped down.

"Speak on it," Twila said, "so Kimberly can stop trying to fix my life."

"I'm not," Kimberly said.

"Yes, you are. I can see your brain cells formulating a solution."

"Okay, you're right."

"I know I'm right," Twila said. "So, fix Hahna."

"I don't need fixing," Hahna said. "I said something stupid and hurt a friend. It's fine, though, I've apologized."

Kimberly and Twila stared at Hahna, waiting for her to elaborate. Hahna stared right back.

"I'm not telling y'all what happened. We're here to talk about the wedding," Hahna said.

She reached into her bag and pulled out her tablet and pressed the screen a few times.

"This is the color and fabric of dress we decided upon. The designer is Vashena, and we can buy online or go into boutiques to order," Hahna explained as she passed the tablet to Kimberly.

"How much are the dresses?" Kimberly asked.

"They start around three fifty," Twila said. "Some of the variations top out at around six hundred."

"Six hundred for a bridesmaid dress?" Kimberly said. "That is a lot."

"It's reasonable. Prom dresses are more than this," Hahna said. "We do realize that Debbie and Samantha might need help paying for theirs. We're willing to help."

"Here's the thing with Samantha though," Twila said. "It's not that she can't make a way to spend the money, she just doesn't want to. She's not broke. Debbie has kids and deadbeat daddies. What the hell is Samantha spending her money on?"

"Definitely not clothes, shoes, or her car?" Hahna said. "Her retirement account must be on swole."

Kimberly sat quietly waiting for Hahna and Twila to run out of steam with their insults on Samantha. Kimberly was still upset about Samantha's judgey statements, but listening to Hahna and Twila, maybe some of it was closer to the truth than she was willing to admit.

"Samantha dropped out of the bridal party," Kimberly said.

"I knew she was gonna do this shit," Twila said. "Let her go."

"What was the reason she gave?" Hahna asked.

"I'm not even sure of her reason. I asked her if she wanted to do the bridal shower and she just kind of went off on a tangent about strippers and Jesus."

Kimberly decided to leave out Samantha's specific issues about Twila and Hahna. That was nothing more than jealousy, and it wouldn't help anything. It would only cause more drama.

"She's just mad that you didn't ask her to be Maid of Honor," Hahna said. "I can't believe that she dropped out."

"I think it's about more than that. I blame myself for some of it. I'm a different version of myself when I'm with her," Kimberly said. "I feel like I'm being fake sometimes."

"Why? Because you don't talk about men and sex around her? Because you don't cuss around her?" Twila asked. "That's not being fake. That's respecting the boundaries of that relationship."

"She doesn't see it that way. She thinks that because I am open to strippers at my bachelorette party that I'm going to hell."

"We don't have to have strippers," Hahna said. "I mean I don't know what she was expecting, but it wasn't going to be all that raunchy."

"She's an evangelist, Hahna. She preaches and teaches the women's Sunday school. She's not going to be a part of anything with a stripper," Kimberly said.

"But here's the thing. No one is requiring that of her," Twila said. "We all understand and modify our behavior around her. No one would've been angry if she didn't come to that."

"I just don't want to lose her as a friend behind a bachelorette party. She's a bit judgey, but she's a prayer warrior. When y'all are ready to ride or die, she's on her face praying."

"We *all* love her," Hahna said. "She wants you to value her friendship above ours, though. And that's where I have the issue."

"Do you think she could be lowkey jealous that you're even getting married?" Twila asked. "I think she's just resigned herself to being saved and single, and that you two would be going to women's retreats together for Jesus until y'all get old."

Kimberly hadn't thought about this possibility at all. Was Samantha hiding her jealousy behind her righteousness? They had always been the plus-sized friends with no or few dating prospects. Samantha had made peace with that for her life, but Kimberly never had.

"Do we know anyone we can hook her up with?" Hahna said. "Maybe she just needs a date."

"I wouldn't inflict that upon any brotha I know."

"She's brilliant and pretty," Hahna said.

"But she's gonna show up on the first date wearing her evangelist collar around her neck. She's too anointed for all the guys I know."

Kimberly shook her head. "We don't need to find her a date, but I don't want to leave things this way. I just don't know what to do about it."

"You should do what Samantha would do," Hahna said. "You should pray about it."

"You're right. What else do you want to show me on this tablet?"

Hahna swiped to a different page. "Here are potential shoes and accessories. Do you want to be uniform with all of these?"

"No. We don't have to be uniform, but can you all approve everyone's selections? Most of us have good taste, but . . ."

"We won't let Debbie wear stripper shoes," Twila said.

"Thank you."

"Do we need to help anyone with travel? We're almost to November, and the wedding is in March," Hahna said. "We should be getting airfare. Does everyone have a passport?"

"If a grown woman in her damn forties doesn't have a passport," Twila said. "I'm throwing the whole heffa away."

Kimberly exhaled through her nose. She was sure that Samantha didn't have a passport. She didn't travel much. She'd talked about taking a trip to the Holy Land, but the church had cancelled the trip for lack of interest.

"Hahna, maybe you can poll all the ladies on that," Kimberly said. "Just to make sure."

"Should I include Samantha in these communications?"

Kimberly nodded. "She didn't announce to you guys that she dropped out of the bridal party, so just keep her in the loop in case she changes her mind."

Twila rolled her eyes. "Let her ass go, for real. I know y'all are close, but she's irritating."

Kimberly made eye contact with Hahna, and Hahna nodded.

"Y'all think I didn't see that little look," Twila said. "I always see those looks."

"No, you don't, 'cause we're slick with them," Kimberly said.

"Okay," Twila said.

"For real though, we can't just act like Samantha isn't important," Hahna said. "She's our line sister. We don't leave our sisters behind."

"She is important," Kimberly said. "But I don't know how to get her past the hurt feelings."

"Why don't you let me try?" Hahna said.

"Be my guest."

Kimberly trusted Hahna to at least help and not hurt. She wondered if that would be enough to fix what she'd broken.

Chapter 34

HAHNA

Samantha had ignored every one of my calls and texts about the wedding, so I was going to corner her somewhere I knew she'd be. The Women's Ministry meeting at church.

When she walked into the sanctuary, I started walking in her direction. As soon as she saw me, she looked over her shoulder at the door as if she was contemplating an escape. I definitely could run faster than she could, so if she wanted to make a break for it, I would give chase. I didn't like how sad Kimberly's face looked just because this heffa was trying to ruin her wedding plans.

"Hey there Evangelist Samantha," I said loudly so that the other women in the church could hear me.

She rolled her eyes as I closed the space between us. She could be annoyed if she wanted to, but this was one conflict she wasn't running away from.

"Praise the Lord, Hahna." If she had said that any drier, she would've choked on the words.

"Yes. He's worthy!"

I might've been a sinner from time to time, but I could out-church the churchiest of them all. We could go back and forth with church greetings all night, or we could have a conversation.

"Surprised to see you out tonight. You haven't been at the ministry meetings in over a year."

The church shade was real.

"Well you know . . . the Lord blessed me with the gift of giving. When I can make it into the building, I also give my time," I said.

"Mmm-hmm, well, like I said, good to see you in the house of the Lord."

"I wondered if I might have a word with you in the foyer."

Samantha looked up at the clock on the wall. "We start in a few minutes. We might have to wait until a better time."

"This will only take a few minutes. I haven't been able to catch you by phone or text . . ."

"I was probably working."

"Then, I'd appreciate if I can just have a few moments now. You know the bible says, when you have an issue with your sister, you should come to her."

I knew this would get the attention of the nosy women's ministry members. Several of them pretended not to be listening but had leaned a little closer to me and Samantha. Wasn't nothing like church gossip. If we had the conversation in their hearing, the whole church board would know about it before we got home.

Samantha gave me a frustrated glare but turned and left the sanctuary. I followed her.

"What is it, Hahna?" she asked as the sanctuary doors closed.

She had dropped her syrupy-sweet Evangelist Samantha tone and got right down to the Samantha I knew.

"I just wanted to make sure everything was okay with you. You haven't responded to any of the bridesmaid communications. Do you need help with paying for anything? How can I help?"

"Kimberly didn't tell you? I'm no longer in the wedding."

I gave my best fake surprised face. "What? Why aren't you in the wedding? Did you and Kimberly have a disagreement?"

"No, we didn't. I don't fit in with the rest of you, and I don't want to force it. I'm fine just being her friend."

"How do you not fit in with the rest of us?"

"I don't want to do any of the things you all have planned. I'm not going to get all glam with makeup artists, weave, and fake lashes."

"Do you think Kimberly doesn't know this about you? She knows exactly who you are, and she still asked you to be one of her bridesmaids."

"She asked me to be a bridesmaid because we are line sisters in Gamma Phi Gamma."

"You really think that's the only reason? You're her prayer partner, Samantha. And you're always there when she needs you. Heck, when any of us need you. You were there for me."

Samantha chuckled. "Oh, I get it. You're the emissary from the bride tribe. You're here to get me back into the fold. You might first want to go lie on the altar and repent for your sins before launching this kind of mission in His house."

I knew she was going to say something offensive at some point. Jesus was her defense mechanism. She thought when the bible said to put on the full armor of God that meant she was supposed to take shots in the name of Jesus.

"I die daily. Isn't that what Paul said. But this isn't really about the status of my soul. It's about your friendship with Kimberly. Don't give that up because you have to sit out of a couple events during the wedding shenanigans. Everyone respects you for being principled."

"It doesn't feel like respect. I honestly feel bullied. It's a hostile environment around y'all," Samantha said. "Everyone drinks alcohol, curses, and talks about all manner of nasty things. I don't want any part of that. I was afraid that if Jesus had come back while we were having that bridesmaid's meeting that I was going to be left behind."

"Oh, my goodness."

"I'm exaggerating of course, but you get it. I just don't like any of those behaviors, and I'm not going to pretend I'm okay with it for Gamma Phi Gamma, Kimberly, or anything else."

"What if I told you that we would have at least one bridesmaid's meeting a month right here at the church?"

"Really?"

"Yes. As long as you don't try to preach to everyone. When they're in the house of the Lord, no one will do any of those behaviors."

"Not even Debbie?"

I swallowed. I couldn't make any promises about Debbie. She was the wild card.

"Lemme say this. Debbie grew up in church like the rest of us. She's not gonna be disrespectful in a church."

Samantha stared at me.

"Or at least, I don't think she will," I added. "But the rest of us will be fine."

"I still want y'all to live right and repent. That message doesn't change."

"I'm not saying your message should change. Just meet everybody where they are. Some of us could really use some of your prayers right now, to be honest."

"Like whom?"

"Well, I'm not going to say who, but someone in the group was sexually assaulted a couple years ago, and she is having a hard time getting over it."

Samantha threw her hand over her mouth. "The blood of Jesus. I will send prayers up."

"So, if we have the next bridesmaid's meeting here next week between Sunday services, do you think that will work?"

Samantha took a long pause before responding.

"Come on, Samantha. I am my sister."

"I know. My sister and I are one."

"Don't break the sisterhood."

"Okay, I'll stay in the wedding. And I'll do the bridal shower too. We can have it here at the church. The ladies in the singles' ministry would like to host."

Lord, I was going to have to sell this hard to the rest of the bridesmaids. The bridesmaid's meetings, the bridal shower, all of it. But at least Kimberly would be happy. We hadn't left one of our sisters behind, and the sisterhood was intact. Kimberly didn't need this stress anyway. She had enough on her plate dealing with Sabrina—the ex-wife from hell.

Chapter 35

KIMBERLY

Even though Kimberly hadn't officially agreed to participate, Sabrina had continued to push the issue of family counseling with Ron. She had made it a contingency for Ron picking up the girls for Thanksgiving, which was three weeks away. Kimberly was only going for Ron's benefit. She didn't give a damn about Sabrina's comfort or any other feeling she had.

The counselor, a woman named Dr. Washington, could've been Sabrina's sister. She had the same long dark hair and the same super thin yoga build. Carly and Kayla weren't at the session, so it was just Kimberly, Ron, and Sabrina.

The doctor's office was small but felt even smaller with all of the tension in the room. Since Sabrina had situated herself on the biggest couch in the room, Ron and Kimberly were crowded into a loveseat. It would've made sense for her to choose the smaller seat since her husband hadn't come, but Kimberly was sure she wanted them to feel discomfort. At least the room was brightly lit and scented with candles. That part helped to calm Kimberly's nerves a bit, if not completely.

"Sabrina, your husband, Frank, wasn't able to make it?" Dr. Washington asked at the beginning of the session.

"He doesn't feel comfortable meeting with Ron until we deal

with a few things first. He feels we need to level set without him, and he'll join at a later date," Sabrina said.

Kimberly's face twisted into a scowl. This was Sabrina trying to take control again. She was dictating both Kimberly and Ron's actions, and they weren't receiving any reciprocity. This was Sabrina letting everyone know she was in the driver's seat.

"To be honest, I'm only here because Sabrina is trying to make this a requirement of my daughters spending the Thanksgiving holiday with me and Kimberly," Ron said.

"That's not true," Sabrina said. "I just mentioned that I'd feel more comfortable if we did this."

"If I have to be here, your husband should have to come," Kimberly said. "Maybe we need to reschedule until Frank can find some courage to sit in a room with Ron."

Sabrina narrowed her eyes at Kimberly. "This isn't about courage. Ron threatened his life and has yet to acknowledge that or apologize for it. He doesn't have to sit across the room from someone who threatened him."

Dr. Washington scribbled furiously on her little pad, while Ron tapped his foot on the floor. Kimberly rubbed the small of his back to show her support of him, but she would have to be careful not to let Sabrina create a negative narrative about Ron.

Dr. Washington looked up from her notes and smiled at Ron. "Ron, do you want to respond to what Sabrina said?"

"I did threaten him, and I don't apologize or take it back," Ron said.

"Please elaborate," Dr. Washington said.

"I promised Frank that if he laid a hand on either one of my daughters that I would make him regret it. And yes, I promised physical violence."

"Many people would say that is a reasonable expectation of a father in response to any violence against his young daughters," Dr. Washington said.

"Except that he had no reason to threaten Frank. Frank would never harm Carly or Kayla. He wouldn't like it if I threatened Kimberly."

Kimberly's nostrils flared at the amount of stank and emphasis that Sabrina put on her name. She said it with such disdain, Kimberly felt attacked.

"You could threaten me if you like," Kimberly said. "I wouldn't be much concerned about it. It definitely wouldn't stop me from showing up somewhere."

Sabrina rolled her eyes. "You know what I mean, Dr. Washington. Of course, she isn't afraid of me. That's not the point."

"What does that mean?" Dr. Washington asked. "If you threatened Kimberly, it would be exactly the same as Ron threatening Frank."

Sabrina laughed. "Okay. I see what we're doing here. We're going to ignore the obvious."

"Please share," Dr. Washington said.

"You're trying to make me sound like a racist, and I'm not falling for it. Ron threatened to hurt my husband, for no reason, and that's what we need to deal with."

"The threat was only if he did something to my children. If he has good intentions, he has absolutely nothing to be afraid of," Ron said. "She acts like there are not men in this world who prey on women with young children."

"And you still don't trust him?" Sabrina asked. "What does he have to do to not have a threat hovering over his head?"

"Listen. I have no issues with Frank. The girls seem to love him, and he hasn't done anything wrong that I know of. All he has to do is keep his hands off my daughters. I didn't have a choice in where they live, because you made the court think we had domestic violence issues."

"Dr. Washington, would a non-violent person threaten a person with violence?" Sabrina asked.

"That's not a fair way to ask that question, Sabrina. I would venture a guess that you are also capable of violence when it comes to your children. If someone hurt or attacked them, would you not spring into action?"

Sabrina sighed. "Ron only threatened Frank because he was angry that I was getting remarried. He begged me to stay with him, and when I refused, he got angry and violent. Whether he wants to admit it or not."

"But you haven't sought out family counseling until now," Kimberly said. "Interesting timing seeing that now Ron is getting remarried."

"Well, Ron made himself comfortable by threatening Frank. That is not how I operate. *This* is the way I obtain a comfort level with you."

"Can we stop with the, 'Ron is violent' narrative," Ron said. "You keep trying to make that point and no one is on board with it."

Sabrina fumed and glared at Ron. She seemed determined to make him a villain in front of the therapist. And for what reason?

"Why do you want to make that point so badly?" Kimberly asked. "Do you think you'll convince me not to marry Ron? Is that what you want to happen?"

Sabrina scoffed. "I don't care who he marries. I just care about my children."

"But you said you were overwhelmed by our engagement party. Because you saw many of the people who were at your wedding," Kimberly said. "So maybe you don't care about who he marries, but it does bother you that he's marrying."

Dr. Washington seemed intrigued by this. "Let's pull that thread, Sabrina," she said. "We need to get to the root of your discomfort. There doesn't seem to be a threat to your children from Ron or Kimberly."

"We don't know that," Sabrina said. "I don't think Kimberly likes me because I'm a white woman."

"Where is this coming from?" Ron asked. "Just a few months ago, you were fine with Kimberly combing Carly and Kayla's hair. Kimberly even made you a video so that you could stop ripping their hair out when you comb it."

"Yes. She assumed that I didn't know how to do their hair because I'm white."

"No," Kimberly said. "The girls told me you hurt them when you comb their hair. I was only trying to help. Dr. Washington, I have a company that makes products for natural hair, and we used my products on their hair."

"And you thanked her for the video and said you wanted Kimberly to teach all your friends with biracial children," Ron said. "All of a sudden when I tell you we're getting married and that we want the girls in the wedding, you started to act insane."

Sabrina took in a deep breath and exhaled. She seemed frustrated, but Kimberly was glad that she and Ron had tag teamed her ass. That was exactly what she deserved.

"Sabrina," Dr. Washington asked. "What do you have to say about that? Are you upset that Ron is getting married?"

Sabrina looked from Dr. Washington, to Ron, to Kimberly and then back at Dr. Washington. She took in another breath and exhaled once more.

"I don't like that he's getting remarried, but not for the reasons they think," Sabrina said.

"Would you like to share?"

"I don't want my daughters coming second to her. I don't want her calling the shots about how Ron spends his money. Not when it comes to my daughters."

"Why do you think I would hurt them ever? I love what Ron loves," Kimberly said.

"It's just that . . . you're not a mother, so you don't understand what that kind of love feels like," Sabrina said. "It's just easier if Ron isn't married."

"I'm not supposed to have happiness so you can feel comfortable?" Ron said. "That makes no sense, Sabrina. In fact, it's somewhat evil."

Sabrina burst into tears. Kimberly sighed. Here was the primary weapon of the toxic white woman. Tears. No one got up to comfort her, but at least this time she got a tissue. From Dr. Washington.

"Sabrina, when you chose to leave your marriage to Ron, he became free to seek happiness for his life. It may feel frustrating for you, but you don't have any control on how he chooses to move on," Dr. Washington said. "And you cannot use your daughters as emotional weapons against him."

"That's not what I'm trying to do," Sabrina sobbed.

"Demanding family counseling when you've never wanted it

before and bringing up things Ron said when he was at his lowest point is all proof of you trying to maintain control," Dr. Washington said.

"It feels like you're just trying to admonish me," Sabrina said. "What about them?"

"Well, I haven't heard anything that Kimberly did wrong. Ron, it might be good for you to acknowledge that Frank has been a good stepfather to your children."

Ron bit his bottom lip and his nostrils flared. Kimberly could tell he didn't want to acknowledge or say anything, but he was the one who'd agreed to this counseling.

When Ron didn't respond, Dr. Washington continued, "Are you really angry at Frank because he slept with your wife? Maybe the threat came from that place of hurt."

"I can't trust a man who screws another man's wife. I don't know what that man's capable of," Ron said.

"See, Dr. Washington, I told you he was just mad that I left him . . ."

"But," Ron said. "I have to say in the years that they've been married, no harm has come to my children."

Dr. Washington smiled. "That was a start. By the end of the sessions, I think you may be able to acknowledge more, but Sabrina, you need to convince your husband to attend these sessions."

"I will do my best."

"Kimberly, do you have anything else to add before we take a break? I want you all to go have refreshments and breathe for a few minutes before we have the rest of our session."

"I don't appreciate my lack of giving birth being a part of this conversation. That has nothing to do with anything."

"I agree, Kimberly," Dr. Washington said. "We need to make sure that we are all being fair with one another or these sessions will not be successful. The goal is for everyone to feel comfortable with this blended family environment."

"Dr. Washington, do you have children?" Sabrina asked.

"No, I don't."

"Well, then there's no way you could understand what I meant when I said that. I stand by my words, but I'm sorry that you felt offended by them, Kimberly. I didn't mean to imply anything about your character. Being a mother is something you can't understand until you experience it."

Sabrina didn't wait for Dr. Washington's retort. She got up from the couch and walked into the hallway where the snack table was situated. Dr. Washington frowned and shook her head.

"We're not going to be successful unless we all do the work," Dr. Washington said. "Please, Kimberly and Ron, go enjoy some of that expensive tea and coffee that my assistant likes to buy."

Kimberly felt a little lift in her spirit. Although Sabrina had probably chosen Dr. Washington because she thought she'd be a natural ally, Dr. Washington was clearly on the side of things that made sense. While the best outcome of this would be Sabrina dropping all the foolishness, Kimberly would accept Ron having unlimited access to his daughters.

Kimberly decided, even though she didn't know for sure, that she was going to give Ron's babies the best Thanksgiving dinner they'd ever had.

Chapter 36

TWILA

I was distracted in my meeting with Dr. Mays. My mind was racing with so many different thoughts. I was still on an oxytocin high from the ridiculous number of orgasms I'd had since DeAndre first touched me. But underneath that high, right on the other side of it, was my growing fury about Alexander Adams living a regular ass life in my neighborhood.

"Tell me what you are thinking," Dr. Mays said. "You are not here with me."

"I'm sorry. I'm here. What did you ask?"

"I asked about the young man you were interested in. Have you decided to proceed with that?"

I briefly went back to that night in DeAndre's theater room. I don't think I could ever relive that night enough times to make me numb to it. *Love and Basketball* was going to forever be an aphrodisiac.

"I have decided to proceed. DeAndre is almost too perfect, but I'm proceeding anyway."

"What do you mean by too perfect?"

"I mean it's like I wrote everything I wanted in a man down in a diary, somebody stole it, and then delivered DeAndre."

"Do you not think of this as a gift?"

"A gift? Maybe. But I'd be lying if I said I wasn't suspicious of it."

"I understand caution. You are in a place in your life where caution is required."

"I am very cautious, I feel, about everything now. And maybe I'm doing too much with that."

"Twila let me ask you a question. Do you deserve a man like DeAndre?"

I thought about this question. On the surface the response was easy. Of course, I deserved a man like DeAndre. I put my all into every relationship, and it would be a first to have that energy reciprocated. But beneath the surface, was where all of my insecurity lived. Because if you looked at my previous man choices, I might have believed I deserved a man like DeAndre, but I'd never said yes to the ones who were close to being perfect.

"I don't know how I feel about that," I responded. "I want to say yes, but the ones I've chosen have been projects. Or, the ones who weren't projects I think I created flaws that needed fixing."

"I am happy that you have done the work to recognize these things about yourself."

"Thank you for helping me do that work."

"But . . ."

"But?"

"I want to say one thing about a gift. A gift is never deserved. It is simply something you accept."

"I accept then."

"Wonderful."

"I am so happy for my . . . for my gift. It just comes at this time when I'm trying to put myself back together. And I . . ."

Why was I crying? Why were there tears falling down my face just trying to get a sentence out?

"What are you feeling? What is causing this emotion?"

"I have discovered that my attacker . . . rapist . . . attends a church near my home with what I believe is his wife and daughter."

Dr. Mays's eyebrows shot up in surprise. It wasn't easy to shock her, probably because as a therapist, she'd probably heard just about everything.

"I imagine that is a problem for you."

I loved how Dr. Mays never inserted how she felt about a situation, even when I could tell that she felt some kind of way. This wasn't her session, it was mine, so she always made sure the feelings and reactions that we were talking about were mine.

"It is a problem for me. I refuse to press charges because the details are way too salacious to not end up in the public. But I have to do something. What if he rapes someone else?"

"That is sometimes the case. Especially when the rape is as violent as the one you have described."

"Correct. It felt like a . . . violation . . . to see him walking into a church. A place where people trust others."

"You felt violated?"

"Yes, I did. And very angry. That is what the fear is being replaced with. Rage."

"Neither fear nor rage are healthy for an extended amount of time. Sometimes positive change comes from channeling either or both of those emotions."

"I'd like to channel both of them."

"I would advise you to exercise the caution that comes naturally to you. Trust your instincts, and before taking any actions, consider the consequences and the downstream impacts."

"I will. This is why I haven't made a move yet."

I did want to harness both my fear and my rage, but in the case of destroying Alexander Adam's perfect little life, I would be content to focus simply on the rage.

Chapter 37

HAHNA

Now that Sam was really moving in, I had to make space for him. My custom-built, two-story closet was full, but I was willing to purge some things so that my man could feel welcome. Twila was supposed to be helping, but she was engrossed in something on her tablet.

"What do you think about these shoes?" I asked as I held out a pair of designer pumps I hadn't worn in years.

Twila didn't look up from her tablet, so I dropped one of the shoes in her lap. She glared up at me.

"You trying to break my stuff?" she asked.

"No. But you're not paying any attention to what's going on up here. You're supposed to be helping me. Sam is moving in on Saturday."

Twila sighed. "Sorry," she said. "I'm distracted."

"I see, but by what? Since when were you on Facebook all like that? What are you doing? Looking up all DeAndre's old girlfriends?"

"No, girl. Why would I do that?"

"The way you said he put it down, I thought you got dickmatized or something."

"No, not yet. Not looking up DeAndre's page or his exes."

Okay, I know good and damn well that was funny. So, why wasn't this heffa laughing? She didn't chuckle, or even crack a smile.

"Damn, heffa. Why you so dry?"

Twila patted the floor next to her. "Come look."

I sat down next to her and squinted as I looked at the screen.

"What is this?" I asked. "An online church service?"

Twila took the earbuds out of the side of the tablet so that the sound would play on speaker. It was some sort of church session. Not a sermon, but a fireside chat with a pastor I recognized.

"Oh, I know this pastor. He's got a prison ministry that's doing good work in Georgia."

"Shhh," Twila said. "Listen."

The pastor was speaking. "Tonight, we're highlighting this amazing couple who have just become powerhouses for Jesus. We are blessed to have them in our ranks. Brother Alexander Adams and his beautiful wife Fatima have done an outstanding job in our homeless ministry, and I will let them tell you about a holiday fundraiser to help our adopted families at the Rebekah Women's Home."

"Thank you, Pastor Wright," the man on the screen said. "We are excited to share what we're doing for the kingdom."

Twila balled her fists and cried out. Then shoved the tablet across the floor.

"What's wrong?"

Then it dawned on me. The man who'd raped her was white, and she had his identity. And, she'd followed him to church.

"Was that him?"

She wrapped her arms around her knees and pulled them to her body. She nodded.

"That's that mother fucker."

"Give me your earbuds."

Twila handed them to me, and I retrieved the tablet. I listened to the rapist describe all the services they had for homeless women. It was crazy how many church folks had secret lives. No one would know he was a rapist by looking at him.

The comments under the live video were going crazy. Lots of people gave full blown testimonies about what the ministry had done in their lives.

"And Fatima, tell us your testimony," Pastor Wright said. "And about the wonderful things God did for you with this ministry."

"I used to live at the Rebekah Home, and was truly destitute without Jesus. When Brother Alexander came to the home with the ministry team, I received the Gospel of Jesus Christ. Soon, I was baptized and serving as a co-laborer in the vineyard right along with Alexander."

The pastor laughed. "And then you became co-laborers in another way, correct?"

"Yes. Alexander became my Boaz and has been such a blessing to my life."

I looked over at Twila who still was shaken by seeing and hearing her attacker on screen.

"You need to hear some of this," I said. "He found his wife in the homeless ministry at his church. *She* was homeless."

"I'm not surprised. If the arrogant prick had to rape somebody in a sex club, he definitely ain't got game enough to pull a woman who has it all together," Twila said.

I glanced at the comments under the video, because someone with the screen name Christina God's Champion Reynolds was typing in all caps. Yelling at the post. Not everyone seemed to be a fan of good Brother Alexander.

The comments were crazy, but persistent.

FAKE.

GOD AIN'T IN THAT.

STOP PLAYING WITH GOD.

"Somebody's straight up trolling him, Twila. A lady is going in typing in all caps."

Twila shrugged. "You know megachurch pastors have haters."

"Yeah, but I don't think the messages are directed at Pastor Wright."

Twila crawled across the floor and I held the tablet out to her while still reading the screen. Then, a comment popped up that made Twila snatch the tablet out of my hands.

BOAZ MY ASS. BOAZ DIDN'T RAPE RUTH.

"The wife, Fatima, called Alexander her Boaz," I said. "These messages are for *him.*"

"Is this Christina person saying that Alexander raped her?"

"Sounds like that to me."

Twila set the tablet down on the floor. "I was waiting on God to show me a sign before I made a move."

"You were waiting on God?"

Twila rolled her eyes. "Listen here. You know I still pray, and I even go to church sometimes."

"I didn't say anything. No judging here."

"Anyway, I talked to my therapist about this, and I told her that I had to do something. I couldn't let him hurt someone again."

"I agree with that. He must be stopped."

"I think . . . I think I have an idea on what to do about this."

"Do you need any help?"

"I don't think so, not yet."

The look in her eyes scared me. No matter what, I didn't want my sister getting hurt trying to go after that man.

"Please don't do anything dangerous. And if you do, at least tell the bruhs first."

"I don't think I'll need our fraternity brothers for this one. I've been approaching this the wrong way all along."

"What do you mean?"

Twila scrambled to her feet. "Sorry, I can't help you with the closet. Just throw away half this shit, 'cause you don't wear it anyway. I have some research to do."

I watched as Twila completely transformed from the afraid and bothered to the determined and fierce. Both versions of my sister scared me, but I knew she had to execute her plan and do whatever she needed to do to feel safe and secure again.

I stood ready to intervene though, and so would the rest of our crew.

Chapter 38

TWILA

Right after that fireside chat, I inboxed Christina God's Champion Reynolds. I didn't know if she'd respond or even see the message since we weren't friends on Facebook. Not only had she responded, but she'd agreed to meet me for lunch.

I didn't know what to expect, because from her messages, the woman seemed to be suffering from some kind of mental health issue. Every response she'd sent me was in all caps, and she hadn't used any punctuation. I wondered if I could get any real information out of her, or if she was reliable.

I recognized Christina from her profile picture on Facebook. Her face anyway. None of her pictures were below her neck, and when she entered the soul food restaurant I saw why. Christina couldn't be any less than four hundred pounds, and that was probably a low estimate. I stood up and waved so she could see me, and she approached me with a huge smile on her face.

I wanted to hug her, but we were strangers, so I held out both hands and gave her warm two-handed shake. She smiled some more and sat.

"Twila, thank you for reaching out to me," Christina said. "I knew I was doing the right thing by posting those comments.

Most of the church members have blocked me, but the pastor won't for some reason."

"Do you think Pastor Wright thinks there is truth to what you're saying?"

"No. He just thinks I'm crazy."

"Um . . . oh."

Christina laughed. "I suffer from chronic depression and food addiction, but I'm far from crazy. Plus, I have a disability that keeps me from working."

"I see. And that's how you ended up in the Rebekah Home?"

She nodded. "Yes. I had gotten behind on my rent, and I was evicted. My social worker recommended that I go to the Rebekah Home."

"I see."

The waitress brought a pitcher of sweet tea and water to our table. Christina looked up and smiled.

"Thank you, sweetheart. Is this sweet tea?"

"Yes, it is."

"Do you mind bringing a pitcher of unsweetened?" Christina asked.

"Yes ma'am. Would y'all like to order?"

"I'll have the fried catfish basked with greens and macaroni and cheese," I said. I needed comfort food. I'd pay for it later with a pre-wedding crash diet.

Christina looked at the menu, and said, "I'll have what she's having, except no macaroni and cheese. I'll have the baked sweet potato."

I felt bad eating the worst, fat-filled things off the menu, when this lady who was clearly trying to be healthier was making better food choices.

The waitress smiled and left, and then Christina turned her attention to me.

"Where do you know Alexander from?" she asked. "The request to meet was really weird when I got it. It kinda scared me, to be honest."

"I don't know him. Other than the fact that he raped me."

"So, you don't go to the church?"

"Not that church, no. But Alexander raped me at a night club with a room for swingers."

"Like a room where everybody gets freaky?"

I couldn't help but chuckle at how she said it. "That's exactly right."

"That seems like exactly the place a minister might be," Christina said. Then she burst into laughter. "No shade, I'm not judging you, but it just seems kinda ironic that Alexander would be there."

"Maybe he wasn't in the ministry then. This happened a couple years ago."

"He's been in that ministry for ten years."

The small talk was fine, but I wanted to get down to the facts that I came here to gather. "So, why did you make that comment about Boaz not raping Ruth? Did Alexander rape you?"

"Well, no. I'm not Ruth. He didn't marry me."

I was confused for a second. "Are you saying that . . ."

"He raped his wife? Yes. He raped Fatima when we were both residents at the Rebekah Home. This was before they were married."

So many thoughts rushed through my head at once, but one blared out more than the others. *Why would a woman marry a man who raped her?*

"And you know this for sure?"

Christina nodded. "Yes. We were roommates at the home. He had taken her out on a date. She went with him back to his apartment to pray for her miracle, and he raped her right there."

"She told you this?"

"Yes. She was so broken up about it. She said he used some kind of electric thing on her that made her not be able to move."

"A taser."

"Is that what it's called?"

"Did she report it to anyone?" I asked.

"No, no. He was a minister from the megachurch. No one was going to tell."

"Well, you're telling me now, so how does that work?"

"I'm no longer a homeless woman. We were both desperate for help from that church, and I needed a place to stay."

I sighed and nodded. I understood. They weren't gonna snitch on the one who was helping them, in case the help disappeared.

"How in the hell did Fatima end up marrying him?"

"Something happened to her, when she was younger. She got raped by several men in her family, including her daddy. I think Alexander's rape wasn't that bad in her opinion."

"But marriage though?"

"He offered her more than the apartments the rest of the homeless women were being approved for. He gave her a home and respectability. I heard that they have a child."

The little girl. Yes. She looked at least three, maybe four. Alexander had raped Fatima before that night at Club Phenom.

"She married her rapist. I can't believe it. I wonder what her life must be like."

"I wouldn't know. She's one of the church members who blocked me. We were so close when we were in the shelter together. She left with Alexander and wouldn't speak to me again."

"Did you ever tell her she should report Alexander to the authorities?"

"I did, later on. I thought she should at least tell Pastor Wright."

"What did she say to that?"

"She thought that if she stayed married to Alexander then he wouldn't hurt someone else. She said she could give him what he wanted."

This made me sick to my stomach. Especially the fact that Alexander was parading her around like some sort of ministry mascot.

"I'm sorry about what happened to you," Christina said. "Maybe if I had told someone about Alexander raping Fatima it wouldn't have happened."

"Only if she had been willing to report him too, and it sounds like she wasn't. I appreciate you for meeting with me today, though."

"You're welcome. Are you about to leave? I was really looking forward to lunch."

Even though I was itching to leave and come up with a plan to attack Alexander, I relaxed in my seat. I could use the carbohydrates and down-home goodness, and Christina seemed to need the food and the company. I could pause for a couple hours.

Didn't want to be hasty anyway. Whatever I did decide to do was going to have to finish Alexander, and not leave him free to harm another woman.

Chapter 39

HAHNA

It seemed like this week had flown by. It was already Friday afternoon which meant that in less than twenty-four hours, Sam was going to be living under my roof. Sam had already contracted a property manager to handle the renting and maintenance of his bachelor pad, so there was nothing left for him to do except move on into my home.

Corden and I were working a little late on the Christmas party plans. We needed a theme and quick, because I wanted to start inviting folks before they got invited to other corporate parties.

"How about, Share Data on Christmas Day," Corden said.

"Oh, gross. That is pretty bad, Corden."

"Wait. I've got it. How about, 'Data Baby?' "

I sat blinking at Corden. He was delirious. Long week had him talking crazy.

He got up and did a little dance. "Sir," I said.

"Data Baby . . . we'll fix your data, but there's a fee . . . not free . . . we'll analyze your data tonight!"

He sang this to the tune of "Santa Baby" and again I blinked. In silence. This was more than the long week. I needed to call someone to come care for him. Symone's number was on his emergency contacts.

"You are tripping. That is a great theme."

"No, it's not."

"I can see the party flyer now. You'll be in a sexy white Mrs. Claus outfit on the flyer, but with your smart looking glasses and a computer."

"Am I selling my ass or getting data analytics clients?"

"Will selling ass get us a million-dollar account?" Corden asked.

"If it did, would you be willing to," I asked.

"I thought we were selling your ass. My ass is too pretty to be sold."

"Well so is mine."

There was a light tap on the door. "I thought you said Sylvia left," I said.

"She did," Corden replied.

"Who's there?"

The door opened slightly. "It's me, DeAndre. You had a visitor come in downstairs and Sylvia wasn't here, so I walked him upstairs," DeAndre said.

"Oh, come in, DeAndre."

When he opened the door all the way, I wished I had told him to tell the visitor that our offices were closed for the day. It was my ghosting ex-boyfriend Torian. He was the absolute last person I wanted to see on the eve of Sam moving in with me.

"You need anything else from me?" DeAndre asked as Torian walked over to my desk.

Corden checked out Torian from head to toe and shook his head. What assessment was this? I couldn't tell what Corden was thinking.

"I'm good, DeAndre. Thank you for bringing him up here."

DeAndre left and I looked at Torian. "Have a seat, I guess. How can I help you?"

"You guess I can have a seat? It's like that Hahna? You're going to apologize about saying that before I leave."

"I didn't mean to be offensive. I'm just surprised that you're here."

"Do I need to leave?" Corden asked. "We can finish the party planning next week."

"You're having a party?" Torian asked.

"Just a Christmas networking event. No, Corden, you don't need to leave. Torian won't be here too long."

"Again, you offend me. I have actual business with you Hahna, and you might not need to have a networking event after what I tell you."

"Again, not deliberately. Tell me your business."

"One of my clients, Yorkshire, Summerall, and Schmidt . . ."

"The private equity group?" I asked. Now he had my attention. He should've started with those three names.

"Yes, correct. They're looking for a consulting firm to do some analytics for them. They're trying to acquire a new business and their due diligence person just went the way of consulting and can't help them anymore."

"And you recommended The Data Whisperers?"

"Of course, I did. They want to meet with you next week."

Thank. You. God.

"Is this a one and done or will it be a continuing relationship?" I asked.

Honestly, I was willing to take anything at that point.

"It depends on your proposal with their team. I have a relationship built with them, and I think we could approach this as a services package. We can put together a whole suite of analytics, marketing and accounting for YS&S and they would sell us to their peers."

We?

"We'd have to work together?" I asked.

"Not physically together, no. We'd bill our hours separately too. I just think we can attract more companies like them by offering a suite of products. Maybe that's the key to saving The Data Whisperers."

"My company doesn't need saving."

"Come on Hahna. It does. No shame in saying that, especially when I'm sitting here offering you a lifeline."

"And YS&S doesn't care about what happened with Hale Brexton?" Corden asked. "Because I'm not trying to go through all the work to build a kick ass proposal just to have them pull up some internet story and shoot the whole thing down."

"They know all about slimy ass Brexton," Torian said.

"Corden, can we have the room for a minute?" I asked.

Corden didn't look like he wanted to leave. He stood slowly and gave Torian the evil eye as he rose. But, Corden knew how Torian had broken my heart when he'd disappeared on me. He'd apologized later saying that he'd had cancer, but I'd never tried to validate his story. I'd already moved on with Sam.

"Another thing you need to do," Torian said after Corden closed the door behind him, "is get some fresh blood and talent in here. Corden is played out."

"Corden has never betrayed me."

Torian took a deep breath and sighed. "I hope you aren't thinking of rejecting this because of our breakup."

"We didn't break up. You left."

"You know what I mean. This is what you need right now. To get your confidence back. I want to see you win, Hahna. Always have."

Skeptical didn't begin to describe how I felt about Torian's sentiments or his offer to connect me to YS&S. I mulled it over. We needed the influx of revenue that would come from this engagement. We also needed the reputation salvaging that would happen with a company this large acquiring The Data Whisperers' services.

What I didn't need was Torian grinning in my face, thinking that he'd come to my rescue.

"If anyone but me had walked in your office with this proposition, you'd already be coming up with the best value adding proposal you could think of. I've never been a slouch when it comes to making money."

"Yeah, only at relationships."

"You can't still be bitter about that. You're dating that writer, correct? I saw that he recently got a book deal."

"You're following him online?"

"Set a Google alert. I'm interested in his career."

This was creepy and weird and all the wrong things. Torian had never felt slimy that way. Not to me. Maybe there was a reason my friends had never cozied up to him. Not the way that they'd embraced Sam.

"You don't need to worry about Sam's career."

"Oh, I do. So, that when I catch him slipping, I can get my girl back."

"Your girl?" I scoffed. "Torian we've been over a long time. If this offer with YS&S is just about you rekindling something that's dead, I suggest that you don't get your hopes up."

"It's not *just* about that. I already told you I wanna see you win. You're hanging on by a thread now. In a minute you won't be able to send Rochelle those utility bill checks."

Torian felt just like the devil, and I didn't accept his bleak outlook on my business or my finances.

"Listen, I'll set up the meeting with YS&S. It can be a dinner meeting. We'll go to Ray's on the River . . . my treat."

The more Torian talked the more his voice bothered me. The more his smug demeanor nauseated me. I remembered when I thought this was sexy. I used to think it made him look like a boss. Now, I much preferred Sam's quiet strength and support to Torian's bodacious asshole-ness.

But I also wasn't stupid.

"No dinner meeting. We have a perfectly good conference room here. If you're serious about this, and it's not just some plot to get back in my bed, please have your admin reach out to Sylvia to set it all up."

Torian threw his head back and laughed. "If I wanted you back, I'd already have you. Your new man isn't really competition, is he?"

I stood to signal the end of this meeting or whatever it was. It felt like an attack.

"I look forward to hearing from you about the YS&S engagement."

I hit him with the corporate meeting close. The professional goodbye. I wanted to tell him to get the hell out of my office.

"We'll be reaching out soon," Torian said. "This will be an amazing partnership. The first of many."

The thought of that nauseated me some more. I sat slowly, trying to keep my head from spinning in the process.

Corden stormed back in my office with his arms waving. I knew when he slammed the door that he was furious.

"Don't tell me we're doing this with Torian."

"It's a good opportunity. We don't have much of a choice, do we?"

"We do. He's trying to waltz up in here to save the day like we're destitute or something."

"We're not?"

"No. We are rebuilding."

"So, what, we throw this party, call it Data Baby, and hope top notch clients come out the woodwork looking to work with us?"

"The networking event is a great idea. It was Sam's idea. And you were on board with it before Ghostface Torian walked up in here saying otherwise."

"You're right. Let's have the party *and* meet with YS&S. No problem with flushing out all the options."

"Okay. But if I have to look at Torian across the table, I might get up and throat punch his ass."

I shook my head. "Don't look at him then. We need this."

Ghostface or not, Torian had just brought in the best news I'd had in the months since Hale Brexton destroyed my business with his lies and intentional data breaches. Nothing was going to stop me from reestablishing The Data Whisperers as one of the top Atlanta consultants for data analytics.

Not even the ex-boyfriend who'd broken my heart. Sam and I could toast to this opportunity with wine and strawberries in bed.

Chapter 40

KIMBERLY

The guest room for Kayla and Carly was ready, Sean and his new girlfriend were invited, and the groceries were purchased for Kimberly and Ron's Thanksgiving feast. She was having all of her friends over, including some of the bridal party. Anytime a large meal needed to be prepared, she was the hostess. Hahna and Twila were acceptable sous chefs, but they knew more about hiring caterers than about making parker rolls from scratch.

The only thing she was feeling anxiety about was the hand-off with Sabrina and Ron of the twins. He had requested that Sabrina drop the girls off at Kimberly's house, and she had balked at that. But Ron had a business meeting about purchasing a new commercial property in Birmingham and he wouldn't have time to drive to North Carolina to pick them up. Ron would be there for the drop off, but Kimberly was anxious, nonetheless.

The three family counseling sessions they'd had were fruitful even if they hadn't solved all of their problems. Frank had come to the last one and Ron had reluctantly apologized for threatening violence. He'd also thanked him for being a good stepdad . . . so far.

It hadn't been a resolution, but it had been a start.

Still, when Kimberly extended the invitation to have the twins for Thanksgiving at her home, Sabrina hadn't seemed sold on the idea. In fact, she hadn't said yes until she'd had a separate conversation with Ron—alone. Kimberly didn't like the separate conversations but didn't want to seem insecure by asking them to stop. So, she endured and listened when Ron came back to her with details.

Ron joined Kimberly in the doorway of the twins' bedroom. He kissed her neck and rubbed her back.

"It looks so nice. The girls are gonna love it."

"Where is Sabrina? She said she was dropping them off today."

"She texted me that about fifteen minutes ago. She's twenty minutes away. Stuck in traffic."

"Why couldn't she text that to me? She's coming to my house, and she's aware that I've decorated the room for the girls. I asked her everything that they like."

"I honestly think she's embarrassed about how she's been acting, and she might be just a tad bit intimidated by you."

Kimberly scrunched her face into a frown. "How could she be intimidated by me? She's the perky little soccer mom."

"Kimmie Kim you are amazing. And yes, she is a soccer mom. That's *all* she is. She doesn't have a law degree and a million-dollar business. And you're sexy as hell. You have it all."

"Including you."

"I don't think she cares about that."

Kimberly shrugged. Ron might've been right, but it sure felt like she cared. Luckily, Kim wasn't worried about Ron wanting Sabrina back. If there had been any insecurity there, it would've been a real problem.

"Who all is coming over for Thanksgiving?" Ron asked.

Kimberly knew he was trying to change the subject, and this time she was willing to oblige. She also didn't want to think about Sabrina's potential issues.

"It'll be small. Hahna and Sam, Twila, and our little family. A few of the sorors might stop by too."

"My mama is coming too," Ron said.

"Wait. What? Your mother is coming?"

Ron burst into laughter. "I wish you could've seen your face. Oh, my goodness. My mama isn't coming. She's mad we aren't coming there."

"I didn't know she wanted us to come."

"She'll be fine. I told her how important it was for you to make the twins feel welcome and she was agreed."

"Oh, good."

"She just said we better have our greasy asses there for Christmas."

Kimberly sighed in relief. "Sure will, with gifts in tow."

"You know I was thinking we should give Carly and Kayla some gifts while they're here. Like an early Christmas."

"I haven't done any shopping yet. I don't know that I'll have time."

"Don't worry," Ron said. "I'll take care of it. I never get to see them open their gifts on Christmas morning. Sabrina does this whole Santa Claus thing . . ."

"They still believe in Santa?"

"Yes. They're only five."

"I've got an idea. Maybe we can put up the tree the day after Thanksgiving and have a visit from Santa!"

Kimberly got excited thinking about it. Maybe she would be a good mom, and not just to Carly and Kayla, but to babies of her own.

"Ron, do you think you're done having children?" Kimberly asked.

"The equipment still works. Why? Do you want a baby?"

Kimberly turned to face Ron. She appreciated the tender look on his face that made her feel safe whispering the thought she hadn't yet said aloud.

"Maybe, I do. I haven't seen a doctor to ask about the possibility of it, but I'm not against it. I feel like I'm warming up to the idea."

"I love being a dad, so if we had a baby, I'd be happy about it."

"And if we didn't?"

Ron kissed Kimberly's forehead. "That wouldn't bother me either. I'm here for either scenario."

The doorbell rang, so they would have to finish the conversation later. Kimberly rushed to the door with Ron at her heels. She wanted to open the door. Sabrina was going to acknowledge her whether she wanted to or not.

She swung the door open and Sabrina stood there with the girls. She'd attempted to do their hair, and while it wasn't perfect, Kimberly could smell the signature coconut scent from the CurlPop products.

Kimberly hugged Carly and Kayla and smiled at Sabrina. "Come on in. I want you to see the room I did for the girls."

"We have a room here?" Carly asked. "This is Ms. Kimberly's house."

"Remember we said that Ms. Kimberly and Daddy are getting married?" Sabrina said. "When you spend time with Daddy it will be here."

"Ms. Kimberly is gonna be Daddy's wife," Kayla said.

"And we get to be in the wedding," Carly said. "We're gonna be princesses, Daddy!"

Both girls swarmed Ron like they did every time he saw them. It was most heartbreaking that he couldn't have them every day and had to settle for weekends and holidays. Kimberly hated to see his sadness when he had to take them home.

Kimberly led the way to the twins' bedroom. When she opened the door and turned on the light, both Carly and Kayla started screaming.

"Kimberly this is incredible. They are in unicorn heaven," Sabrina said.

Kimberly had maybe gone a little overboard, but that wasn't out of the ordinary. The walls were pale blue and pink ombre with glitter and sparkles all over. There were two twin canopy beds with unicorn comforters. The carpet looked like pink cotton candy and the pillows were cotton candy blue. Pastel rainbows adorned the walls and the headboards. If there was a unicorn heaven, this was it.

Ron's phone buzzed in his pocket. He took it out, looked at the caller ID and frowned.

"I gotta take this. Do y'all mind?"

Sabrina shook her head. "We're fine, right, Kimberly."

Kimberly nodded but wondered if that was a true statement.

Ron left the room, and there was an awkward silence. Sabrina moved to help the girls look in the toy box and inside the closet where Kimberly had bought them beautiful robes and unicorn slippers. In the closet also hung the flower girl dresses.

"Are these their dresses for the wedding?" Sabrina asked as she took one of them out of the closet to admire it.

"Yes. They still have to be altered a bit, but yes."

"This fabric is so . . . colorful! I've never seen anything like it. Ron said it's an African print. Is it actually from Africa?"

"Yes, I have a Nigerian friend who prepares wedding attire. The girls' dresses match the men's vests."

"The bridesmaids will have this print as well?"

"No. Their dresses are a pale pink. One of the colors of our sorority."

"That is going to be so pretty," Sabrina said as she put the dress back on the closet rack. "I wish I was going to be see it in person."

"You aren't going to be there?"

Sabrina sat in a powder blue unicorn chair. It was just a bit bigger than child size, so her knees nearly touched her chest.

"No, we've decided not to come. I really thought about it, and it's not appropriate for me to be there on your special day."

"Ron doesn't mind. W-we don't mind."

Sabrina smiled slowly. "I know you don't, and I'm grateful for your graciousness there. I realized that I was just using this as a way to somehow punish Ron."

Kimberly's lip twitched. Punish Ron? Hadn't she already punished him enough by cheating on him and then marrying her lover?

"Punish him for what?"

"For moving on, I suppose. You were right to see that, Kimberly. I think I didn't even see it until we sat in that first coun-

seling session. I still have some things to work out about how
our marriage deteriorated . . ."

Yes, you do. You need to work out your narcissistic tendencies.

Kimberly bit her lip to keep any untoward words from spilling out. She was doing a good job of holding it together too.

". . . but what I do know is that I trust you and Ron to take
care of the girls in Jamaica. I always trusted him, and now I
trust you as well."

"Thank you."

"Plus, I think a couple of your bridesmaids have it out for
me. It might not even be safe."

Kimberly's eyebrows shot up, and she started to object on
the basis of the fact that not all black girls had violent tendencies. But since she couldn't, not with a straight face anyway,
argue that Sabrina was wrong, she decided to let it go.

"We'll have a ton of pictures and videos of the girls."

"I would love that. Can you make sure to get one with Sean
and the girls? I'd like to put that in their room."

"Yes, absolutely."

Ron walked back into the room and gave Sabrina a curious
look. She was still seated in the unicorn chair.

"What did I miss?" Ron asked.

"I just told Kimberly that Frank and I have to send our regrets for the wedding. We won't be able to attend."

"Is there something wrong?" Ron looked from Kimberly to
Sabrina and then back to Kimberly.

"Um . . . well . . ." Sabrina couldn't seem to spit the words out.

"They had something come up, but she wants lots of pictures
of the twins and a nice one with Sean to put in their room at
home."

"Okay," Ron said. "Thanks for letting us know."

Sabrina stood and straightened her skirt. "I guess I better get
on the road. I've got a Thanksgiving dinner to prepare myself."

"Really?" Ron asked sounding truly surprised.

"Yes, I do cook. I'm sure I can't put my ankles in some macaroni and cheese, but I am from the south too."

"Ankles?" Ron asked.

"She means foot . . . I think," Kimberly said.

"Yes, foot. That is what I mean. Anyway, I've got to get going girls. Give mommy a hug."

Carly and Kayla gave Sabrina the briefest of goodbye hugs. They were busy creating a whole new world with their unicorn dolls.

"Upstaged by unicorns," Sabrina said.

"They're nice unicorns though," Ron said.

Sabrina shrugged and gave Kimberly an even briefer hug than the ones her daughters gave her. She stopped in front of Ron and gave him a fist bump. This made him chuckle, but Kimberly appreciated the lack of embrace given to her future husband.

Kimberly and Ron walked Sabrina to the door where she waved goodbye and promptly sped out. Kimberly didn't miss the glistening in her eyes when she did so. She even felt a twinge of compassion for her soulmate's ex-wife.

It was just a twinge, though. Not enough to make Kimberly beg her to be a part of their wedding in Jamaica. They could take the co-parenting in small doses and milestones.

"I wonder if they really had something come up," Ron said.

"Naw. She just felt like it wasn't appropriate for her to be there."

"I bet she thought Traci and Abena was gonna beat her ass in Jamaica," Ron said as she pulled down the driveway.

"Maybe she did. I'm just glad she's deciding to stay at home."

"I would've uninvited her," Ron said. "All you had to do was say the word."

"No, it's better this way. Better for her to feel like it was her idea. It feeds her victim narrative."

Ron shook his head and laughed. "You've got her pegged, huh?"

"Sure do. She ain't getting away with nothing over here."

Ron wrapped Kimberly in his arms and squeezed her tightly. "Thank you for the girls' bedroom. They love it."

"Well, I love them. And their daddy, so . . . I'd build five unicorn bedrooms if it means I get to see your dimpled face smiling at me."

Ron glanced in the direction of the girls' bedroom. "You think they'll miss us if we disappear for about ten fifteen minutes?"

"Nope," Kimberly giggled. "In fact, I think you got a good twenty-five, thirty minutes if you ask me."

Ron grabbed Kimberly's hand and led her to the stairs. Kimberly squealed in anticipation, and Ron held his finger to his lips for quiet.

As they ascended the stairs on tiptoe, Kimberly felt a weight lifted from her. Sabrina didn't need to witness their union, because she wasn't a part of their tribe—not really—not their marital tribe. They would have to forge a path to blending their families; oil and water could only mix if there was another substance to bind them together.

The twins would have to be the tie that bound them all.

Chapter 41

TWILA

I stood in line at the Thanksgiving turkey handout. The one that I'd found on Fatima Adams's Facebook page. I picked this event, because it looked like something she was doing with a different ministry group at her church. Hopefully that meant Alexander wasn't going to be there.

I needed to get her alone.

I'd gone through great pains to make myself look less-than-fortunate, but I don't know if I'd accomplished that feat. I'd covered my expensive Thanksgiving weave with a baseball cap, left my jewelry at home and hadn't worn a stitch of makeup. I'd driven my car to the bus depot and taken a bus to the location. I still felt like I didn't fit in with the rest of the people in line.

As I got closer to the front of the line, I could see the women at the table handing out the turkeys. Fatima was there and a few others. On the surface, Fatima seemed happy wearing her ministry dress and sneakers, but there was a sadness in her eyes. I noticed it, but I bet no one else in her circle cared to pull the layers back.

I'd practiced what I was going to say, over and over again, but I didn't know if I could get the words out. I would be unmasking myself and coming out of the shadows. There would be no mistaking that I knew her husband after this, and I had no idea how Fatima might respond to having her new life snatched from underneath her.

Uncertainty almost made me run away from the line. Determination to end this thing kept me there.

When it was my turn, Fatima greeted me with a bright smile. "Praise the Lord. Do you need a small turkey or a large one?"

I shook my head.

"Did you not need a turkey?" Fatima asked.

"No. I'd like to speak to you privately. Can you help me with something?"

The trembling in my voice wasn't an act. I was nervous as hell doing this. What if this girl was as demented as her husband? Maybe she'd stayed with him because she liked who he was.

"Well, today is the turkey giveaway, but I can get you connected with some of our other ministry partners if you have a different need."

I leaned forward over the table and brought my face right up next to Fatima's. "I need to talk to you about Alexander and his toys. Especially the taser that he used to incapacitate me before he raped me," I whispered.

She leaned back and stared at me with wide eyes. Her partner at the table looked at me with suspicion as I moved back to my starting position. I waited to see what would happen next. I'd only planned it this far.

"Is everything okay?" Fatima's partner asked her.

Fatima nodded. "Yes, but can you call up another one of the volunteers to work my spot for a minute. I would like to go and pray with this young lady."

A smile teased the corners of my mouth. Maybe this would go the way I needed it to go.

Fatima came out from behind the table, took my hand and led me into the church. I followed in silence. She took me into a small room that said Prayer Closet on the front of the door. Except I didn't think we were going to be praying in there.

"Who are you?" Fatima asked. "You know me and my husband, so who are you? Are you one of the ladies from the homeless shelter also?"

She sounded . . . jealous. Like a woman confronting her husband's mistress. I looked at the knob on the door and for a second thought of aborting the mission.

"No, I'm not. I'm actually a very wealthy woman. Your husband does not discriminate."

"You say he raped you? When?"

"Two years ago."

"Impossible. We've been together for four."

"Do you think he stopped being a rapist after you married him? You might have empowered him, you know. Validated him in a way."

"I did no such thing. I just gave him every nasty thing he's ever wanted."

"Let me guess, he ties you up and puts you in a cage. Sometimes he hits you with whips. Sometimes with brushes."

"Lower your voice," Fatima said. "We're on the church grounds."

"Sometimes he still uses his taser on you, doesn't he? He simulates rape until he just can't take it anymore and then he goes out and gets the real thing."

Tears poured down Fatima's cheeks. If everything I said wasn't true, it was damn sure close enough to the truth.

"He raped me at a swingers' club."

"Then he will just say you wanted him."

I nodded. "You're correct. You can see my problem now. I've thought about taking him to the authorities, but I don't know if a jury would get outraged enough about what happened to me. There would be at least one person on the jury who thought I'd asked for it by going to that club."

"Maybe you did ask for it."

"Except I didn't. And neither did you when you were homeless and looking for help from a man who was supposed to be a minister. He exploited you for his sick depravity, and he still is."

Fatima sobbed and shook. I wanted to comfort her but couldn't bring myself to touch her. Not when she was lowkey defending Alexander.

"He bought me a house, gave me a ring. We have a daughter together."

"What if he turns his attention to your little girl?"

"No. He wouldn't do that. He doesn't like little girls."

I swooned in the tight space. This woman was just as broken as she was when she was living in the homeless shelter. She just had somewhere to lay her head every night.

"You're right. He likes helpless pitiful women."

I opened the door to the prayer closet. I was done with this conversation. This was a mistake. This woman couldn't help me.

I wasn't helpless or pitiful. Not anymore. And Alexander Adams was about to find out just how strong I was.

Chapter 42

KIMBERLY

It was five o'clock in the morning on Thanksgiving, and Kimberly was already up and cooking. She'd done all of the baking on Tuesday and Wednesday, but Thanksgiving Day was when all the magic happened. Hahna was there, but she seemed barely awake.

"Is there a reason why onions, bell peppers, and celery need to be chopped before the sun rises?" Hahna asked. "I'm still sleepy, and it was all cozy with Sam in the bed."

"They have to be chopped this early, because they go in more than one dish," Kimberly explained patiently.

She was used to reluctant sous chefs. Especially in the morning. Hahna would be fine once she thawed out.

"Where's Twila?" Kimberly asked. "How'd she get off the hook for this?"

"I went to wake her up, and she wasn't there. Maybe she spent the night at DeAndre's house."

"They've gotten to sleepover status? I didn't know."

"I didn't know either. Even after she gave him some, she came back to my house."

"Did you try calling her? You aren't worried?" Kimberly asked.

"She is an adult, Kim. I don't think we have a reason to be worried . . . unless . . . ."

Kimberly set the bowl of smoked turkey necks on the countertop and turned to face Hahna. There was a lot going on with Twila. Some of it that Hahna wasn't telling.

"Unless? What the hell, Hahna."

"So, the guy, the rapist . . . she's found out all this information. Where he goes to church, that he has a wife and kid, and also . . . that he probably raped his wife prior to marrying her."

Kimberly glared at Hahna. She'd picked a hell of a time to stop telling secrets. Twila had been a loose cannon since the rape happened. There was no way they shouldn't have been monitoring her every move once Twila had those revelations.

"You don't think we should be keeping our eyes on her? Making sure she doesn't do something crazy?"

Hahna rolled her eyes. "Okay, Mama Kim. She's in therapy and she's dealing with her issues. I honestly think she's close to going to the authorities. Now that she has some evidence that this wasn't a one off, and that he's done it before."

"If she doesn't show up in a few hours, I'm asking Ron to go out looking for her."

"That's crazy. Where are you gonna send him? To her office? To the gym? She probably went to work out and will be back in bed in a couple of hours."

"You'll call Sam to see if she came back to the house?"

"Yes."

"Okay."

Kimberly wasn't insulted at all by being called a mother hen. Oh well. Twila was fragile, and she'd been dealing with a trauma that she hadn't told anyone about until recently. The fact that she hadn't moved back home yet showed that she was still in a precarious state. Precarious with Twila equaled the potential for violence.

"Is Samantha coming today?" Hahna asked.

"Maybe. Thank you for talking to her. I don't know what I said, but she's back on board for the wedding."

"I just told her that we would have some of the bridal party meetings at the church. We're meeting in the middle."

"Did you tell Traci and Abena they were going to have to go to the church?"

"No, not yet. I'll deal with them when the time comes. I think they'll be cool with it. They're a lot more flexible than Samantha is, that's for sure."

"Thank you, Hahna. I appreciate you so much for taking the lead in all this."

Hahna put her piles of onion, celery, and pepper into separate storage baggies. She took a long sip from her coffee and looked relaxed. Kimberly laughed at her. The work was only getting started. It wasn't break time yet.

"Now, you can get those yams over there and peel them."

Hahna looked at the mountain of washed yams in the pan and groaned. "How many people are you trying to feed?" she asked.

"Believe it or not, the yams shrink down small when they cook. That pile of yams will serve all of us with just a few leftovers."

"Twila's gonna show up when all the hard work is done, I see," Hahna said.

"It's okay. We'll make her put the food away and clean up."

Hahna smiled. "Perfect."

At around ten o'clock, Kimberly was in the full swing of activity. Pots were bubbling, and the kitchen smelled like collard greens, gumbo, and the cinnamon of the yams baking in the oven.

Ron emerged from upstairs with the twins fully dressed in blue jeans and Thanksgiving sweaters.

"We're going to breakfast with Sean," Ron said. "And then I think we're going to go and look at the Christmas decorations downtown."

"Good. You'll be gone a few hours then?" Kimberly asked.

"Yes. We'll be out of your way, Madame Chef."

"Thank you. Make sure to check your phone periodically in case I've forgotten anything or need you to pick up one last thing."

"Roger that. Where's Twila? I thought she was coming too."

Kimberly looked over at Hahna and Hahna shrugged.

"I haven't heard from her yet," Hahna said. "Maybe we can reach out to DeAndre to see if he's seen her."

Ron looked worried. "Do we have a Twila emergency? Do I need to do some stretches and lift a few dumbbells this morning?"

Kimberly laughed at this, and so did Hahna. Ron's heroics had to come in and save the day for Twila before. He sounded ready to do it again if necessary.

"Hopefully not," Kimberly said, "but I will keep you posted."

"Well, let's get everyone else on speed dial too. That guy she's dating now is buff right? I might need some backup. I'm old."

"You aren't old baby," Kimberly said. "You're just grown and sexy."

Ron kissed Kimberly's cheek. She looked over his shoulder and caught the twins sneaking Thanksgiving cookies.

"Are we having cookies before breakfast?" Kimberly asked.

Carly and Kayla looked at her with wide eyes, probably wondering if they were in trouble. They looked so cute, that Kimberly couldn't even pretend to be angry.

"We're sorry, Ms. Kimberly," Carly said. She was always the voice of the two.

"I think it's a holiday, so cookies before breakfast might be just fine," Kimberly said.

The twins looked at each other and giggled before taking an extra cookie from the dish and putting them in their little unicorn purses. They didn't care that pinks and blues of their handbags didn't match the browns and oranges in their sweaters. Apparently, unicorns were always appropriate.

"We'll be back soon."

"Don't ruin their appetites," Kimberly said. "There will be so much food later."

"They only graze anyway. A couple bites here, a couple bites there."

"Okay, see you when you get back."

Ron chased his daughters to the front door. They squealed as they scurried, dropping cookie crumbs behind them.

"I'm gonna have to add an extra day to my housekeeper's schedule when they're here," Kimberly said when they left. "They are messy."

"Kids are messy. I don't think I'm going that route, but maybe," Hahna said.

"You know Ron and I talked about the possibility of more children. I don't know, but I might be catching a case of baby fever."

"I wouldn't say I have baby fever. I just wouldn't be angry if it happened. Sam feels the same way."

"Unlike your ex. Torian was a hard no on babies, right?"

"Ugh. Why would you speak of the devil? He was a hard no on everything. Hard no on being faithful, hard no on marriage, hard no on telling the damn truth."

Kimberly laughed out loud. "Okay killa. Tell 'em how you really feel."

"Girl, my bad. He showed up at my office the other day and it pissed me off even seeing him."

"What did he want?"

"To bring me a data analytics engagement with a big private equity group."

"I hope you said yes."

"We have a meeting next week. I just don't know if I want to deal with his ass."

"Can you invite Sam to the meeting?" Kimberly asked.

"I thought about that, because if at some point he finds out I'm working with my ex, he might feel some kinda way."

"Sam seems really chill and secure, though. So, he might not care. Maybe mention the whole thing in passing and see what he thinks."

"I will. I just hate that I have any emotions regarding Torian at all, you know? He should be a non-factor. I shouldn't get angry when I think of him. I shouldn't feel sad. I have the love of my life, so why does he even affect me at all?"

Kimberly saw how worked up Hahna was about all this and suddenly felt like a bad friend. Hahna had been there for everyone. She was holding the bridal party together, counseling Twila, and she had lost someone close to her.

"Are you okay?" Kimberly asked.

"I'm sorry, I'm fine. I just totally vented and dumped on you."

Kimberly walked around the counter and sat next to Hahna on a barstool. "You can dump on me, Hahna. There's been so much going on that I haven't really asked you how you've been since you lost your Uncle."

"I'm okay. Dealing with Rochelle was worse than the funeral. Sam was there for me and he was amazing. I felt so blessed to have him there."

"He has been good for you, and good to you. Don't let any leftover feelings from Torian impact anything you've got going."

"I won't. Torian is dust. Except when it comes to me getting this money."

"And as long as you look at it that way, you'll be fine."

Kimberly wasn't so sure about this, though. Torian was a successful man, much closer to Hahna's financial level than Sam. Sam seemed secure with a healthy ego, but Kimberly wondered if their relationship was strong enough to withstand the rich and dashing ex.

"Make sure you talk to Sam, okay?"

Hahna nodded. "I will mention it today when I go back home to get dressed for dinner. If we show up smiling, it went well. If it didn't go well, I might already be drunk."

Kimberly laughed nervously. She hoped it went well, because they didn't need anything to ruin Carly and Kayla's first Thanksgiving.

Chapter 43

TWILA

Thanksgiving was a day for giving thanks to God for all the blessings you had over the course of the year. I hoped to give Thanksgiving a different meaning for Alexander Adams. It would be the day he thanked God he was still breathing.

He pulled against the restraints I had on him, but the duct tape and ropes held. I wasn't worried about him escaping.

"Oh, are you afraid of the dentist's office?" I asked. "Lots of people are afraid of dentists. You'd be surprised. I have had some of the biggest and strongest men in this chair, crying like a baby."

Alexander didn't answer. He only glared at me. He couldn't respond anyway, not with the duct tape on his mouth. I wrapped it all the way around his head. It was gonna hurt like a bitch to take off.

"Were you shocked when I attacked you? You weren't expecting it were you? A tiny runner in the neighborhood, running up on you with a taser as you took out your trash."

The glaring continued.

"Those tasers are amazingly effective for incapacitating a victim. But, then again, you know that. You've incapacitated victims before."

Alexander stopped looking at me. I watched his eyes darting around the office, trying to get some clue of why he was here.

"You don't remember raping me, do you? That makes me wonder just how many victims you have, you sick fuck."

He ignored my speech and kept looking around my office. Nothing of note there to tell him who I was.

"Maybe you'd know me if I had on a black bustier, and thigh highs. Maybe if I had a mask on and a whip in my hand. Or maybe, if we were at Club Phenom. Would you remember then?"

He slowly turned to me and narrowed his eyes. Finally, recognition.

"Ah, now you remember. That night when I was minding my own business, and you tased me and raped me with your unimpressive penis. I barely felt it."

Alexander struggled at the restraints again, and I waved a fresh taser in his face.

"Keep it up, and I'm gonna make you go limp again. I don't want to get your fresh piss in my dental chair though, so calm the fuck down."

He calmed down. Probably wondered what was next. He probably thought he was going to meet his maker. Maybe he thought I was going to rape him back. I hoped he had all those thoughts, and more.

"You are lucky to be alive right now, Alexander Adams. You are very lucky. I could've just killed you and disposed of your body. Do you think your wife would've made a missing person's report? Maybe, but probably not right away. She knows what you are. You raped her when she was helpless and homeless. Then you bought her off with a house and a title. Wife. I wonder what she'd been through in her life that marriage to you was a come up. Poor thing."

Then, Alexander fucking Adams decided that he was going to laugh. It was muffled through the duct tape, but it was definitely a laugh. Bad idea Alex.

I took out my nine-millimeter Glock and held it to his temple.

"Man, don't play with me. I am legit fucked up in the head because of what you did to me. I go to therapy twice a week. But when I told my therapist what you did to your wife, she didn't stop me from doing this. She knew I was coming for your ass."

The laughter stopped, and his nasal breathing was rapid and ragged.

"Nobody is going to care if I empty this out in your head. And nobody's going to know if I do. It's Thanksgiving. This building is closed. No one here but us. Everyone's home preparing their Thanksgiving dinners."

I wondered where he was supposed to be. After that visit from me, Fatima was probably hoping he never came back. If he didn't, she'd probably liquidate the bank accounts, sell the house and get the hell out of dodge. She'd be the first suspect, especially when her friend Christina got questioned by the police for her threatening Facebook comments, and she told everyone the truth.

"Do you think Fatima is gonna care? I talked to her, you know."

He *did* know. His nostrils flared when I said this. Fatima had confronted him. Maybe threatened divorce.

"She'll leave at some point. When she gets on her feet. She's using you now. It's unfortunate there's a child involved. The fact that you procreated and put your rapey genetics into the gene pool is very unfortunate."

Tears leaked from the corners of Alexander's eyes. I burst into laughter. He had the audacity to be crying? What a weak ass he was. I wasn't surprised, though.

"Aw, are you feeling remorseful? Or scared? Which is it? I know I sound like a crazy bitch. I am. So, you're right to feel scared."

The glaring returned, but his breathing slowed. Maybe he could tell that I wasn't going to kill him. He might've been plotting his escape or even his revenge.

"Okay, Alexander. Let's not drag this out. Let's get to what your next steps will be, shall we? I have a Thanksgiving dinner party to get to. Wouldn't want my friends to be worried."

The fury and rage in his eyes was priceless. It matched my own.

"First thing you're going to do, when you find yourself back at home, is you're going to put your house on the market. You're leaving Atlanta. After you do that, you have twenty-four hours to be packed up and gone."

Alexander grunted and made noises. I supposed these were objections. I didn't care about the logistics; I just knew his ass better be gone.

"If you don't pack your shit in a van and get out in twenty-four hours, reports of the women you've raped in the homeless ministry will be given to your pastor. There is a woman who will substantiate the claims for me, so that I won't have to talk to anyone."

The fear in his eyes told me my suspicions were real. He had raped more women at that homeless shelter. I didn't have to produce them, I just had to give enough evidence to the pastor to start an investigation. The stain of it would be enough even if he was never convicted.

"Who knows? Maybe your wife is talking to your pastor right now. That would make this all easy for me, and you. You wouldn't have to find a new place to live. The state of Georgia would have one for you. Three hots and a cot."

He started to struggle against his restraints again. This was getting tiring. He wasn't going to escape, but he was obviously still obstinate. I straddled the dental chair and held my gun between his legs.

"Calm the fuck down before you make me kill you."

He stopped moving and I got off the chair. I wasn't going to kill him. Wasn't going to go to hell for this demon. He could go there by himself.

I opened the drawer and pulled out a syringe. Alexander started grunting and making noise.

"Will you please shut up? It's just propofol. It won't kill you. It'll make you take a long nap though. Long enough for me to put you in that wheelchair and get you out of here. When you wake up, you'll be a little disoriented, but you'll remember. Put your house on the market and get out of Atlanta in twenty-four hours. If not, I'll be back. And I might have to hurt you."

Alexander continued to struggle until I'd administered the injection. Then, it was lights out. Thank goodness for heavy weightlifting. He couldn't have been more than one hundred sixty pounds. It was harder lifting him when he was unconscious, but not impossible.

I cut the tape away from his mouth so that he could breathe freely and freed him from the chair. I lifted him into the wheelchair and covered him with a blanket.

If anyone cared to look at the security footage from this, they might have some questions about what was going on. But since one of the brothers of Omega Phi Gamma owned the building, I wasn't too worried about that.

It was easy to wheel Alexander to the parking lot and haul him into the backseat of my car. Dumping him would be harder. But I'd already found a secluded area in Atlanta—a strip club parking lot on Thanksgiving Day.

I left Alexander there on a bench outside, covered with the blanket. He looked like a man who'd had too much to drink and slept it off on the bench or a homeless person. Either way, when he woke up, he'd be able to get home. I hadn't taken his wallet, or phone, although I'd put it in airplane mode and disabled the GPS.

It wasn't a perfect crime, I was sure. Luckily, it didn't have to be. It wasn't like Alexander was going to press charges, or even tell anyone what had happened to him.

If he did, I would take it to the next level. And if necessary, I'd bring in professionals. He was not going to rob me of my life, my peace, my sanity, or my home. Hell no.

And he damn sure wasn't going to rob me of my gift.

I dialed DeAndre's number. He answered on the first ring.

"Hi Twila. Happy Thanksgiving."

"Hey DeAndre. Happy Thanksgiving to you too. You going to your family's house today?"

"No, I think I'm going to chill around the house. My sister's husband's family aren't really my cup of tea."

"Why don't you come with me? We're having dinner at Kimberly's house."

"The bride to be?"

"Yep. She can cook her ass off. We'll have to do two-a-days for the next week to work off all the calories."

"I'm down. I'd love to. Are you going to text me the address? Should I meet you there?"

I smiled. "No, I'll text you my address. You can pick me up from my place."

Nope, Alexander Adams wasn't taking another moment from me. He was done terrorizing my life. And I was about to share my gift with my friends.

Chapter 44

HAHNA

My back and feet hurt from working so hard in the kitchen with Kimberly. I would remind myself to never work for her in real life. Not to mention that Twila had never shown up for her duties. She'd called and said she had an emergency patient, but I was skeptical. I think she just didn't feel like cutting onions.

"You need the shower, babe?" I asked Sam as I set out a fresh towel in the bathroom. "I may be in here for a while. I think it'll take me forever to get the onion and celery scent out of my hands."

"I took a shower earlier. Do you want tea or coffee? I can have it ready for you when you get out."

"Wine. I need wine."

Sam laughed. "Okay. Chilled white wine it is. You know, there's time for you to take a bath if you really want to relax."

"There is time, but I need not get too relaxed. I might just fall asleep and go over for a leftovers plate in the morning."

"She did have you up early."

"Five o'clock! And she was already going when I got there. Kimberly is amazing in the kitchen though. I ate a slice of pound cake earlier and almost fainted it was so good."

"I can't wait. I love a good home-cooked meal."

"Babe, I've got about five things I can cook well. Outside of that, your home-cooked meals will come from a caterer."

"And I'm not mad about that. You have other strengths."

Sam punctuated this thought with a yummy French kiss. If he convinced me to crawl into bed with him, we definitely wouldn't make it in time for dinner.

"Speaking of my other strengths, I got a really good lead for a new client at work."

"Really? That's great. Do you think it'll be something you could announce at the Christmas party?"

"Yes, if it goes well."

"Why wouldn't it go well?"

For a second, I considered not telling Sam about the Torian connection, but Kimberly was right. At this point, Sam might think I was hiding something if I didn't tell him.

"My ex-boyfriend, Torian, is the one who brought the lead. It's a private equity group he's been doing business with. He recommended The Data Whisperers."

"Hmmm."

I couldn't tell what that meant. Did he not care?

"What do you think?" I asked.

"This is the guy who ghosted you, right?"

"Yeah, the one who claimed he had cancer later."

"Claimed?"

"I mean, that's what he said. I don't have evidence that he had it, but I don't have any reason to think he was lying."

"Sounds like you don't trust him one hundred percent."

"I don't trust him fifty percent."

"But you're letting him bring you business?"

"Corden and I talked about it. We want to at least explore it. It's too promising to not investigate. It could be a several million-dollar engagement."

"If you don't trust him, you should be careful."

"Do you want to come to the meeting?" I asked.

Sam scrunched his face into a frown. "Why would I join your business meeting? I don't know anything about data analytics."

"No, but you're good at reading people. I value your opinion."

"I am good at that, but so are you. I don't think you need me there."

"Okay."

Sam rubbed his hands in his beard and stretched the hair. He did this when he was thinking. His expressive eyes confirmed his pondering.

"Are you inviting me because you think I'd be jealous?"

I let out a huge sigh. I was kinda glad Sam had identified that elephant in the room.

"Would you be jealous?"

"No, no. I wouldn't. I'm not that kind of guy, Hahna. If you're mine, then you're mine, but only because you choose to be. I'm not in the habit of fighting for a woman's love."

"I definitely didn't mean to imply that. I just don't want to mess this up. I love you, Sam. I have never had a bond like this."

"I love you too. More than anything. I want your business to be a success. If this guy can help you with that, I'm not concerned that you used to date him. I trust you implicitly."

I threw my arms around Sam's neck and kissed him. I don't know why I let Corden or Kimberly make me doubt my Sam.

"Now, get in the shower so we can get to the food. A brother's getting hungry."

"You sure you don't want to join me?" I asked as I kissed him again.

"Don't tempt me with a good time. I want some turkey!"

I laughed and rushed into the bathroom for my shower. Over and over this man proved to me how amazing he was. Torian and his stacks of cash had nothing on Sam and his infinite capacity to love me.

With Sam's vote of confidence, I knew that Corden and I would be successful in landing this account with YS&S. I just hoped Torian didn't have any tricks up his sleeve, but since he was the devil in the flesh, I wouldn't be surprised if he did.

Chapter 45

KIMBERLY

Kimberly sipped a glass of red wine as everyone fellow-shipped prior to dinner. The dinner was completed, and Twila had texted and said she was on her way, so Kimberly felt relaxed and calm. She watched Ron play cards with his children, including Sean, and she felt an incredible sense of peace. Even the foreboding that she'd felt about Twila had dissipated.

Hahna looked refreshed in her brown jumpsuit. Kimberly felt a little twinge of jealousy at how good she looked. It was Thanksgiving, and her wedding was at the end of March. Even if she lost an impossible one hundred pounds by then, her body wouldn't look as good as Hahna's. She knew it didn't matter, because the bride would be the most beautiful on her wedding day, but she still wished that over the years she'd finally buckled down and found her discipline. Weight loss was the hardest thing she'd ever tried to do. Harder than getting her law degree, running a business, or even finding a man.

She wasn't helping herself by making the decadent Thanksgiving meal, but she wouldn't worry about that on the holiday. She'd start again, at the top of the year. And whatever happened, would happen. She would be smaller by the end of March, or she wouldn't. She was still going to look into Ron's eyes and say, "I do."

Hahna bounced over to Kimberly. "What are you thinking about?" she asked. "The food coma everyone is going to be in when they're done eating?"

"There will be food comas to go around. Yes."

"Did I tell you I invited one of our frat brothers for Samantha? Is she still coming?"

Kimberly's jaw dropped. Samantha was not a person she hooked up with men. It was terrible for the man and pointless for Samantha. Her list of qualifications was impenetrable. That was why she hadn't had a date in ten years.

"You know Samantha is crazy when it comes to guys, right? Who in the world could you hook her up with?"

"Brandon Tyson. He just planted a church in Decatur."

"Oh, yeah, I know him. His pastor loves him and gave him a full blessing in breaking off to start the new church."

"That's what the church streets are saying. Plus, he's an eligible bachelor."

Eligible was debatable. Brandon was a big man, probably over four hundred pounds, and he had a slew of health issues. Diabetes was the one Kimberly knew about, because he'd been hospitalized after a church conference.

"I don't know if Samantha is looking. Everyone's not looking, you know."

"Well, even if she's not, it's kinda awkward for all of us to be coupled, and her being her as the odd woman out."

"I guess."

"Should I not have invited him?"

"I mean, we're gonna be drinking over here, so is he cool with that?"

"Brandon's a frat. He knows what it is. He'll pray for us and wash his turkey down with all your lemonade and sweet tea."

"Jesus. If he has a diabetic attack because of all this food, I'm blaming you."

"You aren't blaming me. He's grown. He knows what he can and can't eat."

The doorbell rang, and Kimberly walked toward the door, but Ron beat her to it.

"Sit down, baby," Ron said. "You've been cooking for two days. You don't have to lift another finger."

"He loves you so much," Hahna whispered. "I can't wait for the wedding."

Twila walked into Kimberly's living room looking like she didn't have a care in the world, and with her new man in tow. Kimberly marveled at the healing properties of therapy and penis.

"Doesn't she look like she didn't lift a finger in the kitchen today," Hahna said. "Hair all laid, feet unswollen."

Twila laughed. "Y'all not gonna worry me. My patient thanks you both. Y'all know I only know how to chop stuff anyway. I don't cook."

"DeAndre, you cool with that?" Hahna asked.

"The not cooking? She doesn't have to cook. I've got more than one chef in the rotation."

Everyone laughed.

"So, DeAndre, you haven't met Big Ron yet. He's Kimberly's fiancé. These are his little girls Carly and Kayla, and his older son Sean. You've met Sam and Hahna. Everybody, this is my man, DeAndre."

"You've been promoted since the last time we chatted," Hahna said as she gave DeAndre a hug. "Congratulations, brother. Welcome to the circle."

"Yes, welcome him, y'all," Twila said. "He's coming to Jamaica with us too."

"I am?" DeAndre asked.

"Yes, but we haven't talked about that yet. Kim and Ron are getting married in Jamaica. You are my date."

"Oh, cool then. I love a bougie black people wedding," DeAndre said.

"You play spades?" Ron asked. "I'm trying to get a game together. You can be Sam's partner."

"Absolutely," DeAndre said.

DeAndre went to the table, and had a seat while Ron moved Kayla and Carly out of the way. Hahna grabbed Twila and dragged her to the kitchen. Kimberly approved of this action, because

Twila wasn't just happy and free, she was extra. Like she'd already drank all the Henny but without the stumbling.

"Girl, what is up with you?" Hahna asked when they got into the kitchen away from the guys' ears.

"What do you mean?" Twila asked. "I'm good."

"I'm gonna be honest," Kimberly said. "You're a little much today. Like that one time you took uppers during finals week."

"Oh my god, that was crazy," Hahna said. "We had to peel her off the walls. Have you taken something? Sniffed some nitrous with your patient?"

Twila laughed. "Y'all are hilarious. I just feel really good. I had DeAndre pick me up from my house."

"Wait. You went home?" Kimberly asked. "Are you okay?"

"Better than okay."

"And Alexander?" Hahna asked.

"Handled."

Kimberly and Hahna exchanged a look. Twila laughed and poured herself a glass of wine.

"I saw that look," Twila said. "You guys should practice that look so it's slicker."

"Did you kill anyone or order a hit?" Hahna asked.

"No. But if I had, I wouldn't tell you. Plausible deniability."

"Well, then, how is it handled?" Kimberly said.

"Alexander was persuaded to put his house on the market and leave Atlanta."

"Persuaded how?" Hahna asked.

"You ask too many questions. Let's go have Thanksgiving dinner."

Kimberly wanted to interrogate her more, but the doorbell rang again. More guests had arrived.

"We're not done talking about this," Kimberly said. "You are giving me details."

"I am giving you this," Twila said as she shimmied her middle finger in front of her wine glass.

Hahna's jaw dropped as Twila laughed out loud. Kimberly shook her head and went to see who'd gotten to her house. Thank goodness it was her sane friend, Samantha.

Kimberly set her wine glass down and went to hug Samantha. "I'm so glad you came, girl."

"I know you're over here cooking up a storm. My aunt has retired from cooking," Samantha said.

"DeAndre, this is our sorority sister Samantha. DeAndre is Twila's boyfriend."

Samantha smiled. "Nice to meet you DeAndre."

"Likewise," he said, as he slammed an ace of hearts on the table.

"Girl, come on in the kitchen with the women. They are over here killing the card table."

Twila poured herself a second glass of wine as Kimberly and Samantha walked into the kitchen. Samantha waved and smiled. She seemed in better spirits than previous times they'd gotten together.

"Hey Samantha," Hahna said as she hugged their sorority sister.

"Hey girl," Twila said.

Kimberly was kind of glad Twila hadn't hugged Samantha too. That would've been overkill.

"Twila, does your new boyfriend have a brother?"

Twila laughed. "No girl. Only a sister. But I didn't know you were looking. I know quite a few guys who you might be interested in."

Kimberly tried to give Hahna a sneaky look, but Twila laughed, so she knew it wasn't sneaky enough.

"I'm not actively looking, but if someone who looked like that fell out of the sky and at my feet. I wouldn't be opposed to an exploration."

This seemed to tickle Twila more than anyone. She threw her head back and hollered.

"You sound like me, talking about an exploration," Twila said.

"I'm sure you're doing more exploration than I am," Samantha replied.

"Call me Dora. 'Cause I wanna go on a trip with my backpack every day."

They all deteriorated into laughter then. Even though Kimberly was still leery, this was the version of Twila that she loved. The one who could make everyone laugh, from Evangelist Samantha to Debbie.

"So, check this out," Hahna said. "I have been meaning to tell y'all about this. I offered to buy Debbie her plane ticket for Jamaica, because she had been complaining about the cost."

"Oh, good. Thank you for thinking of that, 'cause she would wait until the last minute and have someone paying three thousand for her ticket," Kimberly said.

"Well, she already had her ticket, and she showed me the receipt for her dress."

"Really," Samantha said. "I just knew she would be the last one, and I could get some grace."

Hahna laughed. "Well, she met a guy. An NBA player, and I don't know what she did, but he's fallen hard."

"I know what she did," Twila said.

"Teach me!" Samantha said.

Twila sipped her wine and laughed. "Jesus might not approve."

"Oh," Samantha said. "Give me some of that wine then and let me ponder my options. I might need to change up."

No one questioned Samantha asking for a glass of wine. The sorority sisters wouldn't make her feel like a hypocrite for having a glass. They all knew she was kidding about changing up anything regarding her chastity. A taste of wine was one thing, giving up the goodies was quite another.

"When are we eating?" Samantha asked. "Is everything ready."

"Yep. We're just waiting on one more person, and we can start," Kimberly said.

"Before he gets here," Hahna said. "I think I should warn Samantha."

"Warn me?"

"Well, I wanted to invite a single guy for you to chat with, so I invited one of the frats that I thought you might like."

"Oh, how sweet of you. No one ever thinks to do that," Samantha said.

"You're cool with it?" Hahna asked.

"Sure. Even if I don't like him, we can still have good conversation."

Hahna exhaled. "Oh, good. I thought you might be mad at me."

"Not at all. Does he look anything like DeAndre?"

"Ummm . . . well . . . he's chocolate. Yep, he's chocolate."

Twila burst into laughter. "Girl, who the hell did you invite?"

"Brandon Tyson . . ."

Samantha joined Twila laughing. "Well, this should be interesting. He's been trying to get at me for years."

"You betta let him catch you," Kimberly said. "He's a good brother."

"How he gonna catch me? His big self would be outta breath trying to chase me."

The doorbell rang at the wrong time, because they couldn't stop laughing. Ron let Brandon in and at the sound of his voice, all four sisters were in tears. Kimberly waved her hands in the air.

"We have to stop. We can't be laughing like this. He gone think we're laughing at him."

"We are though," Twila said.

Kimberly marched out of the kitchen and called everyone to the dining room table. She had place settings at the table for ten, and a tiny table in the kitchen for the girls.

Everyone except Kimberly, Twila, and Hahna took their seats. The three best friends brought the final trays of food to the table, and then joined the rest of guests.

"Before we start this Thanksgiving feast," Ron said. "I just want to thank my baby, Kimmie Kim, for working for two days straight in the kitchen. She is the thing I'm most grateful for. I have everything I need under one roof. My woman, my children, and gravy. God is in the blessing business."

Kimberly gave Ron a chaste kiss on the cheek. "Thank you, baby. I'm grateful for you too. And I'm grateful for my sorors being here. Not just today, but for our wedding. I don't know what I would do without y'all."

"Your life would be incredibly boring without us," Twila said. "And my life would be off the rails without y'all. I am thankful for y'all keeping me together. All day, all day."

Kimberly laughed. Only Twila would throw a Kanye West lyric at the end of her Thanksgiving testimony.

"I am thankful for new opportunities," Hahna said. "Sam has a book and movie deal, so I might be A-list in a couple years. I'll make sure you all have my new number."

Everyone laughed. Sam kissed Hahna's temple and she patted his hand. He was always so modest about everything. The only area where Sam was over the top was loving on Hahna, and no one was going to argue with that.

"She's talking about my opportunities, but Hahna has a meeting with a big private equity group," Sam said. "I'm thankful there are extra saved people at the table who can pray for the success of that meeting."

"Mission accepted," Samantha said. "Glad to hear it. I am thankful for good friends, for understanding, and for grace. Even the extra saved folks need it, and I'm glad my sorority sisters have enough of it to go around."

"I'm thankful that my dad is happy," Sean said. "and that I get to spend a holiday with my little sisters."

Kimberly blew her future son a kiss, and Ron gave him a fist bump across the table.

"I am thankful that Hahna, after running eighteen background checks, felt comfortable enough to rent me office space," DeAndre said to a round of laughs from everyone. "If she hadn't, I wouldn't have met Twila. She's the best thing that's happened to me in a very long time."

Twila gave a little sassy nod and drank a sip of wine. Hahna and Kimberly didn't even try to hide their "secret" look. They were just happy for their friend.

"I am thankful for all this wonderful food that has attacked my senses with aromas like my mama's house," Brandon said. "So, can we stop talking and start eating?"

"Man of God, bless the food," Kimberly said.

As they all bowed their heads and listened to Brandon's spirited prayer, Kimberly felt full. There was still lots of excitement to come for them over the next few months, but it felt like her sisters were close to okay. With Hahna's business losses and Twila's trauma, it hadn't felt that way in a while.

Next on Kimberly's agenda, was landing Hahna some new clients. She wasn't going to let Torian think he saved The Data Whisperers. If it was up to Kimberly, Sam's party idea was going to save the day. Kimberly had her sister's back and her future brother-in-law's too.

Chapter 46

HAHNA

We had gone over the proposal for YS&S multiple times. Corden had prepped me and grilled me with a ton of questions about our due diligence strategy. We'd done our homework and discovered the company YS&S wanted to acquire. It was an athletic apparel manufacturer that had lost two major retailers in six months. Several others were looking to jump ship. Without a sufficient overhaul in strategy, it wouldn't be a good acquisition.

"Remember not to give them too much," Corden said.

"I'm not going to give them too much."

"So, we know the acquisition isn't necessarily a good idea for them. Just lead them to the water."

I shook my head but didn't get upset, because I knew Corden was as invested in us getting this client as I was.

"You know they're going to ask about what we've put into place regarding data security," Corden said.

"That'll probably be the first question if they've done their homework."

"Right. You're good on the response?"

"Yep, I am. Calm down Corden. We got this. And if we don't land this engagement, it'll be good practice. We're going to be good again."

Torian walked into the office wearing an impeccable blue suit, and a little bit too much cologne for my tastes. I typically didn't wear any fragrances in a business meeting, but maybe that was a rule women adhered to and not men.

"You certainly love your Tom Ford cologne, huh?" Corden asked.

I closed my eyes and chuckled. Corden just couldn't help getting a dig in when he didn't like someone.

"You like that?" Torian asked. "It is one of my favorites."

"Let's hope everyone at YS&S feels the same way," Corden said. "Boss, I'm going to make sure the catering is on the way. We are at minus one hundred twenty minutes."

"Thanks, Corden."

Corden left me and Torian alone in the conference room. It didn't bother me like it had bothered me before, because I had talked to Sam about it and had his blessing.

"How's your little party planning going?" Torian asked. "Got many RSVPs yet from Atlanta's elite?"

"I feel like you're saying this as a joke, but I'll respond anyway. We're getting lots of RSVPs. Atlanta loves a party."

"Let's hope you don't spend all that money in vain. It's not like you can afford it."

"Are you an ally or an enemy?"

"I can't believe you're asking me that. How could I ever be your enemy?"

He asked that question with such tenderness and compassion that if I didn't know him, I might've thought that he was sincere.

"You have done things to me that weren't exactly friendly. But I don't want to rehash any of those things right now. I'm trying to keep my mind right for this meeting."

"Oh, okay," Torian said with a chuckle. "Do I need to send my PowerPoint deck to your manservant?"

"Corden is not a servant. He is my right hand. If we land a few more engagements, I might move him up to partner. Sylvia is my admin if you have admin-level tasks you need to accomplish."

"Okay."

"Okay," I parroted back.

I understood that maybe Torian had regrets about our breakup, but I didn't. He'd left me, and I was better off without him, especially since Sam had come into my life.

"Hahna, I don't want things to be tense between us. I brought this potential engagement to you with the best of intentions, and to make both of our businesses money."

"I appreciate you for thinking of us. I don't think things need to be any way between us. Not tense, not friendly. We don't need to have a rapport. We can recommend each other's businesses without that."

"Wow. Are you serious?"

"I am serious that I don't want your friendship."

Torian gave a wicked chuckle. "I get it. Your man told you to come in here and lay down the law. Let the ex know that there won't be any shenanigans. You were always loyal like that."

"What would you know about loyalty? Anyway, my man has zero concerns about you or this meeting. I told him about it, and he shrugged and asked me where we were going for dinner."

"Okay, whatever. You're right. We don't need a rapport. Let's just get through this and get our money."

"Perfect."

Corden returned with the caterers who in a flurry set up the continental breakfast items, juice and coffee station. If this was an actual client and not potential client, the buffet would be more robust, but if they hadn't spent any money, they got muffins and juice.

"All right boss. Are you ready?" Corden asked.

"Yep. You ready?"

"Sure am."

Torian watched our interaction, shook his head and laughed. We ignored him.

Sylvia poked her head into the room, "The client just buzzed in at the gate."

"Thank you, Sylvia. Corden, you want to go and escort them in?"

"Yep. I'm on it."

While we were waiting for Corden to bring back the YS&S delegation, I tried to get in my zone. I was used to this. I'd spoken to some of the top managing partners in some of the top corporations and firms in Atlanta. I was well known, and I was respected. I had nothing to prove, except that I had a viable security strategy—and I did.

When Corden opened the door, Torian and I stood to our feet. Immediately, I knew that something was wrong. From the look on Corden's face, he knew it too. The YS&S team was too young and unfortunately, too black.

There were three of them. One black guy who couldn't have been more than twenty-five, one black girl, who was about the same age, and one white woman who was under forty.

Torian and I shook hands with them as they sat at the table. I watched with interest as they shuffled papers and folders amongst themselves before giving me and Torian each a folder. Mine had a bent corner and a coffee ring on the front.

"Thank you for taking the time to come out to The Data Whisperers office today," I said. "I'm Hahna Osborne, owner and this is Corden Johnson my senior data analyst. Torian tells me that you have some data analytics needs that we may have solutions for."

The young man spoke first. "Thank you for the invite. I'm Ryan, and my colleagues are Dawn and LaKeisha. Torian and I hoop together and when he told me the amazing stuff you've been doing over here; I knew we had to get in on the ground floor."

I stretched my face a bit to keep from scrunching my nose in confusion. No last names or titles given. That was telling. What amazing stuff? What ground floor?

"So, what kinds of analytics products are you looking for?" Corden asked.

It was a level setting question. What did they know about data analytics at all? Because neither one of us wanted to waste our breath and energy if they didn't even understand the analytics space.

I gave Corden an approving nod. I would've asked the same kind of question next.

"Well, we know that we want to make data driven decisions," Dawn said. "We want to be able to say to our clients, this is what we say we do, and here are the numbers that show we do what we say we do."

My eyes widened a little. I couldn't help it. It was a tossed word salad with none of the toppings I liked.

"We need dashboards," LaKeisha said. "Everyone is using dashboards to get their points across these days, and we need to have that same kind of cutting-edge technology. It's the dashboards for me."

I looked at Torian and flipped open the folder in front of me. There was an introduction sheet for the YS&S team. I pulled it out while more buzzword bingo happened.

I felt my nostrils flare as I read their titles. LaKeisha was a junior associate. Dawn was an associate. Ryan, the one who'd made this meeting happen, was a paid intern.

Torian had me clear my calendar, do research, and put on new pantyhose for a paid intern. This wasn't just a waste of time. It was an insult from YS&S.

I stood to my feet. "Thanks for coming out to meet with us. You can ask Corden any additional questions. Feel free to enjoy the buffet."

"Y-you're leaving?" Dawn said. "Torian, you assured us we could get facetime with the owner of the company."

"I was here. You've got your facetime."

"But I have questions for you specifically about how a data breach can destroy a company," Dawn said. "I am writing a dissertation you see. I've been trying to get a meeting with you for months."

I gave them all a tight nod. "Corden can answer any questions you might have."

"Well, can I get a quote from you?" Dawn asked again. "I'm sorry, no one knows Corden Johnson."

"I don't give quotes. Have a good day."

I rushed out of the conference room, so that I could make it to my office before the tears fell. I barely made it. I locked the door, and put do not disturb on my phone, and had a good cry.

I knew Torian hadn't done this on purpose. He was way too arrogant to sit in a meeting with junior staffers. He also thought that decision makers were coming to the table. Those three probably weren't even authorized to speak on behalf of the company. Meanwhile, Corden and I had prepared a kick-ass proposal for YS&S and they probably weren't ever going to hear it.

So, it was time to look harder at the party and list of RSVPs. I'd lied to Torian about that. There wasn't as much interest as I'd hoped. Part of me wanted to throw in the towel and become Sam's full-time cheerleader and hype girl. I would be good at that, and I didn't have to worry about my reputation or a data breach.

Okay, pity party over. I'd given myself thirty minutes to wallow in it, and now I had to get up and dust myself off. Plus, I had to buy a dress for the party. I was going to do something off the rack, but now I was thinking Chanel.

I had to look like we were winning, even if we weren't.

Chapter 47

TWILA

From my hiding spot on one of the hills in our subdivision, I watched as the movers packed up Alexander Adams and his family's belongings. The FOR SALE sign was in the yard, just as I'd instructed, and they were soon going to be gone. Alexander had probably already hit the road. If I was him, I'd already be in the wind.

I felt peace wash over me, but it was incomplete. In the back of my mind, I kept thinking that wherever Alexander Adams went he might very well rape another woman. But I knew that I couldn't get him prosecuted without any victims willing to come forward. That was the only piece that was missing. He was still free to perpetrate another crime.

But I had to let that go. Even if I did follow through with my threat to tell the pastor, Fatima was going to lie. I could see it in her eyes. She liked her life and didn't want to end up back on the streets.

There was nothing I could do to put him behind bars.

Away from me would have to be enough. I would make it enough.

I looked down at the time on my phone. DeAndre was coming to my house for breakfast. I hadn't entertained in my own space in months. I hadn't had a man over since Marcus the Instagram thot. This was a next step.

I climbed back into my car and drove down the hill to the other side of the subdivision where I resided. I resisted the urge to look over my shoulder as I pulled into the garage. I didn't need to do that anymore. The danger had passed.

Inside my kitchen, I arranged the items that Katie had prepared for our breakfast. Shrimp and grits, sous vide eggs, little bagels with smoked salmon, cream cheese and capers, and miniature fried chicken and waffles bites.

The doorbell rang, and I jumped. I forced myself to breathe slowly and calm down. I peeked through the peephole and it was DeAndre. He had roses and a bottle of Prosecco. Mimosas on tap.

I swung the door open and hugged him as he stepped over the threshold. Then, I quickly closed the door behind him and locked all three locks. My hands shook as I fumbled over the locks.

"Are you sure you're ready to move back home?" DeAndre asked. "You can come and stay with me if you don't want to go back to Hahna's. You can have your own room and everything. No pressure."

"I appreciate you for that, DeAndre, but I have to do this. I have to take my power back. If I don't, I'm going to be afraid for the rest of my life."

He nodded. "I understand. Just know that the offer always stands. You can show up at two in the morning if you want. I'll always answer."

DeAndre was incredible. He was a gift and he kept on giving. I wanted to skip right over breakfast and take him to bed.

"Let's make mimosas and you can give me the tour of your house," DeAndre said. "What I see so far is very impressive."

"Nothing like your mansion, but I love it. I picked out every feature while it was being built."

I grabbed the orange juice, two glasses, and went to my dining room bar, because we needed Grand Marnier for mimosas. I set the glasses down and started to make our drinks and De-

Andre sat on my armchair. Then, I realized that it was the chair with my pistol underneath the cushion. I didn't want my new man sitting on the pistol.

"Wait, don't sit there," I said.

"Why not?"

Instead of responding, I went to the chair, lifted the cushion and set the pistol on the lamp table next to the chair.

"Whoa. Weaponry," DeAndre said.

"Yeah. It's all over the house. I guess I need to purge some of this stuff."

"There's nothing wrong with having things to protect your home."

"I might have too much."

"Well, why don't you show me. We can purge it now."

My lip trembled and I felt the tears start, but I nodded in agreement. It was time to purge.

I walked over to the sofa, and lifted the middle cushion, and took out a machete. I set that on the floor in front of the sofa. Then, I got on my knees and reached under the sofa. I pulled out the brass knuckles and knife taped there. Next, I walked over to the standing lamp and reached under the lampshade. From there I pulled out a switchblade.

I looked at DeAndre to see his reaction. He hadn't flinched.

"Is that all in here?" he asked.

I nodded.

"Then let's go to the next room," he said.

DeAndre followed me all over my house, to every room, while I removed nearly one hundred fifty weapons from hiding places. In my bedroom, I had thirty different items including six guns and a sword. It was beyond excessive. It was obsessive and compulsive. If Dr. Mays had known about this, I might've gotten that prescription medication that I sometimes thought I needed.

About halfway through the purging, DeAndre helped me make a pile of weapons in the living room. One by one, we unloaded the guns, put the bullets in boxes and placed them in the middle of the floor.

I think I'd lost count of how much stuff I'd bought. I knew

where everything was, but once I'd gotten past fifty weapons my mind stopped adding to the number in my mental inventory. Maybe something in my mind was trying to protect me. Trying to help me hold onto my sanity.

When we were done, we just stared for a moment looking at the pile.

"I've never seen anything like this," DeAndre said. "You could've killed a crew of assassins."

"For some reason, even though I'm not a drug kingpin, I thought the assassins were coming."

"So, which one gun do you want to keep? I think you should have one. You're a woman who lives alone, and clearly you know how to use it."

I didn't even have to think twice about this question. I needed my Glock. I loved how it felt in my hand, and it was what I used to get Alexander Adams out of my life for good.

"How about my Glock, and my taser."

"You need more than one?"

"Well, I'm killing someone with the Glock. A taser will incapacitate a fool, but they can live to stand trial."

DeAndre laughed. "Okay. You should keep both."

"How do I even get rid of the rest? I feel like if I showed up at a police precinct with all this, they'd arrest me on principle until they could run ballistics on all the guns."

"True story. But your boyfriend's an entertainment attorney who dabbles in criminal defense. I know a couple of police officers who'll take them off your hands. I can make a few calls."

"Thank you."

DeAndre stepped over the arsenal and walked to the kitchen. "Let's have breakfast. I'm starving."

I took a tissue from the box on the coffee table and wiped away any remaining snot bubbles. Then, I followed my man into the kitchen. The peace that washed over me was now complete.

"Let's talk about this Jamaica trip," DeAndre called from the kitchen. "Are we flying first class or what?"

And with one question, DeAndre let me know that this compulsion I had, hadn't scared him off. Nothing I told him about my flaws had made him run away. He'd seen all my good qualities and decided that they were worth having in his life, and because of that I yearned to have him too.

He felt perfect, but I knew he wasn't. I knew that some flaw would emerge, and that I would give him side eye. Like maybe he flicked toenails across the room (dear God no, please don't let him do that), but I wasn't going to flinch, just like he hadn't.

I thought I'd give Dr. Mays a call and let her know I was stopping my therapy for a while. She would leave the light on for me though in case I ever needed to come back.

Hahna's party was going to be fun. It would be our coming out party to Atlanta's elite. We were the next power couple that no one knew about yet. Maybe I'd start taking those calls from those cable network reality shows.

Then, I glanced back at the pile of weapons, and thought better of it.

Chapter 48

KIMBERLY

Ron walked into the bedroom with his bow tie hanging around his neck. Kimberly beamed with pride at how delicious her dimpled man looked in a tux.

"Are you almost ready?" Ron asked. "We'll need to get going soon if we don't want to get stuck in the weekend traffic."

"Yes, I am almost ready. I'm just nervous."

Kimberly looked in the mirror and admired her green sequined dress. She'd lost twenty pounds, not that anyone would notice, but she felt good about it. It wasn't her look that she was nervous about though.

"Can you tie my tie for me?"

Ron stood close to Kimberly and she expertly looped the fabric. "You smell good."

"You do too," Ron said. "But tell me what's wrong. What are you nervous about?"

"I've invited a few people to this party. The partners at my former law firm, a board member from Atlanta General Hospital, and a few others. I hope that they show up for Hahna."

"You're always trying to save someone," Ron said. "It's not your job to save the day all the time."

"I know it's not. But if I can help, I have to do something. Do you know how much Hahna has been a force multiplier for

CurlPop? Twila too, and she doesn't even wear her hair natural. They made sure to shout me out anytime they had the opportunity."

"Gamma Phi Gamma showed up and showed out for Hahna too."

"Yeah, but the sorors have already moved on. After that initial push, they're onto the next mission. They haven't stayed the course."

"Okay, I will hope with you that your efforts haven't been in vain and that all of the people you invited show up. But you can't hold yourself responsible if nothing happens. If she can't recover in the next six months or so, Hahna might need to start thinking about how she can go back to corporate."

"No. She's the one who convinced me to launch out on my own. I won't let this happen to her."

Ron kissed Kimberly and then kissed her again. She knew those kisses were to turn the page on the conversation. But Ron didn't understand how strongly Kimberly felt about this. He didn't realize that she'd never leave Hahna behind.

They showed up to the party right before the start time, and Kimberly was psyched at the number of cars lined up for the valet. The worst thing that could happen to an Atlanta businessperson was for them to throw a party and no one show up.

"Looks like she got a good turnout," Ron said.

"Let's hope that means she'll get some new accounts."

Inside the party, Kimberly and Ron mingled with the guests, some of whom Kimberly knew, some she didn't. It was a networking party, so she proudly introduced Ron to the movers and shakers in Atlanta. The upper echelon. Where the money lived, and the deals were made.

When Kimberly saw Hahna, she waved from across the room, but Hahna beckoned them over. When she got closer, Kimberly realized why. Hahna was talking to one of Kimberly's favorite customers, a woman named Renita Chalmers. She'd won the lottery a decade ago in another state and had been secretly funding ventures in theatre and music. She called herself philanthropic, but really, she was trying to buy her way onto the A-list. It wasn't an impossibility in Atlanta. Checks spoke louder than credentials at times.

Kimberly wondered why Hahna was wasting time on Renita. She wasn't a potential client for The Data Whisperers.

Kimberly and Hahna shared hugs and kisses, and the men shared fist bumps.

"Kimberly you already know Renita, but I'd like you both to meet her date, William Bottoms. He's a managing partner at Yorkshire, Summerall, and Schmidt."

"It's a pleasure to meet you, William," Kimberly said. "Renita, you and I need to catch up. I didn't know you were on the dating scene again."

William laughed. "I, for one, am glad you didn't know she was dating. That gave me a chance to shoot my shot."

Kimberly giggled at the thought of this little sixty-something trying to shoot his shot at Renita. Ron smiled heartily and shared a few words with William while Kimberly tried to read Hahna's facial expressions. She had a smile on her face, and that's all that Kimberly needed to see.

"Ron and I are going to work the room," Kimberly said. "Renita, let's definitely link up later."

Kimberly dragged Ron to the other side of the room and got both of them drinks off a tray being passed around the room. She could barely contain her excitement as she sipped the strong mixed drink.

"It's happening. Can you tell?" Kimberly asked Ron.

"What's happening."

"Black girl magic. It's floating all through this room. Hahna's walking out of here with money, I tell you. And a restored business."

"Well, wasn't this party Sam's idea?" Ron asked.

"It was."

"Then, I will say that it's some black boy magic that caused this. Y'all can't just be claiming everything."

Kimberly tilted her head back and hollered. But she didn't argue with Ron. It didn't matter where this magic originated, it was here. Hahna was going to be all right and The Data Whisperers would be back.

Kimberly felt proud of herself and of Sam. They'd fixed the fixer. When Hahna figured that out, she was going to marvel at it, but by then she'd probably be off to fix Kimberly's or Twila's next catastrophe.

Oh, wait. It would be Kimberly's, of course. They still had a whole wedding to execute.

Chapter 49

HAHNA

There was always a risk in asking Samantha to host the bridal shower at the church. The danger was that it would be a holy and sanctified event that wasn't any fun. As I looked at the decorations in the church's fellowship hall, I was sure that the risk had been realized.

The theme was a tea party, and everyone was supposed to wear their fanciest tea party hat. What it looked like from the doorway was the Mother's Day brunch at church where the children gave their mothers roses and the men's ministry made runny eggs and cold grits.

It was well-attended though, so that was something. All of Kimberly's singles' ministry friends were there, and some of the women's ministry. They were all wearing pastels even though it was wintertime. The closest I could come to the Easter egg foolishness that I saw in this room was wearing a winter white sweater dress.

Twila walked in right behind me and gasped. She didn't even do it quietly like I had.

"Shhh!" I fussed, but Twila just sucked her teeth and shook her head.

"What the heck? Is this the scholarship brunch, Easter morning, or a women's convention?"

"We said we weren't going to do this, remember? We're going to support the event, because we're making Samantha feel like a valued bridesmaid."

"I don't value this. Not at all," Twila said.

"Come on girl. Let's go sit down."

We sat at the bridesmaid's table, although I was tempted to take a seat near the door so we could escape when we'd had enough.

Who was I kidding? I'd already had enough, and I'd just arrived.

I pulled my phone out of my purse when I sat, so that I wouldn't accidentally make eye contact with any of the church members. It was too early on Saturday for me. Sam and I had gone out the night before, and my eyes were still red from the Hennessy. I would have it out of my system by Sunday morning, and that was usually good enough.

Since I was bored, I went to the local Atlanta gossip blog to see what shenanigans Atlanta's D-list was getting into.

"Twila," I said when I saw a huge headline on my favorite site. "Look at this. Isn't this the pastor at that church?"

"What pastor at what church?" she asked as she took the phone from my hands.

Twila read the page and her jaw dropped. I knew it was the pastor from the church Alexander Adams had attended.

"Both Pastor Wright and parishioner Alexander Adams have been arrested on charges of human sex trafficking and multiple counts of rape stemming from allegations from several women taking part in their church's homeless ministry operation. Wright was arrested on the church grounds, and Adams was apprehended in Tallahassee, Florida. They are both being held without bail while awaiting jury trial."

"Who do you think pressed charges?" I asked. "Do you think the wife finally came to her senses?"

"I don't know, but this is the best news ever. I felt free enough to throw out all my weapons, but now I could just literally fly across this room I feel so light."

"You got rid of your arsenal?"

"Yep. DeAndre helped me too."

"He must really be digging you if he saw all that and stayed with you."

"He sure is digging me, and I'm digging him right back. He got us first class tickets to Jamaica. You and Sam should upgrade your flight."

"Sam would get so mad at me for buying first class tickets. He's way too thrifty for that."

"Has he ever flown first class though? I think if he flies first class just once, he'll be won over."

"Maybe."

"That settles it. We're going to get an upgrade at the airport. I know some people who know some people."

I laughed. A free upgrade might not be enough to convince Sam to splurge in the future, but Twila wouldn't understand, so I didn't try to explain.

Twila pointed at the gift table. "Now what do you think are in those big ole boxes over there?"

"Definitely not lingerie."

"I'm going with crock pots and air fryers," Twila said. "As if Kimberly doesn't have all of that in her house."

"Uh oh. The rest of the bridesmaid posse is in the house."

Debbie, Traci, and Abena walked in as a trio. The befuddlement on their faces was hilarious.

"Did we look that crazy when we walked in?" Twila asked.

"I think we probably did."

All three of them had missed the theme memo. There wasn't a hat between them, and Debbie was wearing a track suit, like she was on her way to the mall after the shower was over.

Twila scooted over to make room for all three of them at the bridesmaid's table. Samantha looked over at us and frowned, probably because of the dress code. I wanted to tell her to be happy they were there, especially Traci and Abena, who had no use for church these days. Debbie always stayed connected just in case she needed that benevolent fund to pay a utility bill.

"It's the Data Whisperer," Abena said as she gave me a high

five across the table. "I heard you still over there signing on new clients."

"Yes, we are. I had to hire two new staffers."

"Look at God," Traci said. The way she said God it sounded like it had a t on the end of it.

We had not only landed the YS&S account on the strength of my proposal to Renita's date William, but we'd signed Atlanta General and Knight Time Records. Those referrals came from Twila's doctor. My sisters hadn't let me down. They'd hooked me up with the assist, and Corden and I had made basket after basket.

Kimberly walked into the bridal shower with widened eyes and a slack jaw like the rest of us. She'd known the theme was tea party, but I don't know if this was what she was expecting.

Kimberly looked over at our table and waved. We all waved back, and I added a shoulder shrug. I didn't want her to think that I had anything to do with this.

"You get the seat of honor," Samantha said as she ran out of the kitchen.

The seat of honor was at the center of a long table that was meant for more than one person, but Kimberly settled in and waited for the festivities to begin.

"Is it okay if I put a little something in my tea from my flask?" Abena whispered.

I reached over Twila and smacked her hand down. "No, girl. Put that away, why would you bring that to the church?"

"We're not actually in the church. This is the building next to the church," Abena said. "And we always put vodka in our tea."

"Y'all are not about to have Samantha telling me off. Behave yourselves."

"Samantha telling you off about what?" Samantha asked. I didn't know the heffa was standing behind me.

"Nothing girl," I said in a much calmer tone. "Everything looks beautiful. You did a great job."

"Do you want to be the game master, Hahna?" she asked.

I shook my head. I didn't want to be the game master. I wanted to sit and observe, and silently laugh at people.

"Not my thing," I said.

"Come on. I don't have anyone else," Samantha said.

How could she say she had no one else? She had a whole table full of bridesmaids. But I understood. I wouldn't want to ask these heffas to do anything either.

I got up from my seat and mastered the games. All of them. And they were the corny bridal shower games too. The make a bridal gown out of toilet paper game, and the pin the bow tie on the groom game. And finally, not to be left out, was the make a hat out of the gift bows for the bride game.

Interestingly enough, there was not one crock pot or air fryer in the boxes. One of the church mothers had surprised us by giving Kimberly a box of thongs and wet wipes. I could've done without her description on what she'd do with the wipes.

As churchy as this bridal shower was, Kimberly seemed to enjoy every minute of it. That seemed to bring Samantha joy. I'd never seen that side of Samantha, at least, not since she'd been an evangelist. I wanted to see more of her that way, enjoying her sisters in Christ and smiling, rather than scowling and judging.

"She seems a lot nicer at church," Traci said, unaware that her observation agreed with my thoughts.

"Sure does. Maybe we should visit more often," Abena said.

They shared a look similar to the ones Kimberly and I shared when we were communicating silently about Twila.

"Nah," they both said simultaneously.

"Thank goodness we're still giving her a bachelorette in Jamaica," Debbie said. "Are we getting a Jamaican stripper?"

I rolled my eyes at her. "You didn't teleport yourself out of church, girl."

"I mean, God knew I was thinking about it. What's the point of not saying it if He's inside my head?"

"It's a matter of respect for God and the people who worship here," Twila said. "And no, to the stripper. Kim doesn't want one."

"She doesn't?" Traci asked. "Who doesn't want to behold a naked Jamaican in his glory?"

I pointed at Kimberly who was thanking the church mothers for showing up to her bridal shower. Everyone nodded in understanding.

"Don't worry y'all," Debbie said. "When I get married, we getting a whole room full of strippers."

Traci and Abena high fived each other and the rest of us laughed. I hoped that Samantha was happy. We showed up at church, in a range of church readiness and with varying levels of etiquette. But dangit, in the spirit of sisterhood, we showed up.

If this didn't make us harmonious in Jamaica, then nothing would.

Chapter 50

KIMBERLY

Kimberly was speechless as she stepped into the vacation rental they'd gotten for the wedding. The pictures on the website hadn't done the twelve-bedroom villa justice. Each bedroom had either a king-sized bed or two queens and its own en-suite bathroom. There were two half-bathrooms on the first level to accommodate the wedding guests.

The space for the ceremony was as stunning as the lodgings, with covered seating for one hundred fifty, a raised dance floor and a long walkway for the bridal party's entrance. The flower and party decoration team had arrived a day before the bridal party and had already started transforming the place into a sea of pink, blue, and white flowers.

Kimberly was blown away.

"Baby, all your planning paid off," Ron said as he toured the castle with her. "This place is truly spectacular."

As beautiful as the castle was the view of the Negril cliffs and the ocean. The waves crashed off the side of the building and there were even little steps that led right down into the ocean from the front side of the castle.

It was a few hours before all the bridal party arrived on staggered flights and separate cabs carrying them the two hours from the Montego Bay airport to Negril. Kimberly got to hear a new round of excitement every time someone new entered the castle.

"Do I know how to pick em or nah?" Hahna said as she and Sam walked through the front door. "Which one is our room?"

Kimberly led them to the bedroom she felt was second best after the master bedroom. With a full view of the cliffs and a canopy bed, it was better than any hotel room that they could've procured.

"This is amazing," Hahna said as Sam set their bags down.

Ron appeared in the doorway. "Sam, my brother, we're doing a tequila toast downstairs. I know you just got here, but are you down?"

"Definitely. Be back babe," Sam said.

Kimberly and Hahna laughed as he scampered out of the room behind Ron. Their men got excited about good tequila, so excited that they brought their own to the island. In Jamaica every brand and type of rum was available, but the good tequila was scarce.

"Can you believe you and Ron are getting married?" Hahna said. "Just under a year ago we were crying and making pacts talking about there weren't any good men, and that maybe we should lower our standards a little."

"And then we found out that we didn't have to lower our standards at all."

"Exactly right. And the thing with DeAndre and Twila?"

"Crazy," Hahna said. "She wouldn't have even met him if my business hadn't momentarily fallen apart. Our sisterhood facilitated that one."

"True story."

"Well, let me go and manage these wedding workers. I don't want you to worry about anything. I will handle any and all shenanigans as they arise."

"They better not arise," Kimberly said. "Everybody better get here and act like they got some damn sense."

Hahna lifted her eyebrows and smiled. Of course, there would be shenanigans. Debbie, Traci and Abena were on the way. How could there not be?

* * *

The day of the wedding had finally arrived. Ron had been sequestered into the guest house on the property, where he and the groomsmen would get ready. The women needed the run of the house for their team of makeup artists and hairstylists.

Kimberly opened her eyes after a restful sleep. She reached for Ron and he was already gone. On his pillow was a note. Kimberly sat up in the bed to read it.

My Kimmie Kim. In just a few hours we start our forever. I promise to love you more and more every day, though I don't know how I could love you any more than I do right now. My love for you surpasses anything I've ever felt. Thank you for being who you are and for loving how you love. See you in a few hours beautiful.

Love you forever,

Big Ron

The note started the waterworks, but they were the most joyful tears Kimberly had ever had. The anticipation of walking down that path to meet her prince was almost overwhelming. She breathed deeply to keep the tears at bay. She didn't want red and puffy eyes in their wedding photographs.

Later, after breakfast, in the bridal suite, Kimberly was surprisingly calm. Twila and Hahna entered wearing the specially crafted bridesmaid robes that Kimberly had gotten for all of them. Their hair and makeup were done, and they both looked incredible. Like two sun-kissed goddesses.

"How are you feeling honey?" Hahna asked.

Tears flooded Kimberly's eyes and Twila dashed for tissues. "Girl you can't cry off your lashes yet."

"Y'all look so beautiful, I couldn't help it. I-I never thought you two would be *my* bridesmaids. I only dreamed of it being the other way around."

"Fold the tissue and dab with the corner," Twila said, "if you're about to have all these waterworks."

The makeup artist smiled and took a break while Kimberly got emotional. She'd just have to fix any damage that was done after the bride had a moment.

"Are DeAndre and Sam enjoying the castle?" Kimberly asked.

"They are in heaven," Twila said. "Can you imagine all the couples' trips we're going to be taking?"

"I can't wait!" Hahna said. "All those years we showed up in the Caribbean longing to have men of our own . . ."

"Dreaming of island peen that would come and rock our worlds," Twila said.

Kimberly and Hahna shared one of their signature looks.

"Whatever," Twila said. "Y'all not gonna act like I had those dreams all by myself."

"I was just thinking about how you gave up that dream and brought your own peen last year," Hahna said.

They all burst into laughter thinking about Twila's electronic thingamajig that promised to love her all night long. Or at least until the batteries ran out.

"Well, I don't need my battery-operated boyfriend anymore, thank you very much," Twila said. "DeAndre is handling all of that."

"He over there working you out, huh?" Kimberly said.

"Child. We christened that little beach area last night."

"I hope you didn't get any of y'all juices into the wedding decorations," Hahna said.

"What about you and Sam?" Twila asked. "You just worry about what y'all nasty selves doing."

"Sam and I are taking advantage of all the . . . amenities in our room."

The laughter continued until Kimberly's tearful moment had passed. "Thank y'all for being here with me," Kimberly said.

"Of course, we're here. We'll let you finish getting made up," Hahna said. "Do you need anything? Any champagne? More breakfast?"

"No, girl," Kimberly said. "I can't keep eating and drinking all morning if I want to fit into that dress."

"You'll be fine. We don't have a problem greasing you up with coconut oil and sliding you in," Twila said.

Kimberly laughed. She had so many different girdles and equipment, that no one would have to grease her up, but they might need a team for her to go to the bathroom once she was in the dress.

"Thank y'all. For everything."

Hahna winked as she and Twila headed for the door. "It's not over yet. The fun part is just starting," she said.

Kimberly knew Hahna meant the fun of the wedding day, but to Kimberly it had a deeper meaning. She'd waited her entire life to feel like the other girls. She'd looked longingly at couples having fun at skating rinks, movie theaters, and restaurants and wondered if, not when, she'd ever have her own fun. And now in her forties, her fun part was just starting.

And what a time it would be, she and her friends were ballers in love. That meant there would be adventures and shenanigans for decades to come.

Chapter 51

HAHNA

It was time for the wedding to start, and everything was ready. No, everything was perfect. Every flower, every dress, and every eyelash. Ron's little girls, Carly and Kayla were so cute in their African print dresses that matched the men's vests, and the bridesmaids' dresses all fit like they were custom made.

I couldn't wait for Ron to see Kimberly. Twila and I had nearly lost our shit when we saw her in her dress. There were no words for how beautiful she looked. It was like she shone from the inside out. All that love she had for Ron emanated from her being until she glowed.

"Y'all ready to do this bridesmaid walk?" I asked as our sorority sisters lined up.

Traci, Abena, and Debbie were struggling with minor hangovers from the night before, and the morning of drinking, but they were gorgeous regardless. Samantha's face was fresh and pretty, looking much younger than her forty-two years. That was the result of clean Holy Ghost living, and good genes.

"If they ain't ready, they better get ready," Twila said. "We gotta marry this girl off right now."

The music started, and Samantha led the way. She met with her groomsman and they traversed the path down the ramp to where the guests were assembled. We all followed one by one, remembering to smile for photos.

My eyes locked with Sam's and he gave me the most loving smile. I knew that when we married, it wouldn't be like this. It would be something private, for the two of us, because I wasn't letting Rochelle and Shady Falls come through and ruin the joining of our lives.

Ron stood at the bottom of the ramp, already blinking back his own tears, as his little girls descended. I could only imagine what he was thinking, but maybe he never imagined himself having this kind of joy after two failed marriages.

Kimberly emerged from the top of the ramp and met with her older brother who would give her away in place of their deceased father. I could see the tears glisten in her eyes as she came to meet her groom.

When she arrived at the altar, Ron took both of Kimberly's hands and kissed them. He didn't let them go for the whole time the minister spoke. In fact, Ron never took his eyes off Kimberly, and he never stopped smiling.

Right before they exchanged their vows, I stepped to the altar with the best man, and helped Ron and Kimberly bind their wrists together with ropes in the African custom. They were bound in this moment and they would be through this life and the next.

Kimberly said her vows first. "Big Ron. My Ron. You were the one from the first time I saw you on the yard. So skinny you wore sweatpants under your jeans to look a little thicker, but with the most handsome face I'd ever seen. I could look at those dimples forever. And then, we became friends, and my attraction to you became more than physical. We connected on a soul level, so much so that when life took us on different paths, God saw fit to bring us back together. I promise to always love you with everything in me. I will love you with the God in me, and that love is pure. It is patient, kind, peaceful, joyful, and gentle. It is long suffering and it forgives. This love is all I need. It is complete."

There wasn't a dry eye in the place, but Ron was so sweet

with his tears. He'd tried to stop them but had given up. It was funny how everyone kept passing him tissues. Now it was time for him to share his vows.

"Kimmie Kim. I remember when I gave you that nickname. You hated it at first, but you grew to love it, because it was the beginning of our special language. You always got me, and with you I always feel understood and seen. I am my best self when you love me and that's because you love me with your heart, and with your spirit. I vow to reciprocate that love every day of our lives. I will see you, understand you, and protect your heart. You can be vulnerable with me, and I with you because we are safe with one another. Our love is perfect, and I will never leave you. You are my twin flame, and I will spend a lifetime stoking your fires, as mine can never be doused. I love you, Kimmie Kim. You are everything to me."

That was it. We pretty much were done. We even ran out of damn tissues from the crying. The minister pronounced them married and they kissed. Everyone laughed when Ron dipped Kimberly like an old school lover. And then the sisters of Gamma Phi Gamma strolled, and the brothers of Omega Phi Gamma stepped, in the tradition of the yard. Atlanta wasn't the motherland, but it was the birthplace of our adulthood, and this was our own kind of African dance. This was the most perfect union of our Gamma Phi Gamma and Omega Phi Gamma.

At the reception, after the cake was cut and the first dances were done, Sam and I took a walk away from the guests. We went out to the stairs overlooking the cliff, and I finally exhaled. The day had gone by in a blur and now was finished. My girl was married off, and my Maid of Honor duties were complete. I'd reflect on those duties later, and probably look back at pictures wondering what I was thinking or feeling at a given moment.

"You tired, babe?" Sam asked.

"Oh my God, you have no idea. I can't wait to put my feet up and take off this girdle."

"You don't even need a girdle," Sam said. "Why do you torture yourself?"

"For beauty. And because I'm too lazy to keep going to the gym like Twila."

"You are beautiful."

"You say that to me every day, and I never get sick of hearing it."

"I asked you to come out here, away from everyone." Sam said, "because I think it's the tackiest thing ever when dudes propose to their girls at someone else's wedding."

"Wait . . ."

Before I could connect the dots, Sam was on one knee and holding out a ring box. I think I snatched the box out of his hand even though my hands trembled.

"Sam . . . I . . . oh my goodness . . . I . . ."

"I hope there's a yes in there," Sam said with a laugh.

"There's a yes. There's a hell yes. Hell yes!"

Sam and I kissed to the sound of the waves crashing against the cliff. The ocean had been the only witness of this proposal, but it was the perfect audience. The ocean applauded our love.

We didn't rejoin the wedding celebration that night. We slipped into our suite and had a celebration of our own. There was so much love in the atmosphere that I'm sure no one missed us. Especially the new lovers Twila and DeAndre. They'd probably beat Sam and I to their own secret hideaway.

People, women particularly, were always talking about the things they'd tell their younger selves, at sixteen or twenty— ages that were pivotal to building their esteem and self-worth. But if I could, I'd only need to go back one year. When I was crying over a romance that was never meant to be, I'd tell myself that there was still love in the world. And that soulmates were still finding one another, and that mine was coming. I'd tilt my chin up and tell myself to stand in the sun, because my joy was on the way. And then, I'd go and whisper the same things to my sisters, and we'd stand in the sun together.

In anticipation.

Don't miss the previous book by Tiffany L. Warren that introduced sorority sisters Hahna, Twila, and Kimberly . . .

All the Things I Should Have Known

They are forty-something, successful, financially set . . . and done with trying to find "perfect" husbands. So why *can't* Hahna, Twila, and Kimberly have men strictly for friendship, companionship—and especially mind-blowing sex? Their solution: be sugar mamas to gorgeous young studs who promise the best of having it all. But the ladies soon find that real lust and no strings is way more complicated than they thought . . .

All-business *and* all about the money, Hahna is drawn to Sam, an aspiring writer. He's content with his work and Hahna, but her determination to make him appreciate the finest things in life could easily tear them apart. Cautious Kimberly is swept off her feet by handsome adrenaline-junkie Shawn—but an old flame from her past sparks an even more dangerous passion. And for Twila, a smokin' hot Instagram model is fulfilling all her scandalous, insatiable dreams . . . until his high-maintenance demands and jealousy throw her life into chaos. Now Hahna, Kimberly, and Twila need to trust their instincts and their hearts to reclaim their joy—and the love they truly deserve.

Available wherever books are sold

Chapter 1

A year ago today, Torian was a ghost.
Hahna's Facebook page reminded her of this fact. Was there a filter on Facebook to delete the bad memories and only remind you of the good ones? She slowly scrolled the page and remembered. That fateful morning, she'd woken up to a note. Five words had changed her life.

Baby, I can't do this.

Hahna had no idea what this one thing was that Torian couldn't do, because his note wasn't specific. She had a few ideas, though. He couldn't be faithful. He couldn't commit. And he damn sure couldn't tell the truth.

Or maybe it wasn't just one thing. Maybe Torian couldn't do any of the things she wanted him to do—or be any of the things she wanted him to be. Just because he was a chocolate-covered demigod who made her quiver with a glance; and just because he'd showered her with expensive shoes and jewelry and vacations; and just because they'd probably make cute kids—it didn't mean that Torian Jackson truly wanted to have a life with her.

So, he'd disappeared, and he'd left a note as a good-bye.

Hahna placed her phone facedown on her huge cherry-wood desk. The desk she'd splurged on when her consulting firm, the Data Whisperers, exceeded twenty-seven million dollars in annual revenue. The desk that made her office smell like old money, even though the money that bought it was brand-new.

Hahna walked over to the large bay window that she'd had custom-installed to give her a panoramic view of the lake and magnolia trees behind the old-style Buckhead mansion that she'd renovated and turned into her company's main office. She met with clients there and gave them gracious Southern hospitality. Sweet tea, biscuits and honey, and proposals that opened their eyes to all the ways their small companies could use the data they hoarded on laptops and tablets.

Hahna gazed out the window, twirled her right index finger through her honey-colored curls, breathed, and found her peace. Those small actions had become muscle memory for her. She'd made it a habit to calm herself when anxiety threatened to consume her spirit.

Sylvia, Hahna's assistant, stepped into her office. "Hahna, I ordered the car service to take you to the airport. Is there anything else you need me to do before I get out of here for the weekend?"

Hahna looked over at Sylvia and smiled. It was only Thursday, but Hahna was giving Sylvia a long weekend because she was taking one. Her annual spa retreat with her best friends, Twila and Kimberly. They would make her forget Torian, the ghost, and make new memories for her Facebook timeline.

"You're free to go, Sylvia. What do you have planned for the weekend?"

"My grandbaby is coming over, and we're making jewelry and having a fashion show."

Hearing Sylvia talk about her granddaughter made Hahna feel warm inside. The idea of doing fun activities with a little person was a dream that Hahna used to have—before she hit forty and her ovaries decided that they wanted to turn their full-time job into a part-time I-show-up-when-I-feel-like-it gig. And before she had a ghost boyfriend.

But this weekend was not about the ghost, or her sometime-y

ovaries. Spending time with her girls was about rejuvenation, restoration, and relaxation. Some of her favorite *r* words.

"You have a good time with your beautiful granddaughter. I'll see you on Tuesday morning."

"Tuesday? You're being generous."

"I decided that I won't be back until Tuesday, so you get the benefit of my wanderlust."

Sylvia laughed. "Wander on, baby, but be careful about that lust. Don't come back here from that island with one of those green-card seekers."

"I can't import a man? You don't care about me importing furniture, but you won't let me bring back some hot chocolate."

They shared a long laugh that felt good. Laughing, along with breathing, twirling her hair, and gazing out of her bay window, held Hahna together when her cracks started to show. That's why the spa retreats were so important. She was going to laugh, probably at Twila's antics, breathe in the ocean air, and twirl her hair while gazing upon every fine piece of sculpted chocolate that passed her on the beach.

"You don't need to import a man, sweetie. God is going to send you one."

Hahna accepted this as fact because Sylvia believed it, not because she had any evidence of God being concerned with her singlehood. This blessed man who might fall from the heavens was clearly on God's time.

"I know. If I put out positivity, I will attract positive energy."

"Unh-uh. Don't start talking to me about the universe and attracting. You know good and damn well, I'm talking about Jesus. 'Bye, chil'."

Hahna chuckled some more as Sylvia muttered, *My sweet Jesus* and *Oh, the blood of the Savior,* all the way down the stairs. Sylvia loved the Lord but would also cuss you out about Jesus.

Hahna walked back over to her desk and shut down her laptop. For a half second, she was tempted to bring it with her, but then she quickly changed her mind. There wouldn't be any relaxing, rejuvenating, or restoration if she was checking emails all weekend. Plus, if any emergencies popped up while she was out of the country, her staff was more than capable.

Corden, Hahna's senior data analyst, peeked his head into the office.

"Oh, good," he said, "you're still here. I thought you were gone already."

"Almost. The car service will be here in a bit. What's up?"

"Just a teeny-tiny client issue."

Hahna read Corden's body language. His usually tucked-in button-down was half out of his skinny jeans. He shifted his weight from one foot to the other, and his nostrils were flared. This was not teeny-tiny. He wouldn't be standing in her office, fifteen minutes before her car whisked her away to vacation, if it was.

"Do I need to sit down?"

"No . . . well, maybe . . ."

"Shit."

Hahna sat down, placed her hands on the desk, and waited. She hoped it would be quick. She didn't want to miss her flight.

"Aliyah mistakenly sent table data from Shale Accounting to We Work Employment Agency. It was an honest mistake, but the data had sensitive personally identifiable information of Shale's customers. Should we disclose the data breach?"

"Shit, shit, shit."

"I know."

Hahna never strategized on this type of thing without sleeping on it first, but there was no time to sleep on it this time.

"We have to disclose it. To both parties. We Work and Shale. The issue is how we do it. We don't want them to lose confidence in our processes."

"Right. So, Aliyah was sending a dashboard with sample table data over to Shale's database analyst for review. She started typing the name Regina, but Renaldo popped up. She was going so quickly that she didn't realize the email address was wrong."

"Have we already asked We Work to delete the data?"

"Yes, we sent a communication that said the information was

sent in error, and we requested that they delete it as soon as possible."

"So, here's how we will handle Shale. First, create a new secure process for sharing data with their staff. I suggest we use our secure upload site. Then, explain what happened, and assure them that their customers' data is secure."

"Are they going to believe it?"

"I've got a good relationship with Julian Cortez, one of the partners at Shale. I think that I will be able to smooth over any rough edges when I get back."

"Thanks, boss, I hate to bring this up right before you leave for the beach."

Hahna relaxed in her chair, although she was anything but calm about this situation. If Julian and the other partners at Shale felt strongly about this data breach, then they could end up losing one of their biggest clients.

"Also, finish their damn dashboard this weekend. I don't care how many hours y'all have to work. Take some days off next week when I get back. We can't deliver bad news without that dashboard being completed. And I mean ready to go, not in pilot mode. How close is Aliyah to finishing?"

"She's close. I think if I work with her, we can deliver the dashboard and the email on Monday."

"You're not just blowing smoke up my ass, are you?"

"No. She has been testing every page on the dashboard and is only working out a few quirks. We'll get it done. Go enjoy the beach."

"I'll try."

"No, you will. Did you get that bathing suit you showed me?"

"The low-cut white one?"

"Yes, *that* one. The husband maker."

Hahna cracked up. The swimsuit was sexy, and she'd asked Corden what he thought. The man had impeccable taste, and although he had a longtime fiancée and a daughter, he felt more like a girlfriend than a male subordinate.

"It's in my bag, Corden, I don't know if I'll be bold enough to put it on."

"If Twila sees it, you will. You have fun, honey. I'm gonna go catch Aliyah before she leaves and let her know it's gonna be a long weekend."

"Thanks for holding this together."

"This is what finances my comfortable lifestyle. We're not losing this client."

Hahna jumped up from her desk and hugged Corden. He had been with her from the start and was as invested in the Data Whisperers as she was.

"Have fun, boss lady."

Corden left Hahna's office to round up Aliyah, and Hahna exhaled. That could've been a vacation-cancelling emergency. If it had happened a couple of years ago, no one could've convinced her to get on a plane. But she had developed her staff, and she trusted them.

Hahna gathered her luggage from the closet when she heard the SUV pull up in the drive downstairs. As soon as she got to the airport, the shenanigans would commence.

Relax. Rejuvenate. Restore. Her mantra for the weekend, even if/when Twila pulled up with drama.